THE FELL OF DARK

THE
FELL
OF
DARK

CALEB ROEHRIG

Feiwel and Friends
New York

A Feiwel and Friends Book

An imprint of Macmillan Publishing Group, LLC
120 Broadway, New York, NY 10271

Our books may be purchased in bulk for promotional, educational, or
business use. Please contact your local bookseller or the Macmillan Corporate
and Premium Sales Department at (800) 221-7945 ext. 5442 or by email at
MacmillanSpecialMarkets@macmillan.com.

Library of Congress Control Number: 2019940846

ISBN 978-1-250-15584-9 (hardcover) / ISBN 978-1-250-15583-2 (ebook)

Book design by Mike Burroughs

Feiwel and Friends logo designed by Filomena Tuosto
First edition, 2020

10   9   8   7   6   5   4   3   2   1

fiercereads.com

For my mother-in-law, Māra Trapans.
I aspire to make people feel as special and loved as you do, and I'm
so lucky to call you my family!

One can't build little white picket fences to keep nightmares out.

—Anne Sexton

THE FELL OF DARK

CAST OF CHARACTERS

HUMANS

August Pfeiffer: Aka Auggie. Good at art, bad at math, possibly Earth's only chance to prevent the apocalypse.

Daphne Banks: Auggie's math tutor, a college student whose vampire-hunter parents taught her a few tricks of the trade.

Adriana Verdugo: Auggie's best friend, an aspirant witch.

Hope Cheng: The only other student in Auggie's independent art study, and the girl of Adriana's dreams.

Ximena Rosales: Adriana's grandmother, an experienced bruja. The best cook in Fulton Heights, Illinois.

Gunnar Larsen: Mostly competent barista, partial to cool dude-necklaces. The boy of Auggie's dreams.

The Brotherhood of Perseus: Aka "the Brotherhood," aka "the Knights," aka "the Perseans." A chivalric order of mortal knights, established in the twelfth century, with a sacred mission to protect humankind from the undead. A secret society that continues to this day.

Grand Duchess Anastasia Nikolaevna Romanova: Youngest daughter of Tsar Nicholas II, the last emperor of Russia. Executed with her family in 1918.

Marie Antoinette, Queen of France: Wife of King Louis XVI, wearer of enormous wigs. Executed in Place de la Révolution in 1793.

Anne Boleyn, Queen of England: Second wife of King Henry VIII, mother of Queen Elizabeth I. Executed at the Tower of London in 1536.

Mac Bethad mac Findlaích: Mormaer of Moray, later King of Scotland, killed at the Battle of Lumphanan in 1057. The inspiration for Shakespeare's infamous tragedy, *Macbeth*.

VAMPIRES

The Syndicate of Vampires: An ancient association of undead bloodlines. Headquartered in the Carpathian Mountains, it is the closest thing the undead have to a governing body.

The League of the Dark Star: Aka "the League." An undead society founded in the sixteenth century by Erasmus Kramer. Now led by Viviane Duclos, it is devoted to the myths of the Corrupter.

The Mystic Order of the Northern Wolf: Aka "the Order," aka "Northern Wolf." A Corrupter cult established in the early twentieth century by Grigori Rasputin. Dangerous and unpredictable, its membership is unknown.

Jude Marlowe: Born ca. 1590 in London, England, and Turned in 1607, he works for the Syndicate of Vampires. His bloodline is led by Hecuba.

Viviane Duclos: French sorceress, leader of the League of the Dark Star. Born in 1662 outside Chantilly, France, and condemned to die in 1681, she was rescued from her jail cell and Turned by Erasmus Kramer.

Grigori Rasputin: Russian mystic, faith healer for the Romanov family, founder of the Mystic Order of the Northern Wolf. Born in Siberia in 1869, he was Turned ca. 1916, shortly before his officially recorded death.

Hecuba: Age unknown. Having gone by many names, she is one of the twelve original Syndics who formed the Syndicate of Vampires.

Erasmus Kramer: German mystic, founder of the League of the Dark Star. Age at death unknown. He rescued Viviane Duclos from certain death during the Affair of the Poisons but died sometime in the late 1700s.

OTHER

Brixia, Ket, and Sulis: Free agents. Origins unknown; ages unknown; agenda unknown.

The Nexus: A convergence of two ley lines at the exact coordinates of Fulton Heights, Illinois. Nothing but trouble.

The Corrupter: Also called the Dark Star, the Endless One, and the Shining Immortal. A spectral entity that supposedly returns to the earthly realm once every generation. Unverified. Some venerate it, and some fear it; but if the legends are true, it portends the actual apocalypse . . .

Yekaterinburg, Russia

1918

EVEN BEFORE SHE OPENED HER EYES, THE GIRL KNEW THAT
death had come for her. Again. The dark air was thickened with its
pall, tangible as humidity and just as lush, and it settled over her
with a gentle caress. This body was healthy and young, and it could
have had a long life. But instead it would be sacrificed in a grab for
power—that much had been written on the wall for months, years—
because the only thing mortals prized more than the preciousness of
life was their ability to destroy it.

"Your Highness?" A man hovered at her bedside, one hand on
her shoulder. It was Botkin, the physician, his high forehead lad-
dered with concern. He was a kind man, loyal—and doomed. The
second she met his gaze, the fate that awaited him unrolled in her
mind's eye. It would be ugly. "You need to get up."

"Is something wrong with Alexei?" The question came automatically, dredged from the grooves of instinct and a rebellious part of
her consciousness that wouldn't let go.

"It . . . the tsarevich is fine, Your Highness," Botkin answered
soothingly. Across the room, Olga was already on her feet, and
Tatiana was stretching her limbs. "But it seems we're being moved
again. There's been violence in the city, and they fear it will get worse."

Taking a deep breath, she let the thick air coat her tongue and fill
her body, her senses crackling. Rage, and hatred, and—*yes*, violence.

But not in the city; it was here. Under this roof. It gathered like a thunderhead, and soon it would burst. Casting her covers aside, she sat up. "All right, then. I'll get dressed."

They moved quickly. Of the four sisters forced to share this room, she alone realized what was to come, and there was no point warning the others. Foreknowledge would be its own torture, and there was nothing to be done about it, anyway. *She* could stop it, of course, if she wanted to. But what would be the point? As healthy as her body was, it wouldn't survive what would be required of it, and it might make things harder next time around. *Next time.* A pity. She was hungry for chaos now.

With care, the four girls strapped themselves into corsets, the fabric panels packed tightly with precious stones—a fortune in hidden diamonds that the revolutionaries would have seized, had they thought to look. *Bulletproof*, the girl observed grimly, death so close she couldn't shut out the visions if she'd wanted to. And then the guards came for them.

They were hustled through the dining room, with all its ostentatious furniture, and something whispered across her skin. She turned, the sensation tugging her attention, and glimpsed the dark outline of a woman standing in the shadowed passageway leading to the kitchen. Faceless in the dark, the energy she radiated was as clear as a fingerprint.

A smile played on the girl's lips, in spite of everything. The men herding them were drunk on power and self-importance—completely ignorant of how fragile they really were. How small and insignificant, how close to their own deaths. Their lives were as delicate as fairy floss, and one, two, three, they'd all be in their graves before their grandchildren were old enough to remember them. She could see it all, entropy scattering their futures.

Down the stairs and through the courtyard, the girls were

reunited with their parents and brother, and then escorted into a basement room with scarred floors. They were told to wait, and Mama asked for chairs—one for herself, and one for poor, pallid Alexei—and the request was granted. Not for the first time, the girl wished her mother's cleric and faith healer, Grigori, was still with them; he'd been a scoundrel and a fraud, but most unwilling to die. If anyone could have gotten them out of here alive . . .

"Where do you think they're taking us this time?" Olga asked in a worried murmur, perhaps sensing the tension in the air. The younger girl had no answer to give, so she allowed her sister to find comfort in a squeeze of the hand, a listless shrug.

The answer was *an unmarked grave*. It flashed before her— a mineshaft, blankets wrapped around bodies, men woozy with alcohol tossing human remains into the void. The air in the room grew hazy with bloodlust, the smell of sulfur stronger than ever; and deep inside, she came alive. She drank in the caustic miasma of vengeance and loathing that spread as far as her senses reached, poisoning the blood of ordinary people. She felt their rage, their pain, their suffering; into her lungs she drew the intoxicating degradation of it.

The tension finally burst as, unannounced, more than a dozen men poured into the basement, all of them armed. A familiar face, bearded, lean, and lupine, pushed through to the front of the crowd— Yurovsky, their chief jailor. She pulled sharply at his thoughts until he turned, compelled by forces he couldn't begin to understand, and met her eyes.

It took less than a second to dive inside his consciousness and find her way around, to leave sooty fingerprints on his best memories and plant a ring of frost around this night—one that would spread to kill any joy he might ever experience. There was no point trying to stop what he meant to do; but there was no reason to let him live a peaceful life, either. As she pulled back, releasing her influence, she let out a sigh. He had twenty years left, almost to the day, and every last hour of it would now be plagued with misery.

"Nikolai Alexandrovich," Yurovsky began in a loud, crisp voice, addressing her father, "in view of the fact that your relatives are continuing their attack on Soviet Russia, the Ural Executive Committee has decided to execute you."

"What?" Her father started, the blood draining from his face.

In the split second before the roar of gunfire filled the room, before a crew of inebriated men could begin a gruesome and inept act of mass murder, Grand Duchess Anastasia Nikolaevna Romanova closed her eyes. The youngest daughter of Russia's last emperor, she'd had so much ahead of her. But this grisly little scene was not really the end—and she knew that better than anyone.

Death was only the beginning.

1

Fulton Heights, Illinois
Now

The only thing worse than living in a vampire town is having to take Algebra I for the second time. While living in a vampire town. I have a quiz tomorrow on exponents and square roots, and literally the only thing that will keep me from failing it at this point is if I get eaten by one of the undead on my way to school in the morning.

To make matters worse, Fulton Heights, roughly thirty minutes from downtown Chicago, isn't even one of the *cool* suburbs. All we've got is a dying mall, a nexus of weird, mystical energy that attracts monsters, and a handful of abandoned buildings the municipal government can't afford to tear down. Hence the real source of our vampire problem. Empty warehouses make great hideouts for creatures of the night, who need proximity to their food source (us) and a safe place to sleep during the day.

I seriously don't understand why we can't just move somewhere else, but my parents refuse to discuss it. Right now, going on minute twelve of my agonizing attempt to solve for x on question number eight, I'm not sure if dying doesn't have a certain amount of appeal. Reviving a lost argument might be pointless, but it is distracting, so I shout from the kitchen, "Why do I have to learn this stuff when I could get vampired at, like, any moment?"

"About three people in Fulton Heights die from vampire attacks each year, August," my dad calls back from the living room in his stop-being-so-dramatic tone. "That's less than the number of people we lose to heart disease, cancer, and traffic accidents. It's not even in the top ten causes of death for the area! Stop being so dramatic."

Like that's supposed to make me feel better. Pretty much every Fulton Heights resident has those statistics memorized, but for most of us, it's cold comfort. Vampires aren't wild animals that kill indiscriminately, and most of them are smart enough to know that it's in their best interests not to rack up a huge body count and give the frightened townsfolk a reason to get all torches-and-pitchforks about them hanging out in our long-shuttered glassworks factory. But we don't exactly have an armistice, either.

They still need to eat, and we're their favorite entrée. Okay, unlike what you see in the movies, they don't tend to chase us down dark alleys and tear our throats out. A little Undead 101: Along with their superstrength and eternal youth and all that business, vampires also have this special mind-control thing that makes humans all docile and aroused, which renders us easy pickings. You meet a cute boy, he smiles at you—and the next thing you know you wake up all light-headed with a great big hickey and a pint of blood missing from your veins.

Or so goes the rumor. No cute boys have tried to seduce me yet. That's another thing Fulton Heights doesn't seem to have: other gay guys for me to date.

"We should move!" I shout next, because I want to keep this pointless conversation going as long as possible.

"Move where?" my mom responds this time. It's a challenge.

"I think Californ—"

"Earthquakes." She doesn't even let me finish, and I know I've got her. "Heat waves, droughts, brush fires, mudslides . . . Do you know how many people die from *those* each year? Do you know how much property values are, or how much homeowner's insurance costs?"

"No!" I'm on a roll now. "How much?"

"Stop baiting your parents," my tutor scolds, tapping the worksheet in front of me to regain my focus. Daphne Banks is a student at Northwestern University, about fifteen minutes away from here, and my parents pay her to come by twice a week and torture me. "You're not leaving this table until you finish every one of these problems, mister."

"Who cares if seventeen is the square root of three hundred and sixty-one?" I exclaim. "A vampire could chase me down an alley tomorrow and eat me, and it's not like me being barely competent in algebra will scare him off!"

"'Barely competent' might be . . . kind of a stretch," Daphne says, wincing, "and the square root of three hundred and sixty-one is nineteen, not seventeen."

"Ha—gotcha!" Gloating, I scribble down the answer to question number eight. I feel a little bad for tricking her like that, but when you're this bad at math, you need to be really good at grifting. "Thanks, Daph."

"August Pfeiffer, you little swindler!" She reaches out and messes up my hair to teach me a lesson—but the joke's on her, because my hair was already a mess to begin with. "This is important, though, you know? You need to learn this if you want to leave here for college. The odds that you'll get vampired to death are, like, twenty-thousand to one; but if you don't get decent grades, you could end up stuck in Fulton Heights forever."

It's a sobering thought, and I rededicate myself to the soul-sapping practice test. I cannot wait to leave this town, with its empty buildings and guys I can't date, and go live someplace where "Heart disease is our leading cause of death!" isn't a humblebrag. It doesn't have to be California, either. Just a place big enough that the ratio of art galleries to yearly vampire attacks is at least even. The only person I'll miss is my best friend, Adriana. And my parents. And Daphne.

Everyone else can get eaten.

About two hundred years later, I finish the worksheet, and my mom hands Daphne a chunk of cash for putting up with me all evening. Stuffing the money in her purse, my tutor tosses her blond hair with a gracious smile. "Thank you, Mrs. Pfeiffer."

"Call me Monica, please," my mother says for what must be the millionth time. I'm pretty sure Daphne is in a sorority, and she'll have to be held at knifepoint before she addresses my mother by her first name. Delivering a pile driver to my self-esteem, Mom continues, "We're the ones who should thank *you*. So far this year, Auggie's managed to hold on to a C average in a math class, which . . . You know, for your next miracle, can I request that water-into-wine thing?"

"Hey!" I'm mildly affronted. "I'm standing *right here*, remember?"

"I know, sweetie, and you're doing it so well." Mom messes up my hair—because why not get everybody in on the act?—and I scowl at her.

"Auggie's shown a lot of improvement in the past six months," Daphne says diplomatically, as if I had anywhere to go but up after the grades I received last year. "I think he's going to get the hang of this."

"Auggie, why don't you walk Daphne out to her car?" my dad suggests as he enters the kitchen behind Mom, going for the cabinet where he keeps his trusty popcorn bowl.

"That's totally not necessary." Daphne waves the offer away. "My parents used to be vampire hunters, and I'm trained in combat techniques. Honestly, Auggie is safer inside."

"Statistically, vampires are far more likely to approach women walking alone," my dad counters, determined for me to be a gentleman, whether I like it or not. "Besides," he continues, gesturing out the kitchen windows, "there have been a few . . . unsettling incidents on this block recently, and Monica and I would feel better if you didn't go by yourself."

The "unsettling incidents" he's talking about include handprints found on the outside of second-story windows, strange noises at night, golden lights burning in the darkness, and the occasional animal corpse turning up, drained of blood. In the absence of a convenient human, vampires will snack on whatever is handy.

"Does Auggie get to make any decisions here?" I ask, annoyed. "Or are you going to snap a leash around my neck and drag me outside like an animal?"

"Don't be so dramatic, August," my mother says in the manner of someone who is not being sent outside where there are *actual monsters*.

At the same time, Daphne insists, "I'll be fine!"

Then, after a moment, my dad puts in, "We do still have that leash left over from when Scout was alive."

Needless to say, I end up walking Daphne to her car. At the risk of repeating myself, Fulton Heights is a boring town where nothing ever happens—save the occasional death by vampiric exsanguination—so it's not as if she had to fight for a parking spot. Her secondhand Saab is right at the foot of our walk. It's early March, snow still lingering on the ground, and a cold wind rips the breath from our mouths in shreds of white steam.

"It was very sweet of you to make sure I didn't die in the ten seconds it took us to get here, Auggie," Daphne says when we reach her vehicle. My parents have turned on the exterior lights and are watching through the front windows—as if they'd be able to do anything but wave goodbye if we got attacked right now. Wistfully, my tutor adds, "Sometimes I wish you were straight. And about four years older. And better at algebra."

"Two of those things will never happen," I declare emphatically, "and me getting older is about fifty-fifty."

"Well, I guess it is better for me if you stay bad at math." Daphne gives me a hug. She actually smells really nice, and just for a moment I also kind of wish I were straight; but then I remember what Boyd Crandall looked like when he got dared to make a snow angel in his boxer briefs at school on Monday, and I change my mind. She pulls back and points a stern finger at me. "Keep studying those flashcards until you've got your equations memorized, okay? And if you have any questions about your homework, send me an email."

"How about I just send you the homework, and—" I stop, midswindle, when a strange sensation prickles up the back of my neck, like a breath puffed across my skin. Gooseflesh spreads between my shoulders, and I whirl around, convinced something is behind me. The yard is empty, though, without so much as footprints in the snow—human or otherwise.

"Auggie?" Daphne steps closer, peering over my shoulder. "What is it? Did you hear something?"

And then we *both* hear something, and our heads snap up as a gentle skittering noise comes from the neighbor's roof, a shower of displaced snow drifting down from the eaves. It could be anything—a house cat or a raccoon, or maybe a weather balloon caught on a downdraft of swamp gas—but either way, it's my signal to get the hell back inside.

"So I'll see you next week," Daphne says briskly, darting around to the driver's side of her car.

"Drive safe," I chirp in response, and then I'm hurrying up the walk before she's even pulled away from the curb. Halfway to the porch, however, I catch something with my foot and kick it almost onto the front steps. A rabbit, its fur so white it blended in seamlessly with the snow, rolls a few times before flopping loosely onto its back. It's dead, and two deep, bloodless puncture wounds in its neck are all I need to know what killed it. There was a vampire in our front yard tonight.

I sprint the rest of the way to the door, and my heart doesn't stop pounding for another ten minutes once I'm safely locked inside, a crucifix clutched in my white-knuckled fist. Vampires can't enter a privately owned building without an invitation, so I should be safe . . . but I'm not taking any chances.

It isn't until I'm brushing my teeth that the most disturbing fact of all hits me, and my throat goes dry: It's below freezing outside—*but the rabbit's body was still limp.* Whatever dropped it on our front walk must've just left before I stumbled over it . . . barely fifteen feet from the windows where I'd been sitting and doing my homework.

Chilled all the way to my bone marrow, I climb into bed, but it's hours before my eyes finally slide shut.

2

"**A**uggie, you look like crap." Adriana Verdugo has been my best friend since we were both in second grade, but not because I appreciate her honesty. It's between classes at Fulton Heights High, and I have just finished almost certainly failing that algebra quiz.

"I didn't sleep very well." Even after I finally drifted off, all I dreamed about all night was death, one hideous demise after another. Firing squads, decapitation, hanging, burning . . . I would jerk awake just before the final moment, panting and sweating, my heart beating so hard it hurt. Each time, I'd stare at the window, convinced a bloodthirsty monster waited on the other side of the shade. "There was a vampire in our yard last night."

Adriana shudders, leaning up against the locker next to me. "When will the city actually *do* something? It's not like it would cost them much to just burn some of those empty buildings down, right?" Hands on her hips, she states, "I still think we should figure out who to pitch my holy water sprinkler system idea to, because it's brilliant. There are already pipes running everywhere—all they have to do is put in some sprinkler heads and get a priest to mumble a prayer or two at the public works building—"

"The city is ten square miles! They can't even afford to demolish some collapsing warehouses and you want them to put in, like, eighteen thousand sprinklers?"

"Ugh, this place sucks." Adriana sighs in defeat just as the bell rings. Reluctantly, we start for class. "By the way, my abuela wants you to come over for dinner again. She kind of won't shut up about it."

"Abuela as in Abuela Rosales?" For the first time today, I finally perk up. "As in my bestest friend, Ximena Rosales, who will hopefully be making her famous guacamole?"

"Yeah, that's her. So I can tell her you're in?"

"Yes!" I do a little dance move, because Ximena Rosales is possibly the best cook in Fulton Heights. Mentally, I add her to the list of people I don't want eaten. When we reach our classroom, we see the three boys sitting in the front row, and a very familiar combination of fear, envy, and horniness rolls over me.

"Okay." Adriana rounds on me. "Fuck, marry, kill: Boyd Crandall, Dante Gardner, and Kenton Reed."

She thinks this is a stumper, but I don't even have to consider my answer. "Fuck Boyd Crandall, marry Boyd Crandall, and then kill Boyd Crandall and collect the insurance money."

"I'm pretty sure that's cheating," Adriana says, narrowing her eyes. "And *Boyd*? He's, like . . . he's an assclown. And a bro. And a douche." She shakes her head. "He's an assdouche bro-clown, and you're telling me you would seriously do sex to his body?"

"In my imagination, *he* is doing sex to *my* body, and the answer is emphatically yes." My palms are sweaty just thinking about it. Adriana knows all about my lust-hate feelings for Boyd—she just doesn't understand. Apparently, me seriously wishing I could bone someone I don't even like is a concept she finds mind-boggling. Boyd might be an assdouche bro-clown, and I'll never actually date him, but I am about 90 percent of the way toward developing carpal tunnel syndrome after a week of private time thinking about him making a snow angel in his underpants.

"Are you going to be hanging out in the art room after school today?" my best friend inquires now, and her tone is ridiculously casual. As if I don't know why she's asking.

"Yes." I wait patiently.

"Tell Hope I said hi. Or whatever." She acts like it's an afterthought.

"Hi . . . or . . . whatever," I repeat, typing it into my Notes app. "Got it."

Her face turns scarlet, and she rolls her eyes as she precedes me into the classroom. Adriana may have higher standards than I do, but she crushes on as many girls as I do boys—and yet both of us are perpetually alone. At least it's nice to not be the only hopeless case in Fulton Heights.

If Adriana's plan to arson all our hometown's unwanted buildings ever gets any traction, I will humbly propose that our high school be added to the list—with the single condition that the art room be spared. It is literally the only thing worth saving here. The tables and chairs are stained; the walls are covered with yellowing watercolors by students who graduated before I was born; and the air is always gummy with the combined smell of papier-mâché and Murphy Oil Soap. I love it.

Ever since I was a kid, art is the only thing I've really been passionate about. I have dozens of sketchbooks at home filled with my own drawings—from the stick-figure families and their lumpy cartoon dogs I did in preschool, to the complicated sketches I'm working on now. My big dream is to one day illustrate my own graphic novel.

"Ah, my star pupils!" exclaims Mr. Strauss as he sweeps into the room, beaming at me and Hope Cheng, as if we're actually doing him some big favor by making him stay after school to make sure we don't *actually* arson the place. "What are we doing today?"

"I still have my sculpture to finish." Hope gestures at the project she's been working on for the past few weeks, which sort of defies an easy description. She's building a statue out of pine cones and glue, but it honestly looks like a robot made of spiky turds.

"How about you, Auggie?" Mr. Strauss turns to me as Hope empties a bag of pine cones she's salvaged from who-knows-where all over one of the art tables.

"I guess I wanted to practice with the charcoals some more." My big flaw as an artist is that I get easily mired in details, and I'll spend forty minutes trying to perfect a single tree before I finally give up and accept that everything I'm doing is pointless. Mr. Strauss suggested I work with charcoals for a while—a medium that allows for quick sketches that focus on shape and composition rather than minutiae.

Unlocking the supply cabinet, our teacher retrieves all the necessary materials while I clip a wide sheet of paper to an easel. Hope sets up her turd monster on a table across from me, and before I put my headphones on, I clear my throat. "Adriana told me to say hi."

"Oh." Hope tosses her hair, turning away just as a little smile touches her lips. "Tell her I said hi back. I listened to that K-pop group she was talking about at lunch last week, and I really liked them."

"You know, if you want to say hi back, you could always text her . . ." I let my inflection go up at the end—a suggestion and a question. Hope is very cute and totally Adriana's type: ethereal and witchy, all hippie skirts, flowing hair, and mismatched accessories.

"I don't know." Hope bites her lip, swiveling her sculpture

around like she's trying to figure out which part to make worse first. "What if she thought I was trying to, like, flirt with her?"

"*Ugh*, you guys are both ridiculous." I take off my glasses so I can pinch the bridge of my nose. "Flirting is the whole point!" Adriana will totally kill me for going off script, but *come on.* "If you're not into her, that's okay; but if you are, I promise you don't have anything to worry about. That's all I'm saying."

Hope doesn't look over, but I watch as she bobs her head a little, absorbing the information. Finally, she says, "Well, maybe I will text her."

Feeling smug, I slip my headphones on and start my playlist. It's a lot of ambient stuff—background music with a heavy beat to get my blood going. When I start to feel the rhythm, I pick up a stick of charcoal and get to work.

A hand claps me on the shoulder and I jump about a mile, the headphones slipping down around my neck. Mr. Strauss hovers beside me. "Sorry—didn't mean to scare you! It's just that the sun is going to set pretty soon, and we need to lock up."

I blink, my eyes dry and my head swimming. "What do you mean? We just . . ."

My voice trails off as I notice the advanced angle of the daylight shining through the classroom's windows, and when I look over at Hope's workstation, I see her poop goblin has sprouted an entire arm out of nowhere. She's staring at me, too, and I blink a few more times as Mr. Strauss asks, "So what have you been working on for the past two hours? You've been so focused I hated to interrupt."

The past two hours? Dazed—half convinced my favorite teacher is gaslighting me, but unable to deny that the *actual angle of the sun has changed*—I face my easel and freeze. What was a blank sheet not ten seconds ago is now filled edge to edge with a tableau I have no memory of drawing. It's a mob scene of some kind, so dense that the people in it spill into shadowy suggestion in the background. The faces are all vague and featureless, but the attitude is undeniably angry.

"This is . . . Auggie, this is incredible work." Mr. Strauss sounds awed, his fingers tracing the motion of the crowd. "The composition is pretty straightforward, but I can't believe how much emotion you've captured with so few details! Even without expressions, you can sense the rage coming off these people." The scent of rotten eggs tickles my nose, and I sneeze as my art teacher points to a group of figures in the center of the picture. Rendered in heavily layered black, it looks like three women in veils and old-fashioned dresses. "Who are they?"

"I . . . I don't know," I croak.

"Why did you make them the focal point of the image while everyone in the crowd is looking back at the viewer?" He persists. "What are they watching? Why are they angry?"

Staring at the crowd, I feel lost, because I have no idea why. I have no answers to any of his questions. Helpless, I repeat myself. "I don't know."

"Hmm." Mr. Strauss studies the sketch for another moment. "Do you mind leaving it here, so I can take some pictures? You should have high-quality digitals of your work when you're applying to art programs next year."

"Yeah, sure." I'm glad for him to keep it, this ghost sketch that apparently just stole two hours of my life. The horrible dreams that kept me awake last night crash through my brain again—angry mobs, firing squads, faceless executioners. I'm so flustered that it takes me three tries to get my headphones back into my bag. "I should get going. My parents will freak if I'm not home before dark."

Hope is watching me, looking frightened and concerned. "Auggie? Are you—"

"See you tomorrow!" The words are still ringing in the air when

I burst through the door, running for the exit like I'm trying to escape from something.

But what?

My phone confirms that it's two hours later than when I walked into the art room after the final bell. Whatever just happened *really happened,* and my stomach cramps in a very unfortunate, borderline-diarrhea type of way. Shoving through the side exit to the parking lot, I trot past the overhang and into the waning sunlight, gulping down great helpings of crisp air.

"Everything okay?"

Confused and wild, I spin back around to see a guy I don't know leaning against the wall beside the door, a cigarette tucked behind his ear. His dark eyes study me in a way that makes me feel comfortable and uncomfortable at once, and I clear my throat. "I—yeah. I'm okay. I just felt . . . sick for a second. It's over now."

"Cool." The boy points to his cigarette. "You don't happen to have a light, do you?"

His voice is smooth, a British accent curving his vowels into shapes I don't expect, and just like that I'm horny again. He's about my age, and ridiculously handsome: light brown skin, high cheekbones, pillowy lips; dark, fluffy hair cut in a fade; skinny black pants ripped with fashionable precision to show off his knees. How is it possible that he has *sexy knees?* Can knees even *be* sexy? Is this what it feels like to have a kink?

"Uh, I don't smoke." My cheeks are warm, and when his eyes meet mine, it's like he knows what I'm thinking. "And you can get in trouble for smoking on school grounds."

Instantly, I want to throw myself off a cliff. Who *says* that? Why don't I just tell him that I'm a hopeless nerd-virgin rather than supplying him with all these careful hints? He gives me an impish smile, though. "School's out, right? Anyway, I'm not a student here, so what can they do?"

"You're not?" I look around at the mostly empty parking lot. My bike is one of only two left chained to the rack by the sidewalk. "Are you . . . waiting for someone?"

With an enigmatic shrug, he moves his gaze over my body in a way that makes my cheeks even warmer. "Who says I'm not waiting for you?"

An awkward church giggle comes out of my mouth, and I can't look him in the eye anymore. My mind has gone blank. To buy some time while my last two brain cells collaborate on a witty reply, I adjust my glasses and examine his jacket. It's denim, artfully distressed, and under it he appears to be wearing nothing but a thin T-shirt. Inspired, I blurt, "Aren't you cold?"

"Why?" He cocks one of his brows. "You want to warm me up?"

Now my face is an inferno. "I . . . I, um . . ."

"Sorry, that was rather forward of me." He does not look sorry in the least. "My name is Jude."

"Augh—" I begin, and then choke on some saliva, "—ust. August. Or 'ee.' Auggie is, too, also fine. Auggie or August. Is . . . my names." Shutting my eyes, I let out a deep breath. The past sixteen years have been okay, but I am very ready to die now.

"I know who you are, August." His tone is still mild, friendly even, but when my eyes snap open again I see him very differently than before. "I told you I was waiting for you."

His breath isn't clouding the air the way mine is, and he doesn't seem the least bit bothered by the sharp chill in the air, in spite of his thin jacket. The sun dips lower, splashing the parking lot with honeyed light, but the overhang above the side entrance to the school creates a small pocket of lengthening shadow—and Jude hasn't stepped out of it since we started talking. My hands shaking again, I make a show of searching my coat pockets.

"You know what? I just remembered, I *do* have a lighter. It's—

19

aha!" Quick as I can, I yank my crucifix free and thrust it out at him. "Get back, demon of the night!"

Gold light flickers in his eyes and he recoils, flinching at the sight of the cross. Then his features settle into an annoyed frown. "'Demon of the night'? That's very offensive."

"I don't care! You were going to eat me!"

"August, if I had any intention of harming you, I'd have done it the second the door opened—before you knew I was here. I certainly wouldn't have waited for you to get safely into the sunlight before deliberately announcing myself." He plucks the cigarette from behind his ear, tucking it into his mouth. Then he produces a book of matches—which he had *all along*—and lights up. "Believe it or not, vampires are not all brainless killing machines."

"Exactly what a brainless killing machine would say," I snap. "And what was all that . . . seduction stuff? You were trying to mesmerize me!"

"I wasn't mesmerizing you, I was flirting with you." Jude's gaze travels over me again. "I happen to like flirting with cute boys."

"Stop it!" I stammer, my throat flushing with heat again. "Stop playing vampire mind games with me, okay? We had paranormal safety train—"

I don't finish, because his eyes shimmer this beautiful color, and my thoughts suddenly go all warm and gooey. Jude's lips look really soft, I finally seem to notice, and his knees are even sexier than I first thought. There's a clink of metal as the crucifix slips from my fingers and hits the pavement, and I start walking toward the expanding shadow of the overhang. He wants me. And I want him to take my—

He blinks, the trance breaking just like that, and I stumble back again with a sharp gasp. Scooping the crucifix up off the ground, I thrust it at him like a sword, my hands shaking. "*What the hell was that?*"

"That's what it feels like to be mesmerized," he answers coolly. "The only reason you're still standing over there and I'm still standing over here is because I need you to understand that I don't mean you any harm."

"Oh, sure, because you're one of the 'good' ones?" I scoff.

"There's no such thing as a good vampire, August." The blunt candor of his reply actually surprises me. "Just like there's no such thing as a good person. All of us are capable of violence and selfishness under the right circumstances."

"You *eat* people," I remind him, perhaps stupidly. "We're your food, not your friends. Why should I believe that you don't want to hurt me?"

"Because you and I need to have a conversation about something very important." His impish demeanor is gone, and now his tone is all business. It sends a chill clear down to my toes. "Something very bad and very dangerous is happening, August Pfeiffer, and it directly concerns you."

"That's ridiculous." I back away from the ring of sincerity in his voice. If he's bullshitting me, he's spent a lot of time practicing his delivery, because he sure sounds convincing. "I've heard enough, so—"

"You haven't heard anything." Jude steps forward, right to the very edge of the shadow that protects him. "The reason I came to Fulton Heights was to find you and warn you. Darkness is coming, August. The world as you know it, as we all know it, could be coming to an end. And you might be the only one who can stop that from happening."

Another church giggle bursts out of me, because this speech is not only grandiose, but absurd—the oldest and corniest trick in the book. I can't even factor a polynomial, but I'm the key to saving the universe? "Oh, right, sure! Evil forces more powerful than I could possibly imagine, time running out, blah blah blah, and one gullible kid in a shithole suburb of Chicago is the Chosen One who will save mankind. Obviously. When do we get started?"

Jude shakes his head, his expression somber. "Not chosen, August. No one gets chosen for this. You're just in the worst possible place at the worst possible time."

The shadows are even longer now, the sun a broken flare barely cresting the treetops, and soon the daylight will vanish altogether. I back away farther, quick steps toward the bike rack. "Well, look, this has been super fun, but—"

"What do you dream about at night?" Jude demands, not moving a muscle. "Death? People from historical periods you don't recognize?" I freeze, and he must see that he's hit a nerve, because he presses ahead. "Have you experienced unfamiliar memories or lost time? Have you noticed any changes in your body?"

"We're done," I declare, my voice thin and trembling. How could he possibly know about my nightmares and my disappearing two hours? "Okay? This is over. Just . . . stay away from me."

"Very soon, you're going to run out of ways to explain the things you don't understand." He tosses something at me underhand. It's a perfect throw, but I have no coordination, and the object hits me square in the chest, almost dropping to the ground before I get my hands on it. "When you're ready for answers, get in touch. Anytime."

Looking down, I find a disposable, plastic cell phone in my hand—a burner. "Do you honestly think . . ."

But I trail off when I glance back up again, because there's no point in finishing. The light hasn't disappeared entirely yet, but Jude has. He's gone.

3

The three things I actually enjoy about my crappy hometown are as follows: 1) Colgate Woods, a nature area adjacent to our once-thriving industrial neighborhood; 2) The sight of Boyd Crandall in his underpants; and 3) Sugar Mama's, an ice-cream-parlor-slash-café, because everything about it is life-changing. Their Nutella gelato? Life-changing. Their peppermint s'mores mocha? Life-changing! Their gorgeous barista with the cute butt and dreamy blue eyes? *Life. Changing.*

His name is Gunnar, he is sixteen, and he lives in Wilmette—which is about ten minutes away and even smaller than Fulton Heights. He has light brown surfer hair and a cool dude-necklace, and he works Monday and Thursday nights, plus alternating Wednesdays. Which is why I make Adriana meet me for regular and carefully scheduled study sessions at Sugar Mama's each week.

It's been five days since a mysterious vampire ambushed me to say I'm supposed to save the world from Darkness with a capital *D*, and as yet the sun keeps shining. Since then, I've only had one terrible nightmare—a normal one, about spiders—and no more weird blackouts, or whatever it was that happened in the art room. I also passed my algebra quiz by the skin of my teeth, so if there really is some sort of curse on my head, it's failing at its one job.

I'm not trying to sound flippant. I spent roughly forty-eight hours panicking about the possibility that Jude—whoever he is—could be telling me some version of an actual truth. Because, I mean, here's the thing: Either he honestly believes I'm the key to fending off Doomsday, which is scary . . . or he was lying in order to trick me, specifically, for some reason. Which is possibly even scarier.

When I get to Sugar Mama's, Adriana is already at our usual table by the plate glass windows looking out on Main Street, nursing her usual order: a scoop of amaretto ice cream drowned in at least four shots of espresso. I give her a wave and get in line, and when I reach the front of it, Gunnar looks up at me and smiles—and it's a huge smile, one that reaches his perfect, dreamy eyes. "Hey, it's my favorite customer!"

I try not to moan out loud. He's probably straight, and he's probably just being nice—and I'm probably a sad, moonstruck gay boy trying too hard to read the tea leaves of his friendliness. It makes me afraid to flirt with him, lest I poison the well and can never return to my favorite hangout again; but every time I see him I wish I had the courage to try anyway just to see if maybe I really *am* his favorite.

"Hey! It's the best barista!" I exclaim, which is . . . pathetic. Patheticness is my chief export now. "How's, um . . ." Desperately, I search for something to ask about, but my mind is a wasteland. Again. ". . . your week going?"

"You know, it's just going." He does a dude-shrug, bobbing his head a little, and I die inside on an endless loop.

"Awesome! That's totally cool!" Honestly, if that Darkness wants to end the world as we know it, now would be a great time. "So, um, I'd like a—"

"Medium two-pump s'mores mocha with a dash of peppermint, an extra shot of espresso, and a toasted marshmallow," he finishes with a grin that melts me just like Linda Hamilton in that nuclear blast from *Terminator 2*.

"Yes, wow, exactly," I sputter in a high, tiny voice. I was going to ask for whipped cream instead, but if Gunnar the Sexy Surfer-Barista wants to toast my marshmallow, I will allow it. When I pay, our fingers touch, and he winks—he *winks* for some reason—and my coffee and I float all the way across the room to where Adriana is waiting.

"Hey, it's the best barista!" She greets me in an overly enthusiastic tone of voice, and I settle into my chair, pushing my glasses back up my nose with a cool expression.

"You mock, but he winked at me, Adriana." I wave my receipt in front of her. "And he didn't even charge me for the toasted marshmallow."

"You didn't *want* the toasted marshmallow."

"Not the point!" I sniff primly. Hazarding a glance back at the counter, I realize Gunnar is looking *directly at me*, and our eyes meet, and I freeze, and I give him a totally deranged smile and a stiff wave and then turn back to Adriana. "Oh no. Oh no no no. We made eye contact."

"I'm sorry it had to end this way," she sympathizes. "What should I sing at your funeral?"

"He thinks I'm a psycho for sure now." My face is melting like the toasted marshmallow I definitely did not want. "Is he still looking? Tell me he's not still looking."

"He's not looking anymore."

I glance back, and he is totally still looking. "*Adriana!*"

"I'm sorry!" Her giggle fit, however, belies the words. "I was trying to make you feel better! I didn't think you'd turn around again. And anyway, he's not looking at you like he's scared. More like you're . . . interesting."

"I don't know what that means. Is it good?"

"It's good," she confirms. Then she nudges me. "So, what's been going on with you, Auggie? You've been acting weird this past week—and you never got back to me about when to have dinner with my abuela. She's thinking tomorrow night, if you're free."

Picking up my spoon, I poke at the marshmallow floating in my mocha like a bloated corpse. After I fled school last Wednesday, Adriana was the only person I wanted to tell about Jude and his cryptic warning. But by the time I got home, my chest heaving and my stomach all crampy, I couldn't figure out how to raise the subject in a way that didn't scare me to death. I wanted someone to tell me that the whole thing was preposterous, but . . . what if she didn't? What if she took it seriously? What if *I* had to take it seriously?

Nightmares happen, right? I mean, last week wasn't the first time I had dreams about death and stuff—but blinking and missing two whole hours of my life? That's brain tumor shit, and just thinking about it makes my blood turn slushy. For five days I've reminded myself that vampires are known tricksters, that mesmerism is only the tip of the iceberg when it comes to their machinations for luring humans to their doom. The earliest written accounts talk of the undead rising from the grave and returning to their former homes, preying on loved ones' willingness to believe in miracles, for a quick bite.

This Jude dude could have drugged me, or hypnotized me somehow—stolen two hours of my life, so I'd be frightened and susceptible when he showed up three minutes later to tell me I'm Mr. Worst Possible Time—all with the goal of making me a more exciting meal than the usual bite-and-run. It was a ruse. He's an immortal monster looking to amuse himself and fill his eternal hours of free time. That's it.

For Adriana, I finally muster up an answer. "Dinner with your grandma sounds great. And sorry I've been weird. More vampire bullshit."

She shakes her head in disgust. "I know the volunteer hunting squads were a total disaster, but it's ridiculous that the city thinks a few patrol cars rolling around at night with sun lamps and holy-water squirt guns is actually doing anything!" Stirring what remains of the ice cream in her cup, she asks, "What was it this time? More dead animals?"

Before I can answer, I'm saved by the bell over the front door, which jingles as someone we know walks in. I skipped the independent study on Thursday, unable to face the sketch I did and the questions Mr. Strauss has about it, so this is the first time I've seen Hope Cheng in nearly a week. Grateful for the distraction, I wave to get her attention; but she's already headed our way, a shy smile on her face, her eyes focused on Adriana.

"You made it!" my best friend exclaims as Hope sits down beside her. Something passes between them, and I shift awkwardly in my seat, feeling inexplicably like someone watching his bus leave without him.

"Hey, Hope." I cock an eyebrow. "Um, fancy meeting you here?"

"I told her we'd be studying if she wanted to drop by," Adriana says, her cheeks a little flushed, and she offers me a shrug. "I knew you wouldn't mind."

I fight the urge to frown, because now I *want* to mind. Obviously, I'm cool with Hope, but I'd been working up to telling Adriana about Jude—and instead, I'm suddenly the third wheel on what looks like a practice date. Ugh, and *ugh*, because I'm super happy for them—but I can't help it: I'm also jealous.

Over the summer, I downloaded one of those gay dating apps. I know you have to be eighteen to use them, but it's not like they send the FBI to your house to check, and all I really wanted was to see who was out there. My big fantasy was that I would—surprise!—find a secret profile for Boyd, thus beginning a real-life romantic comedy for us. Or a porno. I was not going to be particular on that point.

But I'd wasted both my time and the storage space on my phone, because there was literally no other guy in Fulton Heights on that app. The nearest profile was over ten miles away, and the dude was in his fifties. So I shut it down and deleted it, and I accepted that Adriana and I would be friend-dates to every school dance until graduation and beyond. But maybe *that* dream was unrealistic, too.

"Yeah." I find my voice at last, along with a friendly smile. "Of course I don't mind. What do you want to drink? I'll place your order."

"Oh, you don't have to do that." Hope looks somewhat aghast at the idea of inconveniencing me. "I have money—"

"Give Auggie the money and let him do it," Adriana cuts in. "Seriously, he wants to." Nodding at the bar, she adds, "He has sort of a crush on the barista."

Hope notices Gunnar for the first time, and her eyes go wide as she takes in his perfect perfectness. "Oh. Wow. Uh . . . I think I have sort of a crush on the barista, too."

"Take a number." I snatch Hope's money and get up from my chair. "Fair warning, though: Adriana's grandmother is a witch, and I'm going to ask her to help me put a love and/or sex whammy on Gunnar, so you better act fast."

Adriana frowns. "My abuela is not going to help you put a *sex whammy* on someone."

"What if I say 'pretty please'?"

"What if you just show her his picture?" Hope suggests, her eyes still on the lithe, broad-shouldered boy behind the counter. "I mean, I'm a hundred percent gay, and even *I* kinda want to put the sex whammy on him."

"But, see, though?" I sit back down. "What if I show Ximena his picture and she decides she wants to put the sex whammy on him for herself?"

A yelp of unbridled panic escapes from deep in Adriana's throat.

"Can we *please* stop talking about sex and my abuela?" At the next table over, a mother with three young kids turns to glare at us, and Adriana lowers her voice. "I hate my life so much. Auggie, what's your vampire drama?"

"Vamp— Wait, *what*?" Hope does a double take, her gaze skittering between us. She's not originally from Fulton Heights, and like all newcomers, she still freaks when she hears the v-word.

The problem is, I don't really know Hope very well. She moved here from Minnesota at the beginning of the school year, and she lives with her uncle, but I haven't spent much time with her outside of our independent study. I don't know if I want to bare my deepest, scariest thoughts about Jude and what's either a potentially deadly brain tumor or else a dire, unearthly terror with my name on it. After a pause that lasts a hair too long, I confess a lesser truth.

"They've been finding dead animals in my neighborhood," I report at last, and Adriana sighs heavily, as if she'd known it all along. "Vampire snacks. Mostly birds and rabbits, but a stray cat turned up over the weekend, and I guess some stoners found a deer in the woods on Saturday. Bone dry."

"A deer?" Adriana startles.

Contrary to myth, vampires don't need to drink a lot of blood; they like to eat, of course, and it gives them strength—but as far as anyone knows, starvation is not among the things that will kill them. So generally, they just take what they need and move on; but a two-hundred-pound deer has about as much blood as a similarly sized human, and for it to be completely exsanguinated . . .

"How many bite marks?" My best friend's face is ashen.

"The reports didn't say." I squirm a little. "But cops were going door to door yesterday, telling everyone on my street to be careful— keep your pets inside, don't open the door to strangers, avoid going out after dark . . . the usual."

"'Avoid going out after dark'?" Hope repeats, her voice thin. "It's dark *now*; it gets dark at, like, five-thirty! And nobody came to my neighborhood about this! Why did—"

"Hey, it's okay—there's no reason to panic." Adriana gives Hope's arm a comforting squeeze . . . and then leaves her hand there. Very smooth. "It's a standard response to a spike in vampire-related activity. It happens sometimes, but it usually doesn't mean anything."

"*Usually?*" Hope isn't terribly comforted, and Adriana shoots me a worried look.

When we were kids, there was an undead uprising in Fulton Heights, where a bunch of vampires came to town toting a mystical artifact called the Shield of Baeserta. According to some dubious prophecy, the shield—coupled with a bit of very dark and gross blood magic—would "free the Night's Children from the Curse of Belenus." This was interpreted as a reference to vampires' fatal vulnerability to daylight, in part because Belenus was apparently some kind of sun god, and in part because literally *all* vampire prophecies are about reversing their fatal vulnerability to daylight.

Seriously. They have this major hard-on for being able to walk around and kill people in the afternoon, and every ten or twenty years, some previously unheard-of relic is unearthed, promising them a chance. Most are fakes, because con artists will turn up anywhere there's a way to make money, and the sale of fraudulent antiques and prophecies is a staggeringly lucrative business.

In the end, after the uprising was quelled, art historians were never able to fully authenticate the shield itself. They determined that it was centuries old, but they couldn't tell if it possessed any real magical capabilities, so whether we were all truly in danger of vampires with tans was anybody's guess. Unfortunately, fake or not, the ritual associated with the shield demanded the blood of a dozen humans, so the whole episode was messy.

"It's all pretty normal for this town, trust me." Adriana offers Hope an encouraging smile. "I know it seems really freaky, but the Vampire Shit meter always goes up when we get closer to spring—it's got something to do with the Nexus."

Hope gives an understanding nod. Everybody knows about the Nexus. "My uncle did say its vibrations are heightened around the equinox."

"Yeah." Adriana sighs. "It's great if you practice magic, because it gives your natural abilities a huge boost when you're casting—which is why my abuela moved here in the first place—but vampires get horny for it, too."

"Spring fever: catch it!" I make a rah-rah gesture.

So the Nexus. Basically, the Earth is polka-dotted by mystical axis points where occult energies are heightened and supernatural activity is especially strong; when they're close enough together, these points act like a chain of power plants, amplifying the signal and creating what are known as ley lines. Two such lines intersect at Fulton Heights, which is why our boring suburb gets a double scoop of otherworldly drama.

Adriana waves her hand. "Honestly, vampires are a greater threat to livestock than they are to us. One cow can feed a whole pack of vamps."

"I guess that's nice to hear?" Hope looks like she feels bad for local cows.

Excusing myself, I head to the counter to place her order and ogle my favorite barista some more. Gunnar is talking to a coworker, his attention diverted, so I don't even have to be sly about it. He lifts his shirt to scratch his stomach, exposing a few extra inches of bare skin, and I try not to drool.

"Hey!" Gunnar's eyes light up when he finally notices me. "You're back! You need another marshmallow?" Then, before I can answer, "Wait, I didn't screw up the chocolate, did I? I pumped it twice, like you said, but if it's not enough I can pump it some more."

The thought of Gunnar "pumping it" makes me dizzy, and I have to hold on to the counter for a moment to keep from swooning.

"Haha," I say—like, actually *say*, because I am the most awkward human on the planet. "No, the chocolate is perfect! I, um, need to get a thing for my friend."

"Sure—your wish is my command," Gunnar says, and if only that were true. He looks at me expectantly, and his eyes are so pretty, for a moment I honestly can't even remember how to utter words. While I'm giving my brain an urgent pep talk, I hear the bell over the front door jingle again—and a curious sensation brushes its way up my spine. It's like déjà vu from that night in my front yard; as I break out in goose bumps, I turn around.

A man has entered Sugar Mama's. His hair wild, he kicks the door shut behind him, muttering under his breath. He's probably homeless, looking for a place to warm up . . . but something about him snags and holds my focus. Shuffling along the front of the café, he twitches a little, mumbling louder, and people look politely away. The feeling that crept up my spine is under my skin now, getting stronger, and I watch the man bump against the table of the mother with her three kids. Glaring up at him, the woman snaps, "Excuse me, do you mind?"

My goose bumps spread in a flash, something tugging at the pit of my stomach, and somehow I *know*. A heartbeat before the disheveled man's eyes blaze to life, flaring a brilliant gold—before he grabs the woman and hauls her out of her seat, his jaws swinging wide—I gasp, "*Vampire!*"

The place erupts into chaos as he sinks his fangs into her neck, her children screaming while patrons scramble for the door. There's an emergency kit mounted on the wall—crucifixes, stakes, and holy water, all mandated by local safety codes—and Gunnar starts for it, leaping from behind the counter. He isn't halfway there when the vampire flings his victim across the room, easy as a rag doll, bowling her into my favorite barista. They both crash to the floor in a sprawling, bloody tangle, and the undead monster turns his terrifying golden eyes on me.

Alarm crashes through me, and my heart speeds as the creature flings the table aside, his fingertips stretching into claws. And then he's right in front of me, having crossed the room in the instant it took me to blink, his hands gripping the front of my sweater. My back against the counter, I want to scream . . . but I can't seem to.

"It is beginning." The man's expression is wild and strangely ecstatic, those golden eyes probing mine, boring into me and melting my resistance. "*The Dark Star rises!*"

And then he whirls, letting me go, just like that. Taking off at a sprint, he leaps straight through the broad front window, the thick glass exploding out of its frame; his claws rake the sky as he sails up into the night, rising impossibly, effortlessly.

My veins burn as I watch him finally reach the apex of his jump, backlit by the moon, and begin to arc down again. The buzz under my skin subsides, my heart thumping so hard my ears ring. Adriana says something, but I can't hear her—pressure is building in my head, shadows squeezing my vision into a pinhole as the vampire disappears from sight behind the buildings across the street.

I take a step, and then the pinhole closes, darkness washing over me as I crash to the floor.

4

When Emergency Medical Services arrives at Sugar Mama's, I'm awake again, dazed and suffering a splitting headache. Gunnar insists he's fine, but the woman who got bitten is going into shock—either from a loss of blood, or ... you know, *shock*—so it takes a minute before the paramedics get to me. As they check my pulse and vital statistics, they subject me to a battery of questions, like *When's the last time you ate? Were you bitten? Have you consumed any vampire blood?* I do my best to answer, but I'm rattled by the way they have their crucifixes out the whole time, just in case—even though they know I'm not Turning.

The thing is, Turning involves a whole exchange of fluids; a vampire sucks its victim nearly dry, then feeds them back some undead blood before delivering a killing blow. The body is then interred in the earth, where the immortal blood inside it lives on—replicating, reawakening the lifeless tissue, generating new and horrifying attributes. When the brain is reactivated, the creature rises again, crawling from the grave with its memories and personality completely intact. Only now it lives forever and hungers for blood.

If the organic tissues are too compromised before the victim is buried, the change won't take place—because, as powerful as it is, even vampire blood can't undo a cremation or reattach a severed head. But even a small amount of it can still heal burns and flesh wounds; it can knit bones and close brain lesions; and it can temporarily imbue an otherwise normal human with heightened sensory perception and increased strength.

Unsurprisingly, this is one of the reasons humans hunt vampires as much or more often than vice versa.

I'm given a clean bill of health only moments before my parents arrive, shaken and frantic, and they hug me so hard I'm tempted to ask the EMTs for painkillers. All the way home, I endure a new round of questions—*Are you okay? Are you hurt? Are you okay?*—but I'm not sure how to answer, because now I'm starting to wonder . . . what if I really *am* the Chosen One?

Hear me out: I know it sounds ridiculous, but why not? For as long as there have been supernatural beasties crawling the Earth, there have been legends about humans called to fight them and protect mankind. The oldest records have been purged of almost everyone but the straight white guys—Beowulf, St. George, King Arthur—while the modern accounts tell of warrior girls and goddesses, gifted with otherworldly powers and fated to play a key role in humanity's battle against the undead.

But why can't it be me this time? Why can't it finally be a gay kid with terrible math scores but a good skin-care regimen? After countless folktales about swaggering jocks and brave, beautiful girls, why shouldn't it be my turn?

I *felt* that vampire enter Sugar Mama's. That strange prickling sensation that pebbled my flesh with goose bumps—the same one I experienced the night I walked Daphne to her car, just before we realized there was something on the neighbor's roof—it was a *warning.*

Plenty of legends describe Chosen Ones developing special

abilities to aid in their mission: strength and agility, accelerated healing, extrasensory perception . . . and with the Nexus in play, nothing is too weird or wild to consider. The vivid dreams, these histories I don't recognize could be the result of some burgeoning power connecting to a mystical record of those who once shared the same calling. We're linked across centuries, across lifetimes, and now the torch has been passed to me. No wonder Jude did the whole sexy, come-with-me-if-you-want-to-live act; he must know what I am, what I'm soon going to be, and he intends to stop it from happening.

And maybe he's not the only one. *It is beginning.* The wild-haired vampire looked at me like he was searching for something, and once he'd found it, he smashed clear through a window to escape. What I can't understand is why he didn't just kill me when he clearly had the chance—Jude, too, for that matter. But I'm not exactly planning to look this gift horse in the mouth, either.

I'm also not planning to tell my parents about any of this. Not only will they think I've lost my mind, but if I've truly been chosen by the powers that be, then I need to keep my identity secret. The same myths that tell of swashbuckling jocks and warrior girls also tell of vengeful monsters and heaping piles of dead loved ones.

If I have dreams that night, I don't remember them when I wake up the next morning, my mind still spinning with questions. In the harsh light of day, the thought of being chosen no longer sounds cool. A life of battling monsters is generally a short one—and as far as supernatural gifts go, getting the creeps when vampires are nearby is . . . kind of disappointing.

School is little more than background noise to my mounting anxiety. Adriana can't stop talking about last night, asking how I am and if I'm still coming over for dinner, until I want to jump out of my skin. She means well, but my nerves are utterly frayed. All I can think about is getting to the end of the day so I can go back to the art room.

The afternoon I lost time, I didn't just black out; I went into a trance, or something, and sketched a detailed scene that *felt* familiar, even if I couldn't explain why. It was some kind of psychic phenomenon, my dreams taking over, and I need to know what else is hiding in my subconscious and looking for a way out. I want to draw something else to see if it will happen again.

The art room is empty when I arrive, the lights off, and Hope's dookie sculpture sits abandoned and draped in cloth—and, let's be honest, it's never looked better. Fresh watercolors dry on a clothesline strung beneath the ceiling, landscapes and still lifes in cheery colors; and in a corner, facing the wall, stands the easel I was using last Wednesday.

I move toward it, and my heart flutters. If I see that sketch again, the angry crowd and the women in black, will it return my lost memories? *Do I want it to?* Because there's always a chance that this little plan will unlock something even worse than a two-hour blackout; that I might end up losing an entire day, or somehow conjuring forth whatever apocalyptic nonsense Jude the Vampire was talking about.

Changing my mind, I turn to leave—and smash directly into Mr. Strauss, who was standing right behind me. My heart jumps so high it tickles my sinus cavity, and I let out a little yelp. "Sorry! Sorry, I thought I was alone."

"You were, until I got here." Mr. Strauss grins at his own joke. Under his nerdy sweater-vest and shapeless jeans, he must be built like a brick wall, because I swear I have a bruise from running into him just now. "Sorry if I surprised you."

"I . . . I wanted to keep working with the charcoals today," I manage to spit out as he steps past me, marching straight to the easel in the corner. "I thought, um—"

"You should." Casually, Mr. Strauss swings the easel around. It's empty—of course it is; it's been almost a week since I did that sketch, and who knows how many times that easel has been used since. Earnestly, my teacher adds, "You have a remarkable talent, Auggie, and you should absolutely keep developing it. Have you ever considered applying to a program like SAIC?"

Just like that, I forget nearly everything that happened before his last sentence. The School of the Art Institute of Chicago is a really big deal. "Do you think . . ."

I can't finish, but he doesn't need me to. "I know you've got another year left, and maybe you're not ready to decide what you want to do when you graduate, but you should give some thought to a four-year art and design school. You've got a gift, and an academic environment would provide an opportunity to grow your skills and explore other media."

I take my glasses off and put them on again. "You think I could get in at SAIC?"

"I think you've definitely got a chance." He shrugs, likes it's obvious. "And you've got time to work on assembling a solid portfolio. Is that something you think you'd be interested in?"

"Yes. I—*Yes!*" Honestly, I'd been hoping to get as far away from Fulton Heights as possible after graduation, but SAIC is *SAIC.* "Thank you so much!"

"Don't thank me, you're the one who has to do the work." He grins again, stationing the easel to face the light. "Let me get the paper and the charcoals, and then you can blow my mind again."

As he trots off to the supply cabinet, my head spins some more. Four years at a prestigious school where I can study art and never look at another imaginary number again sounds too good to be true. Now I'm twice as hopeful that I'll have another episode like last week's; ten or eleven more, and I'll have that portfolio in no time.

"Hey." Hope's voice interrupts my daydream, and I look over to see her setting her bag down on the table nearest to me. Her voice is soft, edged with nervous humor as she asks, "So . . . last night, huh?"

"You could say that, yeah." I laugh in spite of myself. "For whatever it's worth, Fulton Heights is garbage, but that kind of thing still doesn't usually happen."

"Well, I'm really glad you're okay." Her fingers are so tight around her bag that her knuckles are white. "I was sure he was going to eat you, and—" She stops short, squeezing her eyes shut. "Okay, that's not helping. To be honest, I'm still completely freaked out."

"To be honest? Me too."

She nods, but her mouth twists a little bit. "Auggie . . ." She stops. Then, "When he spoke to you, did you understand what he meant?"

It is beginning. Numbly, I shake my head. "I think he was just babbling."

"Are you sure?" she says carefully, scrutinizing my face. "You really don't know what he was talking about?"

"No." Something in her tone brings my goose bumps back. "Should I?"

Hope's mouth twists some more until it's nearly sideways. "I don't know. Forget it." She looks down at her bag. "Maybe it just . . . sounded familiar. It's probably—"

"Okay—paper and charcoal sticks, including a few extras, just in case!" Mr. Strauss interrupts us, delivering the announced materials with a cheerful flourish. Turning to Hope, he plops a few things onto her table as well. "For our resident sculptor, here's the epoxy and wire you've been using. Let me know if you need anything else."

He takes a seat within earshot, and Hope turns away, signaling that our conversation is over—which is okay with me. I'm not even sure I want to talk about this, and for now I have an experiment to conduct. Starting my playlist, I pick up a stick of charcoal, rolling it in my grip until it feels right. Breathing in, I center myself, wondering what I'll do with it.

The charcoal snaps between my fingers, and I blink as it drops to the floor, a fierce cramp knotting my hand. Gasping, I stretch the muscles, yanking off my headphones, my heart thumping so hard it hurts. Hope is staring at me, her face ashen, and over the ringing in my ears I hear Mr. Strauss ask me a question; but I can't process any of it.

It happened again.

The light slanting through the high windows has turned golden, and the blank page in front of me has filled itself in the blink of an eye. Nausea twists my stomach into a dangerous shape, and for just a moment, I'm sure I'm about to barf. Hope steps closer, her eyes wide and worried. "Auggie? Are you okay?"

"I'm . . . I'm fine." The statement couldn't be less convincing if I'd delivered it into a video camera while holding up a copy of today's paper, but I can't possibly tell the truth. My skin is hot, my lungs ache, and terror squeezes my throat nearly shut. I don't even know what I'm afraid of, only that I don't want to look at what I've just spent two more missing hours creating.

"You were a demon over here, Auggie!" Mr. Strauss fails to read my mood, stepping up beside me to evaluate my work. "The way you were going through those sticks I was afraid I'd have to bring more. Did you finish your piece?"

"I'm done." I don't know if I finished, but I'll never touch it again.

"This is . . . wow." My art teacher widens his eyes, scanning every inch of the elaborate scene on the page. "You've got . . . kind of a theme going, between this and your last. It's a little macabre, though." This is an understatement; I apparently just spent two hours drawing a person getting burned at the stake—tied to a post, head lolling back while flames roast their flesh like my marshmallow at

Sugar Mama's. My stomach convulses again as Mr. Strauss asks, "What inspired this, if you don't mind my asking?"

"I don't know, it was just . . ." Acid scorches my throat. My heart is finally slowing, but my skin tingles all over, as if sunburned. "It was something from a dream."

"Must've been a hell of a dream." Mr. Strauss leans back, his expression analytical. "The composition is better this time, more interesting. You've set the pyre off-center, which creates a dynamic energy, but it's balanced by the placement of the crowd." He sweeps his hand in a curve, taking in the onlookers—because, once again, I've drawn a mob scene. "I notice you've included that same group of women from your last work."

He phrases the statement like a question, seeking an answer, but I don't have one to give. Watching the corpse burn is a dense group of spectators, and among them is a trio of figures in black. Something inside me flickers with recognition—except I have no idea what I'm looking at, or why I put it there. "I guess I just . . . thought it would look cool."

"The perspective might be the most compelling part of the tableau." Mr. Strauss cocks his head. "We're above the scene, looking down—removed, but not distant. Spectators, like the crowd, but not far enough away to escape the ugly details. It makes us complicit. A god's-eye view."

"It's not a god." I know this much with utter conviction. Somehow, I know I drew this from the viewpoint of whoever was inside that burning body until an agonizing death cast them out. My hands are shaking. "I'm sorry—I have to go or I'll miss the bus."

Shoving my things into my backpack, I sprint from the art room for the second time in as many weeks, the acrid odor of smoke still clinging to my clothes and hair.

5

When I get home, it's just in time for my tutoring session. Daphne is already there, chatting with my mom and pretending not to notice the creepy, blank-eyed rag doll sitting out on the kitchen counter. It belonged to my grandma when she was a little girl, and my mom is convinced it's a valuable antique. Once a month, she pulls it out and gives me nightmares while researching ways to clean it up without destroying it, in the hopes that she can someday get it appraised.

Once upon a time, that doll was the scariest thing I'd ever encountered. But now? Unless Jude really did somehow work vampire magic on me, making me hallucinate all this stuff, his warning was on the level. Dreams of death? Check. Lost time? Check. Changes in my body? If my new undead-sensing ability counts, then checkity-fucking-check.

The world as you know it, as we all know it, could be coming to an end. And you might be the only one who can stop that from happening. But how? And why?

Daphne is patient with me as I stumble through my homework and her prepared exercises, too preoccupied by my growing fears to focus on algebra; and when we're finishing up an hour later, I remind my parents that I'm supposed to have dinner with Adriana and her grandmother. All afternoon, I've been debating whether or not I really want to go. I'm too worried to eat, but Ximena Rosales is an actual factual witch. If there's anyone who can help me figure out what's happening to me, she might be it—if I can muster up the courage to be honest with her.

I came out to my parents freshman year. I'd never really dated anyone, and they'd never pressured me to talk about it, letting me choose when to bring it up. They wanted to give me space to decide if and when I was ready, which was cool; and yet, somehow, all that empty space was also terrifying. It created this enormous platform, full of reverent silence, and it gave me the worst kind of stage fright.

That's sort of what this feels like. I can't tell whether my fears will wreck me faster if I keep them inside, or if they'll do even worse damage once I let them out and no longer have any control over their size, shape, and direction.

"I just don't think I'm comfortable with you going out tonight," my mom says, yanking the cork out of a wine bottle like someone trying to start a lawn mower. "After what happened at the café . . . maybe it's best to just stay inside."

"It's not like Ximena's planning a picnic in Colgate Woods, Mom." Beholden to my nature, the opportunity for sarcasm is impossible to resist. "She's got a whole room in her house just for eating."

"You know what I mean." My mother's eyes narrow. "Anyway, your dad's still working, and I've already had a glass of wine. I can't drive you to Ximena's place."

"I can do it, Mrs. Pfeiffer," Daphne offers politely as she shrugs into her coat.

"Monica." My mother's correction is reflexive. "And I can't ask you to do that, it wouldn't be fair."

"You didn't ask; I offered." Daphne tousles my hair, and my

glasses slip down my nose. "It'll be, what? Five minutes out of my way? We'll watch each other's backs!"

"He'd still have to get home again, and—"

"Ximena can drive me back," I report, holding up a text confirming the claim. I'm still not sure if I really want to go, but winning an argument against a parent is its own reward.

My mom crosses her arms, looking conflicted, but finally sighs. "Okay, then. Just . . . be careful. And text me when you get there so I know you're okay."

Daphne and I are silent all the way to the end of the walk, streetlights gilding the darkness, and I can't help trying to see if I can sense a vampire. Only, I feel nothing but the crisp bite of March air on my face. Either the ability doesn't work that way, or there are no vampires present—or I have no abilities and no idea what's going on.

After we've driven a few blocks, my tutor finally reaches over and thumps my shoulder with a fist. "So what's going on in there, Auggie? Where've you been all night?"

I shrug, having no clue how to reply. *A vampire tried to convince me that the world is coming to an end, and I keep going into freaky trances, and, oh yeah, I was kind of attacked last night.* I don't know how to begin, so I skip to the end instead.

"Do you believe in reincarnation?"

"Reincarnation," Daphne repeats carefully. "You mean like . . . past lives and stuff?"

"Yeah." I shift in my seat. The car is freezing. "When we die, do we come back?"

"Well, when some people die, they come back as vampires, so . . ." She gives me a wry smile, but the look falls off her face when she sees how serious I am. "Jeez, Auggie, I guess I don't really know. You're talking about souls passing on in one form and returning in another?" When I nod, Daphne just offers up a baffled shrug.

44

"But do you think it's possible?" I press. The thing is, I'm becoming less and less convinced that this is some cosmic hand-me-down package of superpowers forwarded to me from a previously known address so I can pick up the torch where the last Chosen One dropped it. I'm not so sure anymore that my dreams of "people from historical periods I don't recognize" are about me tapping into some common frequency shared by those of us who've possessed the same gift.

They're starting to seem like real memories.

It's not like I've never had nightmares before, but lately, they've been getting more intense and more frequent. Just last week, the night before my first episode of lost time, one of the deaths I dreamed about was of being burned at the stake. And I still can't shake the feeling I had while staring at the twisted corpse on the pyre—that I was looking at someone that used to be *me*.

"I don't see why reincarnation couldn't be possible," Daphne allows in an upbeat way, as if she's afraid to argue against it. "It's a central element in certain religions, and that has to count for something. But if you're asking what I believe, personally? I just don't know." A light snow begins to fall, a few flakes catching the high beams and then scattering across the windshield. "I never really got into the metaphysical stuff deep enough to have a real opinion. Not to sound glib, but I feel like every minute you spend worrying about what happens after you die is a minute lost from making the most of the life you have now."

"Yeah. That makes sense," I mumble, but I wasn't really looking for an existential pep talk—and besides, "the life I have now" is starting to scare me.

"Hey." She halts the car at a stop sign, more snowflakes drifting over the windshield, and gives me a perplexed frown. "What are we actually talking about here, Auggie? You've been at some kind of private funeral in your head all night long, and now you're asking about whether souls can come back?"

We're almost at Ximena Rosales's house, but Daphne looks genuinely concerned, and she isn't budging the car from this stop sign. I'm not even sure what it was I hoped she'd say, and now I feel guilty for worrying her. Before I can think better of it, I blurt, "There was a vampire attack last night. Downtown. Maybe you heard about it."

"No." She sits back, brushing some hair behind her ear. "What happened?" I give her the quick version, and Daphne stiffens, reaching for my arm. "Oh shit, Auggie! Are you . . . did he . . . ?"

"I'm fine." I don't tell her what he said. "He didn't hurt me. I was just . . . you know, crapping my pants."

"And that's why you've been thinking about reincarnation, and what happens after you die," Daphne concludes, starting to drive again, and I don't correct her. "Because when a person becomes a vampire, they die; but when their body wakes up again, with all the memories and everything else intact—"

"Is it still the same person?" I play along, grateful for the easy diversion. "Or has their soul moved out, while something totally different moves in? Because the body still uses the same brain, with all the person's knowledge and memories. So does the victim really *become* a vampire, or are they just replaced by an entity that can't tell the difference between itself and who had the brain before it?"

To my surprise, Daphne breaks out in a gale of deep, satisfied laughter. "That is an awesome observation, and I am so mad that a sixteen-year-old kid thought of it and I didn't. Fair warning, mister: I'm stealing all of that for my next independent essay."

She spends the rest of the short drive trying to make me laugh, and I do my best to oblige—but in the back of my mind, I'm thinking about the real reason I asked. *What if I'm not who I think I am?*

I always figured that if reincarnation were real, it would be the kind of thing you needed a spiritual adviser to confirm for you. But the weird dreams and lost time, the "changes in my body," and the unnerving conviction that I *was* that person tied to a post and set on fire? My preferred way to account for it all is the possibility that these are memories of past lives I've led, inexplicably waking up inside me, jarred loose by the Nexus or something.

Because the only alternative I can think of is one I don't even want to acknowledge. If I'm not remembering past lives, or manifesting the supernatural skills of a chosen vampire killer . . . then something far more serious is happening to me.

Something I don't recognize or understand is invading my consciousness.

Daphne stops outside of Ximena's house, but before I get out, she makes me look her in the eye. "Hey, listen. I'm sorry I didn't have the answers you were hoping for about the reincarnation business, but I'm glad you asked. You can talk to me about anything, anytime, Auggie. I know what it's like to have stuff going on that you're not ready to share with your parents, and if you're ever depressed, or overwhelmed, or . . . whatever, I'm just a phone call away." She grins, wiggling her eyebrows. "And lucky for you, I'm a genius about life."

"Oh yeah?" I fold my arms. "So impress me. What's some stuff I should know?"

"First: You will definitely need some flip-flops you can wear in the shower when you go away to college, because people are *gross*." She grimaces. "And second? Your mom's rag doll is haunted as fuck. I swear that thing tried to steal my soul when I touched it."

"At least you don't have to live with it!" I shudder involuntarily, thinking about the expressionless, floppy-necked poppet. "One time I asked my grandma what it was called, and she looked at me all serious, and went, 'She doesn't like it when people say her name out loud.'"

Daphne and I both scream a little, and she shakes all over like she's trying to get spiders off of her. "What the hell, Auggie? Why isn't that terrifying thing buried in a lead box, or trapped in a ring of salt? Your grandma seriously used to *play* with it?"

In the creepiest voice I can dredge up from the bottom of my throat, I intone, "Or perhaps the doll was playing with *her*!"

Daphne screams again, and then laughs, and finally points at Ximena's front door. "All right, get out. Go have dinner—and text your mom so she knows you're not dead."

"Will do, boss." I give her a sharp salute, but before I open the door, I say, "And, um, thanks. It's nice having someone to talk to about stuff."

She points a finger-gun at me and clicks with her tongue. "Like I said: anytime."

The snow is falling heavier when I get out of the car, flakes cart-wheeling on a sharp wind, and the neighborhood looks deserted. I hurry to the front door, and Daphne watches from behind the wheel as I ring the bell. Her presence is comforting—because as I stand there, all alone on the porch, an eerie, whispering sensation steals up my spine. It's exactly what I felt when that vampire entered Sugar Mama's, and I freeze, my skin tightening like a noose.

Maybe the neighborhood isn't deserted after all.

6

aphne's car chugs away at the curb, exhaust piling into the air, and the feeling builds from a whisper to an itch. It tugs at my gut—and I look up. Above, an overhang protects the porch from snow; but one story higher, on the slope of the roof, crouched in the dark beneath a sky robbed of stars . . . I feel it. I feel *him*.

I don't know how I know it's a "him," but I do—and I know that he's moving, a shadow crawling among shadows, descending. It's uncanny the way I can sense this, the hair on my neck rising and shifting as he comes closer, looking for a way down. He knows I'm here, too. *He was waiting for me.*

Stabbing at the doorbell, heart thudding, I swivel toward the street. Daphne is still watching, and it's clear she knows something is wrong, even if she can't see what's waiting where the moon and streetlights can't reach. If I run, the creature will pounce; I won't even make it to the sidewalk. But maybe—

"Auggie?" Adriana's voice spins me back around, the front door opening, and I practically knock her down as I barge into the house. "Uh, it's nice to see you, too?"

"*Shut the door,*" I gasp, even though it isn't strictly necessary. We're inside a private residence now, and whatever's out there can't come in—but Adriana does it anyway, her face turning white in an instant.

"What is it, what's going on? Is one of them out there?"

We both look through the window, but all we see are Daphne's taillights disappearing up the street. The feeling is gone, too, and maybe it was never there in the first place. "I don't . . . I thought . . . I don't know what I thought. I'm sorry."

"It's okay." Adriana lets out a breath and smiles. "I get it. I almost killed Abuela's bathrobe earlier because I thought it was a vampire."

The day we met, in third grade, I was quietly having a panic attack in the middle of class because our teacher told us—very casually—that one day the sun would explode and devour Earth, and Adriana reached over, put her hand on top of mine, and gave me this same look. She didn't say anything, but she didn't need to. Where no one else had seen my distress, she had, and she wanted me to know I wasn't alone.

"Is that Auggie?" a brassy voice yells from across the house. "Come into the kitchen, mijito. I need a hug!"

If there's one thing I don't like about my family, it's that Ximena Rosales is not technically part of it. Just like Adriana, she welcomed me with open arms from day one. When I came out, my best friend was the first person I told; Ximena was the second. Tonight, I find her at the stove, tending to a pan of sizzling vegetables, the air thick as velvet with the scents of garlic, cumin, and oregano.

Adriana's grandmother hugs me hard enough to crack my thoracic vertebrae, and then immediately shoos me away from the range. "I'm in the middle of something here," she says, indicating the stove. "This is gonna blow your mind, kid. Chiles rellenos, champiñones al ajillo, and my famous rice!"

"Guacamole, too, right?" I try not to sound demanding, but it's hard, because I'm being demanding. There are shallots and jalapeños on the counter, and a bowl of avocados is perched atop the fridge. "If you're busy, I can help. Just tell me the recipe, and—"

"Not a chance, cabron." Ximena fixes me with The Eye. She's sixty-five, in a beige turtleneck and wire-framed glasses, but only a fool would assume she's harmless. "You're gonna have to wait until I'm dead to learn that recipe—and I left instructions for my lawyer to destroy it if I die under suspicious circumstances, entiendes?"

I pretend to wheedle, begging to know the secret, and she pretends to be stern—but really we're both having fun. Truth is, I kind of enjoy imagining that her secret ingredient is actual magic—like she mutters a few words and zaps the bowl with lightning from her fingers—and I'd probably be disappointed if I found out that it's really been ancho chile powder and pink peppercorn all this time.

Adriana is in the living room when I return, her face buried in an old leather-bound book, her phone beside her as she studies crowded lines of handwritten text. Glancing up at me, her eyes shine. "Auggie, check it out—Abuela let me look at one of her grimoires!"

I hazard a guess. "That's like a spell book, right?"

"Exactly!" Adriana turns a page, sketches of herbs and phases of the moon surrounding another column of text. "This volume is pretty basic, because I'm still technically a beginner, but there's some really cool stuff in here. This spell is for inviting restful sleep, and if you master it, the next level up is summoning clairvoyant dreams!"

"Sounds practical." The nightmares I had last week flash through my mind.

"It's all about clarity of mind, purity of will, and directed energy," Adriana continues, photographing the page with her phone. "Look at the herbs! Chamomile? Lavender? And the spells are basically just affirmations . . . people practice witchcraft every day without even realizing it." Under her breath, she adds, "But meanwhile, *I'm* the freak."

Sooner or later, living in a vampire town means encountering some extreme special effects—shape-shifting, invisibility, lightning bolts blasting out of fingertips into amazing guacamole—and lots of people think that's what "real" magic looks like. And, I mean, it *does* . . . but in the same way that the Grand Canyon is what a hole looks like.

Wicca is a faith, and its practitioners—like Ximena—work spells that draw on the power of the natural world for stuff like healing, good luck, and preventing others from doing harm. And honestly? Even when the results are mixed, they're no less effective or meaningful than prayer. But in a town used to the kind of bright, sparkling sorcery that has nothing to do with Wicca and everything to do with the Nexus, a girl who carries around a bag of herbs and charms to ward off negativity still gets treated like a weirdo.

It doesn't help that she has zero support at home. Ximena has been a witch forever, and Adriana's mom, Salome, had access to all of it growing up, but she rejected the faith when she met Adriana's father, Martín—a devout Catholic. Now, Martín and Salome Verdugo want their daughter confirmed in the Church, and my best friend has other ideas.

"I'm sorta surprised your grandmother's letting you use that book," I comment lightly. "Aren't your parents, like, dead set against you becoming a witch?"

"Adults." Adriana snorts derisively. "I'm *already* a witch; my parents just don't want to know about it. Maybe they can forbid me from joining Abuela when she meets with her coven, but I know what I believe. They think the Church is the answer because vampires are scared of the crucifix, but witches have, like, half a dozen charms that repel the undead!" Her expression hardens. "I'm pretty sure they think the Church is going to un-lesbian me, too, but let's not even get started on that."

Leaning over, I give my best friend a hug, because it's the only thing I can do. I wasn't raised with religion—Christian, Pagan, or otherwise. Coming out was hard, but only because it felt an awful lot like saying *"Please look at me and consider all the sexual activities that society has trained you to think about when you hear the word gay."* Straight kids never have to experience that; they never have to sit down across from their parents and make a peremptory declaration about what gives them a boner.

"Look at this." Adriana points now to some notes scrawled in the margins, made by different hands. "There are adjustments to each original spell, added by generations of witches in our family line! I mean, this is field testing in action. 'In cases of acute stress, double amount of holy basil and use lemon balm grown close to subject's place of dwelling.'" She gives me a look of abject wonder. "I can't wait to show this to Hope!"

"Will your grandma really let you take the grimoire home?" Shifting uncomfortably, I have another missed-the-bus moment, fear and jealousy corroding my self-confidence. I hate this. I hate this feeling, and I hate myself for feeling it—this resentment because my best friend has found someone and I haven't. Out of everyone in this hellhole town, *she* deserves happiness, and I want it for her. So what's my problem?

"Ha! Not a chance. And anyway, my parents would freak." Picking up her phone again, Adriana captures another snapshot of the book. "That's why I'm doing this. I don't know if Abuela keeps forgetting I can take pictures with this thing, or if she knows and that's the point, but I'm gonna have every spell in this book memorized by graduation."

When dinner time rolls around, the subject matter hasn't changed. The table all but sags beneath a spread of my favorite dishes, but my plate is still dominated by an absolute mountain of guacamole, and I have no regrets. As I stuff my face, Ximena observes, "Sounds like Hope has made quite an impression on you, mijita."

"I guess." Adriana examines her food, cheeks turning scarlet. "It's cool knowing another witch my age. She only started at FHH this year, so we're still getting to know each other, but her element is water—like Abuelo's was. You'd really like her!"

"I'm sure I will." Ximena smiles. "Her uncle is a friend of mine. He's a good man."

"He is?" Adriana and I say it at the same time, only my mouth is full, so it sounds more like, "*HrrrzZZ?*"

"Sure! Most of the witches in Fulton Heights know each other, at least in passing." Adriana's grandmother shrugs. "He's mentioned his niece before. I hope she's holding up okay after last night—I hope all *three* of you are holding up. It must have been terrifying."

"It was," Adriana mumbles, and my stomach shrinks around the guacamole.

"I can't even remember the last time a vampire attacked a human out in public like that." Ximena splashes hot sauce over her food. "Must be a decade ago, at least. It's no wonder they weren't prepared."

Her tone is casually reproachful, an old complaint rising to the surface. For some paranormal reason no one has ever been able to fully explain, the undead can't enter homes without an invitation, but any space open to the public—including stores and cafés—is vulnerable. And crosses and garlic, despite being decent deterrents, aren't exactly bulletproof.

"It happened so fast there wasn't even time to react." Adriana's face has lost its color. "When he went for Auggie . . . I mean, I don't even want to think about it."

"You had quite a scare, mijito," Ximena says to me lightly, tilting her head a little. "Is everything all right? Your energy fields seem off tonight. Disturbed, maybe."

"Abuela!" Adriana sounds vaguely scandalized.

"They do?" I swallow my food, checking the space around me. "What do you mean? How can you tell?"

"I can see your aura," she answers reasonably. "Everybody vibrates at their own frequency, and some people are sensitive to the emanations. For me, they're visible on the color spectrum."

Energy fields. Before I can think twice, I blurt, "I . . . felt something. Like, this prickly sensation, when the vampire first came into the café? Before he even attacked. Could that be an energy field thing?"

Adriana stares at me, surprised, but her grandmother merely shrugs. "Possibly, sure. Describe it for me."

I won't say it doesn't scare me to open up about all this, but once I get started, I find I can't stop. Beginning with Sugar Mama's, I'm soon telling her about my experience on her front porch, and in my own front yard a week ago; then I'm babbling about my dreams, and the sketches I did; and finally, I'm telling someone else about Jude and his mysterious warning for the first time.

When the last of it is out there, Ximena's expression hasn't changed, but Adriana is aghast. "*Auggie.* Why didn't you tell me?"

"It was . . ." But I don't know how to finish the statement. I didn't say anything because I was in denial, and then I was scared—and I'm afraid to admit it.

"He said he found you to warn you, because you could stop the world from ending?" Ximena summarizes carefully, with a trace of encouraging skepticism.

"He also asked if I'd had, like . . . weird dreams and lost time?" My tongue is thick as a jellyfish, I'm terrified that this admission will turn Ximena's attitude around, but the woman just frowns and reaches for her water glass.

"You don't actually think he was telling the *truth*." Adriana has stopped eating. "He's a vampire! Abuela, tell him he's being conned!"

"The truth is, Auggie," Ximena begins flatly, the glass steady in her grip, "you're probably being conned."

"Thank you!" Adriana tosses her hands out.

"But . . . he knew about the dreams—" I begin, and Ximena cuts me off.

"We live under a nexus, kid." She gestures around us. "We're at an unbelievably powerful crossroads of spiritual energy, and it's impossible to overstate the effects of a paranormal flashpoint like this one." Giving my knee a gentle squeeze, Ximena says, "I wouldn't worry. Vampires never tell the whole truth, and I think you'd be shocked to know how many people in this town have strange dreams and experiences. He could have guessed anything and had a fifty-percent chance of hitting the bull's-eye."

"But why me?" My voice is embarrassingly small. "He was waiting for me. He knew my name."

She surprises me by countering, "Why *not* you? I guess you don't know this, but your aura is unusually strong, mijito. Anyone with some magic in their blood can probably sense it, at least a little. And who knows? Vampires think with their fangs first and their private parts second; maybe he took an interest in you because he thinks you're cute."

I happen to like flirting with cute boys. Jude's words come back to me, and my face goes hot to the tips of my ears. Adjusting my glasses, I mumble, "Okay, maybe, I don't know. But then why *am* I having weird dreams? Why did I sense those . . . energy fields?"

"Maybe you're a Sensitive, like me." She gestures again, taking in the art on the walls—landscapes and botanical sketches—reflecting her own element: earth. "With an aura like yours, it wouldn't surprise me. Vampires can feel you, and now you're starting to feel them."

"Wouldn't he know that already?" Adriana puts in, eyeing me like I'm a shaky-looking building that might come down any second. "If Auggie's a Sensitive, how come he's never experienced anything like this before? Why is it suddenly happening *now*?"

"He's at about the right age. As I'm sure you know, Wicca and sorcery aren't the same thing, and anyone can manifest a magical gift. Not all witches are adept at advanced magic, and not all adepts are familiar with basic witchcraft." Ximena makes it all sound mundane, but when she says "sorcery," she's talking about stuff like conjuring, psychokinesis, and transmogrification. "But if you have the gift, it usually makes itself known around puberty."

"I already went through puberty," I state, mortified. Okay, yes, I was kind of a late bloomer, but I've definitely matured in all the necessary places—and, thanks to daily testing, I am confident when I say that my parts function the way they're supposed to.

"The brain isn't fully developed until you're about twenty-five," Ximena returns smartly. A science teacher for the nearby Skokie school district, she is impossible to argue with. "As for dreams and trances . . . overlapping ley lines are volatile, and there's no way to predict how their friction will affect those of us in their shared path. They've stirred up psychic energy, and just your luck, you're an antenna tuned in to the signal."

The nervous heat in my body breaks, a relieved sweat cooling my forehead. "You really think that's all it is?"

"Of course!" Ximena raps the table. "Listen, I'll talk to my circle, and if your parents are okay with it, maybe you can join us sometime. Let some experienced witches help get you sorted out."

"Are you sure?" I ask uncomfortably, glancing at Adriana. Joining her grandmother's coven is her biggest dream, and her parents have forbidden it until she turns eighteen. Watching me get offered exactly what she wants has to hurt.

But Adriana forces a supportive smile just the same. "You should do it, Auggie. It could make a huge difference for you."

Somehow, my best friend and I each ended up with what the other wants most. Nervously, I say to Ximena, "I'll talk to my parents."

"Great! We'll set something up." Reaching over, the woman ruffles my hair. "In the meantime, just keep being careful."

Then, without warning, she rips a couple strands of my hair out by the roots, and I shriek a little. "*Ow!*"

"*Abuela!*" Adriana barks, but her grandmother shrugs it off.

"What? I need it for a protection spell for Auggie."

"You said I had nothing to be worried about!" I glare at her, rubbing my head.

"I said your new abilities are nothing to worry about," Ximena clarifies as she produces a small plastic envelope from one of her pockets, tucking my hair safely inside. "But you've got a vampire taking a special interest in you, and it's better to be safe than sorry. Now eat! I spent way too much time on this food for you to let it get cold."

With that, she turns back to her plate, steering the conversation to lighter topics; but even though I make a good performance of smiling and eating my delicious cheese-stuffed peppers, a sense of cold uneasiness gradually washes over me. I liked everything Ximena said, of course—it was exactly what I wanted to hear. She didn't even blink when she dismissed my fears . . . and maybe the reason I'm beginning to question her assurances is simply because they seem too good to be true.

Or maybe it's because she had that plastic envelope in her pocket when we first sat down to dinner—long before she knew anything about Jude and his "special interest" in me. Like she'd been planning to take some of my hair all along.

I never thought the day would come that I didn't trust an explanation from Ximena Rosales, but as I watch her from the corner of my eye, I sink deeper under the waves of doubt. There's something she's not telling me, I'm sure of it, and unfortunately I can think of only one way to find out what that is. It's a terrible idea . . . and yet it's the best one I've got.

This whole thing started with Jude, and I need him to tell me how the world ends.

7

When my alarm goes off the next morning, I want to fling both the clock and my body out my bedroom window. I might have slept for three hours—a hundred and eighty minutes of sweaty, harrowing night terrors that clung to me like spiderwebs each time I jolted awake.

My dreams were even more gruesome than last week's, a montage of horrific elements: ropes binding me to a pillar of rough wood, flames blistering my skin, smoke burning my lungs and strangling my cries. When I woke up, terrified and gasping, I sobbed with relief when I realized none of it was real. But then I drifted back off, and the dreams resumed, just as graphic: an angry mob, a blade cleaving my neck, and then a weightless fall—my brain still conscious for several precious seconds, racked by unimaginable pain.

My hands are shaking when I fumble out the burner phone that Jude tossed me after school last Wednesday, the list of contacts showing a single number. Before I can second-guess myself, I send him a text: *I'm ready for answers.*

The phone's battery is down to a single bar, and he didn't give me a charger for it. When he said I'd run out of explanations, he knew it would happen soon. I haven't even moved yet when his reply comes through: *Meet me in the food court at Colgate Center after sundown. —J*

It may have once been a thriving hub of local commerce, but the Colgate Center Mall has been dying for almost as long as I've been alive. At least a third of the shops are permanently closed, and, these days, an equal amount of the center's fluorescent lights have been deactivated to save money. The fountain at the heart of the complex was shut off after the financial collapse and converted into a "garden" of dusty plastic bushes packed into a bed of fake dirt just beside the food court.

Unable to face the possibility of reliving another hideous death, I skip my independent art study, reaching Colgate Center well before sundown and chaining my bike to one of the racks in the parking lot. I don't like the idea of pedaling home after dark, but I need answers, and I see no other way. I'll come up with some explanation for my parents—obviously not the truth. Not until I know what I'm dealing with.

If I can believe anything Jude told me, it's that if he wanted to hurt me, he'd have done it already. Choosing a public place for this meeting is a gesture meant to put me at ease . . . but it's all theater, and we both know it. I've finally experienced mesmerism firsthand, and with one shimmer of his gorgeous brown eyes, I'd let him waltz me straight into an abattoir.

I get a mocha at the mall's coffee shop, jumpy and unsure what to do with my hands. The barista looks nothing like Gunnar, and he screws up my order, but I have no stomach for it anyway. *I'm here to meet a vampire.* Before I even started day care, my parents gave me all the usual warnings about stranger danger, explaining the tricks that might be used to lure me into peril. I wasn't to accept candy or get into a car with someone I didn't know—and above all else, I was never, ever to go anywhere alone with someone who had fangs, even if they weren't always visible.

So what the hell am I doing? No matter what the explanation is—whether I've been chosen by mystical forces to save mankind, or I'm developing psychic powers thanks to the Nexus—I'm not sure I care to hear it. What I really want is for all of this to *go away*.

My crappy mocha and I take a seat across from the plastic garden, bad music filling the air. I want to text Adriana, but if she asks what I'm doing, I'll have to lie—and I'm not sure I have the nerve. So I pull out my homework and waste time failing at biology instead. *The world as you know it, as we all know it, could be coming to an end.* If I'm the planet's last hope for survival, then everyone is well and truly fucked, because I can't even remember what a Golgi body is supposed to do.

"Hello, August." The familiar voice, smooth as maple syrup, comes out of absolutely nowhere, and I jolt so hard I almost knock over my untouched mocha. Jude is sitting in the chair across from me, having arrived so stealthily I didn't notice. He's even hotter than I remembered. "I'm glad you got in touch."

"Don't do that!" I splutter, my heart pounding my rib cage hard enough to leave dents. "You can't just . . . sneak up on humans like that! It's not cool, okay?"

"I wasn't sneaking." Jude gives me a blameless look. "You were so wrapped up in whatever you were doing, you weren't paying attention. What *are* you doing?"

"Nothing," I shoot back. "Homework. It doesn't matter."

"Do you want some help?" He reaches for the worksheet, and I snatch it off the table. Arching one of his eyebrows, he remarks, "I've been around for a long time. I bet I know the answers to all those questions."

"I don't care. I'm not letting a *vampire* help me *cheat* on my *science homework*." My glasses slip down my nose as my face gets hot again. I would absolutely let a vampire help me cheat on my science homework—I would let *anybody* help me cheat on my science homework—but these are not the right conditions. "That's not even . . . Why are we talking about this? Stop being all . . . flirtatious and whatever!" That impish grin spreads across his face again, and I scowl. "Why do you keep smiling like that?"

"It's hard not to." He folds his long fingers together on the table. "You're just very cute sometimes."

I glare at him, confused by my spin-cycling emotions. Of course the first hot guy to ever tell me I'm cute would also happen to be an undead monster. "Look, I don't know what's going on, but I don't appreciate mind games. So let's just . . . stick to business."

Jude's smile fades. "I'm sorry. I didn't mean to make you uncomfortable."

"And just in case you get any *ideas*," I hiss under my breath, "I still have my crucifix, *and* I drank some holy water earlier. If you eat me, you'll have a really nasty surprise."

"I've said it before, but I'll repeat it as many times as necessary: I'm not going to hurt you, August Pfeiffer." He looks me square in the eye, no blinking—but who knows how much practice he's had over the years with lying. "For the record, though, I was sick of mind games even before I became a vampire. I prefer to say what I mean. And to flirt whenever possible." His smirk returns, unnervingly sexy. "Besides, isn't honesty the best policy?"

"No vampire is a hundred percent honest," I reply in my court-room lawyer voice.

"Neither is any human," he counters. "You lied to me just now when you said you'd consumed holy water."

"That's different! That was self-defense." My neck goes all hot and scratchy. *How did he know that?* "How did you know that? Were you spying on me?"

His answer turns out to be somehow even creepier. "I can

hear your heart beating. When humans lie, their pulses accelerate. It's the same operating principle as a polygraph machine, actually." Nonchalant, he adds, "Also, the adrenaline levels in your blood increased when you said it, which is—"

"Excuse me, *what*? The *what* in my *what*?" I lean as far back as possible—as if the extra inches make a difference.

"I'm not trying to scare you, August." Jude's tone is measured and silky. "I'm answering your questions honestly. Yes, vampires are predators, and I can tell by your scent when your body secretes adrenaline."

Startled, I shift in my chair, picking at the cardboard sleeve on my terrible mocha. I've been so focused on how much stronger Jude is than me, how much deadlier, that I haven't even considered all the other ways in which I am totally outmatched. My head starts to spin again, my heart beating faster, even as I realize that he's no doubt taking stock of these changes, too. How much adrenaline is in my system now? *What does it taste like?*

"August, listen to me," Jude says, his tone forceful but controlled. "I know you're scared right now, but what's happening isn't going to stop if you run away. You're having the dreams, right? Which ones? A beheading in Scotland, a death by burning in France, a firing squad in Russia?"

My fingers go still around my mocha, and I stare at him, my dream coming back to me. The pillar of rough wood, the blistering fire—ugly words from an angry crowd imprinted on a borrowed memory: hérétique, sorcière, trompeur. *Heretic, witch, deceiver.*

I don't even know French.

"You can feel me, can't you?" Jude asks next, his eyes riveted on mine, drinking me in. I don't even have to ask what he means, because of course I feel him: that scratchy, restless sensation creeping up my spine . . . it's him, his presence, activating something inside me. I don't know why I didn't feel it when he first showed up; whatever it is, it's not consistent. "I lied, August. I did sneak up on you when I got here, because I wanted to see if you would sense me. You didn't at first, but now . . ."

"What—" The words get stuck, dread bottlenecking my throat. "W-what did you do to me?"

He opens his mouth. "It isn't—"

"*Auggie?*" A familiar voice interrupts the tense moment like a car coming through a plate-glass window. "I can't believe it, you're, like, the third person I know that I've run into tonight!" Mentally, I will her to stay away, to turn around and leave, but instead she marches right over to us. "Someone I was supposed to tutor canceled on me at the last second, or I wouldn't even be out here. What are the odds?"

"Daphne," I manage to respond, my voice like a dirty rag caught in a very delicate bit of machinery. "I, I'm . . ."

Her eyes move from me to Jude and back to me again, and her eyebrows do a strange little dance. "Sorry, but am I interrupting? Are you . . . on a date?"

"No!" I exclaim.

"Yes," Jude answers simultaneously, his smile uninviting.

Daphne eyes him, and her lips press into a smile like a paper cut. "Excuse us, but I need to talk to Auggie about something—*alone*." I don't fight her when she pulls me away from the table, dragging me under one of the hidden speakers, some cheerful pop song beating down on us from above.

"Daphne," I begin, but she stops me.

"You do know that boy is a *vampire*, right?" she demands, half under her breath and still somehow loud enough for the entire Chicagoland area to hear her. When I don't answer right away, she grips my shoulders. "Come on, Auggie! He's pretty, but . . . *come on!*"

"It's not what you're thinking." My reply sounds feeble, because I don't know what she's thinking—and I don't know what's going on, either.

"Did he mesmerize you? Are you mesmerized right now?" She actually pries one of my eyelids farther open, and I bat her hand away.

"He didn't mesmerize me, we're just talking!"

"Yeah, sure—*now*." She snorts. "Why is he here, anyway? What did he tell you?"

"It's a long story." I adjust my glasses, the situation spiraling out of my control. "Just . . . I'm not in any trouble, okay? I promise. He says he's not going to hurt me."

"Of course he says that, they all say that!" She shoots a suspicious glare at Jude, who's been watching us this whole time. Can he hear us over the music? Can he read our lips? "Look, Auggie, I know Fulton Heights has . . . limits, and I get it if you're lonely, but *this*? Isn't worth it. Human and vampire relationships don't work out!"

"That's not what's happening," I insist flatly—even though, if I'm being completely honest, I've spent plenty of *private time* this past week wondering if Jude really wants to suck more than my blood. If you know what I mean.

Daphne waits for more, but what can I tell her that she won't feel compelled to share with my parents? So I just shake my head, and she frowns, disappointed; and then, abruptly, she spins around, marching straight back to the table where Jude waits. Pulling out a chair, she drops into it with the force of a comet crashing to Earth.

My anxiety climbing all the way up to my scalp, I hurry after her just as she snaps, "Look, I don't know what's going on, but I'm not leaving him alone with you."

"Doesn't he get to have a say in that?" Jude retorts. "We were having kind of a personal discussion."

Triumphantly, she counters, "You're not a person."

"Well, fair point." Jude grants her a polite smile. "But whoever you are, I assure you you're overreacting. As I've told August— several times now, and I believe to his satisfaction—he's in no danger from me."

Daphne narrows her eyes, unimpressed. "I know how vampires like to trick people into thinking with the wrong body parts, so I intend to see that you keep your teeth and hands to yourself. All right?"

I'm burning alive again, but it's not a dream; when I die and my life flashes before my eyes, I hope they let me fast-forward most of it.

Jude's expression doesn't change—but something predatory glitters in the look he gives her. "That's very bold talk . . . Daphne, was it? But the fact is: I am a five-hundred-year-old vampire, and I could break this table in half with my bare hands. If I really meant to harm August, do you honestly think that you could stop me?"

"Yes," Daphne returns immediately, her voice pitched low, so filled with icy conviction that I actually get chills, "I do." She shakes the sleeve of her jacket, and a slim, wooden stake, whittled into a lethally sharp point, appears in her hand as if by magic. "Besides, you're only four hundred and thirty years old at the absolute most, *Jude Marlowe*. Stop lying about your age."

Jude's eyes go as wide as mine feel, and I take my seat again, because *what the fuck*?

"You're Brotherhood, aren't you," Jude observes—and it isn't a question; his tone is hammered steel. Totally lost, I look from him to Daphne and back again, my hackles rising by degrees. They're locked in a battle of silent glares, and I'm not sure my nerves can take another second of it.

"What is he talking about?" I finally demand. "What the hell is 'Brotherhood,' and how do you know his name? *What's going on?*"

Daphne's eyes flicker to me, and she lets out an unhappy sigh. "The Brotherhood of Perseus. It's a secret society dating to the Middle Ages, a fraternal organization of—"

"Assassins." The word is as cold as an unfired bullet when Jude spits it out.

"*Warriors*," Daphne amends crisply, her fingers tightening around the stake in her grip. "I told you my parents were vampire hunters, Auggie, and I let you think that meant they were part of a volunteer defense squad, but . . . that wasn't the truth. I'm sorry." After a moment, she slumps back, and with another shake of her sleeve the wooden stake vanishes again. "The Brotherhood of Perseus was founded in the twelfth century by two dozen knights who pledged their lives to battling the undead—humans who risked everything against an enemy that could barely be killed. It was dudes only at first, hence the name, but the organization is gender-inclusive these days. Back in the Middle Ages, vampires could attack peasants in the countryside, or raze entire villages without anybody—"

"That hardly ever happened," Jude interrupts crossly. "Yes, there were some bad vampires roaming around nine centuries ago, but they didn't rack up even a quarter of the body count that humans did!" Shaking his head, he lets out a disgusted snort. "Your lot have always exaggerated the dangers of vampires as a means to excuse your own barbarism. Or aren't you planning to address the role the Brotherhood played in the Crusades? Burning down libraries and slaughtering whole families that refused to convert to Christianity—"

"That's vampire propaganda!" Daphne jerks upright, icicles dripping from her tone. "The Knights of Perseus rode in the Crusades, yeah, but their mission was to root out vampire strongholds. People were idiots back then—they thought the Earth was flat, and half of them died of the plague because they believed bathing was dangerous!" She slams a finger down onto the table. "You make it sound like there were six or seven bad, fang-toothed apples rolling around, sucking the blood out of a few women and children at the edge of civilization, but the Knights have extensive records, buddy. Vampires were crawling all over the Holy Land, picking off travelers like birds on a line, and during the Crusades their numbers were cut in half thanks to the Brotherhood."

"A lot of things were 'cut in half' thanks to the Brotherhood," Jude rejoins without missing a beat, "including a few hundred peaceful shepherds and farmers."

"You know what? This is stupid." Turning to me, Daphne states, "I was raised by people who took an oath to protect humankind against vampires." With a pointed glance at Jude, she states, "I don't care what tall, dark, and Dracula here has heard, or thinks he can convince you he knows—the Brotherhood of Perseus has always been a bulwark against the undead. Don't fall for his crap."

"'A bulwark against the undead.'" Jude rolls his eyes. "Give me a break. If you Perseans are so virtuous and steadfast and all that other bollocks, why didn't you tell August the truth about who you are?"

"Because it wouldn't be a *secret society* if we went around handing out business cards, fucknut. While we're talking backgrounds, though, maybe now's a good time for you to tell Auggie about your work for the Syndicate!"

"Th-the Syndicate?" The blood drains out of my face, sinking all the way to my ankles. The undead like to keep humans in the dark as to their organizational structure, but everyone has heard of the Vampire Syndicate.

Blood is what fuels the undead, what spawns their progeny, and what binds them together. If Daphne is right about his age, then four hundred and whatever years ago, Jude was a living, breathing human just like me; until a vampire drained him, fed him, and killed him— thus bringing him back from death.

That means the blood that even now fills the chambers of Jude Marlowe's heart—perennially still, unless he wills it to beat—is spawned from that of the vampire who Turned him. For however long they both walk the Earth, Jude will be linked to his maker on an elemental and psychic level; and because his maker has a maker, and so on up, that link extends all the way to the top of his bloodline.

No one knows when the first vampires appeared, or where they came from, but there's estimated to be a few million of them on the planet today . . . and roughly three-quarters of them can be traced back to a dozen distinct lineages. Short version? At some point in the distant past, a tiny handful of ancient, undead beings—each with considerable sway over their growing progeny—formed a coalition called the Syndicate to safeguard their survival and advance their interests.

"Jude Marlowe was Turned in 1607 at age seventeen by Rudolfo Sanoguerra," Daphne announces. "Sanoguerra was Turned in 1348 by Margit Bertóthy. She's one of the *real* Transylvanians," she adds, and I know what she means. Bram Stoker's notorious 1897 novel inspired by the exploits of Vlad the Impaler was mostly bullshit, but it was so popular that vampires from all around the world suddenly started claiming a connection to the Romanian region where Castle Dracula was located. "These days, Margit's maker goes by Hecuba. She's used dozens of aliases, and no one actually knows how old she is. What we do know is that she's one of the original Syndics; which means that Jude here is only three degrees of Kevin Bacon from the closest thing the undead have to a governing body."

Jude stares at Daphne, shock written across his face. "Who *are* you?"

"I told you the Brotherhood keeps extensive records," she answers smugly. "I've been studying vampire bloodlines since I could read."

"Hello? Can we talk about me some more?" My voice is higher

pitched than I'd like, but I can't help it. *The Vampire Syndicate sent a representative to find me.* "I mean, like, not to interrupt your romantic tension or whatever, but can we skip ahead to the part about why the undead government even knows my fucking name?"

Slouching back, Jude flicks a distrustful glance at Daphne. "I'm not comfortable discussing Syndicate business in front of some Brotherhood gangster—"

"It's not 'Syndicate' business," my tutor interrupts immediately. "It's *Auggie*'s business, and I'm not leaving him alone with you."

They glare at each other, and pressure builds inside me until I can't take it anymore. I don't know if I want Daphne here for this or not, but I barely worked up the nerve to contact Jude at all, and I'm not leaving until I get my answers. Plus, she's some kind of monster-killing knight, and maybe that's what I need right now.

"I'm not promising to keep anything you tell me a secret." I look Jude straight in the eye, my fingers aching from the death grip I have on the edge of the table. "And Daphne's not going anywhere, because no matter how pretty you are, you're still a vampire and I'm still a human and it was probably dumb of me to meet you alone in the first place." Clearing my throat, I state, "You came here to tell me something, so just tell me already."

Jude purses his lips, casts an annoyed gaze to the side, and then shakes his head. Finally, his eyes meet mine, his expression grave. "August, an ancient and powerful entity is rising here in Fulton Heights—now. And *your body* is the vessel prophesied to carry it."

8

His words hang in the air, backed by a jazzy instrumental from the mall's hidden speakers, and I would laugh hysterically if I didn't think my mouth would shoot barf like a busted fire hydrant if I opened it. An ancient entity wants to use me as a *vessel*?

Daphne goes stiff. "What are you talking about? What prophecy?"

"I hate to break this to you, but despite the Brotherhood's best efforts, vampires have still managed to preserve important volumes filled with the auguries and predictions of the oldest ones," Jude explains with a sarcastic lilt.

"Oh, of course, *vampire auguries*!" Skepticism drips from her tone. "Does this 'ancient and powerful entity' happen to have a name, or have you not made one up yet?"

"It has many names, actually." Jude juts out his chin. "The Endless One, the Shining Immortal, and the Dark Star, just to name a few." At this, I jerk upright and stop breathing, the wild-haired man's voice ringing in my ears. *The Dark Star rises.* Cutting a glance at me, Jude adds, "Most commonly it's called the Corrupter."

"The *Corrupter*?" Daphne explodes. "*That's* what this is about? You made this poor kid come all the way out here so you could terrify him with a fairy tale about Vampire Santa Claus?" Kicking her chair back, she gets to her feet. "Come on, Auggie, we're leaving."

Jude stands as well. "You know, I've just about had it with your anti-vampire attitude—"

"Do either of you actually fucking mind?" I'm still thrown, my insides on a hellish carousel ride, and my hands shake so badly I'm afraid they're going to crawl off on their own. "What is the 'Corrupter'? What do you mean my body is a 'vessel'?"

Focusing on me again, Jude sits back down. "I'm sorry if I scared you. Unfortunately, not a lot is known about the Corrupter, in part because the Brotherhood of Perseus set fire to most of the historical records that vampires had compiled by the Middle Ages."

"Oh?" Daphne resumes her seat as well, exuding pleasantness. "You mean those burning libraries *weren't* filled with vital scientific texts after all?"

Jude grits his teeth, but continues, "The surviving accounts refer to the Corrupter as a spectral being that returns to the earthly plane once every hundred years or so . . . taking over an existing human form."

"'*Taking over*'?" I practically screech, my voice ringing out through the mostly abandoned food court, my heart ready to ride that barf fountain right out of my mouth.

"Stop it—stop scaring him!" Daphne exclaims fiercely, her eyes going wide. "The Syndicate doesn't even believe in the Corrupter, so what are you really doing here? What is this actually about?"

"Is that true?" I demand, my throat thick and wet, my face and neck clammy. "The Syndicate doesn't think this . . . *thing* you're talking about is real?"

Jude shoots another dirty look Daphne's way. "It's complicated. The formal position of the Syndicate is that the Corrupter is a myth. Aside from a handful of prophecies and some outrageous claims that can't be verified, there's nothing to prove its existence—and, just in general, the grander a prediction is, the more skepticism it warrants." He sits back. "If the stories are true, then the Corrupter would have corporealized hundreds of times by now—but there are no confirmed firsthand accounts. Thousands of vampires have alleged direct contact over the years, of course, but nothing has ever been verified. There are no records that this thing has ever successfully manifested inside a human body." Turning his palms to the ceiling, Jude says, "After a while, the Syndicate decided that this one was all smoke and no fire."

"Then what are you doing here?" I ask, breathing a little easier. Something is definitely happening to me, but if even the oldest and most influential group of vampires on the planet think "the Corrupter" is fictional, then maybe Ximena was right after all. Maybe I'm just developing some spooky, paranormal sensitivity thanks to the Nexus, and all of this is just more vampire bullshit.

"Yes, Jude, what are you doing here?" Daphne asks with the air of a prosecuting attorney about to spring a trap. "What is it that the Corrupter supposedly does that would be worth your coming all the way out to Fulton Heights, of all places, from the Syndicate's headquarters in . . . where is it, again? Some ski resort in the Carpathian Mountains, right?"

She waits, and when Jude scowls deeply in reply, a glimmer of interest burns its way through the tumult of my anxiety. More than ever, I'm glad Daphne showed up when she did. Reluctantly, the vampire says, "The few writings about the Corrupter that remain all generally say the same thing: It will Rise once in every generation, it will borrow the guise of a living human, and it will . . . free vampires from the shackles of death, bringing them true immortality once and for all."

He mumbles this last part, and after a moment of awkward

silence, Daphne helpfully elucidates, "He means daylight. And fire, decapitation, pokey pieces of wood, holy water, garlic, and all the rest of it, too. The standard package."

Looking from her to Jude, I give him a chance to rebut the claim; when he doesn't, it's my turn to scowl. I'm furious with myself for wasting precious energy freaking out over this. "This is about another sunlight cure?" Disgusted, I get to my feet, my chair scraping the tiled floor behind me. "Are you fucking kidding? I've been panicking for *days* because some vampire showed up, telling me the world was going to end, and now it turns out it's just one more day-walking fantasy? Fuck off. Let's go, Daphne."

As I'm putting on my coat, Jude stands up again. "It's not the way she makes it sound, August—she's twisting the facts out of perspective!"

"You heard him, Fangoria, sit back down." Daphne thrusts a finger at him.

"The Syndicate investigates all supposed 'sunlight cures,' no matter how preposterous they seem—we'd be fools not to!" He gestures around, taking in the mall, that terrible music still chugging away. "You'll notice that the Syndicate sent only one sad little junior member to talk to you, and not a paramilitary squadron."

"As far as we know," Daphne shoots back. "You've told, like, a dozen lies since I first sat down. We've got no idea what else you're hiding."

Jude ignores her. "The Syndicate isn't what you need to be afraid of, August. We aren't the ones taking these nonsense predictions seriously."

"What does that mean?" I freeze in the middle of wrestling my gloves out of my backpack, his tone snagging my nerves like a piece of barbed wire.

"It may be the Syndicate's official position that the Corrupter is a fable, but the Syndics don't speak for all of the undead. They can pass decrees that their respective lineages will be more or less compelled to heed, but they can't direct individual beliefs." He runs a hand through his soft-looking curls. "And the blood bond that ties a vampire to its progeny can be severed at any time, so the Syndics' control isn't absolute, even over their own descendants."

"Just get to the point," Daphne says through her teeth.

"I know you remember the Baeserta incident, August." He waits until I nod, and then continues, "The Syndicate discredited the prophecies about the Shield in the 1800s and pronounced the believers a dangerous cult. There were only thirteen adherents back then, but the membership was up to twenty by the time the group arrived in Illinois, determined to bring about the apocalypse." With a flourish, he folds his hands in front of him. "Only the original thirteen came from untraceable bloodlines; the rest were descended from the Syndics and severed from their lineages."

Daphne rolls her eyes. "You know, when I said 'get to the point'—"

"Vampires are tribal, just like humans," Jude snaps. "Those of us still connected to the Syndics obey a strict code of ethics, but those who fall outside Syndicate bloodlines are free to commit themselves to any cause without any moral principles to get in their way. That's how deadly factions like the Baeserta sect get started: All they need is a charismatic leader and enough followers willing to do their part." His thick eyebrows draw together. "No matter what the Syndicate says, there are vampires out there who are convinced that the Corrupter is coming—who believe wholeheartedly that this Rising will be the start of their brave new world. Most of them are Syndic progeny, constrained by our laws, or tiny fringe groups that lack the resources to be considered dangerous—but some are, August." His eyes dig deep into mine. "We know of two significant cults that have formed around the Corrupter, and they're coming to Fulton Heights. If they're not here already."

My head spins a little as I think about the growing number of dead animals piling up in my neighborhood, the rabbit left in my front yard—about the way that disheveled vampire looked at me right before he jumped through a window—and I glance over at Daphne. "W-what does that mean?"

"It means that even if the Corrupter is as bullshit as the Shield of Baeserta, lots of people could die anyway," she answers bluntly, her scarf knotted tightly in her fingers. "Assuming, you know, that he hasn't just been lying through his fangs this whole time." Turning to Jude, she demands, "What factions? Who are we dealing with?"

But he's finally had enough. Eyes burning with a low golden light, he growls, "I think I've shared everything I'm going to with the Brotherhood of Perseus. You're obviously familiar with the prophecies, and if *you* haven't been lying this whole time, then you've got access to your own research. So hit the books—the ones you haven't burned, I mean."

"I intend to." Daphne's voice is so frigid I could probably skate all the way home on it. "I'm gonna study up on the Corrupter, the Syndicate—and especially on Jude Marlowe." Looping the scarf around her neck, she shakes out her hair. "Auggie, I don't know how you got here, but I'm driving you home."

"I don't have any books!" The words burst out of me on a wave of panicked anger, and both of them glance over in surprise. "I don't have access to research or moldy prophecies, but *I'm* the one that Vampire Santa Claus is supposedly using for a crash pad! So maybe you two can, I don't know, stuff your ancient enmity for a few minutes and finish telling me what the *fuck is going on*?"

"I'm sorry, August." Jude's voice is smooth as a satin cord again when he pushes to his feet. "I wish I could say more, but I can't—not in front of someone who would see my kind purged from the Earth. The Syndicate can help you, though. Back at our headquarters, we have a research center staffed by some of the most knowledgeable mystics in the world, and a fully appointed alchemical laboratory, so if there—"

"You are unbe-fucking-lievable, you know that?" In just twelve syllables, Daphne manages to hit notes across two entire octaves, and she places herself between us. "You come rolling in here with this square-jawed, pouty James Dean act, pretending like you think this whole thing is nonsense, and then it's all, 'come away with me to the *secret alchemical laboratory* in my vampire fortress where you'll be safe'? How gullible do you think he is? And what do you take me for, that you think I'd just sit here while you try to gaslight him into becoming a Syndicate lab rat?"

"I don't take *you* for anything," Jude retorts hotly. "And for the record, you were the one who pointed out the Syndicate's stance on the Corrupter legend." Leaning across the table, dark eyes flashing, he gestures at me. "But something *is* happening to August, and the Syndicate is one of few organizations equipped to figure out what— and one of even fewer capable of offering real protection if vampire cultists target him!"

"As far as I can tell," Daphne says, drawing me back from the table, "the only vampire coming after Auggie is you. Don't follow us outside, or you'll regret it."

We're halfway across the food court, my feet moving on auto-pilot as Daphne hustles me toward the nearest exit, when Jude calls out behind us, "You'll need me again, August. And I'll be waiting."

9

Fresh snow fell while we were in the mall, and now the Colgate Center's west parking lot is a winter wonderland, sparkling under the amber glow of sodium light. I'm shivering beneath my coat, my face burning hot, and I keep coughing on the frozen air as I follow Daphne to her car. I hate how dark it is beyond the penumbra of the lampposts. I hate that I'm terrified of every shadow too dark to see through, and with good reason.

Neither of us has said a word since we left the food court, and the silence swells in my throat until I can't take it anymore. "Do you really think he was just trying to trick me?"

"August Pfeiffer, what the hell were you thinking?" Daphne shouts, whirling on me so fast I jump back, slipping a little in the new snow. "You agreed to meet a vampire *alone*? You have got to be smarter than that! Did you even tell anyone what you were doing or where you were going?" When I don't answer, she covers her face with mittened hands. "What if he'd killed you? What if this had been a trap? I mean, it *was* a trap, but what if it had been worse? You could be in a cage on your way to Romania right now!"

"I'm sorry," I mumble, my eyes on my hands. I'm not exactly sure why I'm apologizing to Daphne, except that she's upset, and it's making me uncomfortable.

Slumping against the side of a parked SUV, she pinches the bridge of her nose for a moment. "I'm sorry, too. I'm just . . ." Trailing off, Daphne shrugs and shakes her head. When she speaks again, her voice is softer, her expression concerned. "What's going on, Auggie? If something is . . . *happening* to you, I might be able to help."

"Are you really part of some, like, secret monster-fighting club?" I ask first. It's not that I doubt her—I just think I need to hear it again.

"The Brotherhood of Perseus isn't a 'club.'" She gives an offended snort, folding her arms over her chest. "It's a centuries-old order of badass vampire-hunting knights, and you have to damn well prove yourself worthy of wearing the emblem before they let you join. My parents met while fighting side by side, and they trained me from the age of six to identify and kill the undead."

"Wow. That's . . . really cool. I can't believe you're not allowed to brag about it."

"Secrecy is part of the membership oath. It's only under . . . extreme circumstances that Perseans are permitted to reveal themselves to outsiders." Glancing back at the lights of the mall, she states, "And this definitely qualifies. Auggie . . . whatever you thought a vampire could tell you, the Brotherhood can do the same, and at a way lower cost."

The problem with sharing a secret is that you can't *un*-share it again if things don't go the way you want them to. But I'm running out of places to look for answers, and Daphne has me wondering if I can believe anything Jude told me at all. As I take a breath, the decision trembles on the end of my tongue. "I've been having . . . dreams. Nightmares. Maybe visions, I'm not sure."

And the rest of it spills out of me with hot relief, a sensation that feels even better than when I divulged the truth to Ximena. Daphne is already taking this seriously, and she knows things that I don't—about Jude, about vampires, and about whatever the "Corrupter" is.

She wants to help me, and the more I focus on that, the easier it gets to talk.

Because I'm starting to fear that I really do need help. Jude might say that the Syndicate doesn't believe in the Corrupter, but he still came to Fulton Heights with my name in his mouth, a list of dreams I'd had, and knowledge of symptoms I was about to experience. That's no trick or strange coincidence, and it scares the shit out of me to contemplate.

When I'm finished, Daphne has a faraway look in her eyes, one hand clutching tightly at her collar. We've been outside for a while now, and while my skin doesn't itch in that "vampire approacheth" way, my toes are starting to go numb. Finally, her gaze refocuses, tension knotting her forehead. "I wish you'd told me about this before."

"Oh, sorry, it's just that I'm not super excited to share it with people!" I exclaim. "And it's not like you told me you were an actual vampire-killing Jedi before, either, you know."

"Listen to me. You can't trust Jude Marlowe, okay? I know he's pretty—"

"That's not what this is about!" I protest, but inside I still feel kind of called out. It's not like I was hoping he'd ask me to prom or something, but he isn't in my *private time* thoughts for no reason. "He knew about the dreams, he said I'd have changes in my body—"

"Big deal!" Daphne throws her hands up. "You're sixteen, your body is changing all the time!"

"I am not still going through puberty!" I shout way too loudly for a public place. Getting a grip, I continue, "Who is he, anyway? Why do you know so much about him?"

"I've been studying the Syndicate and its operatives since forever, and I can probably tell you things about them that they've even forgotten about themselves." Her tone is grave, one mitten curling into a fist. "Jude's father was a British merchant, and his mother was from Algiers. They settled in London in the late sixteenth century, and Jude was born around the year 1590.

"The family was happy, et cetera, but then the plague returned to England in 1603, and things went south. By 1607, Jude had lost his father and two sisters, and he and his mother were dying as well. Lucky for him, his piano teacher and secret boyfriend, Rudolfo Sanoguerra, happened to be a vampire." Settling back against the side of the SUV, Daphne watches snowflakes drift in the yellow light. "Rudolfo Turned the Marlowes to save them from permanent death, but Jude's mother didn't survive the transition. So when Jude rose, reborn, he traveled with Sanoguerra back to mainland Europe and ultimately chose to work for the Syndicate. And now here he is today, trying to sell you a crock of shit so he can kidnap you off to Romania."

"You really think that's what he was trying to do?"

"I don't trust anything the Syndicate says or does, so maybe I'm biased, but I don't buy his story." Sparks flash in Daphne's eyes. "The Brotherhood has access to the same prophecies those vampires do. More than they do, if I'm being honest, because those ancient libraries didn't all burn down completely." She slides a canny look my way. "Everybody knows the Corrupter Rises every hundred years or so, but the only reason the Syndicate—and these supposed factions, if they actually exist—would take an interest in the legend now is because *this* year, the so-called Endless One is supposed to *Ascend*."

"What does that mean?"

"*Rising* is just a fancy, mystical-sounding way to describe how the Corrupter returns to our plane of existence. Allegedly, it takes root in a normal person and gestates, during which time the host develops magical capabilities: clairvoyance, telepathy, subtle forms of mind control—"

"Mind control?" I perk up immediately, thinking about all the math homework I'm going to get other people to do for me. I mean, yes, an ancient entity may be taking over my body and so forth, but at least I won't have to fail algebra again.

"There are also some dubious claims of pyrokinesis and levitation, but—"

"*Levitation?*" My eyes bulge. "Are you kidding me? Like . . . you mean I'm going to be able to *float*? And read people's minds, and see the future, and . . . and I don't know what pyrokinesis is. Some kind of Greek yogurt?"

"The ability to generate and control fire."

"*Seriously?*"

"Auggie!" Daphne laughs a little. "It's not like you'd be turning into a wizard or something. If this is real, if the Rising is really what's happening, you have an entity slowly regaining its consciousness inside of you."

The mood in the air darkens so quickly it's as if the stars are swept out of the sky. Images of Jude—dead, blistered by the plague, the blood in his stomach replicating and spreading—fill my thoughts. "Like what happens to a vampire?"

She looks at me and then glances away. "Not exactly. From what I understand, it's more like . . . possession. The Corrupter expands within the person, alongside their consciousness, sharing their body."

My stomach rolls and vaults upward, and the only reason I don't puke is because of a lump in my throat the size of a decorative gourd. My worst fear has gone from "grandma's rag doll" to "being spiritually double-penetrated by an ancient ghost" in the space of two days. Hoarsely, I manage, "And then what?"

"Well, that's just it—nobody knows." Daphne shrugs helplessly. "Even when it Rises, the Corrupter is confined by the body it inhabits; it's an awakening rather than a transformation. With vampirism, bodies stop aging, they do things that defy human physiology, and they can't be killed except by several very specific means." She shuffles her feet. "If the old records are to be believed, the vessel's mortality is what has ultimately prevented the Corrupter from wreaking total havoc. That contains it, limits its powers, and leaves it vulnerable to all the same things that kill humans. Age, disease, starvation—"

"Executions," I croak out, gagging on the memory of smoke in my lungs. "So that's what the Ascension is? Escaping mortality?"

"Again, according to a lot of sketchy writings from thousands of years ago," Daphne begins, miserable, "the Ascension is when the Corrupter *exceeds* the vessel—possibly meaning that it jumps free, but . . . most likely meaning that it jailbreaks the body altogether from the hold of mortality."

"So a transformation after all. A takeover," I interpret in a stricken tone, feeling hollow inside. It's ironic, I guess, given that my body has apparently never been more full. "Best-case scenario is this thing will pop out of me like a stripper from a birthday cake, and worst-case is that . . . one day I'm just going to *Turn* into Vampire Santa Claus." Stomach roiling, my mouth dry, I ask, "How am I supposed to bring day-walking and true immortality to all the good little vampires, anyway?"

"That's another thing that's missing from the prophecies." She shakes her head. "The most popular theories are that it's either bestowed through touch—some sort of vampiric benediction—or else . . . that the vessel's blood becomes charged with magic, and by sharing it, the Corrupter can imbue the undead with its gifts."

My face is stiff with cold, my hands hurt, and my toes have no sensation at all anymore; but every part still feels like *me*—like *my body*. Is this real? Is there something inside me right now, getting stronger all the time? My throat closes as I whisper, "Why me?"

"There's no good answer to that, either." Daphne's eyes shine with sympathy. "When it comes to the Corrupter, there have always been more rumors than facts, and most prophecies are barely intelligible. But the seers whose visions were the most precise talk about an Ascension taking place in this age." Her mittens come together as she wrings her hands. "They describe a vessel born under certain planetary influences, exhibiting specific traits, living at a meeting point of two ley lines, and . . . well, it's you, Auggie. There's just no one else, anywhere or at any time, that meets the criteria the way you do."

My back goes stiff, every last one of my star-crossed atoms suddenly clanging with alarm—and not because my Leo sun and Scorpio moon are apparently written down in some moldy, supernatural library book, either. Backing up, I ask, "How do you know that?"

"What do you mean?" Daphne drops her hands. She doesn't look as cold as I feel.

"How do you know what 'planetary influences' I was born under?" I step back again. "How do you know I'm the only one who meets the criteria?"

"Auggie—"

"Who are you?" My eyes go hot and blurry, a week's worth of ugly surprises overwhelming me, suspicions as black as the starless sky exploding in my mind.

Her shoulders slump. "I told you who I am. I'm Daphne Banks, I'm good at math, and . . . I'm a Knight with the Brotherhood of Perseus." She doesn't move closer, not even when I take a third step back, and the sadness in her eyes is what finally makes me stop. "I'm sorry I didn't tell you before—I couldn't. The truth is, Auggie . . . I'm not a student at Northwestern. And it's not a coincidence that I'm part of an organization of vampire-killing warriors. The Brotherhood sent me here. I was . . . I'm assigned to watch you."

One tear spills down my cheek, and I scrub it away with

shaking fingers. I'm staring at her, waiting for her to peel off her rubber Daphne mask, or to say that this is some elaborate prank. She's been tutoring me for nearly six months, and the whole time she's been spying on me, keeping secrets *about me*—it's too much to process. "H-how?"

"I'm sorry it's coming out this way." Daphne's forehead knots, her voice thinning with nerves. "I'd hoped that nothing would happen—that you'd pass algebra and never have to know anything about me at all. But the Brotherhood has been aware of those prophecies for generations, and they always meant to place someone on the inside. When it became clear that you were the vessel, they sent me in." Hugging herself, she adds, "Everyone who wears the emblem of Perseus pledges their life to guard humankind against supernatural dangers. The point wasn't to trick you, Auggie, it was to protect you. The only reason the Syndicate is interested is because they're hoping the legends are true, and that they can somehow control the Corrupter when it Ascends!"

"You've been lying to me." My voice is still broken, and more hot tears slip down my cheeks. "For months. How am I supposed to believe you?"

"I'm sorry, Auggie," she repeats, her tone soft and small. "I know this is a lot to take in, but you have to understand that I would never hurt you." Daphne looks me in the eye as she says it, snowflakes feathering her lashes. "Part of the reason I came here was to keep the Syndicate from shutting you away in some secret laboratory where you'd be experimented on. If there's any way to stop this prophecy from coming true, the Brotherhood will find it."

"So you think it's real." A frigid wind gusts across the parking lot, cutting through the fabric of my coat. "Inside you acted like it was a hoax, but now you're talking about trying to stop it—so all of this is bullshit. The only thing you're really here to make sure of is that the Syndicate won't turn into a bunch of unkillable day-walkers who can extend the same power to, like, seventy-five percent of the world's vampires."

Daphne's jaw shifts, and she rolls her shoulders. "All right. Touché. Six months ago, maybe the main thing I cared about was . . . well, that. But I'm not your enemy, Auggie. Just because I agreed to come here and, and . . ."

"And insinuate yourself into my life under false pretenses," I supply coldly.

"And *watch over you*," she amends, "doesn't mean I believe that the Corrupter is anything more than a fantasy—"

"*Bullshit!*" I shout loud enough that Daphne glances around to see if we're overheard. We're probably fifty yards from the mall's entrance, standing in an empty space between an SUV and a compact car, all alone with a bunch of lies and secrets and possibly one slowly metastasizing parasitic entity trying to take over my *entire fucking body*. "Stop bullshitting me!"

"Whether I personally believe in the Corrupter or not doesn't even matter," Daphne finally snaps, mettle sparking in her eyes. "What matters is that there are a lot of incredibly unstable vampires in this world that absolutely *do* believe in it, and with the kind of foaming-at-the-mouth zeal that makes the Salem witch trials look like a fucking game show." She takes a step forward, closing the gap between us, her eyes still locked on mine. "You're not safe, Auggie. That's what I've—"

She doesn't finish. Her eyes go wide, her head jerking up, and she throws herself backward a split-second before something streaks through the empty space where she was just standing. With a thump and a hiss, an object plunges into the front tire of the compact beside us—a blade of some kind, its hilt sticking five inches out of the thick rubber—and the car shudders as air erupts from the sudden puncture.

Daphne doesn't even have time to regain her balance before a black-clad figure glides soundlessly over the top of the SUV. Face hidden by a ski mask and tinted goggles, he drops between us with a second blade clutched in one gloved hand. Gleaming viciously under the electric safety lamps is a foot-long katana—and it's aimed straight at my heart.

10

The sword swings at my neck, and I lurch backward, my feet hitting ice and going out from under me, the blade whistling past by an inch. I land hard, pain shooting through my elbow, and I stare up at my attacker in disbelief. A neoprene bodysuit hugs a wiry but masculine frame, and the gear masking his face makes him look monstrous and surreal. He raises the sword, and I cry out as he prepares to lunge—but that's when Daphne recovers.

With balletic grace and surprising power, she spins backward and slams her foot into the mysterious ninja's hip, taking him off his feet. The man hurtles sideways, striking the rear bumper of the SUV and setting off its car alarm before crashing to the pavement, slewing over ice and fresh snow. Ripping her mittens off and wrenching the second katana free from the ruined tire of the compact car, Daphne shouts, "*Run, Auggie!*"

It's great advice, but where to? There are still plenty of shadows in this parking lot, and even in my panic I have no reason to assume this *actual sword-wielding assassin* came alone. I don't even know what he is, or what kind of friends he might have out there. My skin is crawling again, but I don't know if that means "vampire," or if it means *a ninja is trying to kill me.*

Ignoring Daphne's directive, I scuttle along the damaged compact as she advances on our attacker, putting myself on the safer side of the experienced vampire killer. And as she spins the blade with clearly practiced hands, carving loops out of the snowy air, I have to admit that she looks every inch the warrior she claims to be.

The ninja rights himself, rocking onto his haunches, evaluating his opponent; and then he leaps, springing forward, swiping his katana at Daphne in a deadly arc. She parries the blow with a violent clash of metal, dancing back a step as the man's feet touch the ground, and then their battle truly begins.

They move so fast I can't keep up. The swords blaze under the streetlamps, and their bodies whirl, counter, and collide as the twin blades meet again and again. Twice, Daphne manages a surprise attack—once a kick to the man's knee while deflecting a blow, and then a strike to his midsection as she dodges a forward thrust. But the masked man repays the favor, an unexpected swing ripping through the front of her coat. When she stumbles back, the fabric gapes open, the cut so deep the skin of her stomach is visible.

She doesn't even slow down. They charge back together with two-handed grips, the clanging blows getting louder. I can practically feel the car alarm in my back teeth, and I finally remember my cell phone, wondering if I should call the police. Despite being trained to expect trouble with vampires, the authorities have been historically shitty at fighting them—fangs beat guns every time.

Reeling from another kick to the chest, the ninja regroups and charges, his katana slashing the air. He leaps, kicking off the side of the SUV to vault even higher, and Daphne arches back, dodging the blade as she simultaneously lashes out with her own—piercing the stiff neoprene of the man's bodysuit just as he launches into a sideways flip.

The motion wrenches the blade from Daphne's hand, and when the man hits the ground, so does her sword. Metal rings as the katana spins out of sight beneath the SUV, and the ninja staggers back, looking down at the hole my math tutor sliced open over his right flank. Six inches of pale skin are exposed, along with a bloody but unfortunately shallow flesh wound, and he gazes up at her—his grip tightening on his sword.

"Auggie," Daphne begins, backing away from the man, "you *really* need to run."

The ninja advances, slashing and thrusting, and Daphne somehow manages to retreat from each attack until her heels hit the front tire of the compact and she falls over the hood. Lifting his blade, the man makes to impale her clean through the heart, but she seizes his wrist with both hands just in time. The tip of the sword is an inch from her chest, and the katana quivers as he struggles to drive it into her body.

Electrified by adrenaline, I know what I have to do. Diving under the SUV, I grab the lost blade and scramble to my feet. I've never even thrown a punch before, but Daphne is fighting to save my life—I'm not running anywhere. Wrapping my fingers tight around the hilt, I blank my mind. I hope I don't run him through and end up stabbing Daphne; I hope that if he dies, his ghost doesn't haunt me; and I hope I don't fuck this up.

But I do, of course. I don't make it two steps before he swings around, swiping his katana at mine so hard the blade is knocked from my half-numb hands. He lunges at me, and I almost fall on my ass again, but Daphne springs up from the compact's hood with a vengeance. Kicking the back of his knee, she drops him into a kneel, and in a flash, the wooden stake she brandished at Jude appears in her hand again. Plunging it down, she buries it in his shoulder.

The masked man emits a guttural screech, toppling sideways. Blood splashes the pavement as he scrambles away, one-handed, dragging himself to his feet and limping into a run. Daphne scoops up his sword from where he dropped it and flings it after him as hard as she can, but it crashes against the side mirror of a sedan as the man vanishes behind it.

"Damn it." Daphne bends over, her hands on her knees. "*Damn it.*"

"I can't . . . I can't . . ." I can't figure out what to say. "I can't fucking believe that! That was an actual fucking *swordfight*, and you were amazing!"

"I'm a warrior, Auggie." In spite of everything, she actually manages a faint laugh. Her hair is disheveled, her coat is ruined, and she very nearly got killed by a *ninja* in the parking lot of a dying mall, but somehow she's smiling. "You've got no idea how long I've been training for a fight like that." Then, looking around, "We really need to go."

Even in the mostly deserted lot, the SUV's alarm is attracting attention. People have emerged from the main doors of the Colgate Center, watching from a distance as we race for Daphne's Saab. No matter how I felt when we first left the food court, I've got no problem trusting her anymore—she lied, but she's more than earned the benefit of the doubt.

It isn't until she screeches out of the lot, swerving onto the road leading back into town, that my endorphin high vanishes and I finally lose it. My nose runs, my eyes fill with tears, and I quake so badly it takes me three tries to open my messaging app.

"What are you doing?" Daphne demands, her voice as sharp as the sword she was just fighting with.

"I'm texting my m-mom!" I make a disgusting noise and then wipe my nose on my sleeve, for lack of anything better. Which is . . . also disgusting. "Some guy just tried to *kill*—"

"*Stop!*" Without even glancing over, she bats the phone from my hands, knocking it into the footwell.

I stare at her, sure she's lost her mind. "What the hell? I need to warn my parents—"

"So they can do what?" she challenges, the lights of an oncoming car sweeping across her face. "Think this through, Auggie. What will they do?"

"They . . ." I don't know how to explain what should be obvious. "They'll call the police—"

"Who will come out and stop all the vampires, like always?"

"At least they'll *know*!" I'm vehement, my tone rising. "People with guns and stuff will know that killers are after me—how is that a bad thing?"

"So the mayor mobilizes the Fulton Heights police to act as your personal bodyguard service. That's what you think your parents will do for you?"

Her sarcasm is more than I can handle. "What is your problem? A guy with actual swords just tried to chop both our heads off, and you're trying—"

"I'm trying to make you *wake up*!" She pounds the dashboard hard enough to startle me into silence. "If you tell your parents that vampires are after you, they'll take you out of town!"

"Good!" I declare. "*Good*. I *want* to get out of town! I *should* get out of town. My whole family should!"

"And then you've involved them, and they become obstacles." Her tone is final, deadly. "The Vampire Syndicate has known about these prophecies for centuries, Auggie. They're prepared. They sent someone to sweet-talk you, and you said no, but do you really think they'll let you just fuck off to Ecuador or New Zealand or wherever?" She waits for an answer, but I have none to give. "It's the digital age, and disappearing—really disappearing—isn't easy, especially for a bunch of suburbanites with no training or experience. Credit cards, bank accounts, phones, medical records . . . all those things can be traced. You wouldn't last a week.

"Those who believe in the Corrupter are true fanatics. That's what I've been trying to tell you. You saw that guy back there!" Daphne shoots me a wide-eyed glance. "He came for you, but the second I got in his way, I was fair game. Right now, you're reachable—they obviously know how to get to you without going through your family. But if your parents find out you're in danger, and they remove you from Fulton Heights? They're suddenly in the way, too, and they become necessary collateral. Can they swordfight?"

I freeze, chilled by the picture she's painting. "Th-there's still protective custody—or witness protection."

"You think vampires can't mesmerize cops or FBI agents?" she counters. "Not to mention the fact that you'd have to convince the authorities you're worth spending those resources on in the first place. I don't think you want to try that."

"Why not?"

She lets out a bone-weary sigh. "That guy just now? He was human. Really strong and incredibly skilled, but still just a living, breathing human who really wanted you dead."

"W-what . . ." But I can't finish. I don't know how to ask.

"What I've been trying to tell you is that if the legends of the Corrupter are real, then it's already inside you, Auggie. You can't escape the prophecies. There's nowhere to hide." Her words are blunt and cold as she navigates a corner into my neighborhood. "The Syndicate wants to keep you locked up as an incubator, and when humans find out what you might bring forth, they'll want to kill you before you can hatch."

Daphne's tone is ominous, as if I need special emphasis to understand how extra-double fucked I am.

"Oh." I swallow hard, my throat thick with fear.

"There are all sorts of ragtag anti-undead human militias around the world these days, some more sophisticated than others. The Persean Knights have a lot of company." We reach my block and she slows, pulling up to the curb outside my house. Snow is still drifting down, dusting the porch overhang like sugar, and everything looks so peaceful it makes me want to scream. Quietly, Daphne says, "I left him alive so he can crawl back to his friends, or whoever sent him, and let them know you're protected. It'll buy us some time before whoever it is tries again."

"They're going to try again?" I swivel to her in horror. "What if they come *here*?"

"I'll make some calls, see if I can get eyes on your house when I'm not around," she promises, gripping my shoulder with a comforting hand. "Look, if there's a way to stop the prophecy from coming true, or to prove that it's a hoax, the Brotherhood will find out. In the meantime, I'm going to do everything I can to see that you're protected. I know this is awful, but you've got to do your best to act like everything's normal."

I laugh wildly, shaking my head. "Yeah, sure. No problem."

"I'm serious, Auggie." She meets my eyes, and she looks like the old Daphne—the one I thought she was all along: sweet, sisterly, tough in a kind way. "No matter what happens, you've still got a life to live. Don't waste it by giving in to fear of what might be coming. Don't let a possible future ruin what you've got right now."

"I'll try," I hear myself saying, but that hollow feeling only widens. Someone just tried to kill me, I'm drawing death scenes on autopilot, vampires have books with my name in them, *I'm slowly becoming possessed*, and the only person I can trust is someone who's been lying to me for the past six months. And her sage advice amounts to *Hang in there, baby!* How am I supposed to keep this a secret? How am I supposed to *smile*?

Once again, Daphne waits at the curb, watching me like a guard dog as I shuffle up the walk in a daze. Mounting the porch steps with Frankenstein feet, I dig for my keys with fingers that are still restless with fear. My house is empty right now; my mom is working late, and my dad will be at the gym, so at least I won't have to worry about them being killed in a staged home invasion if that ninja has impatient friends.

At least not tonight.

I'm so distracted by my jittery thoughts that somehow, ironically, I don't even realize that I'm not alone on the porch until it's too late—until the shadows beneath the overhang divide, and a tall figure lurches at me out of the darkness.

11

The keys drop from my hands and I scramble back, my heart slamming into my throat. My heel hits empty space at the top of the porch steps, and I wobble dangerously—my life a Choose Your Own Adventure that's about to end in either Ninja or Gravity—when the figure moves into the moonlight. "Don't freak out, Auggie, it's just me!"

My would-be attacker grabs me and hauls me back to safety. I blink, rapid-fire, not sure I can trust my eyes. The surfer hair, the soft lips, the jawline . . . I recognize him, of course, but how messed up is it that I'm more shocked to find a cute boy on my porch than a deadly assassin? "G-Gunnar?"

"Hey." He grins, his smile as warm as my favorite peppermint s'mores mocha. "Sorry, man, I didn't mean to scare you like that. I got here a few minutes ago and was trying to decide if I should leave a note or just . . . leave, when your ride pulled up."

He jerks a thumb in the direction of Daphne's car, still idling at the curb, her profile a hazy smudge through fogged windows. Can she even see him? I don't want to sound ungrateful, because she doesn't exactly work for me, but I could have just been slaughtered on my front porch! This is exactly what I was worried about.

"I . . ." My brain is still several beats behind. "Sorry, hi. What?"

"I got here a few minutes ago," Gunnar repeats slowly, his dramatic eyebrows slanting upward with worry. "I knocked, but there was no answer, and I was trying to decide what to do. You probably think I look like a stalker now."

"No, you look great," I assure him quickly, because my special talent is humiliating myself in front of cute boys. Sighing, I retrieve my keys. "Sorry. Again. I've . . . had a weird night."

"I'm sure I'm not helping." His grin takes on an abashed quality, and my heart melts just a little. And then, remembering Jude, I try to freeze it back up. Maybe I need to stop being such a sucker for a pretty face.

"I don't mean to sound rude, but . . . what are you doing here?"

"Oh! Sorry," he repeats, and then grabs something off the porch railing, presenting it with a flourish. "You left this at the café the night that, you know, a vampire catapulted through our front window." In his hands, he's holding my US History textbook, and I actually glance over my shoulder at my backpack for a second, as if somehow he swiped it from me while I wasn't paying attention. "I guess we could've just kept it behind the counter—you come in pretty often. But I thought if you had, like, a test coming up or something, you might want it?"

He looks down at his hands as he mumbles the last part, and I accept the book, still staring. I should probably just be grateful, like a normal person, but paranoia keeps whispering little warnings in my ear. "How did you even know where I live?"

"Your name is written inside it. I looked up 'Pfeiffer in Fulton Heights,' and this address was the only result. It's part of why I couldn't decide what to do when no one answered the door. I mean, if it *wasn't* your house, I didn't want to just leave the book."

The explanation makes sense—of course it makes sense. I rub

my forehead like it'll chase away my scrambled thoughts. "Thanks. I hadn't even realized I'd lost it."

"Oh good. Then you didn't need it for a test or whatever."

"No, I mean, I totally did." The test was this morning, and I'm pretty sure I failed it. "That's what we were studying for when Mr. Toothy showed up. I've just been . . . I've had a lot on my mind."

"It was a pretty intense night." He grimaces, and lines appear at the corners of his mouth. Somehow, I find them sexy, and I'm pretty sure something's wrong with me. "Are you doing okay? The way he got in your face . . . you must've been terrified."

I can't think of an elegant reply. "I didn't shit myself, so I'm proud of how I handled things."

"Impressive." He grins, more lines appearing. "I admire intestinal fortitude."

"I might have peed a little, though," I admit.

"I'm not judging—I had it easy." Gunnar shrugs, his eyes comfortably on mine. "I just got wrecking-balled across the room by a screaming, blood-soaked mom. Luckily, all I hurt was my whole entire body."

"Oh yeah. Ouch." I push my glasses up my nose, still discombobulated by the events of the night—by the fact that Gunnar the Sexy Barista is here now, talking to me. "Are *you* okay? No permanent damage?"

"Just the psychological trauma," he replies cheerfully.

"Cool, cool." Furtively, I cast another glance back at Daphne's car. It's still there—she's still watching. The fact gives me a little bit of comfort, but who knows when the next attack might happen? "Um, would you like to come inside? I'm kind of freezing my ass off."

Gunnar hesitates, but then says, "Sure. I shouldn't stay too long, but okay."

My nerves fray even further as I unlock the front door, my

thoughts smashing around like bumper cars. *I have invited a cute boy inside! Whatever's going on here, I am prolonging it!* Already my mind is going blank, and I have no idea what else to say. *WHATEVER YOU DO, DON'T SHOW HIM THE SCARY RAG DOLL!*

"That's my mom's terrifying rag doll," I say the literal second the door is closed behind us, and it's like ripping off a Band-Aid. Naturally, the doll is propped up on the counter, where it watches us like a sentinel guarding the gates of hell. "Try not to look it in the eye."

"Holy shit." Gunnar's brows climb most of the way to his hairline. "Is it a Horcrux? Because it really looks like there's a bunch of souls trapped inside of it."

"Don't ask questions you don't want answers to." Shrugging out of my backpack, I wince, my elbow throbbing; when I get my coat off, there's blood seeping through my sweater. "Shit."

"Oh man, are you okay?" Gunnar steps into me, gently taking hold of my arm and rotating it. He smells like fresh, cold air, and just his touch makes different parts of me start to firm up. His hair is glossy, his lashes curl upward, and there's spearmint on his breath.

"I'm okay," I squeak. "I . . . fell earlier." Repeating myself, I add, "It's been a weird night."

Holding my tricep in one hand and my wrist in the other, Gunnar bends my arm carefully. Looking me in the eye, he asks, "Does this hurt?"

"N-not really." I can hardly breathe.

"Good." He releases his grip and steps away again, but my heart is still fluttering. "Then it's probably not broken. I fractured a bone in my arm falling out of a tree when I was little, and it sucked. Hurt like hell for days—I had to wear a sling and everything."

"I've never broken a bone before." I'm very smug about this. I take off my glasses so I can work the sweater over my head, and my T-shirt rides all the way up with it. As I tug it down, I glance at

Gunnar, and I swear his eyes flick guiltily away from the bare skin of my exposed stomach. Heat rushes through me again, my face tingling. "I, um . . . Do you want anything? I can get you some water, or . . . ?"

"Honestly, I should really get going." He fidgets, picking at his sleeves. "I just wanted to make sure you had your book, and . . ." He trails off, sighs, rubs his face. Then his smile comes back, self-effacing and almost goofy. "*Ugh*, how am I so bad at this?"

"What do you mean?" I ask, wadding up my sweater, my hands acting of their own accord.

He rakes his fingers through his hair. "The reason I didn't just leave the book at Sugar Mama's is because I wanted an excuse to see you. It's like . . . every time you come in, I could swear you're trying to flirt with me—but I'm afraid to flirt back, because if I'm wrong, things could get weird, and you'd never come into the café again. Or you would, and it would be awkward." He glances up at me with a sheepish grin. "And, of course, I've just made sure things will be awkward anyway. *How am I so bad at this?* I'm sorry, I'll—"

"Wait!" I stop him before he can reach the door. "Are you saying that you came over here to flirt with me? Seriously? Like . . . *seriously*?"

Gunnar laughs. "Is that so hard to believe?"

"Well, kinda, yeah." Scrunching my nose, I point out, "You're all . . . you. And I'm all, like, *me*."

"Okay, I have no idea what that means. But I like you, Auggie. You're cute, and you make me laugh, and I never know what you're going to say next . . . I like that you're always a surprise." He shrugs, seeming embarrassed by all this apparent honesty.

My sweater drops to the floor, and I barely notice. Living in Fulton Heights, I've always been different—the gay kid, the art nerd, the weirdo. Plus, I'm a mess, with hair that sticks up all the time, glasses that are always askew, and, you know, a monster growing inside of me. By contrast, Gunnar is all shiny skin and cool dude-necklaces. I'd dreamed but never for a moment truly believed that he would even notice me, let alone—

"You're gay?" I squint at him, still trying to make all this add up.

"Yeah, pretty much." He bobs his head awkwardly. "If I've made things weird, I'm really sorry. I just . . . Well, we only get so much time, right?"

Pulling out one of the barstools at the counter, I collapse into it. "You . . . like me?"

"Yes!" Gunnar actually laughs. "Why do you keep saying it like that?"

"Nobody's ever liked me before," I answer honestly. Except Jude, sort of—but he might have only flirted with me because he wants to stuff me in a cage until I *hatch*.

"Well . . . ta-da!" He does a goofy little dance step, somehow even more attractive than ever. "Listen, if you're not feeling it, that's okay; I should go anyway. But I just thought, you know, if you *were* feeling it . . . we could get coffee, or something. Somewhere that's not Sugar Mama's."

"Like . . ." I scratch my neck where the heat makes it tingle. "You mean, kind of like a date?"

"Or an actual date. If you're cool with it."

For a moment I just stare at him. About twenty minutes ago, a guy with two swords was trying to vivisect me in a parking lot—right after a four-hundred-year-old vampire told me I'm the undead's version of Aladdin's lamp, destined to barf up a wish-granting super being that will give them eternal life; fifteen minutes ago, I was a sobbing, snot-covered wreck, desperate to flee the country and hide forever. I *still* want to run and hide. With four walls around me and a front door that locks, I feel safer . . . but I know it's an illusion. Even if vampires can't get in, ninjas don't need an invitation to pick a lock and katana me to death.

The world as you know it, as we all know it, could be coming to an end. I should really tell Gunnar thanks, but no thanks. As lonely as I am, as lonely as I've been—as much as I'd love to be kissed by a boy just one time before I'm *possessed* . . . how can I even consider it?

Daphne's words come back to me: *You've still got a life to live.* As messed up as that life is, she's right. I'm sick of being told that if I just wait two more years, if I just get into college, I can move to a city where the closest real-life gay guy isn't ten miles away. Most of my straight friends have been dating since middle school, and I'm sick of being told that when I'm eighteen, I might finally get the chance to catch up to them—to hold hands with someone, to know what it feels like to want someone who wants me back.

I might never turn eighteen; I don't know if I have two months left, let alone two years. If the Corrupter is real, and the Brotherhood can't figure out how to stop it from Ascending, my time is already running out. All I have is now, and even though I am definitely on the verge of a panic attack, I don't want to miss out. Not if I'm going to die.

"I think a real date would be very cool," I manage to say, nodding, my face kind of hot and my breathing all funny.

"Awesome." Gunnar smiles again, showing all those perfect teeth. How are teeth sexy? They're pieces of actual *bone* that stick out of your face, but I want to lick them anyway. We exchange phone numbers and then say an awkward goodbye—but he hugs me before he leaves, and it's amazing.

"Be careful," I call out as he skips down the stairs of the porch— but he doesn't even look back. No one is out to kill him.

After he's gone, the house becomes a trap, every pane of glass an easy entry for a masked murderer. The air is so still the quiet hurts my ears, and when I walk, the sound of my footsteps is unnerving. I take a knife, climb the stairs to my bedroom, and turn my desk chair to face the window, so I can be ready.

Shutting my eyes, struggling to concentrate, I think about what I felt on Ximena's porch the other night—what I felt at Sugar Mama's, and sitting across from Jude in the food court. If this ability to sense vampires really comes from an entity developing inside of me, I definitely don't want to welcome it into my consciousness, but right now I'm desperate to know what's out there, and this undead radar is my secret weapon. My only weapon.

For a long time, there's nothing. But then something connects, wires touching in a part of myself I can't identify, and the back of my neck prickles—a rush passing over my skin. And then I sense them—two vampires. One is about ten yards away, the other about fifteen, on opposite sides of the house. They aren't moving.

Ironically, it's the first time all night I'm able to relax. My guess is that the Syndicate is having my house watched, and even though that should freak me out, it doesn't. They can't come in, but they won't want me to get killed by vigilante ninjas—not while my body is still pressure-cooking the Endless One. The enemy of my enemy is . . . okay, well, the Syndicate is still totally my enemy. But as long as they want me to stay alive, our goals are temporarily aligned, and I will gladly let them protect me from assassins.

I wake up slumped in my desk chair, my elbow throbbing worse than ever following a night of mercifully dreamless sleep. All through my early classes, I'm groggy and listless—but I snap out of my daze quick during third period when Leesha Gardner barrels into class, her face puffy and streaked with tears. When she collects herself enough to speak, she shocks the whole class. "M-Mr. Strauss is dead. Someone killed him last night!"

Conversation ripples through the room, and my mind reels as

I struggle to process the news. *There must be a mistake.* And yet the first hit that comes up when I search for more information is a story from the local section of the *Chicago Tribune—Man Found Dead in Fulton Heights*—accompanied by a smiling photo of my art teacher.

Jesse T. Strauss, 29, originally of Richmond, VA, was found dead behind the wheel of his car late last night on Montebello Road. The body showed signs of violence, and according to Fulton Heights authorities, the suspected cause of death is blood loss from a deep wound to the shoulder area. A police spokesperson said that the Fulton Heights High School art instructor probably died between 6:00 p.m. and 7:30 p.m. last night, and that the death is being treated as a homicide. Strauss's car had rolled into the drainage ditch that runs alongside Montebello, and was noticed by a passing motorist, who called 911.

My eyes go hazy for a moment, static filling my ears. It couldn't have been later than 6:30 when Daphne and I were jumped last night—and Montebello Road is less than two minutes from the mall. In my mind, I keep seeing that wooden stake coming down, the pointed end plunging through neoprene and flesh and burying itself in the ninja's shoulder.

That guy just now? He was human.

You should give some thought to a four-year art and design school.

I left him alive so he can crawl back to his friends.

You've got a gift, and an academic environment would provide an opportunity to grow your skills and explore other media.

At the bottom of the article, it says the story is still developing, but I close the tab and delete the page from my phone's history. I'm fighting to breathe, and for a moment I'm sure I'm either going to be sick or black out.

My favorite teacher tried to kill me.

Paris, France

1793

THIS ONE WAS A STRONG BODY, WELL CARED FOR AND well fed, and its original occupant had not surrendered control without a fight. Even now, sitting in the back of the lurching, rolling cart, the Corrupter could feel her deep inside, battling him for primacy. Like a stone lodged in a shoe, she was a constant irritant, and her plight was senseless. In less than an hour, this body would be put to a gruesome death, and the woman knew it.

Mortals could be counted on for nothing so much as acting against their own best interests.

Centuries changed like seasons for him, each subsequent lifetime bursting open with a dazzling newness that tarnished as soon as he realized how dreadfully similar it would be to the last. Fashions evolved, but mortals always stayed the same—their small jealousies, their petty greed, their laughable and unearned sense of pride. A hundred years or more might elapse while the Corrupter slept, and yet every time he opened his eyes, he found himself looking out at a generation of humans that would have reliably learned nothing from their own endless history of warring and bloodshed.

The cart shook, and the deliberately humble cap they'd given the Corrupter itched against his shorn scalp. A filthy mob shouted from the roadside, their rage so potent he could smell brimstone on the air. Secretly, it delighted him. The fury, the elemental rawness of their bloodlust . . . it called to him like a siren's song, stirring the power that trembled inside this moribund shell of meat and bone. To release it would be an indescribable pleasure—the act he'd died countless times waiting to perform. But he couldn't.

This body was strong, but not quite strong enough.

An apple sailed at the cart from somewhere in the crowd, and the Corrupter leaned out of its path, letting it hit the boards near his feet. For all this rage and clamoring arrogance, the only name history would remember from this day would be that of the woman these red-faced rustics were determined to destroy.

Just because he could, he twisted around and locked eyes with the youth responsible for throwing the piece of fruit—a factory worker with pitted skin. The boy's thoughts rang clear as a bell in the Corrupter's mind as their gazes met, a din of hatred.

He had plenty to be angry about, the Corrupter acknowledged, feeling his way through the boy's short and miserable history before their tenuous connection evaporated. The details were a little hazy, but certain facts were quite clear: backbreaking labor, starvation, loss. The young revolutionary blamed the woman in the cart because of what she represented, and because he had no one else to blame. He wanted her to die.

The cart turned again, and then once more, the crowd growing louder and thicker; then they entered a vast public square packed with people. Soldiers with bayoneted rifles, Parisians climbing on statues to get a better view, parents hoisting their children up as if attending a carnival. Their zeal, their desire for carnage, made the Corrupter hum deep in his borrowed throat as the horses pulled him closer to the scaffold and the guillotine.

It didn't have to end this way. With no effort at all, the Corrupter could surface, snapping the fragile tethers of mortality that constrained his body, and give the crowd a show to remember. With a single breath, he could reduce the square and everyone in it to ash, send them all screaming to hell in a bath of fire and blood. This body was strong.

But not strong enough. It would withstand his unadulterated splendor for maybe a hundred heartbeats before it disintegrated utterly. And the Corrupter would, ironically, pass into his next incarnation even faster than if he simply waited for these men with their vicious ideals to finish their overly grandiose execution.

They were all dying anyway. Even without the full range of his power he could see how close to the edge they were. The boy with the apple had a mass in his lung that would take him before two years were out; the cart's driver would drink himself to death shortly before that; and even Maximilien Robespierre, an enthusiastic architect of this grisly little drama, would lose his own head in this very square in just nine months' time. They bayed for blood, believing it would salve the deep wounds of exploitation and abuse, but not one of them would live long enough to see the stable republic of their dreams.

Escorted from his cart and up a flight of creaking wooden steps to the platform, the Corrupter stood resolute as various proclamations were announced and crimes read out to the gathered mob—and then something familiar whispered across his skin. *There.*

He'd been looking for them. For the entire hour it took the cart to travel from the Conciergerie, he'd been waiting for that telltale prickle, knowing they would come. The crowd shifted, parting to reveal three figures like the remains of a dock at low tide. Clad in mourning dress, their faces hidden from the sun behind heavy veils, they stood near the base of a wide pedestal. The Corrupter nodded with a smirk, and they nodded back, a familiar conversation passing over the heads of the mob—over the span of centuries.

Rough hands guided him toward the guillotine, and he stumbled, stepping on the foot of his executioner. Locking eyes with the man, the Corrupter sent out a gossamer thread of cold terror. "Pardon me, monsieur. I did not do it on purpose."

The words were soft and polite, with just a trace of a crisp Austrian accent, and he made the executioner look away first. It was a moment that would linger in the hooded man's dreams for the rest of his unfortunate life. Then the crowd pressed forward as the Corrupter knelt down, stretching out across the block. Everyone wanted to watch as Marie Antoinette, erstwhile queen of France and enemy of the Republic, met her death.

Queen of France. Whether in the terrible inferno of the Ascension, or at the vengeful hands of revolutionaries, she had always been doomed to die; with the first breath he'd taken inside her body, the Corrupter had known his time was already running out— and he'd known that, once again, his own destiny would be deferred. A pity. What a life it could have been.

Next time. The Corrupter made a promise to himself as the blade dropped, crashing down with terrible speed.

Next time.

12

After the announcement of Mr. Strauss's death, the rest of the day passes without my noticing it. I'm too shaken to focus on anything other than my memory of last night, of the sword he thrust at me before Daphne could intervene. I can't stop thinking about all the times he praised and encouraged me. *You should give some thought to a four-year art and design school.* When he said that, he'd already been planning my death.

I keep telling myself not to cry, and then I cry anyway. The art room has been my oasis for years, and aside from Adriana and Hope, Mr. Strauss was the only person at this school I ever looked forward to seeing. He taught at FHH for *a year and a half.* Was he watching me that whole time? Sharpening his swords and waiting for me to start sketching mob scenes and bodies burning alive so he'd know it was time to finish me?

The worst part is, I'm also sad because I *miss* him. How messed up is that?

They don't let us leave early, and when I go to the office to say I don't think I'm handling the news very well, all they do is make an appointment for me to see the school psychologist—at the end of the day when classes are over.

So I white-knuckle it through the afternoon, and then an additional hour with Dr. Janovsky—in which I lie, sweatily and creatively, since he is absolutely not ready to hear about either the Corrupter or how I am 99 percent sure that Mr. Strauss tried to murder me—and then I'm finally free to go. The door to the art room stands between me and the exit, and I pass it at a sprint, ready to dive headfirst into the meltdown I've been resisting.

It isn't until I'm outside, the chilly air snapping its fingers in my face, that I remember: I didn't ride my bike today, because it's still in the mall parking lot, and the late bus won't come for another thirty minutes. I whirl around to catch the door before it shuts and locks again, and yelp out loud when I see who's standing there, leaning against the wall beneath the overhang—again.

"Hello, August." Jude is in his ripped jeans and denim jacket, a stubby cigarette pinched between two fingers. Belatedly, my skin prickles to life, and I dig my crucifix out of my pocket as the door bangs shut.

"Don't come any closer!" My voice shakes a little. It's still technically daytime, but the sky is so overcast I'm not sure it matters. I don't totally know how that rule works.

"For the hundredth time," he begins wearily, dropping the cigarette and grinding it under his boot, "I've no intention of hurting you—no matter what your friend had to say. The Brotherhood of Perseus has its own agenda, and I'm sure—"

"She saved my life."

"From another *human*," he adds promptly, his gaze not wavering from mine. "In fact, no vampires at all have attacked you yet. Have they?"

"I was jumped in the middle of a crowded café," I remind him. It bothers me that he already knows what happened in the parking lot.

"By a vampire that did nothing but look at you." His tone is calm. "I have no hidden intentions here, August. I'm not your enemy."

"You had . . . *henchmen* watching my house last night!" I exclaim, not sure what else to say. His not wanting me dead is great—it's what I like most about him, actually, aside from his pretty face and sexy knees—but I still don't trust him.

"*I* have been watching your house for three weeks." He produces a pack of cigarettes, drawing one out with practiced finesse. "Just me. I would have been shadowing you in the parking lot, too, to make sure you were safe, but after the way things ended, I didn't want to provoke your guard dog." Flicking open a silver-plated Zippo, he lights up. It's all very Bad Boy Vampire cliché. "At the risk of repeating myself—again—I'm the Syndicate's only representative in Fulton Heights."

"There were two vampires in my neighborhood, I could sense them," I shoot back imperiously, my sense of righteousness at catching him in a lie thwarted immediately by the realization that I've just handed him an update on my Corrupter abilities.

"Actually, there were three." He wiggles as many fingers. "That's the reason I'm here. We didn't get a chance to finish talking yesterday, and there's more you need to know."

"I'm not interested." The words come out automatically, and they're absolutely true. I don't want to know any more—I don't want to know what I know already. What I want, with every molecule of my being, is to wake up from all of this. I want to run until *this* can't see me anymore.

But I stay where I am. *You can't escape the prophecies. There's nowhere to hide.*

"Look, August, you're right to distrust the undead. You said it yourself the first time we met—you're our food." Coming from a vampire, it's an unsettling statement. "But vampires aren't some hive-minded monolith. Our brains work the same way yours do."

"That's because they're *our brains*," I point out, arms akimbo.

"And I'm not falling for this reverse psychology bullshit—where you tell me why I shouldn't trust you, and it makes me trust you more."

"No psychology." He lifts his hands, palms out. *Nothing up* this *sleeve!* "What I'm getting at is that the decision of the Syndicate to publicly reject the Corrupter as a myth is a . . . complex issue. Not all vampires feel the same way about it."

"Right. Some of you believe in it a hundred percent. And just in case the stories are real, you want to make sure I'm locked up tight in a Syndicate holding cell, where you and your buddies can use me like a private vending machine for 'true immortality.'"

Jude's brow creases in irritation. "Just for a second, would you listen and stop letting the Brotherhood speak for you? Not all vampires actually want 'true immortality.' Some of us would be overjoyed to prove that the Corrupter is a fantasy, and put this whole thing to rest once and for all."

I stare at him, waiting for the punch line, and when it doesn't come I laugh anyway. "Oh, okay, sure. The most powerful organization of undead creatures on the planet sent a special emissary to my shitty hometown to spy on me and seduce me, but you're totally not interested in day-walking."

"I am not trying to *seduce* you!" he protests with a frustrated laugh. "Flirting and seduction are two different things, all right? I'm a four-hundred-year-old pansexual vampire, and I can certainly find willing partners without having to lure them into it!"

"That's your argument?" I toss my hands out, indignant. "There was a massacre here thanks to a bunch of day-walking wannabes, okay? I know what you're after. You vampires are obsessed with your *almost*-immortality!" Then, struggling *so hard* not to look at where his dick is that I totally look at where his dick is, I mutter, "And, you know, your . . . reproductive parts."

"Vampires can't reproduce sexually," he retorts with a feline smile. "But my parts *are* productive."

My face warms because, damn it, in spite of everything, Jude Marlowe is incredibly hot, and now I'm thinking about him naked. "Stop trying to distract me!"

"Have you ever given any thought to what it means? Living forever?" He considers the smoke coiling up from his cigarette. "I was supposed to die at seventeen—I *did* die—but here I am anyway. I'll be young for as long as I walk this Earth, and unless I do something truly unwise, there's no known limit on how long I'll be here." His eyes shift to mine. "Isn't that immortal enough?"

"Again," I reiterate slowly, "this reverse psychology thing—"

"True immortality means I never check out. Ever." He flicks ash from the cigarette. "Humans are destroying this planet just as fast as they can, because every generation figures it'll be the next generation's problem; what do I do when you all wipe yourselves out, and I carry on for eternity, starving in a parched, baking wasteland? What happens to me when the sun eventually goes supernova? I would endure an inferno, only to be blasted into the depths of space, where I'd just . . . float for eternity—alive, but frozen solid. Just me and my thoughts in airless silence, revolving in the dark, until the end of time."

His eyes are vacant, fixed on the sky, and I just stare at him. What he's describing is existential horror on a level I've never contemplated, and the hairs on the back of my neck are dancing like one of those wiggly armed noodle creatures outside of a car dealership.

"The prophecies say nothing about 'imperviousness,' by the way—just endless life," he continues evenly. "Right now, almost any wound I sustain, no matter how severe, will usually heal within an hour, but if I'm decapitated, that's the end. What if I had true immortality, and some Persean Knight managed to cut my head from my shoulders? Could I reattach it? Or would I be in two parts for the rest of my eternal life?" A grim smile plays on his lips. "If I got blown up by a grenade, would I just exist forever as severed limbs and meat and a pile of mutilated brain tissue that can't die—"

"Okay!" I'm practically gargling bile, my back a Slip 'n Slide of icy sweat. "I get it: True immortality is not the rosy, daytime blood feast lots of vampires always imagine it to be. You can stop painting me the picture now, please!"

"But that's the problem. Lots of my kind do see it that way—even some within the Syndicate." Jude takes one more drag on the cigarette and then stomps it out before it's even halfway spent. "Just as you said, I represent the most powerful organization of undead creatures on the planet. The majority of Earth's vampires descend from the original Syndics, and our strength is such that we're able to compel even those who fall outside our influence to comply with our directives.

"If you've ever wondered why Fulton Heights has so many vampires and yet so few vampire-related fatalities, it's because the Syndicate forbids the unnecessary taking of human life." Jude stuffs his hands into his pockets. "The punishments for breaking that edict are medieval, because I've seen firsthand what happens when humans get scared and start to mount large-scale demon hunts. It goes badly for both sides."

"Oh wow," I coo breathlessly. "Your commitment to policing vampires and protecting humans is so dreamy! Can I feel your muscles?"

Jude's gorgeous face pulls into a frog-like scowl. "That's not—I'm not trying to seduce you!"

"No, you're just feeding me a load of Syndicate propaganda," I return. "You *eat* people. You've got your reasons for wanting to keep some kind of balance between humans and vampires, fine, but you're not Doctors Without Borders."

"All ecological systems with hunters and prey require stability for both populations to thrive." He lifts his chin. "I consume blood; I don't *eat humans*." That feline look creeps back into his expression. "I rather enjoy humans, actually. And biting can be fun for both—"

"Okay, okay!" I stuff my hands in my own coat pockets and punch down, because now he's looking at where *my* dick is, and I kind of don't want him to see it at just this moment.

"But there are many undead who absolutely desire vampire supremacy." Anything coy about his demeanor is gone in an instant. "They are infuriated by their vulnerabilities, find it intolerable that they must hide among shadows while humans run this world into the ground, and are outraged by the Syndicate's control. They want a change in the world order, and the ones who believe see the Corrupter as their chance." A car passes by the side lot, tires hissing against damp pavement. "They are dangerous, August; and for many reasons, we cannot afford to let them get what they want."

"You're telling me," I mumble, but now my cold sweat is starting to break out in a cold sweat—because all I hear is that if the Corrupter is real, Jude's buddies would rather kill me than let me fall into the wrong hands. "Is there a cure? I mean, if this thing is real?"

He shifts, glancing down. "We're not sure. As I've said, there really isn't much information available, and the prophecies are incomplete. Our scholars have done research over the centuries, but never particularly seriously. Most of them honestly don't believe it's real, and it isn't knowledge any of us have needed before."

I reply with a stiff nod. What he's continuing to not say is *We just figured we'd kill you*. The easiest "cure" of all.

"I promise I'll . . . I'll look into it." He winces, seeming to immediately regret saying so—but before I can parse his expression further, he adds, "Listen: I said there were three vampires watching your house last night, and it's important you understand what that means. You need to know about the two major cults that have formed around the Corrupter, because they *are* gathering in Fulton Heights. Now."

A dead deer sucked dry in a farmer's field just past my neighborhood, a vampire purring at me, *the Dark Star rises . . .* I swallow. "Of course they are."

"One is called the League of the Dark Star." Jude steps out from beneath the safety of the overhang. When he doesn't burst into flames, I check a mental box. *Clouds = adequate protection from sunlight.* "The League was founded in the sixteenth century by an undead mystic named Erasmus Kramer, although he's believed to have been killed by Brotherhood hunters sometime in the late 1700s. Since then, they've been led by Kramer's chief lieutenant—a powerful French sorceress named Viviane Duclos, who is notorious for her cunning."

"Oh neat." I shuffle back a few steps as Jude comes closer, wanting to keep a little distance. "And she's been watching my house?"

"No, sentry duty is grunt work. She wouldn't expose herself like that." He pulls out another cigarette, just as I back into the end of someone's car, and he pauses to light up. "No one's seen her for centuries, there are no photographs, and the only portrait of her was destroyed in the eighteenth century. For all we know, she died when Kramer did and the League has been using her name as a false front to spread disinformation ever since."

With a frown, I ask, "So what do you *actually* know about these people? What am I on the lookout for here?"

"There's probably fifteen members, they're all skilled fighters, and they're all very, very smart." Jude leans against a Prius parked across from where I'm standing. "Kramer was choosy, and Duclos even choosier, when it came to building the ranks. They expect to become demigods with the Ascension of the Corrupter, and they don't want that privilege going to just anyone." He folds his arms across his chest. "Mostly they lie low, stay out of trouble. They either abide by the Syndicate's precepts or break the laws in ways we can't prove, so we monitor them but generally leave them alone."

"Okay." I adjust my glasses a little. "They don't exactly sound terrifying. From what you said before, I was expecting a bunch of Baeserta nutjobs."

"Don't underestimate them, August." Jude's brows dip down. "They've spent hundreds of years waiting for this. They've been careful not to make waves, because they couldn't risk giving the Syndicate any justification to crack down on them. But now that they believe their moment has arrived, they're not going to let anything stand in their way. If Duclos wants you in her grasp, she's had since the sixteen hundreds to devise countless ways to manage it."

"Fantastic," I croak. We're outside, the sky spreading everywhere, and suddenly I feel like someone's sitting on my chest. A centuries-old sorceress-slash-vampire is out to get me, and my only protectors are my math tutor and a vampire who might want to stuff me in a cage. "Just . . . fantastic."

"It's the second group that's truly dangerous," Jude goes on, finding the only words that could possibly be worse. "The Mystic Order of the Northern Wolf. They are . . . Well, they make those 'Baeserta nutjobs' look like the Von Trapp family. They make the *Manson* family look like the Von Trapp family." He pushes off the side of the Prius, coming even closer, and I shuffle sideways along the length of the car until I bump against the side-view mirror. "They hold nothing sacred and have no limits. Where the League venerates the Corrupter, Northern Wolf sees it as a weapon—a doomsday device they'll use to annihilate whoever or whatever displeases them."

"Is that their endgame?" My voice sounds like a radio transmission from Mars. "Doomsday?"

"Effectively, yes." He doesn't even blink. "They want absolute power, a world where they're in charge and humans are hunted for sport, and this is their chance to make that dream a reality. What the Corrupter offers them is a pathway to total domination, and they will happily drown the Earth in blood for a chance to seize it."

"Neat." It's all I can manage, my esophagus suddenly in a half-Windsor.

"When I said I don't eat humans, I meant it. From the night I was reborn, I was trained to control my hunger, and the only kills on my conscience were committed in self-defense." He stops right in front of me, casting yet another half-finished cigarette to the pavement. "The vampires of the Mystic Order of the Northern Wolf might as well be feral. Their leader Turns humans on a whim and lets his progeny run wild, because he believes that for a vampire to kill a mortal is of no greater significance than for a mortal to pluck an apple from a tree." He sets his jaw, his eyes cold. "They're reckless and self-destructive, and when they die, their leader just Turns more humans and repopulates his crew. It's nearly impossible to keep track of his membership, because he doesn't care who becomes part of the Mystic Order; he just wants followers—easy to control and impressed by his cheap parlor tricks."

The incident at Sugar Mama's flashes through my mind again: a reckless attack on humans in a public place, a vampire who apparently just wanted to get close to me. Pulling my coat tighter, I ask, "What kind of parlor tricks?"

"Conjuring, localized teleportation, some minor defiance of gravity." Jude rolls his shoulders, sounding bored. "It amounts to magical fireworks, but he was a mystic in life, and it flatters his ego to pretend he's some kind of latter-day Merlin."

"So you know who he is," I observe, certain I don't want to hear any more.

"Yes. He's a newish vampire, Turned in the early part of the twentieth century, and his carelessness put him on the Syndicate's radar almost immediately. In fact, you've probably heard of him, too." The thick clouds overhead are quickly choking off what remains of the daylight, darkness coming on faster than scheduled, and the streetlamps blink on without warning. "Grigori Rasputin. The 'Mad Monk' of Russia."

13

"Rasputin?" I repeat, goggling at him. "Rasputin as in . . . *Rasputin*?"

"The one and only." Jude is unimpressed. "What do you know about him?"

"Not much, I guess." Weeding through the dust of my school-related memories, I hazard, "We did a unit on the Russian Revolution in World History last year, and our teacher said he was supposed to be some kind of spiritualist and healer. And his influence on the tsar was one factor that turned public opinion against the Romanov dynasty."

"He was a charlatan." Jude's tone is sharp and decisive. "A con man and birthday party magician who managed to inveigle himself into the favor of the Russian royal family. Alexei, the tsarevich, was a hemophiliac, and at the time, very little was known about the disorder or how to treat it. It was easily fatal, and because Alexei was the only male heir, his parents were pretty desperate about finding a cure." He sweeps his arms out. "Enter Grigori Rasputin, who used vampire blood to save the boy's life on several occasions, earning himself a permanent place in the Romanovs' household."

"They knew he was a vampire and they didn't care?"

"He wasn't a vampire when he first came to St. Petersburg," Jude answers. "He probably wasn't Turned before 1914, when he was nearly stabbed to death by a peasant. But two years later, he pretty famously refused to die when a nobleman attempted to finish the job. Over the course of a few hours, Rasputin survived being poisoned—repeatedly—shot, and then beaten. Then they put a bullet in his brain and dumped him off a bridge." A cold smile turns up the corners of his mouth. "He finally got the message and played possum long enough to be photographed and pronounced dead, but then vanished. An unidentified corpse was buried in his place to reduce the kind of mythologizing that would have taken place if anyone had known the truth."

My whole body is one giant goose bump at this point. "Wow."

"He's quite dangerous," Jude declares softly. "And I'm pretty certain I know how you're going to respond to this, but I have to say it anyway: There's only so much I can do, watching your house at night. The League and the Mystic Order . . . they've got numbers on their side, and no matter how good I am, I can't keep you safe by myself. Please think over what I suggested yesterday. There's no reason in the world you should trust us, but the Syndicate does have the best chance of protecting you."

I'm more aware than ever of how close he is at this moment as I pick out my words with the care of a bomb squad. "Thanks for the amazing offer, but I'm kind of hoping this will all turn out to be the result of a brain tumor. So until I know for sure that I'm pregnant with an ancient demon, I'm going to have to decline."

"I figured." He gives a half-hearted shrug. "You could at least let me take care of your elbow for you."

"My el— What?" Instinctively, I reach for my sore arm, glaring at him suspiciously. "How did . . . What do you mean, 'take care of' it? How do you even know there's something wrong with it?"

"August, please." He rolls his eyes. "Identifying weaknesses in humans is a basic vampire skill—and, in case you haven't noticed, I rather enjoy studying your body anyway." Jude takes a step closer and I lean back, causing him to let out a frustrated sigh. "Would you please relax? I just want to fix it for you."

"Fix it how?" I demand. "Special lab work back at Syndicate Headquarters in the Carpe Diem Mountains?"

"Carpathian," he corrects, humor glinting in his eyes, "and don't be ridiculous. We don't have to go anywhere. Just a little bit of my blood—"

"No. Absolutely not, no way." I shake my head emphatically. "I am not drinking any vampire blood!"

"August. Literally just a few *drops*, and your arm will heal within minutes. Maybe even seconds. It won't hurt you—it requires a whole ritual for a human to Turn, if that's what you're afraid of."

"It isn't," I insist frostily, even though it's pretty much exactly what I'm afraid of. "I just don't need any favors from the undead!" Squirming a little, I try to look composed. "I mean, no offense. Believe it or not, I'm cool with it healing the old-fashioned way."

"And if it turns out to be a hairline fracture, that could take weeks, during which you won't have full use of your arm. Are you cool with that, too? A psychopath like Rasputin watching your house, Viviane Duclos biding her time and waiting for—"

"*Okay*, you've made your point," I cut him off desperately, already dizzy with alarm—because he's right, damn it. After witnessing the intense battle between Daphne and Mr. Strauss last night, I'm fully aware that I could have a dozen arms or no arms at all, and I'd still be lucky to last five seconds in hand-to-hand combat with any of the killers currently gunning for me. But leaving myself deliberately weakened is unforgivable, especially when a cure is staring me right in the face. "Just . . . what do I do?"

"Well . . ." Jude steps even closer, our toes almost touching. "The most fun way I know is if I cut my tongue just a little bit, and then we kiss until—"

"*No.* No thank you—next idea!" I'm dizzy again, and punching my pockets down again, because there is clearly something wrong with me. I'm being stalked by two different cults, my art teacher tried to sword me to death, and Jude just finished his second attempt at convincing me to surrender my life to the Syndicate, but thinking about sucking on his face *just a little bit* is already giving me a boner? I'm sick! I'm sick.

"Okay." He lets out a sigh. "The boring way, then."

From nowhere, he produces a folding knife, the blade flashing a bright silver as he flips it open. Slicing the pad of his index finger, he then squeezes a bead of garnet-colored blood to the surface. At the time, the thought of making out with him just to heal my hurt elbow seemed preposterously inappropriate, but it's not exactly like it's somehow *less* erotic when he pushes his finger into my mouth, sliding it across my tongue, murmuring, "Suck on it, August."

Nervous and trembling, I do as I'm commanded, blood issuing from the tiny wound with surprising ease. It tastes earthy and metallic, and it tingles as it slips down my throat. *Everything* tingles, all of a sudden. There's a buzzing under my skin, that seemingly paranormal sense I've developed for detecting the proximity of vampires building to an ecstatic hum as this vampire becomes a part of me. And then my veins warm, electricity snapping—and I come fully alive, or so it feels, for the very first time.

"*Oh.*" I let Jude's finger pop out of my mouth. The sky is brighter, the world more colorful, and for a moment I'm transfixed by a halo of fine mist gathered around the glow of a streetlamp. The particles slide and shimmer, a veil of white gold fluttering in the oncoming dusk. I can hear the distant rustle of underbrush, the flutter of wings pushing air overhead, my own heart *thud-thud-thudding* away.

"August?" Jude's voice is deep and wonderful. "What do you feel?"

"Everything." When I look him in the eyes, I'm terrified and fascinated at once. They glow, molten with brassy light, and I fall into them without trying. There's a hidden depth that calls to me and I'm in it before I know what I've done.

He's shirtless, standing above me, brown skin smooth over a frame packed with lean muscle. Candlelight flickers, carnal and rosy against exposed brick and dark curtains, and Jude licks his lips. No matter what happens, *he says, reaching for his belt buckle, his fangs partly extended,* tonight is about us.

I fall out of the vision, gasping, and realize Jude is holding me— one hand on my waist and the other on my cheek. My instinct is to fight him off, until I see how concerned he is. "August, what's the matter? What happened?"

"Nothing!" I'm still breathing hard, still remembering the warm light and the muscles flexing in his shoulders. The memory of a desire that I haven't even felt yet consumes me, and I shudder with pleasure. "It was . . ." There's no way to safely complete this thought, so I shake my head. "It was nothing. I got scared."

"It's an intense experience." He says it soothingly, his thumb rubbing my cheek, but it only awakens more confused feelings, and the pressure in my groin is unbearable. "The first time a human ingests vampire blood can be overwhelming, but you'll be okay, I promise. How's your elbow?"

"What elbow?" I pull cold air into my lungs and carefully guide his hands off my body so I can think again, but my brain is fizzing and it won't cooperate.

"So I guess it worked." Jude steps back, smiling a little, and draws yet another cigarette out of that pack.

"Why do you smoke?" Frantic to change the subject, I jump at the first distraction possible. "It's gross. And you don't even breathe."

"I don't *have* to breathe," he corrects me, flicking the Zippo open with a ping of metal. "But my body is capable of doing anything yours can do. Maybe someday I'll demonstrate."

Jude winks as he lights up, and I blush to my hairline. I can't tell if he's aware of what I saw, if maybe we shared that vision—or if I'm the only one who just lived the future.

Because somehow I know that what I experienced when I fell into his eyes was more than just some sort of dream. It was concrete, as real as the moment we're living right now . . . it just hasn't happened yet. And even as I struggle to make sense of that, I remember Daphne's words: *The accounts document clairvoyance, telepathy, subtle forms of mind control . . .*

Clairvoyance. Perception of the future. But if I accept any of this, it means that someday—possibly soon—Jude and I might have *relations*. It's . . . I don't even know what it is. The words won't come to me. But the wind shifts, and I smell him, a mixture of lemongrass and fresh soap, and I am embarrassingly aroused.

"I have to go!" I blurt madly, punching my coat as far down as I possibly can, as if he doesn't know where every drop of blood in my body is at this very moment. "My bus is supposed to be here!"

It's the least sophisticated exit line of all time, but he doesn't give chase when I sprint past him, heading for the pathway leading to the front of school where the late bus will hopefully be waiting. Before I'm out of earshot, however, he calls after me.

"Hey, August?" His voice is musical, delighted, and I look back at him with sweat freezing at my temples. "You know, if you ever want to taste me again, all you have to do is ask."

His cocky laughter pursues me around the corner of the building and all the way to the front entrance.

*　*　*

I'm hoping for the late bus, but I find the turnaround deserted—save for a single, familiar car parked in the spreading glow of a streetlight, a familiar girl perched on the hood of the trunk. My steps falter when I see her.

"You two boys have a nice conversation?" Daphne asks, deadpan, and for just a moment I could swear she's referencing my horny vision of the future.

"It wasn't what it looked like." This might be a lie.

Sliding off the back of her car, Daphne lets out a weary sigh. "Forget it. I'm not your mom, and you can talk to anyone you want. I just . . . I wish you'd listen to me, Auggie. You can't afford to trust Jude Marlowe, even if you think he's cute."

"It's not even . . ." Frustration robs me of my words. "Why does everyone act like I'm just some walking boner, and that all a guy has to do is smile and I'll forget my life is in danger? For your information, I *don't* trust him, and I told him so. I didn't ask him to come here, by the way. He was waiting when I came out of the school."

"He heard about your teacher?" Daphne's guess, at least, tells me why she's also shown up out of the blue. Her expression turns sober. "I'm sorry, by the way. I can't believe . . . I didn't mean to kill him. The stake must have punctured his axillary artery, or something, but I swear it was an accident."

"He was trying to kill us," I remind her. "It was self-defense."

"Not what I mean." She shakes her head with a glum smile. "I know he wasn't just another teacher for you. You liked him, and he's dead, and . . . well, it would be hard news to take even if the circumstances weren't as completely fucked up as they are."

"Thanks," I manage, my eyes immediately filming over with more tears that I don't want to shed. "It's . . ." I have to wait it out for a moment. "It's pretty fucked up, yeah."

Sniffling, I try to wipe all the tears away before they can really get started, but Daphne crosses the space between us and puts her arms around me. So I cry for a little bit. She doesn't say anything, and I finally realize that this is all I've wanted—just someone to sympathize without demanding that I promise to feel better.

When Daphne steps away again, she runs her fingers through my hair. "Get in. I'll drive you home, okay?"

Once the car is moving and I've got my composure back, I exhale. "Jude . . . It wasn't about Mr. Strauss. He wanted to warn me about some vampires—two groups that worship the Corrupter. They're already in Fulton Heights, and he thought I should have details."

"I bet he did," Daphne grumbles, her knuckles white around the gearshift. "Let me guess: 'They're super dangerous, August. You'd better let me spirit you away to Transylvania where you'll be safe and never heard from again. Tallyho!'"

In spite of myself, I giggle. "First, your British accent is terrible, please never stop using it. And second . . . Okay, it was kind of like that. But I don't think he was just trying to scare me. Some of the things he said kind of . . . made sense."

She frowns sharply at this. "What exactly did he say?" So I start to tell her, but I don't get any further than *League of the Dark Star* before Daphne curses out loud. "Duclos, of course. I wondered when we'd hear from her."

"You were expecting this?" I can't quite keep the annoyance out of my tone, since what the actual fuck? "Why didn't you say something before?!"

"You weren't supposed to know who I was before!" she protests. "This isn't easy, by the way. All the lying and subterfuge and shit."

I run my tongue along my lips and my teeth, refusing to be lured. Daphne saved me, and I trust her way more than I trust anyone who isn't named either Pfeiffer or Adriana, but she lied until her hand was forced. "What do you know about Viviane Duclos?"

"Not much, unfortunately," she growls. "What did he tell you about her?"

"Not much," I echo. "Unfortunately. French sorceress, blah blah, nobody's ever seen her, she might be fake, et cetera. You got anything else?"

Her fingernails tapping the gearshift, she surprises me by saying, "Yeah, actually, I guess I do. The basics are these: She's not fake. Her origins aren't totally clear, but the first time she came to anyone's attention, she was a courtesan in Paris during the reign of Louis XIV."

"Courtesan?"

"A . . . professional companion. Basically like a fancy sex worker," Daphne explains. "That's not what it means exclusively, but in her case it does. Access to the royal court was a big deal back then, and if you had it, you didn't squander it. A lot of high society types—of all genders—who'd been forced to enter into marriages of convenience with people they didn't particularly like, looked for companionship elsewhere. Viviane Duclos was a popular courtesan, known for her shrewdness, her intellect, and her ability to tell the future."

"She was a psychic?"

"She read palms and tarot cards—the usual sort of stuff," Daphne answers with a disinterested shrug. "Apparently, she was good at it. She kind of fell in with a bad crowd, though, and got caught up in one of the biggest and most shocking scandals of the seventeenth century. It was called the Affair of the Poisons, and shitloads of people were implicated, including a former mistress of the king. There were dozens of arrests, and ultimately thirty-six executions—for murder or witchcraft or both." Her eyes dart to me and then back to the road. "Duclos was named and arrested, but before she could be put to death, she was sprung from jail by a German mystic named—"

"Erasmus Kramer," I supply.

"Yeah. Kramer." Daphne downshifts as she navigates a turn. "Nobody knows exactly what went down with the two of them. Kramer was already a balls-to-the-wall believer when it came to the legends, and as best we can tell, Duclos was still fully human when she was sentenced to die by hanging. But the dude got to her in her cell, freed her, Turned her, and she joined his cause forevermore."

"And now she's here." I look out the window, as if I might see her flying by on a broomstick or something.

"So he says."

It's almost dark now, and Daphne's window is fogged again, a ghostly version of my own face gazing back at me. "What does she look like?"

"Nobody knows." Her reply is prompt, corroborating Jude's claim. "She's deliberately stayed out of the public eye—and, you know, she's an actual bona fide sorceress. She might know countless glamours to disguise her age and appearance."

"Great. I'll punch everybody I meet, just in case."

Daphne nods absently, like I just proposed a wise plan. "You said there were two groups. What's the second?"

"The Mystic Order of—"

"*Rasputin?*" Daphne snaps a look at me, and the car swerves. When I gasp, gripping the dashboard, she forces her attention back to the road. "Sorry. Sorry, I didn't . . . Northern Wolf, right? That's what he said?"

"Yeah." I blink a few times, trying to relax again. "He told me Rasputin is an unstable whack-job."

"An understatement." She takes a corner, steering into my neighborhood. "Look, I don't know what Marlowe told you, but Rasputin is real bad news. Even when he was still human, back at the turn of the twentieth century, he was a first-rate con artist and Svengali—grifting his way into the imperial court and taking advantage of the royals' trust to accumulate massive amounts of power. And since becoming a vampire, he's only gotten better at it." Daphne's mouth tightens. "He finds lost, damaged humans, Turns them, and gives them not just eternal life and more strength than they've ever known, but also a *purpose*. They worship him, and he worships himself—and there's nothing more dangerous than that."

"If I promise you I'm already scared out of my fucking mind," I say, my heart beating so hard I can see my retinas pulsing, "will you please stop talking now?"

"I'm making this worse—I'm sorry." She pulls the car to a stop, and I look up at my house. The lights are on in the front window, my dad moving around in the kitchen, and my heart lurches. As if reading my mood, Daphne says, "I already asked for backup, just in case Strauss had other friends, but I promise I . . . I'll figure out a way to keep your family safe. I pledged to protect you, Auggie, and that goes for them, too. You have my word."

"Thanks," I whisper, unable to speak any louder; then I bolt from the car—three different vampires registering on my silent radar before I even reach the porch. The night watch has already arrived.

14

Almost a week passes where nothing actually happens—no bad dreams, no deadly attacks, no impromptu visits from the undead—and gradually my anxiety subsides to a more manageable level. I won't pretend that I'm not still scared, though, or that I don't still look over my shoulder every five minutes, expecting a bony, greasy-haired giant with a scraggly beard and pinwheel eyes to come leaping at me out of the darkness.

Because, oh yeah: I've looked up pictures of Rasputin, and each one pretty much screams HUMAN REMAINS FOUND IN AREA MAN'S FREEZER. I mean, axe-murdering cannibal mountain men would cross the street if they saw this guy coming.

Over the weekend, the number of vampires surveilling my house went from three to six, and now I'm sensing them everywhere—even during the day. A car will drive by me while I'm on my bike, its windows tinted so heavily I can't see inside, but that familiar, conclusive ripple will pass across my skin; or a sudden tingle between my shoulder blades will tell me I'm being watched from one of the empty houses between home and school. Maybe it should unnerve me, but instead it's having the opposite effect. They're keeping their distance, and even though each side is just trying to make sure the other doesn't get to me first, they're all otherwise leaving me alone.

On Tuesday, Daphne makes good on her word to protect my family in a way I didn't expect: Out of nowhere, my mom receives an email from an appraiser interested in her hideous rag doll, having heard about it from an unnamed colleague. The twist is that he wants to see it in person, but he lives in London and isn't capable of traveling. The twist on the twist is that my parents have always wanted to see London but haven't been able to justify the expense, and the twist on *that* twist is that, seemingly overnight, their frequent flier account tripled—to the point where their tickets would be all but free.

I don't know how the Brotherhood pulled it off, or how they'll keep my parents safely out of town long enough to see things through to the end, but I'm already planning to name my first pet Daphne out of gratitude.

If I live long enough to have a pet of my own. *The end* might be anytime. Someday, maybe soon, I could wake up and find the Corrupter in control of my body.

But I'm still in command of all my parts on Wednesday when Gunnar texts to ask me on that official date: *Hey! How do you feel about ice-skating?* I'm afraid to be honest and tell him it scares me—especially because it's a silly thing to fear after I literally almost got murdered—so I reply with a thumbs-up emoji, an ice-skate emoji, and an explosion emoji, which is vague enough to signify either excitement or imminent calamity. And I'm still very much me when I get home from school on Friday, my stomach so packed with butterflies they don't even have room to flap their wings, so they're all just crawling around in there until I'm pretty sure I'm going to barf.

After my shower, I spend a few eons agonizing over what to wear—because what outfit says *I'm into you, but I might die soon, so let's not play games?*—and then a few more trying to make my hair look cool. Eventually I give up on that dream and try to settle for "messy, but maybe it's intentional," and then . . . I'm out of time.

I graciously allow my parents exactly two minutes to speak with Gunnar when he arrives, and then I'm pushing him out the door again, promising to honor my dad's routine exhortations to be careful. Regardless of the statistics, Fulton Heights is still a vampire town, and I still have a crucifix in my pocket. The night air is crisp but wet, following our third straight day of rain, and all the snow is gone. Around us, I feel the undead watching, shifting restlessly when they realize I'm not alone.

"It's good to see you," Gunnar says, pushing a hand through the tousled waves of his hair. It's shiny, and I have a feeling it would be soft to the touch if I were in the right position to pull on it. The thought does funny things to my insides, and in spite of myself I'm suddenly horny again. He reaches over and tugs the lapel of my jacket. "You look really cute tonight, by the way."

"Thanks. So do you." I might start floating. I've never been able to say that out loud before, and the words taste almost guilty on my tongue, my head buzzing with satisfaction. *This is what being on a date feels like.* "I see you wore your best dude-necklace."

It's a silly thing to say, but I can't keep my thoughts contained, all of them running together. Gunnar just looks down in surprise at the pendant resting against his T-shirt, a fragment of stone on a leather strap, and laughs. "My dude-necklace—I like that." He smiles at me sideways. "I found this on a beach in Iceland—it's my good-luck charm."

"Does it work?" I ask as he opens the passenger door of his car for me.

"I guess we'll find out," he murmurs, his breath soft against my ear, and by the time he shuts the door and circles around to the driver's side, I'm buzzing *everywhere.*

*　*　*

Gunnar's mouth is amazing. And I mean this purely from an aesthetic standpoint, because no kissing has happened (yet). But I'm thinking about it a lot while he talks. It turns out he has three different kinds of smiles: the mild one, where the corners turn up; the intermediate one, where his teeth show and a tiny parenthesis appears in each cheek; and then his advanced smile, when he really laughs, and his eyes crinkle and his whole face becomes animated. That one's my favorite.

We talk about music (which feels like a trap until I realize he's genuinely interested in hearing what I like), and he asks me about my art and I ask him about Iceland, and against all odds, by the time we get to where we're going, I'm almost relaxed again.

He pays for our entry and helps me hobble out onto the rink, but there's little help for me once we're moving—our whole bodies balanced on millimeter-thin blades of metal, hurtling pell-mell across *actual fucking ice*. I fall six or seven hundred times in the first ten minutes, my ass bones shattering like Christmas ornaments, while children zoom by us, skating in loop-de-loops at light speed and shrieking with laughter.

"Are you okay?" Gunnar has actual concern in his voice after hoisting me to my feet one time too many. "I thought maybe this would be fun, but I don't want you to get, like . . . actually hurt."

"I'm all right." I force a smile, glad I haven't landed on my face yet. Bruises can heal, but my dad will freak out if I break my teeth or my glasses. "You stop feeling it after the twelfth time."

He grins—an intermediate smile—and says, "Okay, how about this: We skate together. Grab on, and we'll go slow."

He holds out his hands, his grip firm when I reach for them, and then we start to move. He skates backward, smooth and languid, and I find that if I keep my feet more or less planted and let him tow me along, it's just not-terrifying enough to be sort of pleasant. Letting out some nervous laughter, I observe, "Hey, what do you know? Not falling down is almost like having fun!"

Gunnar laughs—an advanced smile, warming my insides with victory—and eases us to a gradual stop. "Okay, I'm starting to think this was maybe not the best idea for a date."

"I'm sorry." I wish the lights around the rink were a little dimmer, because I'm sure my face is bright pink. "I should have said something, it's just . . . you seemed really excited about it. And, also, I kind of didn't want to admit that I was scared."

He reaches over, tugging at the zipper of my jacket—a playful gesture that still somehow feels intimate—and shrugs. "You were scared, but you did it anyway. That's more impressive than being a good skater." Our eyes meet, and we stay that way for just long enough to make my heart race before Gunnar suggests, "How about a snack or something instead? The food here is . . . gross, but it'll kill you a lot slower than snapping your spine in half on the ice."

"Music to my ears," I reply, already hobbling along the raised guardrail that circles the rink, heading for the exit. It's an indoor facility, with a bunch of small tables and a greasy-looking concession stand to one side. I claim our seats while Gunnar gets the food, and it's only a few minutes before he joins me again, lumbering over the rubberized flooring in his skates.

He sets down a tray bearing two Styrofoam cups of something pale and brown, and a cardboard container of tortilla chips covered in bright yellow goo. "I'm pretty sure this stuff is supposed to approximate cheese, but I wouldn't swear to it in court, and the hot chocolate is just a powdered mix—I actually watched her rip the packet open myself."

"Made fresh!" I return enthusiastically, stirring it with my plastic spoon. Scummed with foam the color of dirty sand and just shy of boiling, it tastes like burned dried milk that someone watered down while whispering the word *chocolate*. "I haven't had this since middle school."

"Probably for good reason. Also, you have a little . . ." He leans over and swipes a finger across my upper lip. I freeze, my nerves going haywire, and Gunnar shows me a dollop of foam on the pad of his index finger. His eyes still on mine, he licks it off. "Yum. The best part."

Breathless, I struggle to come up with a reply. "The foam is not the best part."

"I wasn't talking about the foam." He grins—well beyond his advanced smile—and my brain turns upside down. I take another sip of my grotesque hot "chocolate," forgetting that it's only slightly hotter than the surface of Venus, and cough a little while pretending to act cool. Folding his hands on the table, Gunnar states, "So. Here's what I know about Auggie Pfeiffer: He likes to make his friends laugh, he maybe failed a history test recently, and his mom has a cursed doll that will someday be bought at a garage sale and kill an entire family of good, God-fearing folk somewhere in Oklahoma."

"It might kill them as close as Indiana." I pluck a nacho from the tray.

"Tell me three things I don't know about you, and I'll tell you three things you don't know about me," Gunnar suggests—and I realize for maybe the first time that I know almost nothing about him. I've been so worried about making a good impression, I didn't even think to ask.

"Um, okay. So, first . . . my mom is super allergic to bees—"

"That's not about you!"

"Hold on," I protest. "Mom is allergic to bees, and when I was, like, ten, I declared myself her protector. My dad made me a suit of armor out of cardboard, and I scared bees away from the garden with a plastic sword and a spray bottle of water. I called myself Spider-Bee-Man."

"'Spider-Bee-Man'?" Gunnar's whole face lights up. "That's . . . adorable. Did it work?"

"She hasn't been stung since," I answer smugly, popping another nacho into my mouth. How can something composed of one hundred percent recycled plastic taste so *good*? "Um, okay. Number the second: I've never broken a bone." *I think.* Instinctively, I flex my formerly injured elbow, remembering Jude's insistence that I heal it with some of his blood—and how Gunnar examined it the night it happened, his gentle touch giving me goose bumps as big as Tesla coils. "I mean, I haven't broken any before tonight. I'm pretty sure I left fragments of my spine and pelvis all over the ice out there."

"Don't worry about it." Gunnar waves his hand. "They've got a whole huge machine that gets rid of all the bone pieces at the end of the night."

"And third, um . . ." *I'm a mystic vessel cursed to bring forth a vampire deity that will doom humankind forever!* I scramble for anything else to say, and, unfortunately, what I come up with is somehow even worse. "This is . . . my first date."

Gunnar waits politely for more, and when I don't add to the statement, his expression undergoes a change. "Your first date. Not, like . . . you mean . . . ever?"

Shrugging nervously, I try to make it a joke. "Well, I went to a dance with Leesha Gardner in middle school. But that was mostly as friends, and by the end of the night we'd both confessed to having secret crushes on Boyd Crandall. So." Gunnar smiles—mildly, this time—and heat steals into my cheeks. "Anyway, sorry. I didn't mean to make things awkward. I just . . . I'm kind of a menace to society. Forget I said it, okay?"

"Auggie, you don't—"

"The real third thing that's interesting about me is I can fit my whole fist in my mouth!" I announce haphazardly, not even sure if this is true. Then, as I attempt it, I discover that it is in fact absolutely *not* true, but the misadventure finally brings a more genuine laugh out of Gunnar. Wiping the saliva off my fingers, I say, "Okay, your turn. What are three things I don't know about Gunnar . . . whatever your last name is? And if you tell me your last name, it doesn't count as one of the things!"

"Larsen. It's Gunnar Larsen." He looks down at the table with a shy grin. "Okay. So, for starters, English is my second language. I'm originally from Norway, although I've pretty much lost my accent by now."

"Wow!" I blurt, genuinely impressed. "Say something in Norwegian!"

"Du er søt," he replies, his tone soft. Before I can ask what that means, he adds, "The second thing is, this necklace isn't actually a good-luck charm. I just found this stone that looked like . . . well, the whole truth? I was trying to make somebody jealous." His fingers can't stay still, worrying each other or stirring his hot chocolate or combing through his hair, and I finally realize he might be as nervous as I am. "I'd had kind of a shitty breakup, and I knew I was going to have to see the guy again sooner or later, so I decided to give myself this whole huge makeover. I got a leather jacket and started wearing 'dude-necklaces' with mysterious origin stories . . . Ugh." Gunnar rubs his face, wincing at the memory. "It's so embarrassing now. Like, I sincerely believed he'd see me again and think I was more interesting, and wonder what he was missing out on."

My heart goes out to him. I've never had a breakup, of course—good, bad, or otherwise—but I really know what it's like to want someone to notice you and *feel* something about it. "So what happened?"

"Nothing." Gunnar smiles, hitching one shoulder. "We saw

each other again, he was polite, and he didn't say anything about my dude-necklace or my clothes or anything else. And that was it." He fidgets with the nachos, pulling out a chip and then putting it back. "And I felt stupid for thinking he would care enough to be jealous, but then . . . it turned out I kind of liked the New Me? And it wasn't about the jacket or the necklace or whatever—it was about the fact that I'd decided to become someone who was happy without him. So I kept the necklace, because it reminds me that I'm strong enough to pick up the pieces."

"Wow," I repeat. The lights mounted around the rink make his bottom lip shine, and I really want to kiss him all of a sudden. "It kind of sounds like it *is* a good-luck charm."

"Maybe." Gunnar tugs at the stone around his neck, rubbing it with his thumb, the fingers of his other hand drumming the table. "But anyway. Thing number three."

He looks around the room, fingers tapping away. His eyes find mine, and then they dance away again, and finally he sets his jaw. Unease is prickling the back of my neck by the time he finally manages to spit it out, his eyes filled with regret.

"The third thing is . . . I'm a vampire."

15

I t's my turn to wait for a punch line, and his to sit in an uncomfortable silence until I realize he isn't joking. I try to believe I've misheard him, but I know I haven't. "What the hell is that supposed to mean?"

"I'm sorry I didn't tell you before, but—"

"Prove it." I've made the demand before I've considered what I'm asking, but Gunnar gives me a guilty look, and gold lights spark to life in his eyes. At first they're just pinpricks, but they expand rapidly—and, just as quickly, they retract and vanish. He opens his mouth to speak, but before he can get out a word, I shove myself back from the table and clamber to my feet. "*Stop.* Just . . . stay there! Don't come any closer."

"Auggie, I'm not going to hurt you," he says quietly, fingers knitted together in his lap.

"No, that's right. You are absolutely the fuck not going to hurt me!" My crucifix is in my pocket, and I wrap my fingers around it hard enough for the metal to bite into my skin. "What was all this, anyway? Some kind of sick game? You thought you'd see how many things you could get some pathetic human to do without having to mesmerize him into it?"

"It's not like that." His tone is still quiet, his expression misera- ble, and suddenly I want to cry. This was supposed to be my bucket list night, going on an actual date with an actual boy before I die—or worse—but it's all been a lie. Clearing his throat, Gunnar gives me a plaintive look. "All I wanted was . . . I didn't realize this was your first date."

"Apparently, it's not." My voice catches, anger and sadness crash- ing together in my chest, and I start hobbling for the desk where Gunnar exchanged our shoes for these ice skates when we arrived.

He's on his feet in an instant, moving easily beside me. "I wasn't trying to mess with you, Auggie, I swear. Please—can you just give me a minute to explain?"

"No! I'm sick of listening to vampires *explain* shit to me," I snap, hobbling faster, as if he has any idea what I'm talking about. As if *I* have any idea. "Just stay away from me. I'm going home." Infuriatingly, he follows me to the desk, exchanges his skates alongside mine, and then follows me to the parking lot. When we're outside again, alone in the chilly darkness, I finally yank the crucifix from my pocket and force him to back away. "*Stop. Following me. Okay?*"

"You don't need that." His shoulders sag. "And you don't need to be afraid of me. I drove you here, I'll take you home."

"Yeah, right." A few heavy flakes of snow fall from the sky, dis- solving as soon as they hit the ground. "How could you possibly think I'd trust you now?"

"Auggie, I turned sixteen in 1962," Gunnar finally blurts, tossing his arms out. "I lived in a small, shitty town in California, full of small, shitty people, and I didn't even know what 'gay' was—just that I was *different*. The kind of different that meant everyone who was supposed to care about me kept trying to hurt me." His fingers return to the stone pendant, stroking it compulsively while he speaks. "And then one day I met this guy, a really cute guy my age, at this crappy

143

diner. Just by chance. He was different, like me, and I . . . it was the first time I realized I wasn't the only one, you know? My whole understanding of the world changed."

"Why are you telling me this?"

"Because it's important." He hasn't moved from where he's standing, letting me put as much distance between us as I want. "This guy . . . I fell for him, really hard. Maybe because he was my first everything, I don't know, but when he said he had to leave California—that there was too much sun and he couldn't take it—I didn't even ask what he meant; I told him I wanted to go with him, that I hated everything about my life, and I didn't want to lose him." Gunnar rubs his face with both hands. "And he told me there was only one way we could stay together. One way, but it meant we could be young and happy forever."

"He was a vampire." The conclusion comes to itself, but it seems like I'm supposed to say it aloud anyway.

"I've been sixteen for sixty years, and you know what, Auggie? It really kinda sucks." He laughs, loud and bitter. "My big love story didn't even make it to the eighties, and lemme tell you, the vampire dating pool is toxic as shit. Meanwhile . . ." Gunnar sweeps his hands around, taking in the brightly lit rink. "I mean, I'm glad I lived long enough to see all of this, but sometimes . . . sometimes it just makes me so fucking *sad*."

"What do you mean?" Without realizing it, I've lowered the crucifix—because he really does look sad, and I'm starting to feel a little ridiculous.

"I had to hide and lie about who I was when I was mortal. But now . . . there are places where guys get to hold hands in public, go on dates, and say 'I love you' out loud. They get to go to movies about other guys who hold hands and say 'I love you.'" The loose, melting snow is gradually soaking his unruly hair, and he runs a hand through it to get it out of his face. "I might be the only vampire on the planet who actually misses being human, but there it is. I wasn't trying to lie to you, I just . . ." He turns his palms up. "I just wanted to go out with a cute guy. To flirt and have fun, and maybe . . . you know, make out, if it felt right. I like doing those things. But I didn't know this was your first real date, and I don't want you to go through what I did. I'm honestly sorry if I hurt you by not telling you before."

Another silence passes, Gunnar looking at his feet while I search for something to say. I've heard stories about vampires "mainstreaming" before, having jobs and friends, and defiantly going around like normal people—almost always in major cities, though, and never in Fulton Heights. All of our vampires have only ever wanted world domination.

But it's not like he hasn't had countless opportunities to mesmerize me. I invited him into my home, for Pete's sake. I showed him an open wound on my elbow, and not only did he control the urge to feed after smelling my blood—something that supposedly drives vampires into a frenzy—he actually tried to help me. And he resisted sinking his teeth into that poor woman at Sugar Mama's, even after she was thrown on top of him, spilling blood all over the place.

"If you really want to," I begin, before I can change my mind, "you can drive me home."

I don't regret the choice. By the time we're in his car, I'm soaking wet and shivering, and the heat that blasts from the vents is a godsend. Once we're on the road again, he says, for the third time, "I really am sorry, Auggie."

"It's okay." I can't believe I'm apologizing to a vampire. "I . . . you didn't really lie to me. A lie by omission, maybe, but"—*I never told you I only said yes in the first place because I wanted to kiss a boy before getting taken over by an evil spirit*—"you told me the truth when it counted. And I guess I never really considered what it would be like to . . . you know, *be* a vampire."

"Sometimes it's cool. Most of the time, actually." A real smile turns his mouth up—intermediate. "I'm strong, I'm fast . . . I speak six languages now, and I'm learning two others; I never get sick and I never get old, but . . ." Gunnar hitches his shoulders. "Well, like I said. I can't do normal stuff. I used to love surfing, but I can't anymore, except at night. And I . . . I made the mistake of falling for a human once, too. I mean, total cliché, right?"

"What happened?"

"He was seventeen, and I was sixteen. Then he was eighteen, and I was sixteen. Then he was twenty, and I was sixteen. And then . . ." Gunnar lifts a hand and lets it drop, like the story is too heavy to hold on to. "Well, I learned the hard way what it's like to be on the other side of my Great Love Story. 'There's only one way we can stay together!' It sucked."

"I'm sorry." Hesitantly, I reach over and put a hand on his arm, just to show him I'm not really afraid—to show him . . . I don't know. Maybe I *should* be afraid, and letting my guard down is the stupidest decision I'll never live to regret, but my life is in so much danger already that a brooding vampire with sad eyes and perfect lips is the least of my worries. "And . . . I'm sorry I freaked out. I've kind of got a lot going on right now, and—"

"It's okay, don't apologize," he cuts me off with a wave.

"All I wanted tonight was to go out with a cute guy, have fun, and maybe make out." I use his words with a grin, but my face is hot enough that I have to turn the air vent away. "If I'd known you were a vampire, I'd have probably said no, but . . . I guess I'm glad I didn't."

I trail off into silence, not even sure what I'm saying. My whole life, I've been taught that vampires are predators, that they're dangerous, that even if they're careful and do their best not to kill humans,

I can never forget what they are. But, lately, my own understanding of the world has been turned upside down.

"For whatever it's worth," Gunnar says wistfully, slowing the car as we reach the front of my house, "I'm glad you didn't, too." We come to a stop, and then we just sit there for a moment. I reach for the handle and let go, reach for it again, and let go again, my stomach thundering with nerves. His voice gentle, Gunnar finally asks, "Auggie?"

"You said . . . I know things didn't go as planned, but . . ." I swallow a lump in my throat the size of Jupiter, feeling just like the one and only time I ever rode a roller-coaster—that same sense of bone-shaking terror threaded with a scintilla of excitement—and I wonder how people just *do* this. *I could wake up dead tomorrow*, I remind myself. *Just go for it*. "Maybe this is totally inappropriate, but if you . . . s-still wanted to kiss, I would like to kiss. Very much. Um, tonight."

"Really?" Gunnar straightens, his eyebrows going up a fraction of an inch. "I mean, are you sure? Because if this is your first—"

"It is. But what if I'm already sick of waiting for my Great Love Story? What if I never get one?" I shove my glasses up my nose, nervous sweat making my temples damp. "I'm kind of a mess, I know that, but . . . I've wanted to kiss you since the first day I saw you at Sugar Mama's. And I . . . I think I still want to. You know?" I swallow again, and my throat is so dry it actually squeaks. "I mean, if you don't want to kiss *me*, that's different, but—"

"I do," he interrupts immediately, breaking into a smile that shows his perfect teeth. I should be scared of those teeth, but right now, it's everything else that terrifies me—his experience and my lack thereof, how I've got no idea what I'm supposed to do with my tongue, how my breath probably smells like microwaved cheese and burned milk—but Gunnar just leans toward me, his eyes on mine.

"As long as you're sure this is what you want, Auggie Pfeiffer, I would be honored to be your first kiss."

"I want," I whisper, breathless, and then . . . his lips meet mine. They're cool, but not cold—gentle, but not passive. They're plush and smooth, and they have a grip, tugging at my mouth and nudging it open. My tongue lifts to meet his, instinctively, and then . . . then the *1812 Overture* is blasting away in my brain, drums and strings and horns and cannons, and I've never felt anything like this. I could eat a whole meal of just kisses; I could power the Earth on the energy surging through me just now.

Gunnar's hand finds my waist and slides up, and I tangle mine in his hair. He makes a soft noise, deep in his throat, and the pressure between my legs is unbearable. He kisses me harder, his other hand closing around the back of my neck . . . and when the noise in his throat curves into a growl, more animal than human, he lurches back with a gasp.

Gunnar's eyes glow a bright gold, the angles of his face sharper and more dramatic than before. His brows and cheekbones catch new light, and the tips of his partly extended fangs show between swollen lips. I'm staring, frightened and fascinated, and he turns away. "Sorry—I'm so sorry! I didn't mean . . . This happens sometimes, when I get . . . excited. Please, just, don't be scared? I wouldn't hurt you, I promise, I—"

"You can look at me," I say, when I finally rediscover my voice. After a moment, he does, his eyes like embers in the darkness of the car. His face is still altered, and I resist the urge to reach out and touch it, just because it's unfamiliar. "I'm not scared."

"I don't usually lose control like this," he admits, a sheepish smile exploring the new limits of his facial structure. "Most people aren't . . . Well, I try not to show mortals this face too often."

"I understand." The last time I saw a vampire this far into his transformation was at Sugar Mama's—right after he'd bitten open a woman's neck. But somehow I'm really *not* scared; I even kind of like that Gunnar is this . . . excited. And somehow it's still beautiful, his exaggerated features finally cast in a way that makes sense. "I think I kind of like it."

"You do? You mean . . . you would still kiss me? Like this?" Gunnar plants his hand down on the center console, and I note that his fingers have not yet started to turn into claws. That might be my red line.

"Guess there's only one way to find out." I let him come to me this time, half-certain I'm making a fatal misjudgment—but he fits his mouth to mine and kisses me with renewed hunger. He's aggressive and athletic, the growling in his throat quickly starting to sound more like a leonine purr, and my tongue slips harmlessly against the points of his fangs.

I've never felt sexier in my entire life, and when he finally breaks away again, I swear I'm only two seconds from losing it. *In my pants.* Deliberately placing his hands on the steering wheel, Gunnar closes his eyes, quelling the brilliant golden light. His face is still changed, his eyeteeth longer and his brow bones even more arched. "Okay. Okay, I think now is a good time to stop."

"You're . . . hungry?" I'm breathless and tingling all over, but I still slide one hand into my coat pocket, searching for that crucifix.

Gunnar laughs a little. "I've got a lot of urges right now, and feeding is barely, like, number ten on the list. Don't worry, I can resist them all, it's just . . . not very fun."

"Oh. *Oh.*" My voice squeaks again. But I don't jump out of the car right away. In the back of my mind, I'm thinking about *things*. If I could weaponize the disorienting power of my dick, I could probably bring whole countries to their knees.

"Thank you," Gunnar finally says, and when he opens his eyes, the light in them is gone. His fangs retract, and the shape of his face slowly returns to normal. "For going out with me tonight. For listening. For . . . you know, this."

"Thanks for being honest with me. And for not eating me, and stuff." I mean it sincerely, but he laughs really loudly, and immediately I pretend like I was joking all along. "If you wanted to go out again sometime, that would be cool," I say as casually as possible. He glances over, but before he can speak, I add, "No Great Love Story, I promise. Just . . . fun. And make-outs."

Gunnar opens his mouth, hesitates. Then, "Actually, there's an underground party tomorrow in one of the abandoned buildings near the woods? Well, I guess it's more like a rave." His brows contort into an adorable questioning expression. "It would be . . . kind of cool if you came?"

"A rave?" I try to imagine myself at a rave—only I have barely any idea what a rave looks like. The images that come to mind are neon body paint and glow sticks and people shoveling drugs into their mouths with those scoops from the bulk candy store. "Is this, like . . . When you say it's underground, do you mean it's a vampire thing?"

"It's hosted by vampires, but it'll be a mixed crowd," he answers. "You might be surprised, but there are lots of mortals who like to party with us. Most of them are weird, but some are actually pretty normal."

"I've heard of stuff like that before." Just like vampires who choose to mainstream, there are humans out there who fetishize and even worship the undead. Most of them, of course, don't come from towns with unusually frequent deaths by exsanguination. "I didn't know there was anything like that in Fulton Heights, though."

"A lot of stuff happens—here and everywhere else—between vampires and humans that neither side likes to publicize too much."

Gunnar reaches over and brushes his fingers against my cheek, and I go all tingly again. "You'd be totally safe if you came. And I don't just mean because I'd protect you. There's a lot of rules and plenty of security."

"Can I think about it?" This is my polite way of saying, *Not a chance in hell.* Making out with Gunnar was one thing, and I totally don't regret it, but walking into a vampire party? I'm dumb, but I'm not stupid.

"Yeah, of course." Gunnar's thumb grazes my lip, and I kind of want to jump his bones again, but I say good night and get out of the car. There are seven vampires watching my house tonight, each presence as tangible as a mosquito bite on my skin, and I shiver as I race up my front steps. But it isn't until I've unlocked the door and am waving goodbye, watching Gunnar pull away from the curb, that it hits me. Seven vampires . . . but none of them are *him.*

I can't sense Gunnar.

16

That night, I can't sleep, trying to understand what it means that Gunnar doesn't register on my radar—trying to figure out where I can turn for answers. I can't ask Jude, because the Syndicate might expect some sort of cooperation in return, and I'm honestly not sure the Brotherhood is much better. Daphne I trust, but she's promised to have her organization investigate a dozen different things for me, and so far they've come up with nothing.

I don't understand how the sensor works, and I can't even be sure it's 100 percent effective, but I'm afraid the actual explanation has something to do with the fact that both of the undead cults gathering in Fulton Heights are led by known magic-workers. If anyone understands how this entity works, and how to successfully jam the radar I've developed because of it, it's someone who's spent lifetimes studying the Corrupter.

Pretending to be a cool-dude-necklace-wearing human might only be the tip of the iceberg when it comes to Gunnar's deceptions.

With Jude and Daphne out, the only other person I know who really understands supernatural stuff is Ximena Rosales; but I tried her once, and all she did was steal my hair for a "protection spell." If she knows something, she's already lied about it. No matter what her reasons were, I can't trust her to suddenly tell the truth now . . . and if she's capable of magic beyond regular witchcraft, I can't even be sure she's using it in my favor.

My head is throbbing with questions by mid-afternoon the next day when I receive a text from an unfamiliar number: *Hey, Auggie, it's Hope. I know this sounds weird, but can I send you something?*

Immediately, I'm intrigued—and also anxious, because I'm starting to realize just how much I hate surprises. I haven't seen Hope since the day I drew a flaming corpse and our art teacher died trying to murder me, and I can't imagine what she wants to talk about. Nervously, I send her a *sure*, and her reply is prompt.

It's a photo of what looks like a medieval woodcut printed on parchment, labeled with words in a language I don't recognize. The image itself depicts six slender figures with their arms raised, gathered around what looks like a man being struck by lightning. After a moment, I type: *?????*

My video chat activates with an incoming call, and when I accept, Hope's face fills the screen. "Hey. I, um . . . How are you?"

"Confused? Why did you send me a picture of a guy getting electrocuted?" I ask. "I mean, not to be rude. It's nice to see you!"

Hope squirms a little, her mouth in a knot until she says, "Before I explain, you need to promise me you won't tell anyone about this. I could get in deep shit, and . . . I mean, you can't even tell Adriana."

My eyebrows lift slowly. "Okay . . ."

"So remember when I told you that something about what the vampire who jumped you at Sugar Mama's said sounded familiar?" she asks—and I do. I've been a little curious about it, but couldn't figure out how to ask her questions without revealing more than I wanted to. Besides, I like Hope, but . . . what could she possibly know?

"Yeah, sure."

"This is the reason. My uncle has a lot of books on the history of magic and witchcraft, and this picture is from one of the oldest. He would literally kill me if he knew I was showing it to someone outside of the family—especially someone who isn't even a witch."

"I get it, total secrecy," I assure her. "But what's the point?"

Hope takes a deep breath. "This image is titled 'The Rising of the Dark Star.'"

I freeze. "The . . . what?"

"It's from some ancient lore, basically a fairy tale about this legendary sorceress coven from, like, thousands of years ago." Hope waves an apologetic gesture. "I don't know if they were even real, but . . . that's what the guy said, right? 'The Dark Star rises'?"

I feel myself nodding. "Yeah . . . um. I think so."

"The text under the picture is so damaged it's hard to read, but it says something about an 'arcane ritual' and something called 'the Corrupter.'" She pauses, watching me carefully through the phone. "Does that mean anything to you?"

"I don't know." I can barely feel my hands.

She watches me a moment longer, and then looks away. "I asked my uncle about it, but he wouldn't say much. Apparently, it's some mostly forgotten tale about six witches who kicked ass and took names back in, like, the Bronze Age, or something. I don't know." She gives me a meek smile. "I'm basically talking nonsense, right?"

"N-no, you're fine," I insist automatically. Clearing my throat, I try to sound casual as I ask, "What do you mean, an 'arcane ritual'?"

"I don't know," Hope repeats helplessly. "That part's missing— which is weird, because magic-workers love to document a ritual." Misreading my expression, she grimaces. "Ugh, I'm sorry. This is some billion-year-old witch myth, and he was a vampire . . . Who knows what he was talking about?"

"It's okay." I force a laugh. "Never a dull moment in Fulton

Heights! I bet you don't regret moving here at all." After an awkward pause, I say, "Um, I appreciate you sending it, anyway. And don't worry, I won't tell."

"Thanks, Auggie." She smiles. "Have a nice day."

"You, too," I say, and it takes me four tries to close the app.

For a long while after we hang up, I can't move, reexamining the woodcut over and over. *The Rising of the Dark Star*. The nature of the "arcane ritual" being depicted is too unclear to decipher; it looks like they're zapping the unholy shit out of the poor bastard who was that century's vessel, killing him before it was too late . . . But maybe what I'm really looking at is the Corrupter being directed *into* a vessel for the first time. Maybe this Bronze Age coven actually started the once-a-century nightmare I'm living today.

Instinctively, my fingers jump to the spot where Ximena Rosales pulled out my hair—for a protection spell she was planning before she knew I needed protecting. If vampires and monster hunters have passed down knowledge of the Corrupter by word of mouth for generations, why not witches, too? And if Adriana's grandmother knows something, then I can't be sure she's not one more enemy to add to my growing list.

I sit for a while longer, coming up with bad ideas followed by worse ideas—realizing that if I really want answers, I need to look anywhere and everywhere I can, even if it's reckless and stupid. I'm drowning, surrounded by nothing but bricks, and I have to grab onto something. If I do nothing, I'm dead, so I might as well die tilting at windmills.

Getting off the bed at last, I head for my closet, trying to figure out what the hell you wear to a vampire rave.

I know I'm dressed wrong the second I answer the door, and find Gunnar on the porch in a tank top and jogging shorts, with stripes of UV-reactive paint on his face. Even though he's standing right in front of me, I still can't sense him . . . but the muscles of his chest and arms make bells ring in my stomach. With some effort, I successfully wrestle my libido under control and arch a brow. "Is this party in Florida?"

"I don't really feel the cold," he explains with the same bright, easy smile that made me all swoony for him in the first place, and I try to detect artifice in it now. "But it actually gets pretty warm at these things. You might want to change."

He follows me upstairs, because I can't think of a decent excuse to keep him waiting on the porch, and I watch him explore the territory where I spend most of my time. I've never had a boy in my room before. My parents are out at a fancy dinner to celebrate their upcoming trip to London, and I'm acutely aware of how empty the house is—of how sexy he is, even if I can't completely trust him.

I'm increasingly self-conscious as I go through my clothes, until Gunnar finally takes over, pulling out the tiniest pair of shorts I own. "These are perfect."

"Isn't it, like, forty degrees out?" My face warms a little.

"Trust me," he says unironically. "If you wear pants tonight, you'll be miserable."

Walking outside in the middle of March, however, wearing nothing but a T-shirt and tiny shorts, is plenty miserable itself. My teeth are chattering by the time we make it to the car, and I've only just started to thaw when we're already parking again. Gunnar stops on a lonely stretch of curb on the "bad" side of town, where the empty, shuttered buildings that the city can't afford to demolish have become the favored hideouts of the undead.

Music pulses faintly in the air, and we follow the sound to a blocky edifice of whitewashed brick. Its weedy lot separated from the foliage of Colgate Woods by a frail chain-link fence, I recognize the former Trapans Glassworks factory, and send off a discreet text. As I slip my phone back into my pocket, I catch Gunnar's watchful eye and give him an innocent smile. We're playing a game, but I don't want him to know that I know it.

At the rear of the building, where thick shadows keep a multitude of secrets, a line to get inside stretches for at least twenty yards. Gunnar pushes past the crowd, all the way to the velvet rope, where an undead bouncer screens the would-be entrants, his frame packed with muscle he doesn't need. Lacing his fingers through mine, Gunnar whispers something to the doorman—and, just like that, we're waved past the crowd and into the party.

Inside, down a flight of concrete steps, is pandemonium. The cavernous chamber is alive with a sea of dancers, strobe lights beating against storm clouds of artificial smoke, and the music is so loud the bass makes my lungs vibrate. There's a DJ on a raised dais, and massive speakers tower in the gloom. When I look over at Gunnar, his teeth gleam just as brightly as the UV paint that luminesces on his cheeks.

"This is it, Auggie," he shouts, and I see the golden light smolder to life in his eyes. "I know it sounds dumb, I know this is just a bunch of drunk losers in a basement, but . . . it's beautiful, right? It doesn't matter who's human and who's undead—nobody's scared here, nobody's in danger. It's just . . . *joy*."

I can barely make out any faces in this mob, but their body language testifies to what he's saying. On Halloween, Kenton Reed threw a party at his gigantic house, and basically the entire school went—from the jocks and the horse girls all the way down to the freshman band kids—and his basement looked a lot like this: people feeling the music, dancing close and not caring who was beside them. Boyd had backed into me by accident, his perfect butt actually touching me, and when he realized it, he'd *laughed*.

Our hands still twined together, Gunnar pulls me down into the thick of the rave. What looked like smoke is really a perfumed vapor, billowing through the crowd, clinging to my skin. The din is too loud to hear over, but as soon as we're on the dance floor, strangers' hands brush my arms in a silent welcome; someone hands me a glow stick, someone else kisses my cheek, and the beat thumps like a shared heartbeat.

I'm definitely out of my element, and I have no idea how I'm going to learn what I came here to learn, but the energy in the room is intoxicating. The factory was gutted long ago, and the space opens up, up, up, massive windows high on the wall letting the starlight in. I've never danced to this kind of music before, but it's too dark to be self-conscious about my movements, and nobody seems to be judging me anyway. I sway and I jump . . . and I feel the joy.

"You're beautiful, Auggie! Do you know that?" Gunnar shouts at me, his eyes glowing in the darkness—and for the first time in maybe my whole life, I think, I *feel* beautiful. The beat thuds, laser lights finding exposed brick walls through fog and shadows, and the rhythm surrounding us threads its way into my blood. I embrace it, fall into it, becoming one more essential piece in the great machinery of the dance floor.

At first Gunnar keeps his distance, but soon we're pressed close, his hand at the small of my back, his lips grazing my ear, my cheek, my jaw. His eyes burn bright, but the only thing he seems hungry for is pleasure. He's not alone, either; throughout the room, golden lights echo his own, beacons identifying the undead. But there are no screams or victims at this party; no matter how many new people I collide with, all I see are happy faces, humans and vampires sharing the moment.

Time slides together, and I don't even notice I've become separated from Gunnar until I realize I have no idea how long we've been apart. Everyone around me is unfamiliar but friendly, a stranger's hand on my hip, another's fingers running through my hair. It's hedonistic and thrilling and scary, all my inhibitions drowned out by the buzz of being wanted. I've never been drunk, but this has to be what it feels like—this buoyant looseness, this blur. For the first time in weeks, I don't care what happens next; I only care about right now, about the gentle hum beneath my skin getting stronger the longer I dance.

"August?"

The blur snaps into focus, a handsome boy with glowing eyes, dark curls, and a British accent suddenly taking shape. Jude Marlowe smiles curiously, his touch gentle on my elbow, and a rush of mixed emotions eddies through me. The shirt he wears is sleeveless, and high on his shoulder is a crescent-shaped scar—one I recognize from the vision I had in the school parking lot. *No matter what happens, tonight is about us.*

I still have no idea what that premonition means. I'm not sure I trust Gunnar anymore, but I trust Jude even less—and a month ago, I would have laughed at the idea of getting naked with a vampire. But sparks are zipping through me, surging where his skin contacts mine, and the memory of a night that hasn't happened yet makes my body react.

"Fancy meeting you here." My voice is thick and dreamy.

"Are you . . ." Jude scrunches up his nose, and it's very cute. "Are you on something?"

"Nope." Someone brushes past us, a vampire, and he winks when I catch his eye. Another shiver, one that has nothing to do with the supernatural, runs up my spine.

Jude notices with a knowing smirk. "Just boys?"

Trying not to blush, I shrug. There are plenty of guys dancing together here, more than I've ever seen in the same place. I feel like I'm somewhere I don't stand out—where I belong—and it's amazing.

Jude takes hold of my shirt, giving it a gentle tug, and I let him draw me closer. The sparks turn into fireworks when his fingers graze my cheek, when he fits his hips to mine, moving with me. My thoughts fly into a million pieces, like the tiny lights spraying off the mirror-ball above the DJ's platform. Something inside of me is starting to make noise I can't ignore, and Jude's touch is a magnet, pulling it to the surface.

"Auggie? There you are!" Gunnar's voice breaks through the static in my thoughts, and my chin snaps up, our eyes meeting as he takes in the sight of me and Jude—together. I freeze, guilt heating my blood. Regardless of my motives tonight, no matter what I suspect about Gunnar, this was supposed to be a date.

"I—this isn't . . ." But I don't finish, because I don't know what I'm doing—why I've let *either* vampire get this close.

The frosty look that hardens Gunnar's face, however, isn't directed at me. "Long time no see, Jude."

Jude turns, his smirk blooming into a feline grin, bicep flexing as he pushes a hand through his hair. "Gunnar. I was wondering how long it would take for our paths to cross."

"No, you weren't." Gunnar's face darkens, mouth pulling down. "If I know you at all, you've been planning this moment for days. Possibly longer."

The tension in the air is even thicker than the artificial smoke, but it's somehow clearing my head. A bad feeling creeping over me, I step back. "You know each other?"

Jude's grin widens even further, the sharp ends of his teeth radiant with black light. "Of course. Gunnar is my ex-boyfriend."

Simultaneously, his scowl deepening, Gunnar snarls, "Jude is the one who Turned me."

17

The side of the factory that faces the moonlight is lonely and deserted, people and vampires reluctant to congregate where they might be seen and recognized—but this is exactly where the three of us wind up to hash out this extremely awkward situation.

I came to an undead rave, hoping my date would reveal something about a cult that worships the monster I'm slowly turning into, and now I'm caught in the middle of vampire ex-boyfriend drama. I miss when I thought this town was boring.

"Wow, what a coincidence that you both ended up in Fulton Heights, trying to seduce me at the exact same time," I remark flatly, hugging my arms across my chest. It's fucking freezing out here.

"*I* have not been trying to seduce you!" Jude tosses his hands out, exasperated.

"Don't listen to him," Gunnar interrupts. "Of course he's been trying to seduce you—that's what he *does*. It's his whole MO."

Jude grunts loudly. "Are we really going to have this conversation again? For the millionth time?" He turns to me like I'm going to play referee. "Gunnar and I were together for nearly twenty years. Does that sound like a seduction to you?"

"I don't care what it sounds like!" Gunnar's voice is rising.

"Twenty years or twenty minutes, it makes no difference with you. You sweep in with your cool British accent, all flirty eyes and 'I'm bad, but I can be better,' when all you actually care about is what you can get away with! As soon as you're bored, it's all 'see you later'!"

"That's such a load of one-sided horseshit," Jude retorts, glaring at him. "And do I really need to point out that *you* were the one who dumped *me*?"

"Because you were already done! You just made me be the—"

"Here we go. 'I have no agency! None of my mistakes are my fault! All my bad choices are because somebody else did a mean thing one time!'"

"*Fuck you*, Jude Marlowe!" Gunnar snaps, eyes aflame. "You were over me long before we broke up, but you didn't want the guilt of ending things after Turning me, so you just pushed and pushed and acted like an ass until I couldn't take it anymore. So fuck you!"

Jude just nods, a sarcastic smile on his face. "Like clockwork. Every time we see each other, it's the same old story: I ruined your life, and you'll never forgive me for Turning you. Fine. But for once, just this one time, admit that you asked me to Turn you. You hated your life in that rancid pit toilet of a town, dying by degrees while you waited to inherit the family dirt farm or get murdered by homophobes when you couldn't hide your secret anymore. You said you'd rather I just kill you than leave you behind. You cried when you asked me to take you—you fucking *begged*."

Gunnar struggles to answer, and when he speaks, his voice is rough and thin. "I didn't know. I didn't know what it would mean to be . . . like this. Forever." He rubs his eyes, and when he opens them again the golden light has gone out. Wounded and vulnerable, he says, "You didn't tell me the truth. You told me you loved me. You said we'd be together forever. Those were lies and I believed you."

"I never intended for things to turn out the way they did," Jude says quietly, after a long moment. "I don't regret the choices we made, and I'm still grateful for what we had. You won't believe me, but I did love you. And you'll always matter to me."

There's another thick silence as their words settle—interrupted only by the chattering of my teeth, because *it is cold out here*. "Not that it isn't heartwarming how you two are working through your boring emotional baggage after all this time, but there's an actual demon trying to claim squatter's rights in my actual body, and I'd like some fucking answers *right now*."

Jude faces me, the humor gone out of his expression. "Everything I've told you is the truth, August."

"Are you really the only representative the Syndicate sent here?" I demand. "Humans want me dead, two cults led by murdery sorcerers are hanging around town tearing shit up, and you're really the only guy they sent to check things out?"

Jude hesitates just long enough for me not to trust his answer. "Yes."

"That means *for now*," Gunnar interprets. "He's the only one *for now*. The Syndicate is a bureaucracy, and they love nothing more than sending in a mid-level functionary to do some scouting before they decide how many resources to expend on a problem."

"Excuse me, I am not a 'mid-level functionary'!" Jude is even more outraged at this slight than when Gunnar accused him of rigging their breakup. "I am Hecuba's man-at-arms, with the full trust of the board of Syndics, and they sent me alone because they knew I was capable of assessing the situation!"

"Pro tip," Gunnar says to me in a mock aside, "if you ever want to royally piss Marlowe off, just criticize the Syndicate or question their right to rule over every single vampire on the face of the Earth."

"Someone has to maintain order." Jude crosses his arms over his chest, the sinew in his shoulders rippling. Both of them are dressed for a day at the beach, and appear just as comfortable, but in about two minutes I'm going to look like one of those dead bodies floating in the ocean at the end of *Titanic* with frost on its eyeballs.

"And it might as well be you?" Gunnar retorts.

"Yes," Jude answers just as bluntly. "It might as well be us. You know better than most what kind of chaos there'd be if we weren't out there 'ruling over every vampire on the face of the Earth.' You've seen the kind of uprisings we've had to quell." With grim satisfaction, he adds, "It wasn't even that long ago that you agreed with the Syndicate's mission."

Gunnar casts his eyes down, uncomfortable. "I was linked to you then."

"You still are. Just because you severed from me, that doesn't change. No matter what, you'll always be mine." Their eyes meet, and something meaningful passes between them.

"Can you two hug this out later? I am literally about to freeze to death!" I wrap my arms as tightly around myself as I can, and, wordlessly, both vampires bite into the flesh of their wrists, offering me their blood. I take a step back, instinctively repulsed—but I catch myself before I can say no.

That afternoon in the parking lot, when Jude cut open his finger and urged me to drink, I became aware of my surroundings on a level I hadn't known possible, and when I looked into his eyes, I saw something I still can't explain. I don't know if it was a power that came from the Corrupter, or if it had to do with vampire blood, or if maybe it was both. What I do know is that if this clairvoyance thing is legit, it's one of the few advantages I might have in this situation.

Plus, I'm cold as fuck out here.

I choose Gunnar, because he's the greatest mystery right now, and because I want to see if whatever magic that keeps me from sensing him will break when I know what he tastes like. Gingerly, I take hold of his arm and bring the wound to my lips. He can control his pulse, push out as much as he wants to; when I close my mouth on his wrist, his blood oozes freely over my tongue.

My scalp prickles, and that caffeinated feeling crashes through me, nerve endings I'd forgotten about waking up one by one. Everything jolts into focus, shadows fading as my eyes tune to the darkness. Closing them, I listen, and I *hear* where Gunnar and Jude are standing—the wind whispering as it passes around them. I listen harder and pick up voices from the crowd on the opposite side of the building, people and vampires waiting to enter.

". . . think she'll be here tonight? She told me . . ."

". . . not a fucking *blood orgy*, you prejudiced asshole . . ."

". . . weird if I'm only into boys when they're undead? Is that a thing?"

The wind shifts again, and a scent catches my attention—something distant, but familiar: unwashed flesh, old blood, soiled clothes. I see him in my mind: wide, golden eyes, wild hair, and then—

"Auggie?" Gunnar's voice brings me back, and my lids snap open. He's watching me, his brows furrowed, as he gently withdraws his arm. "Did that help?"

"I'm not cold anymore," I murmur, although it might be more accurate to say that the cold doesn't bother me. But my attention is focused on him, on the darkness at the center of his eyes—on the resistance I feel there. But after only a few heartbeats, I break through, falling into a maelstrom of images that flicker and unfurl.

Two boys on the beach at night, one human and one undead, their fingers touching discreetly in the sand as fireworks explode against the stars; a dark stone on a stretch of rugged coastline, the fragment shaped like a shark's tooth; a tablet computer showing the image of a guy with glasses and screwed up hair, and a pang of deep regret—he's cute, but doomed; incense casting a ribbon of smoke into candlelit air, a needle kissing a fingertip, and blood dropping into a bowl held by the same guy.

Held by me.

I fall back out of the vision, gasping for air, the night sharpening around me. Both vampires regard me with curiosity, and once again I have no idea how much of what I just experienced was shared. My thoughts are hyper but occluded, something heavy pulling them in a direction they don't want to go.

I wish I could just forget that night on the beach.

The voice isn't mine, but it rings in my head, and I gasp again as I struggle free of it. I *feel* him; I feel Gunnar's memories like soot coating my hands, like I've been touching something forbidden and the evidence is all over me. I blink up at him, startled and afraid I'm going to fall right back in again, but the thread tying us together finally breaks.

"Auggie, are you okay?" Whether he knows I've been prowling around in his head or not, he sounds concerned for my well-being. And, if anything, it only serves to piss me off.

"You're one of them, aren't you? The Corrupter worshippers?" That picture of me flashes bright in my thoughts, his sense that I was cute, but doomed. Was that the past or the future? I haven't held a bowl of blood yet, so the visions were at least a mix of the two. "I'm going to guess the League, because you don't exactly look like a Rasputin groupie."

Gunnar is dumbstruck, those dramatic eyebrows jumping halfway up his forehead, leaving Jude to grin with sly satisfaction. "*Ding ding ding*—a correct guess on the first try! Looks like I'm not the only one who has a problem telling the whole truth."

"Fuck off, Marlowe!" Gunnar snaps.

"Everything he said about the Syndicate is straight from Duclos's pitch to new members," Jude continues. "She's got him completely brainwashed. In fact, I've always wondered if she was the one who pushed Gunnar into severing with me."

"*Shut the hell up!*" Gunnar shouts loud enough to be heard from the road—on the other side of the building. "You don't know the first thing about Viviane *or* the League. You've never even met her!"

"I know you used to think that vampires who pursued the Corrupter were fools, and now here you are, spying and doing Viviane Duclos's dirty work." Jude gestures at me, and I just about boil over.

"You're *both* spying on me! You're both doing someone else's dirty work, so stop acting like only one of you is the bad guy!" I'm vibrating with fury, vampire blood like rocket fuel in my veins. "I'm the bone you're playing tug-of-war over, telling me whatever you think will make me trust you—but no matter who wins, I lose. Neither one of you actually cares what happens to me so long as I *die*."

Tears sting my eyes, the pressure too great to resist, and both vampires freeze in place. They exchange a mortified glance, and Jude begins, "August, that's not—"

"I'm dying. I'm being . . . *occupied* by some thing I don't understand, that I can't begin to fight—I mean, does that sound familiar to you, Jude fucking Marlowe?" When I glare at him, the sadness in his eyes is a quicksand trap that almost pulls me in. "Tell me how it felt to be seventeen years old and dying of bubonic plague."

"August . . ." But that seems to be all he's got. His mouth opens and shuts a couple of times. "I . . . Okay, I understand what you're going through, but—"

"No, you don't," I counter immediately, "because when you were dying, you weren't surrounded by people rooting for the fucking plague!" With a gesture at Gunnar, I continue, "You didn't have people preying on your loneliness, trying to make sure it was their arms you'd die in, just so they could have control over what you left behind!"

"Now, wait!" Gunnar puts his hands up, his expression horrified. "That's not—"

Jude doesn't let him finish. "Gunnar? What did you do?"

"Nothing! We just . . . we went on a date."

"And he kissed me," I add, sounding petulant.

"Of course I kissed him—he's cute!" Gunnar is exasperated. "And I told him I was a vampire before it happened, by the way. I didn't trick him, or hypnot—"

"Yes, you did! You never told me who you really were—you never said that the only reason you asked me out was so you could get closer to me!"

"That isn't why I asked you out, Auggie. Fuck!" Gunnar's voice is rough, and he drags his fingers through his hair. "All I was supposed to do here was observe you, okay? To protect you from threats, and see if you showed signs that the Corrupter was starting to Rise. That was it. I wasn't supposed to involve myself in your life, and I don't think you have any idea how much shit I'm going to be in when Viviane finds out I kissed you."

I look to Jude, wondering if he'll call bullshit or not, but he's just staring at Gunnar in confusion. Unsure how to react, I default to sarcasm. "Oh, sure. Well, obviously, I buy your story without any questions. Sorry I ever doubted you."

"It's not that simple. None of this is simple! I asked you out because I was *lonely*, all right?" Grimacing, he shoots a humiliated glance at Jude. "I've spent months watching you hang out with your friends, and flirt with me, and do funny things when you didn't know anyone was looking. And I was sad, because everything *sucks*—and then . . . then you left your book at the café." He tosses his arms out and lets them slap down at his sides. "It was a bad idea. I know that now. But I wanted one night to pretend everything was different, and I thought . . . I thought I could give you that, too. Just in case everything is about to end."

These final words linger like the chill in the air, and it's Jude who musters an embittered retort. "How selfless of you."

Irritation brings my voice back with a quickness. "You're one to talk—you've been using my fears against me since you got here. 'Come into my secret laboratory, August! The Syndicate's blood-thirsty, undead scientists will definitely work on a cure for you!'"

"Is *that* what he's been saying?" Gunnar emits a bark of unpleasant laughter. "Wow. Well, then, let me assure you that 'everything he's told you' has not been 'the truth.'"

"What does that mean?" I look at Jude, but he avoids my eyes.

"Think about it. The prophecies have been around for thousands of years . . . Do you really think there's anything the Syndicate hasn't learned yet that they're suddenly going to figure out now?" Gunnar shakes his head. "What could they possibly learn from studying you in Romania that they couldn't learn by sending their scientists here, instead?"

My insides are cold again, my heart a dead weight. "I don't know."

"You can't stop the Corrupter," Gunnar finally says, his expression etched with sympathy. "He's not a disease you can study under a microscope, or treat with antibiotics—and nobody even fully understands how the Ascension works, to begin with." He rubs his wrist, the wound already closed again. "I'm really sorry, Auggie, but the prophecy can't be prevented or undone. The future has been written, and it's only a matter of time."

18

nly a matter of time. It's what I've told myself, what I thought I believed. But now that someone has said it out loud, chaos barnstorms my nervous system. My heart races, and my arteries are freezer-burned with a surge of adrenaline. *You can't stop the Corrupter.*

All the empty promises and sales pitches, the days I've spent waiting for help and trying to think of new places to search for answers . . . it's been a waste of time—a precious commodity I'm running out of at a pace I can't even predict. The truth of it crashes over me like a wave of dark water, cutting off my air. How fucked up is it that the only person who had a real solution to this problem and tried to do something about it was Mr. Strauss?

"August?" Jude steps forward, tense with concern. "Don't panic, all right? Not even the League of the Dark Star can prove the Corrupter is real, *or* that you're—"

"*Stop it!* Just stop!" I still can't breathe. "I can *feel* vampires, and I've been having visions of the past and the future . . . I saw you, okay?" Accusatorily, I point from one of them to the other. "Both of you—on the beach, touching your fingers together, hoping nobody else noticed. There were fireworks . . . Was it New Year's?"

Gunnar blinks. "You saw that?"

"August." Jude takes another step closer. "What else have you seen? What else have you experienced?"

"It doesn't matter, does it?" I laugh, the sound utterly unhinged. "I mean, I'm already dead, right? Either someone kills me, or my body gets hijacked by a ghost that will doom humanity, and you both know it. You've known it all along, and you've treated me like some prize in a game show!" My chest catches. I refuse to let them see me cry. "Fuck you both."

They call after me as I turn and run, but I'm done listening. The only completely true thing either of them ever said was that I shouldn't trust vampires. Will I still be me when my parents get back from London? And if I'm not, will they be able to tell? Someday soon, I'm going to wake up in the back seat of my own body—*if I'm lucky*—and a being with my face will introduce the world to a nightmare no one will wake up from.

By the time I reach the dark side of the abandoned factory, panic and despair have given rise to a sense of unstable recklessness. If my fate is sealed, then who cares what I do? What have I been waiting for all this time? While everyone else was living their lives, I was hanging onto the promise that one day mine would finally start. I can run home and await the inevitable . . . or I can do whatever I want, because what do the consequences matter?

I march straight to the bouncer at the velvet rope, giving him a cocky smile that feels as if it's wearing me, and he waves me back inside. Within moments, I'm lost in the crush of bodies again, dancing, making contact. If this is all the time I've got, then I'm going to live it as hard as I can.

The air is muggy with the sweetness of the artificial smoke, and my temperature rises as I throw myself around. This great big rock is hurtling through space, and we're all trapped on it until

I cough up the apocalypse, but right now, this dance floor is my whole universe. Strangers smile at me without menace, matching their rhythms to mine, and then we move on to new strangers and different rhythms. Soon, a dreamy buzz is damping the hard edges of my fear.

I dance with a girl, and then a boy—and then two boys, and the hum gets louder. Maybe it's the vampire blood pumping through my system, or maybe it's something else, but everyone I touch stays with me when I move on. The girl is mad at her friends, and her anger is a fleck of ash caught under my tongue; the boy is a vampire, recently Turned; and the couple's desire leaves me confused and aroused, my body a network of sparks.

The electricity is too much for me to contain. I can sense when it erupts from me—when the hum leaps beyond my skin and touches someone else, our connection as secure as if we're holding hands. And it spreads like smoke, enveloping one dancer after another until I contain multitudes, until I'm delirious with connectedness. The crowd is a mess of emotions, but I get to choose which ones I put my hands on, and I choose *bliss*. All these people are one with me somehow, part of a seamless current that runs through my blood, and I pick up their thoughts like coins from a fountain.

. . . finally in love . . .

. . . didn't know it was possible to be happy . . .

. . . hope I remember this night forever . . .

"Auggie!" The voice pierces my haze, and I look up to see that Gunnar has found me. "Look, I'm so sorry I didn't tell you the whole truth. I've got no idea how I can make it up to you, but this . . ."

He trails off as the spreading euphoria touches him as well, pressing against his defenses. Whatever armor he's wearing, it's strong—but when I touch him, the barrier dissolves, his emotions rush into me, and I know the truth at last. He's attracted to me; he thinks I'm going to die, and it makes him sad; he never fully believed in the Corrupter until now, and he's both excited and scared; he's glad we kissed . . . but he also regrets it, because he really does care what happens to me.

The electricity grows stronger, the shared bliss of the crowd spilling into both of us. His eyes flash gold, his expression going first bright with surprise and then dark with lust. He steps closer and I let him, welcoming him into the circuitry, and his hands find my waist. "Auggie . . . I really want to kiss you again."

"I know." I touch his jaw. "So why don't you?"

He pulls at my hair, forcing my head back, and when his lips meet mine, the circuit flares. His mouth is exquisite, and more memories pour out of him: a guy at a diner, with brown skin and soft curls, who smiles when he catches Gunnar staring; losing his virginity on the beach at night, the water freezing, but the stars endless and perfect; teeth sinking into his neck, and a single thought pulsing in his mind, *Yes, yes, yes* . . .

"What's happening?" Jude stands before us, eyes glowing and heavy-lidded, caught in the same honey trap as the rest of us. His thoughts tingle when they touch me, and I move closer as he asks, "Why do I feel so . . ."

When I take his hand, a shudder passes through both of us. He wasn't lying about his reasons for flirting with me, and he wasn't lying when he said he'd look into ways to stop what's happening to me—but he doesn't think it can be done. He tells people he doesn't believe in the Corrupter, but he's always suspected, and deep down he's afraid the only way to stop it is for me to die.

And lately, unexpectedly, he's not sure he wants that to happen.

I pull him closer, pushing the thoughts aside, because I can. The stress, the anxiety, the conflict . . . it's endless and unbearable. If I wake up dead tomorrow, I don't want my last night to be drowned in suffering—and underneath it all, buried by his own self-imposed miseries, Jude's bliss cries out for freedom as well. So I give it a tug and bring it forth.

His eyes blaze, and he stumbles closer. "August?"

"It's okay." I've never meant anything more sincerely. A week ago, I'd never been kissed, and tonight . . . "I know what you want. It's okay."

He moves in, and when our lips touch, his memories erupt in my mind: his sisters singing a duet; a debonair vampire helping him out of a shallow grave; a gallery of faces; a mudslide of emotions I shrug off.

Jude's kiss is even more aggressive than Gunnar's, like it's our only chance and he wants to make it count. His hand drops to my waist, where Gunnar is still holding onto me, and their fingers knit together. The air thickens, and our intimacy spreads throughout the room—other mouths colliding, other tongues, other hands—and all of the sensations pass back into me. Whatever drug this is, I'll never get enough.

When Jude pulls back, his cheekbones are sharper, his teeth extended. He and Gunnar stare at each other, and then finally reconnect. Their hands are still together at my waist, and I'm tied to their emotions, a kite caught in a turbulent sky. Their history storms and surges, love and hurt and want, and their desire builds until the pressure between my legs is almost too much to bear.

And that's when one of the massive windows high above us explodes, daggers of shattered glass raining onto the dance floor. The crowd shrieks and begins to scatter, just as a figure with bony limbs and long hair plummets down among us, making a dramatic three-point landing. The party crasher looks up, right at me, his eyes bright as molten bronze and his fanged teeth bared in a twisted smile. The spell of bliss broken, my blood runs cold as I recognize him from all my late-night research.

It's Grigori Rasputin—the Mad Monk of Russia.

19

Whatever magic was holding this crowd together, it dissolves in an instant. More glass shatters overhead, figures flying through the windows and plunging into the cavernous basement, while dancers—human and vampire alike—panic and try to take cover. Instinctively, I trip away from Rasputin, his freaky pinwheel eyes still fixed on mine, and the crowd surges with me. A body flies overhead, and then another, and a wave of frightened screaming sweeps through the mob.

Suddenly, there's a stampede for the exit, and I'm swept into it like a toy boat in a whirlpool. The music cuts off, but the lights continue to pulse and flash, fake smoke rolling while the horrific sound of tearing flesh and spraying blood fills the air. When something warm splashes my arm, adrenaline sends me into survival mode, and I start shoving.

Another vampire drops out of nowhere, touching down only a few yards to my right, and the crowd diverts again. I'm brought off my feet, nearly carried into a concrete wall—but a hand grabs my elbow, an iron grip yanking me back to safety in the nick of time. When I look up, gasping for breath, Daphne glares back at me, irate disbelief in her eyes.

"*Really*, Auggie? 'I'm going to a rave with a bunch of vampires at the glassworks factory, you might need to come save me,' *really*?"

"You got my message?" I could actually cry, I am so grateful to see her right now.

"Yes, obviously!" She pulls me closer as the frantic exodus swells, bottlenecking at the bottom of the stairs. People are starting to get trampled, and now vampires who came to party are starting to throw down with the ones who came to eat. Knuckles white around her stake, Daphne demands, "What were you thinking? Why the hell did you come here?"

"I wanted answers!" My voice catches, and I blink tears from my eyes. Chaos rages around us, and I've lost the ability to choose bliss. "I'm dying, or . . . *something*, and the boy I thought I liked is actually a vampire, and he's part of the Dark Star cult, and—"

"Auggie, what—" She's cut off when two vampires, eyes burning, claws sunk deep into each other's flesh, slam against the wall beside us. Grabbing me, Daphne spins me behind her, backing away, deeper into the shadows. "Never mind—tell me later. We're getting the fuck out of here."

"But that's the exit!" I point to the stairs, where bodies are piling up, blood spilling over concrete.

"There's always another way out, Auggie," she whispers, herding me through fragrant mists into heavier and heavier darkness. "Never forget that."

I don't know if she's been here before, or she's just a damn good guesser, but she pulls me through the gloom and into a lightless passage somewhere at the back of the building, a dark void closing tightly down around us. The space is narrow and the floor uneven, strewn with rubble and trash that I keep tripping over, and the terrified clamor of the dance floor chases us deep into its recesses. The chance that we could be ambushed in this stifling rat maze is all too real, and my ears ring with danger.

We hit the end of the passage, and Daphne kicks hard against something—a door, metal scraping against damaged concrete as she forces it open—and then we're in a stairwell. Moonlight weeps through filthy windows, and my bodyguard shoves me up the steps ahead of her. At ground level we find an exit; it's chained shut, but the links are so rusted that they shatter under a few blows with a chunk of broken flooring. And then we're out in the night air again, the frigid damp a welcome embrace.

Just as we round the building, heading for a break in the perimeter fence facing the road, a figure drops out of the sky in our path. Landing with the force of a comet, fracturing the asphalt as it slams down, it's another vampire. Eyes burning, her hair a mane of untamed curls, she shows us a fang-toothed grin. "Where do you two think you're going?"

Daphne has her stake out in an instant, spinning it like a baton, demonstrating her skill. "Back up, you undead bitch. You're not the only one in the mood for blood tonight."

The vampire peers around her, though, looking straight at me. "Don't leave so soon, baby, the Master wants to talk with you!"

"The *Master*?" Daphne blinks, spluttering with laughter. "Did you seriously just call him *the Master*? You have got to be kidding me."

"*You* are irrelevant." The vampire snaps ferociously, her cheekbones sharpening as she glares at my protector. "If you put down your weapon and walk away, no harm will come to you. But the Master wants August Pfeiffer."

I take a step back, metaphorical violins shrieking in my ears, even as Daphne retorts, "Oh wow, I'm so relieved. You promise you won't hurt me? Actually, you better come over here and show me how to put this down, just to make sure I don't do it wrong!"

"Keep making jokes," the curly-haired monster snaps, eyes burning brighter. "Might as well get them out while you still have a throat."

"Mmm, okay." Daphne pretends to think. "Got one! Why did the chicken cross the road?"

A sudden impact shakes the ground behind me, and I whirl to find that we've been joined by two more of the undead. The first is a man with boot-black hair and a leather duster—it's beginner Goth nonsense, but I can't laugh about fully extended fangs and black-tipped claws. He sways toward me, and I nearly swallow my tongue as the second vampire is revealed behind him: my old friend from Sugar Mama's.

"Auggie, get back," Daphne commands, all business now, her expression hard as flint.

The Goth vampire lunges first, and Daphne feints a retreat before meeting the advance with a kick to the sternum; at the same time, the girl vampire tries to seize the advantage of distraction but is knocked back when that chunk of broken flooring shatters across the bridge of her nose. What follows is even more dizzying than the altercation I witnessed in the parking lot of the mall. Daphne spins, kicks, and blocks simultaneously, somehow managing to fight both attackers at once while keeping me on the outside.

All the while, the man from Sugar Mama's hangs back and watches, like he was only sent to observe—or maybe to keep me from running. If I separate myself from Daphne, I won't get far, and if they overpower her . . . well, I'm a goner either way.

Twice, Goth Guy lunges for me while Daphne is fighting Curly, and both times my erstwhile tutor deftly intercepts him. On his second attempt, though, she swings him around, driving her stake into his chest. He stumbles back, his body going stiff—and Daphne has already spun away again when his death catches up to him.

Here's the thing: Vampire deaths are *gross*. Whoever this guy is, only the arcane magic of his blood has kept his body from deteriorating since the day he was Turned. Now, that magic dispelled by a stake to his heart, the forces of the natural world are making up for lost time. He rots in seconds, his flesh withering to the bone while his skin sloughs off in revolting clumps—and finally he collapses, his skeleton disjointing completely.

When he hits the ground, his head detaches and rolls right at me. I'm winding up for the loudest, shrillest screech I've ever let pass through my lips, when Daphne swoops in and grabs it. Hooking her fingers into the dead man's now empty eye sockets, she whips around and flings the skull at Curly's face. The undead girl parries with a hard block, shattering the missile entirely—just as Daphne lunges in for her second kill of the night.

There are still pieces of broken skull hitting the pavement when the girl vampire reels, clutching the hole in her chest. The glow in her eyes goes out—and then her eyeballs shrivel altogether, her lips peel away, and she gurgles as her throat and lungs desiccate. When her bones hit the ground, scattering like jackstraws, Daphne rounds on the man from Sugar Mama's . . . but he's already gone, leaping away into the night.

Frozen, waiting for the other shoe to drop, I manage, "Where is he—"

"Doesn't matter," Daphne answers blankly, her gaze skittering around the vast lot, her fingers turning the stake in an agitated revolution. We're on the moonlit side of the building, and people are scattering across the lot in a witless panic. Their screaming fills the air—and above it, the wail of approaching sirens keens ominously. "Come on, we're getting the hell out of here."

Grabbing me by the wrist, she takes off again, moving so fast I can barely keep up. We're both expecting more vampires to drop out of the sky at any moment, and when we make it to the fence without being attacked, I think we're both surprised. The first police cruisers are veering into sight as Daphne braces her hands together to form a springboard—and then she's launching me to the top of the fence.

She touches down on the other side right behind me, actual cops shouting at us to stop, but we take off at a sprint as the street floods with people escaping the factory. Cutting a corner, racing past the pumps of a gas station, we pelt into a residential neighborhood I don't recognize. I'm gasping for air when we reach her car, and I've never been so glad to see the dented, rusting shitmobile in my entire life.

I've barely got the door closed as we peel away from the curb, and all the traumas of the past hour hit me like a flash flood. I bury my face in my hands so Daphne can't see me cry, and I try like hell not to sniffle, but her awareness is hotter than the plastic-scented air blasting from the vents. "I know you're upset, so I am seriously trying not to yell at you, Auggie Pfeiffer, but *honestly*. What the fuck were you thinking?"

I have to work the knot out of my throat in order to reply. "*I'm sick of dying.*"

"And you thought partying with vampires was the road to a long, prosperous future?" Her jaw is set so tight I can see the muscles shifting. "What if I hadn't gotten your text? What if I hadn't been able to drop everything and save you from fucking *Rasputin* and his gang of homicidal henchmen?"

"So what if you couldn't?" My voice is as wrecked as I feel.

"What is that supposed to mean?"

"Has the Brotherhood figured out how to stop what's happening to me?" I counter with another question. "Have they come across any spells or rituals or even *superstitions*, for fuck's sake?" She has nothing to say, her hand flexing on the gear shift, and I make an ugly noise. "So that's a no. We're all just waiting out the clock. What happens when this thing takes me over, Daph? Will you still be protecting me?"

"Auggie, I don't—"

"I can *feel* it!" I finally blurt, my voice breaking. "Before, it was just these weird episodes—strange dreams and sensing vampires—but tonight it was . . . part of me." My glasses are fogged, and I take them off, tears making it too hard to see anyway. "I was inside people's heads, experiencing their emotions and stuff . . . I was connecting people."

Daphne glances over, her eyes sharp. "What do you mean? What exactly happened?"

"I could, like, read their minds," I whisper. "I knew their memories, and what they were thinking, and . . . maybe I even saw parts of the future, too, I'm not sure."

This is a lie. I'm positive it was the future, but I don't want to have to explain what I saw—bowls of blood, and Jude taking off his pants. I'm still confused by both visions. But Daphne isn't going to let me off the hook that easy. "This vampire, the one you said was part of a Corrupter group . . . did you read his mind, too?"

"A little bit. I saw . . ." *He lost his virginity on a beach at night, terrified and ecstatic; he tells people his necklace is about finding the strength to move on, but he still isn't over his ex.* "He thinks I'm going to die. He wasn't even sure the Corrupter was real until he met me, but now he believes, and he's depressed about it—if you can believe that." I laugh, wiping my eyes. "Jude thinks the same thing. The only way this ends is with my death."

"Jude Marlowe?" Daphne's hand slips off the gear shift. "You *partied* with *Jude Marlowe*?" She doesn't even wait for a reply, exclaiming, "What have I tried to tell you? You can't trust him, Auggie! Of course he thinks the only way to stop this is to kill you—it's either make you serve the Syndicate or make sure you can't serve anyone else, and considering how much power they've got already, I'm not sure they care either way!"

"I . . . I don't think that's his agenda." I can't put it any clearer than that. I didn't read all of his thoughts, but the flavor of them still lingers. "He doesn't want the Corrupter to Ascend, Daph, bottom line. But the stuff I saw in the future . . ." His skin warmed by candle-light, *tonight is about us.* "He doesn't want to hurt me, either."

"Don't be so gullible," Daphne snaps, her voice surprisingly cold. "He's over four hundred years old, and there's no way a Syndicate ambassador hasn't encountered mind readers before. I'm sure he knows how to protect his thoughts. What else did you see?"

For a moment, I stare out the windshield, trying to formulate an answer. The ribbon of incense, Gunnar saying words I can't remember as his finger drips into a bowl. "Why would a vampire mix his blood with mine?"

"*What?*" She cuts a look my way that actually scares me, her face taut with alarm. "You saw yourself taking a blood oath with *Jude Marlowe?*"

"I don't—" I choke, her anxiety contagious, and don't correct the misunderstanding. "What's a blood oath, what are you talking about?"

"It's a covenant—a ritual, where your blood binds you to your word. You make a pledge, and magic forces you to honor it." Her hands squeeze the wheel so hard her knuckles pop. "If Jude gets you to swear your allegiance to the Syndicate, and seals it with your blood, you're theirs forever, Auggie. It doesn't matter who or what is in charge of your body—as long as the same blood flows through your veins, you're on a mystical leash until the end. If there *is* one."

Her meaning sinks in, and I grip my seat belt. I've got no idea what this entity will want when it busts me open and spreads its wings—but it won't be good. After generations of Rising and failing to Ascend, surely the Corrupter will have its own plans for what to make of its glorious return. But if any of these vampires can compel me to sign some mystical contract in blood, I'll tie the Endless One to their agenda for a literal eternity.

"What if I take an oath to the Brotherhood?" I blurt. "Then the Corrupter's hands are tied, right? Even . . . even if it Ascends, the world would still be safe."

She opens her mouth to speak but doesn't have a chance to. At that exact moment, something crashes down onto the roof of the car, the impact sending us out of control. I gasp as Daphne jerks the wheel, our tires slewing over rain-slicked pavement, and we spin for a sickening moment. Then she hits the brakes hard, and I lurch forward against the resistance of the seat belt.

The thing on the roof tumbles over the windshield and slams onto the hood, just as Daphne hits the gas again, yanking the wheel and veering into the oncoming lane, trying to dislodge it. But it spears a set of black-tipped claws through the car's metal skin, holding on tight as we swerve back and forth. My eyes reel as I make sense of what's right in front of me, nothing between us but a sheet of glass—the mantis-like limbs, the scraggly beard, the eyes that glow ferociously when they meet mine.

For the second time tonight, I'm face-to-face with Rasputin.

20

The photos I found of the Russian cleric were freaky, but none of them prepared me for the terrifying thing crawling across the hood of Daphne's Saab, vampirism turning an already frightening figure into a nightmare on steroids. His face is gaunt, his hair tangled by the wind, but his eyes are dazzling—deep and golden, they move without moving—and as he drags himself closer to the windshield, one handhold at a time, my vision tunnels on those two bright spots of light. The car swings from side to side, but the motion is lulling, the air warm and pliant.

"*August Pfeiffer.*" His lips don't move, but his voice fills my head, a soft, rasping purr. "*You have no idea how long I've waited for you. Our time is at hand.*"

I breathe deep, and a knot inside me loosens, weeks of stress dissolving. For the first time, I know the answer to my problem, and the relief is indescribable. The Order of the Northern Wolf needs me, and I need them, and only if we're together will I ever be truly safe. Lightness travels through me, and I'm practically floating as my fingers seek the release for my seat belt. He'll catch me if I climb out the window, and then—

"*Don't look at him!*" Darkness falls instantly, Daphne's hand clamping over my eyes, and all the heaviness and pain slams back into my body. I gasp for air, dizzy, the car still weaving and skidding over the road. "Don't look at anything—just keep your eyes shut and hang on!"

When she peels her fingers away again, I do as I'm told. Two seconds of eye contact, and I was so deep in the hypnotic thrall of an undead cult leader that I was prepared to literally fling myself into his arms. Daphne hits the gas, the car leaping forward again, and I yelp with terror when my side of the vehicle smashes into something.

We rebound from the impact, fishtail, and straighten out. A blow hammers against the windshield from the outside—once, twice, the glass cracking loudly—and I whimper like an animal. Am I going to be ripped out of my seat by a claw-handed monster, dragged off to Vampire Jonestown with my eyes squeezed shut the whole way? Once again, Daphne's voice breaks through the dark spiral of my thoughts, clipped and urgent. "Brace yourself, Auggie, this isn't going to be fun."

The engine revs, the car hurtles faster, and I sink into my seat. Rasputin's fist comes down on the windshield again, the glass shattering; then the wheels meet resistance, the vehicle bucks up, and—*impact*. I'm slammed forward so hard the seat belt rips skin from the side of my neck, and I cry out as glass, metal, and plastic are crushed together with a deafening roar. My head bounces against the side window, lights flashing, pain cutting a path from my scalp to my stomach.

For a moment after the car settles again, I grip the dashboard, convinced I'm about to vomit or die. The air stinks like gas, my ears are ringing, and my thoughts won't fit together—puzzle pieces with all the wrong ends trying to join up. My right side hurts so badly I can't move, and when Daphne puts her hands on me again, I let out a pitiful moan. "Auggie? Auggie, I'm so sorry, but you need to take these."

She tucks something into my mouth—two fat, smooth capsules that she places between my back molars, before pressing my jaws together to split them open. Fluid rushes across my tongue, thick and coppery, and I'm swallowing it before the bright tingle it leaves behind registers. Vampire blood. My eyes open in surprise, the car a swirl of foggy colors that snap into focus as the substance races to my stomach and begins to spread.

"Auggie!" Daphne snaps her fingers, pulling my attention. The pain in my side is already dulling, my thoughts unscrambling as the static in my brain dissipates. Our eyes locked, Daphne reaches down and unbuckles my seat belt. "Listen to me: As soon as you get out, you need to run, okay? Head straight home, don't stop—we're only about a mile away, and those capsules should give you enough juice to make it in a few minutes."

"What do you mean? What's happening?" I reach for the torn skin on my neck, and feel it close under my fingertips. The windshield is destroyed, the front end of the car wrapped around the trunk of a massive oak, and my door hangs open. At first, I don't see Rasputin—but then movement catches my eye from the middle of the road, a dark shape flung some twenty yards from the crash, slowly twisting its limbs back together.

"I told you I'm going to protect you, and I meant it." Daphne leans over and kicks hard at her door, forcing it open with an angry croak. "I'm going to keep him busy, but . . . I don't know how long that's going to work. So I need you to watch out for yourself. The second you get out of the car, just run and don't look back. Understand?"

I blink, the words clear but confusing. "What do you mean, you don't know how long it's going to work?" She opens her mouth, and for a moment I think she's going to tell me something . . . but then she looks away. My voice rising, I demand, "Daph?"

Instead of answering, she reaches across me, grabbing hold of my injured shoulder and rolling it. The sudden pain makes me gasp, bones and tendons crunching back together as she manipulates the joint—but when she releases it, the throbbing ache is gone entirely. With a smile, troubled and brief, she says, "Don't be a hero, and don't wait for me."

And with that, she turns and clambers from the car. Panicked, I roll out on my side, tumbling onto someone's lawn—lights springing on up and down the block as people react to the crash. Rasputin is just beginning to stand when Daphne advances on him, and even from thirty feet away, I can see malevolence in the feral grin that sharpens his face.

Getting to my feet, I start to run . . . but guilt slows my pace. *Don't be a hero.* How can I run away, seeking cover while Daphne fights this battle on my behalf? She knows she's outmatched, we both know it—and despite what she said, I can't help but look back, watching from half a block away as she squares off with a hundred-and-fifty-year-old vampire.

When she gets close, she twirls, slashing at him with the stake. But he vanishes, blinking out in a puff of vapor—only to reappear instantly, right behind her. Before I can shout a warning, I realize she's anticipated the trick, lashing out and slamming her foot into his pelvis just as he materializes; he reels, but when she dives back to bury the stake in his chest, Rasputin counters with a blow that sends her flying through the air.

He turns toward me, then, those horrible eyes burning brighter than the streetlights, and I hear his voice thundering in my head. *You'll join us, August Pfeiffer.*

"Keep running!" Daphne shouts, scrambling to her feet. She charges a second time, leaping into a spin kick that catches air when Rasputin relocates again—but once more she's anticipated the feint, the point of the stake catching him in the shoulder when he reappears on her opposite side. He growls, his face darkening, and Daphne screams, "*Go!*"

Fire blazing in his eyes, Rasputin lunges straight at her—and disappears in a dark smear, just as before. The trick is old now, and Daphne anticipates it . . . but when she spins around to catch him, her stake finds nothing but air. Reappearing in the exact same place he vanished from, Rasputin catches her arm in midair, and the sound of bone snapping is as horrifying as our head-on collision with the tree.

Shock pulls all the blood from my head and pushes my stomach into my throat, and the night wobbles as Rasputin rips the stake from Daphne's limp hand, crushing the wood into splinters. And then I watch, frozen, as he wraps a hand around her chin and twists her head, viciously and effortlessly, to the side. There's a nauseating *crack* . . . and Daphne drops to ground, limbs sprawling. Her blond hair streams over the wet road, her eyes half open and turned to the sky—glazed and unfocused.

Dead.

I gag stomach acid, tears flooding my eyes, everything too bright, too real. The vampire blood surges and snaps in my veins, anger and grief hurtling up out of the darkness—and deep down, in a place I can't name, I sense the Corrupter's power. He likes the chaos inside me. My fingers itch with the desire to rip Rasputin's head clean from his body and watch him crumble into nothing but dust and bone.

But when I meet his golden gaze, my hands squeezing into fists, the air between us darkens and narrows. Again his eyes move without moving, and pressure builds in my head. He's trying to mesmerize me, and only a slender membrane of resistance—maybe the vampire blood, maybe the Corrupter—is holding him back. Just like that, I know I'm not strong enough to fight him; I'm barely strong enough to fight *this*.

A window slams open somewhere nearby, a high, thin voice shouting, "Whatever's happening out there, we've called the police, and they're on their way!"

Rasputin glances sharply in the direction of the sound, and I spin on my heel, obeying Daphne's final command: *Go.*

She was right about the extra juice—I'm moving like Mario with an invincibility star, trees blurring as I skid around a corner and sprint for my own neighborhood. It's one mile, and with every foot of ground I cover, I expect Rasputin to drop on me out of nowhere. I expect him to materialize in front of me, to close in on me from behind, but both times I allow myself a glance over my shoulder, the streets are dark and empty.

I don't understand it. I don't understand anything. By the time my house comes into view, my chest is heaving, and not from the exertion. Daphne's last moments hurl themselves constantly against my memory, a moth trapped in a jar, and the only thing holding me together is sheer, unbridled terror. I have to get inside.

But the night isn't done with me yet.

My hands are shaking as I stumble up the front steps, my keys dancing as I struggle to find the right one. Only three vampires are watching my house tonight—but who do they work for? I don't believe Rasputin would just let me escape like that, and I can't accept that he did. He followed us from the rave and killed Daphne right in front of me—why am I not in a cage right now? What does he have planned?

Throwing open the storm door, I'm just about to jam my key in the lock . . . when, once again, I realize I'm not alone on the porch. Something moves in my peripheral vision, a shadow more solid than the rest. Whirling, I yank my crucifix free so fast the stitching of my pocket tears—but then: "Auggie?"

The voice is so familiar, yet unexpected, that I almost drop the cross. The darkness under the overhang is a black quicksand, swallowing everything, but the vampire blood lets me see her face anyway. "A-Adriana?"

"I didn't think you were ever going to come home." She shivers, her breath coming out in a machine-gun stream of ragged puffs, and worry is written in the set of her brow.

"What are you doing here?" I demand, unlocking the door as quickly as possible, sounding angry when what I really am is frantic—grief-stricken. My throat is a fist closed tight around my tears, and every breath I take is a reminder that Daphne is dead, and Rasputin is somewhere behind me.

"Waiting for you," she answers with vacant simplicity, stepping out of the shadows and blinking as if the moon hurts her eyes. "I must have fallen asleep. It's . . . it's really cold, Auggie."

A horrible thought comes over me, like a centipede crawling up my arm, and I shove the front door open and hurry inside. The house is warm—and empty, and silent, but it's a safe zone of a sort, and just standing inside it makes me ready to weep for a dozen more reasons. I turn back, my breath tight, the crucifix still biting into my fingers. "I mean, yeah, it's cold. It's the middle of the night. Why were you waiting for me?"

"I . . ." She blinks again, still framed by the doorway. "I don't know. I just . . . wanted to see you, I guess." And then she steps inside, uninvited, closing the door behind her. I hold my breath for a beat . . . but nothing happens, and finally I let it out, inexpressibly relieved. I couldn't *feel* her with that undead radar I've got . . . but, then, I can't feel Gunnar, either. I don't know who to trust anymore.

Adriana's cheeks are bright pink with cold as she kicks off her shoes, and then takes two steps past the threshold and goes rigid. She gasps, her head snapping back, her fingers splayed until the tendons in her hands stand out like the guylines on a tent.

Her eyes roll up until only a crescent of glistening white is visible beneath the lid, and her mouth opens. The voice that comes out of her is deep, gravelly—and thick with a Russian accent. It's not hers, but I recognize it immediately, and my head swims.

"August Pfeiffer, we have your parents. If you wish to see them alive again, you will pledge yourself and your blood to the Mystic Order of the Northern Wolf, before the vernal equinox on Friday. You have until Thursday to decide."

As soon as the statement is out of her mouth, Adriana's body collapses to the floor.

OUTSIDE IN THE NIGHT, BELLS RANG THE LATE HOUR, AND A breath of wind teased the candle that flickered by her elbow. Another day ended, another hour closer to her appointed death, and all she felt inside was empty.

No, that wasn't entirely true. Inside she felt . . . *something*. And it troubled her greatly.

It wasn't so very long ago that her destiny seemed bright as the sun and poised to soar as high; but the sun always sets, and the future is rarely more than a trick of the light. The past six months had been an unremitting parade of degradations, and now she found herself here. How strange, how villainously poetic, to be held prisoner in the same chamber where once she awaited her coronation.

The wind stiffened, making the candle gutter, and she shielded it in the curve of her palm. Then, because the perversity of it was irresistible, she asked the flame to burn brighter—and it leaped an inch. She shuddered, discomposed by her own uncanny magic, and withdrew her hand in an instant to let the wind claim its bounty.

The flame blinked out, smoke slithering off the wick, and darkness spilled across the pages before her. Leaning back in her chair, she let out a nervous breath. Other candles burned in the room, casting their shifting light against the walls, and for a moment she let herself believe the dancing shadows were spirits welcoming her to her eternal reward. What a thing to look forward to.

Soon. But maybe not soon enough.

The scrape of metal against metal brought her up short, a key turning in the lock, and she twisted sharply to face the door. It was late, and she knew of no visitors she was scheduled to receive that night. There were very few she might expect, even in the worst of cases, who could simply enter her chambers without a show of asking permission first.

And so she was utterly nonplussed when the door opened and a single, delicately built man sidled into the room. His clothing was unremarkable, the material dark and the quality modest, and his face—high cheekbones, expressive eyes, a tidy beard—was unfamiliar. Despite some cleverness in his expression, he was the kind of man she'd have passed without notice . . . were it not for the fact that her very skin crawled in his presence.

"My lady," he began, with a deep and humble bow, a sly and private smile turning up the edges of his mouth. "I ask that you please forgive the unannounced intrusion."

"Who are you?" she demanded with an imperious air, rising to her feet. While she had been uncontestably stripped of her dignity, her title remained, and she could insist upon at least an empty demonstration of respect for it. "How dare you enter these chambers uninvited?"

"Again, I beseech your forgiveness," he said, his eyes humbly on the floor, his words clipped by a German accent. "Had there been a more appropriate avenue to seek your audience, I would certainly have pursued it, but circumstances are . . . such as they are, and I am afraid that what I have to say cannot wait."

"How are you here?" She drew back, closer to the window, although he had made no overt threat to her safety—though death was perhaps the last thing she feared just then. Through her window, she could see the fortified walls that ringed the Tower, and she knew her rooms were watched night and day by the guards. They were out there even now, they had to be. "Why did they let you in?"

What she really wanted to ask was why he made her *tingle* so, but she was afraid to articulate the question aloud. Unaccountably, one of the few contrived charges that had not been leveled against her was witchcraft, and she lived in perpetual fear of performing some unaccountable feat in front of witnesses—such as making candle flames dance, or perhaps floating in her sleep, as she'd done twice this week already.

No, for many reasons, death was not what she feared the most.

"My name is Erasmus Kramer, Your Highness." He sank lower into his bow. "And they let me in for the simple reason that they had no other choice." At last he looked up, meeting her eye. "I am a mystic and fortune-teller of some renown—and many other things, too—but the reason I am here is to explain what *you* are."

She meant to step back . . . but instead, her feet drew her closer. Too many nights had passed with strange and terrible dreams that defied understanding, and too many minds had opened up their secrets to her curiosity like flowers blooming at her touch. The glint in his eye bespoke a knowledge that she craved. "What, exactly, do you mean by that?"

"You are, quite possibly, the doorway to the future," he answered, a smile turning up his mouth. "Within you is the remedy to a terminal sickness that infects the Earth, and I believe you have the strength to manifest that cure. But more time is needed."

"Time, Herr Kramer," she said dryly, "is a luxury the condemned are not permitted. Not even ones of my station."

"I could give you that time, though." His smile spread, teeth stacking up in the sharpened corners of his grin. "With the same ease that I came in, I could take you out."

She stilled, only a foot away from him. "To what purpose? What is this sickness you speak of—and who are you, anyway?" When he did not immediately reply, she decided to seek the answer for herself and pushed her way into his thoughts. What she saw there was impossible and shocking; things that should not be. Pulling away, she stumbled back, her fingers trembling. "You're a revenant."

"And many other things, too," he replied simply.

Revenants. The returned ones. Those who went to their graves, and then somehow . . . came back. She'd heard stories about them growing up, and as part of the royal court had played audience to knights with heart-pounding tales of the battle against unholy creatures who had already proven once how they would not die. But the accounts told of fangs and claws—neither of which the spindly gentleman before her possessed.

"It is time that you explained your business with me, Herr Kramer." She settled her lips into a grim line.

"Are you not afraid?" He seemed surprised, perhaps even a little dismayed. "Most mortals run screaming when they learn what I am."

"As you can well see," she began with a sweeping gesture around her tidy and comfortable prison, "I have nowhere to run. And even if you were to take my life, you would only beat the king to my neck by a matter of days. But you speak of taking me out of the Tower, and I wish to know why."

"I offer a condemned prisoner a chance to escape the axe and she wishes to question my purpose." He gave a dry chuckle. "Very well. I shall be blunt: I know who you are, of course, and why you're here—"

"I failed to birth a son," she interjected bitterly. "Whatever you've heard, *that* is the reason I am here. His Majesty required a male heir, and my body could not produce one."

"What if I told you that your body is destined to produce something so much greater than a mere prince? That in a matter of days, perhaps a week, you will change the very world as we know it—that you will reduce this king and his kingdom to nothing?"

"I would say that I am come to doubt your credentials as a fortune-teller," she answered smartly. "In a week's time, I shall be dead."

And so he told her about the *something* she felt inside of her. He called it the Dark Star, and he explained its reach back into time so ancient that no written record of its origin existed. His vision was apocalyptic, and his belief in the truth of what he said was total.

At the conclusion of his tale, he renewed his offer. "This does not have to be how your story ends. Come with me. Spare yourself from the wrath of a spiteful and petty king who could not remain faithful to you for three whole winters."

"You need not remind me of the weakness of my husband's flesh." Even now, he was planning his next wedding—to her own maid of honor, the conniving vixen. "You wish me to leave this place with you, to trade one hour of death for another, and my only reward is to become the mechanism that . . . does what, again? Permits the dead to rule the Earth?"

"Your death would have meaning, my lady." His brows came together, irritation showing on his gaunt face. "Stay here, and you will die only to satisfy the capricious lust and self-glorification of a tyrant; if you come with me, you will die on your own terms."

"I will die on *your* terms," she corrected. "I've had quite enough of acquiescing to the demands men make of my body in order to further their private ambitions, Herr Kramer, and what you've not done is convince me that *my* needs are best met by your proposal."

"You have a daughter. My people would gladly pledge to protect her."

"She has people pledged to protect her now. What benefits me from leaving behind a legacy of invulnerable revenants?"

His mouth turned down. "My people would also quite gladly target your daughter."

She surprised him with a throaty chuckle. "I've no doubt! And you certainly wouldn't be the first. Those who guard her include Knights from the Brotherhood of Perseus, and I understand they have safeguards against even the peculiar seduction your kind exerts over human minds."

"I could force you," he noted darkly.

"Physically, perhaps, although if it were that simple, we'd already be well away from here. I believe, however, that you require my allegiance—which you can neither force without leverage, nor compel with even the sorcery you worked to infiltrate these apartments." Of the many tales she'd heard from the Persean Knights, this one detail had been particularly interesting. To look into a revenant's eyes, they said, was to fall under its control, but magic required desire and intent to work, and no spell could succeed when worked by one without free will. "The small bowl that sits at the forefront of your mind, the one you wish my finger to bleed into while you speak the words that will seal us together . . . I'm afraid it shall remain empty."

A storm passed across the man's face, his angles lengthening and a baleful light smoldering to life in his eyes; but just as quickly, the storm cleared, and Herr Kramer took a step back. "I suppose, then, it is time for me to depart. Again, please forgive the intrusion."

"Just like that?" It was her turn for surprise. "You're conceding defeat?"

He shrugged serenely. "I am a better fortune-teller than my lady wishes to acknowledge. And although you are one of a precious few to bear the gift of the Dark Star . . . you will not be the last. And your death shall simply mean a new beginning."

With those words, Erasmus Kramer left the way he came, and when he was gone, the prisoner returned to her writing table. A bowl

of blood was not the most disquieting image she'd seen in the revenant's vision of the future, and she shuddered at some of the horrors
she'd brushed against while exploring his mind. If this Dark Star was
truly capable of such dire work, then she was almost glad for her
slender neck and her husband's reckless selfishness.

With a simple glance at the candle, she induced the wick to
ignite itself again, and she finished the letter she'd been writing. At
the bottom, she signed her name—Anne Boleyn.

How odd to suddenly hope she would die before it was too late.

21

When Adriana regains consciousness, she's disoriented and scared, and I set her up on the living room sofa to recover while I suffer a complete mental breakdown. I try my parents' cell phones at least a dozen times each with no answer, and I'm such a mess that it takes me fifteen minutes to remember what restaurant they were eating at tonight. My call reaches a recorded voice, telling me the place closed an hour earlier, and I go into free fall.

I'm on the kitchen floor, hugging my knees to my chest, ugly-crying when Adriana finds me. She doesn't say anything, just sits down beside me and puts her arm around my shoulders. We stay like that until I'm capable of speaking again, and I can finally tell her everything—from the beginning.

"Why didn't you say something?" She stares at me in a daze—shocked and angry, but perhaps most of all hurt.

"I didn't want you to have to be part of this," I whisper, my voice rough and broken. "I didn't want them to come after you, too." It seems a useless thing to say at this point. But Daphne is dead, and my parents are gone, and there's no time to think of something better. "What happened? What did he say to you?"

"I don't know. I'm sorry, but I can't . . ." She's pale, still trembling as though she's cold, although we've been inside long enough for her to warm up by now. "The gate in our back fence was banging in the wind, and my dad got mad at me because he said I must've left it open. So I went out to shut it, and when I got there—"

"Rasputin?"

"I didn't even see him at first." Her voice shrinks. "He wasn't there, and then . . . he was. Just this tall, bony, goblin-looking-ass dude, *grinning* at me, and I was sure I was dead. I saw my whole fucking life flash before my eyes, and then . . . I don't know." Adriana squeezes her hands so tight her knuckles pop. "Everything gets fuzzy after that. He told me something, then the next thing I know, you're coming up your front steps and I've been sitting there so long my feet are numb. But I don't know when I got here, or how long I was waiting. It's all a blur."

"Is there a spell for that? Some way to bring back your memory? Or, like . . . I mean, he spoke *through* you! Like, he planted his words in your head. Maybe there's some way to reverse that and use it against him?"

She frowns, but her eyes are distant and thoughtful. "Like how?"

"He used magic to do it, so there must be some kind of counter-spell, right?" I barely know more about magic than I do about math, but I'm desperate right now. "Magic is all about balance and harmony, and equal and opposite reaction, and stuff, right? If he zapped you, there *has* to be a way to zap him back!" I'm practically pleading. "Your grandma has all those grimoires full of big-deal spells . . . Maybe there's something in one of them!"

"Auggie . . ." Adriana shakes her head, stricken. "Even if there is, I can't summon the kind of power something like that would require—and if I tried . . . Remember the time in sixth grade we decided to make lasagna and ended up setting your whole oven on fire because we had no clue what we were doing? It would be like that, except with my brain."

"He has my parents. I have to do something." More tears roll down my cheeks, and I wipe them away with the back of my hand. It's the first time I realize that my glasses are missing—that I lost them, and didn't even notice, because I don't seem to need them anymore. *You have until Thursday to decide.* The Nexus always goes hyperactive on the vernal equinox . . . Is that when my time runs out?

Suddenly, my best friend shoves to her feet, her fingers worrying into fists. "I think my abuela knows something."

"What do you mean?" I finally stand up as well, shaky inside and out, remembering Ximena's plastic bag—thinking about Hope's freaky woodcut.

"Don't tell me you didn't notice her acting weird the night you came over for dinner," she replies with a snort. "She snatched some of your hair, and I let her convince me it was for a protection spell!"

"It wasn't?" My voice reaches for the stars.

"Well . . . I don't know, maybe it was!" Adriana exclaims. "There are lots of spells that require stuff like that, but . . . it's the way she's been asking about you, the way she wanted you to come over for dinner in the first place—even before that scene at Sugar Mama's went down. I didn't think anything about it at the time, but now . . ." Adriana trails off and then shakes her head, coming to a decision. "She's going to be so pissed I told you this, but . . . my grandma isn't exactly who she says she is."

My eyebrows ratchet up slowly. "She's in witness protection?"

"No, you doofus." Adriana rolls her eyes. "What I'm saying is . . . look, there's a difference between a witch and a sorcerer, right?"

"Yeah, I know," I answer hastily, hoping to forestall another diatribe against people who belittle smudge sticks because they remember the time the Baeserta cultists brought down two feet of snow on

Fulton Heights. In July. "Anyone can become a witch, but you have to be born with the gift for sorcery—like the X-Men." I swallow. "Are you trying to tell me that . . . Ximena is one of the X-Men?"

"I don't even know what she is," Adriana returns. "Witches who can do actual sorcery try not to advertise it, because it scares people—and because history hasn't exactly been awesome toward minority groups with a little power." Fingering the zipper on her coat, she adds, "Abuela's afraid to even show *me* everything she can do. It's part of the reason she and my mom fell out."

"Really?"

"Abuela can do serious, hard-core magic, and it scares Mamá. She thinks it's dangerous, and she doesn't want me involved with it." Adriana looks down at her hands with a regretful smile. "You know what's really messed up? I couldn't get involved even if I wanted to, because I don't have the gift—but I refuse to admit it to my mom."

"So . . . what are you saying, exactly?" It's a question I'm not even sure I want to ask, because there's only one good answer . . . and lots and lots of really bad ones. In my head, all I can see is some dude either getting zapped to death or possessed by an eternal monster while a bunch of witches rejoice.

"I'm saying that I think she already knows about all of this. She kept bugging me to invite you over, she took your hair for a spell . . . and she didn't *tell* me!" Adriana blurts. "I know she wants to keep the sorcery stuff under wraps, but there are lots of protection spells that don't require that kind of magic—and you're my best friend!" She pushes trembling hands through her hair. "She's hiding something. And it has to do with you."

I'm hiccupping with nerves, and I don't want to go any further, but now I *really* need to hear that one good answer. "Do you think there's a chance she can stop the Corrupter?"

"Auggie." A big, fat tear rolls down Adriana's cheek. "What if the only way to stop him is for you to *die*?"

I nod mechanically. Jude thinks so; Gunnar thinks so, too, and the Brotherhood never found an alternative. At this point, I'm out of straws to grasp, and it's almost a relief. "What if it is? Honestly, at this point, what difference does it make?"

"Please don't say that," she whispers, more tears rolling.

"I don't want to die." Admitting it is hard, because it feels futile—because mortality isn't something I'm supposed to be grappling with right now. It isn't fair, and I want to scream and cry and rage at the injustice of it all. "But the only thing worse than me dying is this thing getting loose in the world. You've got no idea what kind of plans Rasputin has for a future where he's in charge and invincible, but it's really, really bad."

"Okay." Adriana takes my hands and squeezes them so hard my fingertips turn white. "We'll talk to my abuela."

We don't sleep much. I don't want to be in the house alone, and neither one of us wants to go outside again, so convincing Adriana to stay the night is relatively easy. The problem is that she doesn't know how she got here, or where her parents think she is, and she's afraid that if she calls home, she'll get in trouble for something she can't safely explain.

"Let me try something," I suggest, taking her hands again. What I'm about to attempt is something I've only done before while hopped up on vampire blood—and not only is it something I'm unsure I can manage, it's something I'm unsure I *want* to manage.

My ability to go walking through people's minds, to visit their memories and spy on their futures, is obviously coming from the entity currently trying to carjack my body. How do I know that every time I draw on the Corrupter's power, it doesn't pull the entity closer to the surface? Adriana, with all her talk about balance and harmony in the universe, might even say that if I'm borrowing from it, I'm almost certainly giving it something back.

But once again, I'm caught between a rock and a much bigger rock, and if I can control this mind-reading thing, it's an advantage I can't afford not to cultivate. So I breathe out, look my best friend in the eye, and reach down deep. I remember what it was like in the club, surfing through the consciousness of an entire crowd without even having to think about it . . . and a moment later I'm tumbling into Adriana's thoughts.

We're hurtling backward, skipping from our fraught moments in the kitchen to her collapse just inside the door—and then her memory thickens, time growing fogged and slippery as I relive her night with her in reverse. *An eon passing on the front porch, the air getting colder, golden eyes floating in the distant dark; a long, purposeful walk, every step a relief, because there's a message for Auggie; sneaking out the back door, must be quiet, can't get caught, there's a message for Auggie; standing motionless behind a closed door, waiting for the coast to be clear.*

Then. *Two eyes, bright as searchlights—pulling in and swallowing up, inescapable.*

A message for Auggie.

My heart thuds, and I manage to hold steady in Adriana's memory at the moment she looked Rasputin in the eye. She was at the Verdugos' back gate, the moon fighting through a grease-stained sky, when he created a channel between their minds. I wish I knew what I was doing, because I want to shove my fist through that channel until I punch his fucking brain out.

"Your parents don't know where you are," I report when I let go, stepping out of her thoughts and back into my empty home. Then, shutting ourselves in my bedroom, we set an alarm for sunrise and climb into my bed with our clothes on.

I try to keep Daphne's death from playing on a constant loop in my thoughts, but I fail. Grief is a freight train, flattening me, forcing the air from my lungs—and even after everything, even knowing what I know about why she lied to me, my sorrow is still muddied with resentment. She could have warned me all of this was coming. Maybe she couldn't have saved me, but at least I would've had some time to get ready.

No matter how hurt I am, though, I can't help but think of all the times she took my side when my parents were annoyed with me, how she'd casually get me off the hook; I think about how she liked to tease me, but in a way that made me laugh rather than feel bad; and I think about how she would still be alive if I hadn't expected her to be my lifeline when I stupidly went to a vampire rave because I was scared and desperate for answers.

She was my tutor and my secret guardian, the older sister I never had and a stranger I was only just getting to know. If the Brotherhood can't find a way to prevent the Ascension, what will they decide? What would Daphne have had to do if she were still alive when the time came?

What if the only way to stop him is for you to die?

I cry as quietly as possible so I won't wake Adriana, and it's a long time before I fall asleep.

22

driana promises that her grandmother is an early riser and rarely has anywhere to be on Sundays, so in the morning, we head out as soon as the sun is high enough that we're sure the streets will be clear of vampires. It's only a partial comfort for me, of course. The single direct attempt on my life throughout all of this was made by a human—and the person who saved me from it is dead.

The walk is quiet but tense, my nerves stretched to the breaking point, and when we get to Ximena's house, climbing the steps to knock on the door, I'm almost hoping no one will answer. For all I know, sorcery is how this whole thing got started. Jude says I wasn't "chosen" as the vessel—that it's just my shitty luck—but what if he's wrong? *An arcane ritual . . . the Rising of the Dark Star.* What if a bunch of X-Men witches stuffed this being into me in the first place? There are plenty of reasons why humans would consort with an entity promising true immortality.

But *why me*? According to Daphne, some ancient prophecy describes my "planetary influences" and "specific traits," and yet no one has told me which ones; no one even seems to care. If a bunch of witches really singled me out and squeezed me full of the Corrupter like some kind of hideous Halloween dumpling, I want to know *why*.

Footsteps sound inside, the knob turns, and Ximena Rosales appears before us, her eyes registering surprise for only a moment before they settle into resignation. With a weary nod, she steps aside. "I was wondering when this moment would come."

"So I take it ESP isn't one of your big, scary sorcery powers?" I can't help the sharpness with which the words roll off my tongue. Before now, I would never have dreamed of speaking to Ximena like this—but I'd never felt betrayed by her, either.

On all sides, I've been surrounded by people dealing in deception, trying to outsmart each other at a game where I'm the grand prize. Gunnar, Daphne, Mr. Strauss . . . and now even Ximena, a woman I've known almost my whole life. I get why she didn't tell me she's an actual sorceress, because I never would've been able to keep it a secret—but she knows something, and when I turned to her for help, she deceived me.

The amazing irony in all of this is that Jude Marlowe is the only one who never lied about what he is.

"It's early," Ximena remarks when we're all gathered in the living room, Adriana and I side by side on a love seat near the front window. "Would you like some coffee?"

"Sure. Do you have sugar, or just *more lies*?"

Adriana shoots me a nervous frown. "*Auggie.*"

"No, mijita, it's okay. He has a right to be upset." Ximena seats herself in a high-backed wing chair—one Adriana's grandpa used to favor when he was alive—and she picks up a mug of coffee from the table beside her. "So, Auggie. What is it you'd like to know?"

I scowl deeper, annoyed, the question designed to back-foot me. "How about we start with why you really yanked out my hair."

"I needed some of your hair for a spell to determine whether or not the Corrupter was truly Rising inside you," she says evenly, her eyes on mine. "But given the circumstances, I'm guessing you already know that."

"Why didn't you tell me?" My eyes film over, and I struggle hard not to fall apart, but that's a battle I almost always lose. I didn't mean to ask this question so early, to go right to what hurts me the most. From a lifetime of being "different," I know how dangerous it is to expose your insecurities at the beginning of a confrontation. It's the equivalent of handing your opponent a sledgehammer and a guide-book to your kneecaps.

But Ximena's expression softens immediately, and she sets her coffee aside. "What *could* I tell you? It would have been cruel to say something before I was certain, to fill your head with scary stories that I couldn't explain without first fessing up to something I've worked hard to keep hidden all my life. And after the spell was cast . . ." She falters, glancing away—and what's left of my hope drops through a trapdoor and into a moat filled with alligators. "It's not easy news to give someone, and there's still a lot you don't understand."

"What does that mean?" I'm tired of everybody knowing more than me. "What don't I understand yet? Because I'm dying! This thing is getting ready to replace me—and, meanwhile, a bug-eyed vampire from 1915 kidnapped my parents and threw Adriana's brain at me like a ransom note tied to a brick!"

"Mijita?" Straightening in her chair, Ximena shoots an alarmed look at her granddaughter, and Adriana squirms uncomfortably.

I'm not done yet, though. "He wants me to take a blood oath and join his apocalyptic death cult so he can call the shots when this thing finally does a Kool-Aid Man through my actual soul, so if there's something I don't understand, it would be awesome if you would explain it." I'm breathing so hard my hands tingle. The fact is, she's had lots of time to volunteer explanations . . . and she hasn't, which is an explanation itself. "There's no way to stop this thing, is there?"

Her expression stricken, Adriana grips my hand. "Of course there's a way, there has to be—there's always a balancing force in magic! If this thing is from the magical world, then there's a magical solution, right, Abuela?"

"We're not talking about hexes and charms, here, Adriana," Ximena says gently, and my friend's fingers dig harder into my flesh. "Vampires have a magical cause, too, but if there were any way to 'solve' that problem, sorcerers would have discovered it eons ago. Balance is about equilibrium—systems keeping each other in check."

"So what's the bottom line?" I demand, my voice gritty with exhaustion. There's an 80 percent chance she's going to tell me I need to die—and a 20 percent chance she'll tell me to shut up and incubate faster, because she's pro-Ascension—and I'm just waiting for her to say it either way.

Ximena sets her coffee down again and stands up, pacing restlessly to the window. "Don't get mad, but I'm going to answer that with a story." She turns to face us. "I was about your age when my abilities started to manifest. We knew there was sorcery in our bloodline, so my parents weren't shocked, and they knew where to find people who could help me learn about my gifts." Absently, she runs her fingers through the fronds of a potted fern. "That's how I ended up here, in Fulton Heights. I moved in with some family friends and started mastering my element. The Nexus amplifies magical power, and training under it is like being an athlete preparing for the Olympics.

"A few years ago, I was approached by a group of witches—the last members of what was once an incredibly powerful coven." Ximena turns her gaze out the window, arms crossed at her waist. "They said that they were looking for certain elementals with extraordinary potential, and that they believed I might be the earth witch they needed to complete their circle."

"For what?" I ask, because I already know this story eventually comes back to me, my mind filled with terrifying images. *An arcane ritual.*

"They told me a story," she answers after a moment, "about an entity that appears on Earth once in a generation, finding a host and taking it over. They showed me a prophecy foretelling just such an event within my lifetime . . . and they told me where the Corrupter came from. The thing inside you isn't a monster or a ghost, Auggie." She turns to face me again, her eyes hollow and razor-edged. "It's an angel."

23

blink for what must be a full minute. "It's a what, now?"

"An *angel*?" Adriana's jaw drops open so wide I'm afraid it's dislocated.

"You mean, like, with wings and a halo and . . ." I fumble for what I know about angels, but I'm panicking. "And a line of greeting cards?"

"An angel," Ximena confirms, "but not some rosy-cheeked cupid from a Christmas pageant. We're talking about *real* angels— *warriors*—beings of incredible strength and power, capable of raising the dead and shaking the earth with their voices."

"I didn't think you believed in angels. Or *anything* from the Bible." Adriana is having almost as much trouble wrapping her brain around all of this as I am.

"Since they were first written down, the scriptures have been edited, curated, and reinterpreted, over and over, by men with an agenda," Ximena states flatly. "But what I believe in is complicated. I think humans have become arrogant creatures with little respect for the natural world—and Wicca provides a path in the opposite direction."

"At the risk of sounding like an arrogant creature," I interject, "can we talk about me some more? Because you just said my body is going to crack open and spew out an *actual angel!*"

Ximena crosses back to her chair and sits down, leaning over her knees. "His name is Azazel. He was thrown out of heaven alongside Lucifer—the Morning Star—for rebelling against God. But while Lucifer and his demons claimed dominion over hell, Azazel—the Dark Star—ended up here, in this realm. So, in a sense, he and the entity you know as Satan are colleagues. Equals, in a manner of speaking."

"Cool, cool." My mouth makes a dry, clicking sound when I speak. "Fun information."

"What he's known for is 'corrupting the Earth.'" She gives me a meaningful look. "But what those accounts don't spell out in so many words is the form that corruption took."

Adriana and I exchange a glance, our eyes bulging.

"Just like Lucifer, he wanted his own kingdom, and he meant to build one here among the mortals," Ximena continues. "But his attempts at creating an army, sharing his blood with his human disciples, produced something monstrous and deadly." She takes a deep breath. "Auggie . . . Azazel is the source of vampirism."

"Are you serious?" Adriana squeezes my hand even harder until I'm afraid the bones are going to crack.

"His blood is endless, truly immortal, and it continues to pass from one vampire to the next up to this very day—although Azazel hasn't had a body of his own for millennia." Ximena leans back in her chair. "Ages ago, when their coven was whole, the witches I told you about tried to work an occult ritual on the Corrupter, but even as powerful as they were, the magic was still too intense for them to wield successfully. One of the witches died, and the spell went wrong, resulting in . . . well . . ." Her voice drops, and she runs her fingers along her upholstered armrests. "According to them, that's how the father of all vampires was removed to an unknown plane, able to return to our realm only every hundred years. His blood is still here, and it still calls to him. He'll keep coming back as long as he can, aiming to build the kingdom he was denied."

"How long ago are we talking?" I ask next, on the edge of my seat, that damned woodcut doing cartwheels in my brain. "'Ages' like bad hair and bell-bottoms . . . or 'ages' like, like . . . 'ugh, me hungry for mastodon'?"

"I don't know. But if I had to guess . . ." Ximena looks me in the eye. "I'd say they remember what Salisbury Plain looked like before Stonehenge was built."

"That's not possible." Adriana's face is gray. "How is that possible?"

"Magic takes energy, mijita, you know that," Ximena says quietly, "and sorcery requires far more than ordinary witchcraft. To work the strongest spells, even with the support of a full coven . . . it's like running a marathon. You have to prepare, you have to know what you're doing, and it still drains you." Her hands move, agitated. "These were some of the most talented witches history has ever seen, and they failed in part because the six of them together couldn't handle the power they needed to channel."

"But vampires have heightened strength and stamina," I point out dully. "And their blood boosts their ability to work basic magic."

"They heal almost immediately, too," Ximena adds, "which means they can recover the energy they lose from casting almost in real time. So, yes. They say that, knowing their mortal weakness would always prevent them from succeeding at this ritual, the surviving witches found a vampire who would Turn them . . . and they joined the undead."

"You're working with a bunch of *vampires*?" Adriana clearly can't believe what she's hearing. "My whole life you've told me the undead can't be trusted, and now—"

"You watch your tone, Adriana Verdugo," the woman snaps, fast as a cobra, and my best friend's mouth clicks shut. "Don't speak to me like that."

"Why *are* you working with them?" I demand, because Ximena isn't my grandmother, and I don't even know if I trust her now. "Whose side are they on?"

It should be an easy question to answer, but the woman gets a pensive look, her mouth shifting. "To be honest, I'm not sure."

"You're not *sure*?" Adriana squeals, and her grandmother glares at her again.

"I don't need you to lecture me, young lady. I've only trained with them because they've made me stronger in my craft than I ever dreamed possible. But I've always questioned their motivations and tried to anticipate their end game. I meant what I said the other night, when I reminded you that vampires never tell the whole truth." She sighs. "They didn't reveal to us until last month that this was to be the year of the Ascension, and it was only a few weeks ago that I learned Auggie was the intended vessel."

"Whose side do they *say* they're on?" I try again, growing exasperated. My parents are missing, I'm pressure-cooking Satan's office buddy, and she needs prompts?

"According to them, they've sacrificed everything to save mankind from the Corrupter. They've spent millennia tracking him from one Rising to the next, hoping to confront him again and cast him into hell once and for all." Her wedding ring clinks against her coffee mug. "Only three of them remain now, and they've been grooming me and two others for years to replace their fallen sisters."

Immediately, my mind flashes on the sketches I did in the art room, and the trio of mysterious, black-clad women that figured into both. "If that's really their plan, then why haven't they done it yet? If this thing comes back every hundred years, they've had shitloads of opportunity!"

"A ritual of this magnitude can't be worked on a whim." She sets her mug aside, crossing her legs. "It requires a confluence of factors that can't be forced, and a balanced circle with experienced magicworkers . . . They say the circumstances necessary to pull it off didn't come together until just now. And all of that is true enough, as far as I can tell."

"You keep saying stuff like that—'according to them,' and 'as far as you can tell.'" I tuck my hands under my thighs so the sofa can absorb the sweat from my palms.

"I'm not sure they're being honest with me." Ximena gives her granddaughter a meaningful look. "They're very secretive, and provide information only when they deem it necessary, and . . . I've come to realize that they're not above telling me what I want to hear in order to gain my cooperation." Finally, she gets to her feet again, pacing back to the window and then spinning around. "The fact of the matter is that, even if what they've told me is true—even if they once lost control of a spell meant to banish Azazel and sacrificed their humanity so they could prepare for a rematch—it means they've been undead for thousands and thousands of years."

"That's a long time," I mumble, my dry mouth making gross, sticky noises.

"Much longer than they were ever human, of course." She smiles with her lips pressed tightly together. "Long enough to have changed their minds about finishing what they claimed they started. It bothers me that they won't explain the details of the ritual when we're running out of time to perform it. It bothers me that they won't say *why* they won't explain the details."

"Abuela, there's no way you can keep training with them!" Adriana practically screeches. "What if they're dangerous?"

"Don't worry about me, mijita." Every inch of Ximena exudes a confidence I wish I'd ever felt. "Believe me when I say I can protect myself—even from these women. Right now I'm worried about Auggie." Both of them turn to look at me, and I feel the color drain out of my face. "Because there are no written accounts that exist, I only have the witches' word that they were human when they dealt with Azazel the first time. For all I know, the ritual they botched— the one they want me to assist them with now—wasn't meant to stop him. *They might have been trying to help him Ascend.*"

23

In the movies, this would be the big moment where the hero decides to take matters into his own hands. Some cockamamie plan would come together, he'd find an unexpected ally, and together they'd snatch victory from the jaws of defeat. But I've got no plan, and no allies I haven't tried. All the information I have about the Corrupter comes from people with reasons not to tell the whole truth, and there's nowhere I can think of to look for more allies.

All I can do is try to choose some smart strategies, even if it feels like giving up. Even if it means accepting that the best-case scenario is one in which I never live to see if my plan even works out. I have no way of contacting the person I need to see, but instinct tells me to check the mall, where I learned of the Corrupter for the very first time. I can wait as long as it takes; it's not like I'll get in trouble with my parents.

Ximena offers to let me stay with her, but I ask her to drive me home. Maybe she's trustworthy . . . but maybe she's not, and I can't afford the luxury of making a mistake about it. The second she drops me off, I pull out my bike and start across town, the sky a shield of low-hanging clouds that makes the sun feel farther away than ever. A week and a half ago, I was fantasizing about a future at SAIC—a dream stoked by a man who was already plotting my death when he suggested I apply for their program.

Obviously, Mr. Strauss recognized the meaning behind my sketches—knew what was happening to me, saw my art as proof. What scares me is the possibility that there are more humans out there who want me dead, while I'm fresh out of humans who want to protect me. Vampires might watch over me by night, but who's left to keep me safe now?

When I reach the mall, I'm not sure I'm even surprised to find Jude already waiting for me. Sitting alone at the same table as before, he turns a coffee cup around in his long, slim fingers, and that familiar prickle trails up the back of my neck as I approach. When he looks at me, it's with an expression that suggests he's heard terrible news. "I was wondering if you would turn up here."

"The burner phone died and I didn't remember your number," I reply awkwardly, still numb as I take a seat. "The only places I could think to look for you were here or the school parking lot, and I don't know if it's cloudy enough for you to be outside. I don't know how that works."

A smile flits across his face. "It's cloudy enough for me to get around, if I take certain precautions. But I don't generally like to risk it. Frankly, I ought to be asleep anyway."

This is actually a point I've always been curious about, and I might as well ask. "What happens if vampires don't sleep?"

His smile stretches until it's almost genuine. "They get tired."

I look at his hands, remembering the way those fingers felt on the bare skin of my waist. "I could have checked out the last place we saw each other, too, but I sort of figured that wasn't the best idea."

Jude actually flinches. "Listen, August, I'm sorry."

When he doesn't add anything more, I almost laugh. My friend is dead, my parents are missing, my surrogate grandmother might have accidentally joined a Corrupter cult, and my time is running out. "You're gonna have to be way more specific."

"I'm sorry that I kissed you," he answers, and he seems so sincere that I'm at a loss for words. "Given the circumstances, it was inappropriate. I know humans think all vampires are louche, amoral sociopaths who only care about satisfying our various needs, but that's not the case. At least, it's not for me. I should have shown better sense."

"It wasn't your fault," I finally manage. "I was . . ." My throat catches, the truth hidden by a scab that doesn't want to come off. "This thing, the Corrupter . . . it's getting closer to the surface—I can feel it now. And last night, when I had some of Gunnar's blood, I . . ." Focusing on the tabletop so he can't see the embarrassment in my eyes, I blurt, "I don't know how I did what I did, but I just wanted to feel happy. I wanted *everyone* to be happy, and I . . . made you feel that way. You wouldn't have done it if I hadn't been messing with your brain. I'm the one who's sorry."

"It's very noble of you to apologize," Jude says, tilting his head, "but you didn't make me feel anything. The Corrupter isn't known to plant thoughts in people's heads; he merely . . . calls forth what's already there. And even with you tugging at my desire to kiss you, as a vampire, I do have the ability to resist compulsion."

This is something I didn't know before, and I wonder if it has something to do with the fact that this thing inside me is the source of his talent for mesmerism—for plucking at people's memories and emotions, and guiding their will. But I don't know how many of the undead are even aware of their true origins. The Syndicate has officially written Azazel off as a myth, and if Ximena's witches are even remotely on the level, they are quite possibly the only beings on the planet old enough to know the truth.

Setting the coffee cup aside, Jude clears his throat. "I could have resisted, but I didn't want to."

I think back to the bright waves of golden bliss I drew from the crowd last night, the honesty of the emotions that poured through me. Jude *did* want to kiss me—almost as much as he wanted to kiss Gunnar—and I helped him forget his reasons not to. "Okay, well, I'm not sure what we're supposed to say here. I forgive you for kissing me if you forgive me for turning into a magical brain monster that made everybody horny. I was a mess—I'm always a mess—but that's not why I came looking for you."

"I see." He scratches at the tabletop. "If this is about what *else* happened at the party last night, rest assured that—"

"I want to take a blood oath to the Syndicate." I force the words out before I can swallow them forever, before I can think twice. He doesn't say anything, just stares at me with shocked eyes, until I add, "I mean, before the Ascension can happen."

"I know what you mean," Jude says softly, "but do you?"

"If I do this, it means I'm committed, right? Magically?" I try to remember what Daphne told me when I described my vision of Gunnar and the bowl of blood. "I make a promise that I can't break, even if . . . I die?"

"It means your body is bound to your word, so long as the same blood is in your veins," he answers, his brows knitting together with . . . concern? Suspicion? "It could potentially mean that you'd be indenturing the Corrupter to the Syndicate's whims. Forever."

"But the Syndicate doesn't want true immortality." I pick at my sleeves, my fingers shaking. "You told me all that stuff about severed heads and body parts living forever . . . and your whole *thing* is maintaining a balance between mortals and the undead, right? Punishing vampires who step out of line, and all that stuff?"

"I . . ." He struggles for a moment, rotating his coffee cup a little faster. "That's the mission statement at the moment, yes."

"All I want is for my parents to be safe," I whisper, my voice lumpier than oatmeal. "If there's no way to stop this thing, then I want to make sure it can't hurt anyone I care about. Rasputin killed Daphne last night, and he kidnapped my parents. If you can promise that the Syndicate will save them and protect them, then I'll take the oath." Tears heat my eyes and spill over. "I mean, let's be honest, you know? I'm not getting a happy ending. The best way this goes for me is I don't feel it when the end comes. But people I love will be left behind and I don't want them to suffer, either."

"August . . ." Jude looks away, and he pops the knuckles of his left hand. "Something you should understand is that no one actually knows what will happen to your body during the Ascension. You might keep your blood . . . and you might not. Even when humans are Turned, their bone marrow remains the same, and when reactivated, it continues producing enough red cells to keep them bound to the oaths they swore in life." Cocking his head, he adds, "But we don't know what's being introduced to your body, or what a change will look like. You might be transmuted into something else entirely."

"Oh, okay." I lick my lips, and my tongue is so dry I almost taste the sparks. "Thanks for making it sound so pants-shittingly cool."

"I'm sorry. What I'm trying to say is that a blood oath might not even work." His eyes are on his hands. "And you might not want it to."

"Um . . . what?"

"The only reason the Syndicate has ever cared about striking a balance is because, historically, we've risked annihilation every time we've grabbed for power. Vampires might be faster and stronger than humans, but we are drastically outnumbered, and our vulnerabilities—chiefly to fire and sunlight—make it hard for us to centralize our power." Hunching his shoulders, Jude scratches the tabletop more vigorously. "The reason the Syndicate is headquartered in the Carpathians isn't some silly homage to Vlad Dracula; it's strategy. The castle was built at a time when isolation, inaccessibility, and clear vantage points meant the difference between surviving through daylight hours and waking up engulfed in flames while delighted villagers watched us burn.

"In the age of satellite technology, we're more discoverable than ever. Targeted missiles, long-range bombs, aircraft . . . Militaries around the globe already have protocols in place for wiping us out when the opportunity presents itself." He lays his hands flat and leans closer. "Today, the only difference between life and death for the Syndicate is our reputation for stringently policing our own kind, enforcing regulations, and keeping humans as safe as possible."

It sounds an awful lot like a warning. "All the more reason for you to be in control of the Corrupter, right?"

"You don't understand." He speaks quietly, but with an edge sharp enough to cut my fingers on. "The kind of power the Corrupter promises . . . If the Syndics had *that* to share among their lineages, there would be no reason to maintain balance—no need to fear death at the hands of men, and no need to perform our cooperative submission."

Ice spreads through me. "So it was all a lie? All that stuff about the Syndicate not believing in the Corrupter and true immortality being a curse—"

"It wasn't a lie," he interrupts. "Myths of the Corrupter have been around forever, and there's way more fiction than fact out there. Besides that, the oldest Syndics have been alive since pre-Christian times, and they've never encountered the so-called Endless One." Jude shrugs, but it's a weak gesture. "Many of them don't want true immortality, but if this is really happening . . . it's a game-changer, August. Consensus won't matter anymore—and once word gets out, humans will employ their protocols against us, and that will make joining the ranks of the truly immortal a survival imperative for vampires everywhere."

"Oh." Who knew this situation could actually get worse? "So Daphne was right. Your whole plan all along was to get me into your secret lab so you could harvest the Corrupter when the time comes."

"No, that's not what I'm saying." He gives up an anguished groan, rubbing his face. "I was sent here to assess the situation and report back, period. My objective was to keep the situation from spiraling out of control, and to protect the Syndicate's interests from hostile parties. I wasn't . . . Last night was a big mistake." He makes an emphatic gesture with his hands. "I shouldn't be telling you any of this. It's a complete breach of my duties, and if Hecuba finds out—*when* she finds out . . ."

"Why *are* you telling me?" I need to know this as much as I need to know anything else.

"I don't want any of this," he declares flatly. "Neither does Hecuba. I meant everything I said about the horrors of true immortality, and no one can afford a world where unstable, unkillable vampires get to make all the rules. Anyone who sees a massive, overnight paradigm shift as a road to peace is a madman or a fool, and the catastrophe this could bring down on all our heads is unimaginable. We lobbied hard for me to get this assignment *because* we don't want any of this.

"The Syndicate isn't an elected body; it's an association of lineages represented by their progenitors, and each bloodline has its own agenda. Collectively, the Syndics want to maintain their influence over the world's undead . . . and some of them think the Corrupter could be a tool to that end. Hecuba is not so gullible. She knows that the Ascension poses a dire threat to everything she's spent her considerably long lifetime building, and her desire—our desire—is to see that the status quo is maintained." Leaning forward, he states, "I came to Fulton Heights hoping and believing this would be just another false alarm in centuries upon centuries of false alarms."

"But?" I prompt wearily.

"Do you know what syzygy is?" My blank look tells him I don't, so he fills me in. "It's an astronomical event, celestial bodies moving into alignment, and it can augur a tremendous focusing of power—just like the ley lines that intersect over Fulton Heights." Jude points upward, past the frosted glass of the dome ceiling above the food court. "Right now, Pluto, Uranus, Jupiter, and the moon are all moving into formation, and the way they're affecting the energy under the Nexus . . . I've never experienced anything like it."

"So the moon is in the seventh house, and Jupiter is aligned with Mars, and I'm about to get donkey-punched by the universe?" I summarize.

"I'm sorry." He looks helpless. For the first time since I encountered him outside the school like two weeks ago, he seems uncertain of his position. "I wish I knew some way to suppress the Corrupter, or alter his course."

"What *is* the Corrupter?" I ask quietly. I have Ximena's answer, and I have one from Jude as well . . . but I want to see if his has changed—if this is another thing that's been kept from me all along.

But what he says is: "I don't know. I'm sorry, August. There have been so many false accounts over the years, so many reasons to disbelieve the entire myth, that the Syndicate has long since given up on finding a concrete answer to that question at all."

"What if I took an oath to the Brotherhood of Perseus instead?" I don't know why I'm bringing it up with him, except that . . . who else do I have? "When they realize what happened to Daphne, they'll probably have someone else contact me. If I pledge myself to their cause, then it keeps the Corrupter's power out of the hands of *all* vampires."

"If the oath works," Jude reminds me cautiously, something

troubled lurking behind his expression. "And only if they don't have something else in mind."

The way he says it is so ominous I expect lightning to strike. "W-what else—"

"Truly, I've been trying to understand the Brotherhood's angle in this all along. Not to mince words, but even though you're human, you're also a threat to humanity—*the* threat." Jude drags a hand through his curls. "I assumed they had access to materials we didn't and were working on a way to divert the Ascension, or that maybe they were simply protecting you until the last possible moment, hoping for a miracle."

It is by the grace of God that I don't diarrhea myself as I supply, "*But?*"

"I haven't just been sitting on my hands these past weeks. When your art teacher tried to kill you, I took a deep dive into his background." He shifts his jaw. "Jesse T. Strauss was born in Richmond, Virginia—and died three months later from an undetected abnormality in his heart. The man who came to Fulton Heights using a deceased infant's name and social security number, and some expertly forged documents and professional references, was named Kyle Galloway. He was from old money in New England . . . and he became a Knight with the Brotherhood of Perseus when he was nineteen."

"That's . . . not possible." It doesn't even make sense. "If he'd been with the Brotherhood, Daphne would have known! Even if he went rogue and tried to ninja me to death on his own, they would have found out afterward!"

"Maybe they did," he suggests, too lightly. "Maybe they told her and she kept it from you, because she didn't want to shake your faith in the Knights' ability to protect you. But," Jude adds, his brow tensed, "someone set him up with that ID. The documents, the references, the deep cover . . . He was here for a year and a half. That would be hard to pull off without support."

"So what does *that* mean?" My stomach gurgles some more. "They sent him to watch me, too, and he decided to change the mission?"

Jude looks down at his hands, taking a moment to choose his words—a long moment—which makes what's left of my stomach curdle into cottage cheese. Finally, "Your tutor's name wasn't really Daphne Banks."

"Okay." I stay perfectly still, even though the entire mall capsizes.

"I mean, it makes sense," he adds cautiously, "since the Brotherhood seems to prefer false identities for Knights working undercover—but I couldn't find a paper trail for her at all. She wasn't a registered driver in the state of Illinois, she wasn't enrolled at Northwestern, and the car she was driving belonged to a ninety-six-year-old woman in Skokie who's been bedridden for three years." He shrugs in a performance of confusion. "Why would the Knights craft a detailed alter ego for one operative, and send the other out with . . . literally nothing?"

"Because she wasn't the one trying to get a job at a public high school." I can barely breathe the air I need to say the words. "She didn't need all that stuff."

"Maybe." Jude studies my face. "Or maybe Kyle Galloway isn't the one who went rogue."

24

It's the second time I've shoved myself up from this table, drawing attention from other people in the food court. "You don't know what you're talking about. No matter what her name was, Daphne saved my life!"

"That's exactly what I mean," Jude says, getting to his feet as well. "I'm sorry to put it like this, but the most obvious way to protect humankind from the Corrupter is to kill the vessel." His tone is modulated, careful. "She knew that. If your body dies before he can Ascend, his time on Earth is over for a generation."

He peters off awkwardly, and the silence between us is made from barbed wire. It's not like I hadn't considered this same issue—I even asked Daphne herself about it. But Rasputin intervened before I ever got my answer.

If Daphne and Mr. Strauss were both with the Brotherhood of Perseus, then one of them wasn't following orders; and if Jude's telling me the truth, then only my art teacher's background is confirmed. Meanwhile, I can't even prove Daphne was who she said she was when I first found out she *wasn't* who she said she was. Why would she have protected me, saved my life three times, and finally died so I could escape Rasputin, if she worked for an organization that wanted me dead? And if she didn't work for them . . . *who was she*?

Jude rubs his jaw, stretching out his long, elegant throat, and I stare at it. A few centuries ago, human and terrified, he decided that vampirism was the least of two dire fates—better undead than just *dead*. My pulse is going berserk, my skin hot and cold at once.

If I die, the Corrupter dies with me . . . but what if I *come back*?

"What happens if I Turn?" I ask before I lose my nerve. This isn't even something I'm sure I want—to live like Jude or Gunnar; to figure out how to break the news to my parents. But I don't want to die. "We could stop the Ascension, and I wouldn't have to—"

"No, August." Jude stares, eyes filled with pity. "I'm sorry, but I . . . I can't."

"Why not?" I'm fighting the urge to scream it.

"For one thing, the Syndicate has strict rules about that. I'd need their approval—and I won't get it, specifically because of their conflicting views on the Corrupter. And if I do it anyway . . . well, there are, in fact, fates worse than death, and those of us who don't die easily can suffer the worst of them." Jude shakes his head and gives me a beseeching look. "You don't really know what you're asking, August. You'd never see the sun again, you'd never see your parents. Eventually, you'd bury them, along with everyone else you know and love." He sits back down heavily. "Gunnar wanted to Turn, too, you know. His life was dismal, and I couldn't say no to him, even though I knew it was a mistake. And look how that turned out. He hates me now, and sooner or later, so would you."

My voice is almost too rough to pass through my throat. "All I ever wanted was to get out of high school so I could live a normal life, like everyone else."

"I'm sorry." His expression is sincere, beautiful. "You know, Gunnar's not the only one who remembers what it's like to be

229

mortal—who misses it. Everything is new: your first kiss, your first dance, your first time reading Emily Dickinson or trying foreign cuisine . . . It's intoxicating and exciting." He gazes out across the food court. "It's what got me in trouble when I met him. I fell for Gunnar so hard, and Hecuba blew an absolute gasket when she found out I'd become involved with a mortal while out on assignment."

"What happened between you two?" I ask, because I've got nothing to lose by being nosy at this point.

"Everything. Nothing." Jude gives a listless shrug, lost in the past. "It's all so hopelessly tangled now. But in the beginning, it was like seeing the world again for the first time." He looks back at me again. "That's what I want. Not a world where vampires and humans battle each other until the subjugation of one or the extinction of the other; not a world where the *only* alternative to a horrific end is a deathless existence until the end of time. I like the world." He shrugs with an open, helpless smile. "And I liked kissing you. If we'd met under different circumstances, it could have been fun. Not the kind that would get me in trouble with Hecuba, but the kind where we would have kissed again. Maybe a lot."

No matter what happens, tonight is about us. I'm running out of time for that future memory to take place, and I still don't know what it means. Was it ever even real?

"Rasputin has my parents, and one way or another, I'm going to save them. If I have to take an oath to the Order of the Northern Wolf, then so be it," I declare. It's a stupid threat to make. The Syndicate might disagree internally about whether the Ascension should be celebrated, but Jude wants to stop it, and he's already divulged the only effective plan he's got. "I have until Thursday to decide."

Jude studies my face, and I school my features into a deadpan glare. I don't think he believes I'll go through with it—my poker face is bullshit—but he gives me a nod anyway. "I'll see what I can find out about Rasputin's operation and where your parents might be. Give me a day or two, and we can talk about a plan to rescue them."

It takes me a moment to realize what he's saying. "Just like that?"

"Unfortunately, no." He rises to his feet again with a funerary air. "I had to report last night's attack to the Syndicate. It was a serious breach of our protocols, and they'd have learned of it regardless. They're sending reinforcements, and in a matter of days I'll lose the advantage of being able to make decisions and justify them later." His eyes travel over my face, my lips, and he looks away. "Hecuba wants to bury the Corrupter forever—even as a rumor, it's caused nothing but trouble. Supposing you died, August . . . all it would do is reset the same conditions. She hasn't given up on looking for some way to stop him permanently, and I haven't, either. I'll do everything I can, for as long as I can, to keep you from having to make this choice. You have my word."

With a final, sober nod, he turns and leaves me at the table, disappearing from view while I try to figure out if I've just moved forward or backward.

It looks like the Brotherhood actually wants me dead, and that Daphne defied them by protecting me. It's chilling, because even if I can't figure out why, I'm less safe than ever now that she's gone. Conversely, Hecuba apparently wants a way to stop the Corrupter that goes beyond just executing me like vessels of yore—and as one of the original Syndics, she clearly has a lot of influence. That doesn't mean she cares about keeping me alive, of course, or that a way to thread that particular needle even exists . . . but at least she doesn't want me dead. Yet.

The chair beside me scrapes the floor as someone joins me at the table, and when I look up, I freeze all the way to my marrow. A familiar face, a familiar voice, a familiar smile. "Thank God; I thought he would never leave."

My lungs constrict, fear stretching its sharp claws in my chest. I push away instinctively, and she closes a hand over my wrist, her grip enough to bring me to a trembling standstill. I refuse to believe my eyes. I won't. "*No . . .*"

"Don't lose your shit, Auggie," Daphne says with an amused look. "You should know by now that I'm not going to hurt you."

Riveted in place, I just stare at her, aware of nothing but the pressure of her confident grip—of that telltale whispering sensation that never went away when Jude departed. Her features are off somehow, her cheeks a little sharper and her hair a darker shade of blond, but it's unmistakably Daphne Banks. And she is unmistakably a vampire.

"What did he d-do to you?" I barely get the question out, my insides rioting, all my fluids wanting out by their most convenient possible exits.

"You mean Rasputin?" Daphne gives a derisive snort, rolling her eyes. "*Please.* He got lucky because I was pulling my punches. If you'd run when I told you to"—she gives me a reproachful look—"we wouldn't even be sitting here right now. His pathetic, three-card-monte ass would be a pile of bones."

"You're a vampire," I whisper.

"Okay, Auggie, I'm really sorry to have to do this, but I need you to calm down so you can hear me out." Daphne looks me in the eye, gold light shimmering across her irises—and just like that, she's in my head.

It's as familiar as her scent, the delicate way she plucks at my thoughts, a harpist searching for the sweetest notes; and a bottleneck forms where I fight against the bliss she wants to let into my body. This is what I did to the crowd last night—this is what Jude said he could have withstood if he'd wanted to. And as the pressure builds, a tranquil happiness spreading wide and waiting to envelop me, I understand why Jude gave in to it.

When I stop fighting, the tension floods out of me in an instant. Even as my heart rate slows, my body relaxing with a rush of dopamine, I know this is all false. I'm being manipulated, but I don't care, because for the first time all day I'm finally not drowning in terrified misery. Taking a breath, Daphne exclaims, "Wow! That was some impressive resistance, mister. Pretty soon, I bet tricks like that won't work on you at all."

"You had vampire blood in your system." The noise in my brain quiet at last, I'm thinking things through. I remember the capsules she forced into my mouth after we hit the tree—when my shoulder was almost certainly broken, and my only hope for recovery and escape was to borrow power from the undead. If she'd done the same for herself, to boost her strength, and then she died . . .

"It takes vampirism twenty-four hours to gestate," Daphne interrupts my thoughts patiently. "Or thereabouts, depending on where you are. Sundown to sundown, anyway." Gesturing at the domed skylight above us, the panes a bleak gray-white from the cloud cover, she notes, "And the sun's not down yet."

I take a breath, and finally just ask the question. "Who are you?"

"Just so you know, this isn't how I wanted to have this conversation," she begins apologetically. "I mean, there was never going to be a 'good' way to get this out in the open, but I'd at least hoped for better circumstances than these. Hell, I did my best to *plan* better circumstances, but . . . well . . ." Daphne squares her shoulders and meets my eyes again. "Auggie, my name was never Daphne Banks. That was an alias I adopted so I could get closer to you—closer to *him*. My real name is Viviane Duclos."

25

The universe whirls, a mad carnival ride with us at its axis, and I hold tight to my chair to keep from being thrown clear. With one move, she's shaken out the past, forcing everything into a new alignment. Rigidly, I croak, "That's not possible."

Viviane Duclos—official cult leader of the League of the Dark Star. Jude's ominous words go on a military parade through my brain: *A powerful French sorceress . . . notorious for her cunning . . . if Duclos wants you in her grasp, she's had since the sixteen hundreds to devise countless ways to manage it.*

"I'm sorry." She almost looks sincere. "The truth is, we were never supposed to get to this point. You were never supposed to know me as anyone other than your math tutor—and after the Rising, I would be here, waiting for the Dark Star."

She looks dreamily into the distance, and I try to understand how this familiar face could be someone I never knew. It seems silly to feel hurt in this moment by the pettiest of her deceptions, but I can't help it. My voice dripping with accusations, I state, "You told me you were with the Brotherhood. You said you were here to protect me."

"Two points," she begins, holding up as many fingers. "First,

I *am* here to protect you. I didn't get into a swordfight and throw hands with Rasputin just to sell a cover story, you know. Keeping you alive is half the reason I'm here at all."

"Yeah, so I can keep incubating the Angel of Death for you," I shoot back.

"Would you have rather I let your art teacher chop your head off?" She arches a brow, offering no reaction to my knowledge of the Corrupter's true origins. "Anyway, Jude Marlowe was the one who brought up the Brotherhood, not me. I saw you two sitting together, and I panicked—I didn't want him to seduce you and kidnap you off to Transylvania, so I intervened. When he accused me of being a Knight, I went with it, because it was the easiest explanation." She flops back in her seat, disgruntled. "I knew the Syndicate would send someone, and I should have figured it would be Marlowe, with his puppy dog eyes and slick vibe. They went straight for your hormones. Predictable."

"And you didn't?" I counter, glad at least that the spell she has me under disguises how vulnerable I feel right now. "Or do you seriously want me to think it's a coincidence that you sent a gorgeous surfer boy to work at my favorite café?"

"Gunnar Larsen, that horny little dipshit." Daphne—*Viviane*—pinches the bridge of her nose. "I want you to know that he was never supposed to approach you. His job was to watch you when I couldn't, and that's all. I didn't even know the two of you had seen each other outside of Sugar Mama's until you told me he'd been at that fucking party last night! Believe me, when I see him again, he's going to get my entire foot up his ass."

I blink a few times, my throat closing up as I whisper, "I thought you were my friend."

"Oh, Auggie." Viviane Duclos clasps her hands together and gives me an abject look, her eyes genuinely sad. "This whole thing got so much more complicated than I ever imagined. I've been chasing the Dark Star for almost three hundred and fifty years, and when I started planning for the Ascension, you were just a footnote in an ancient book—a vessel to be born at a particular time, bearing particular markers." She shakes her head. "I'm sure it won't mean anything to you to hear this now, given where we are, but . . . I *am* your friend. Or I was. I only came to Fulton Heights to find the Corrupter, but I found you, too. And I'm honestly glad."

"That makes one of us." It's a pitiful comeback, but I've got nothing else to fight with.

Viviane nods with resignation. "I wish you could understand. Not everything was a lie. My parents really were hunters—pretending to be Brotherhood was an easy charade, because my father was a Persean Knight in the seventeenth century. So were my brothers. I'd have joined, too, except they wouldn't accept women back then." A flinty look passes across her eyes. "My sister was married off to some grotesque merchant, a man twice her age with a face like a potato—and while my brothers were out swinging swords and riding for glory, I was learning needlepoint so I could become some old man's hausfrau, pooping out babies one after another until I died from it.

"It wasn't a great time for women with aspirations—but I was lucky to be considered attractive, and lucky that my family was respected, because it meant my parents had the connections to send me to Paris." Viviane makes a face. "Mortals have so many hang-ups about sex, but honestly? Being a courtesan was great. I had to be able to read and write, which meant I received an education, and for the first time I was the master of my own person."

"Until you ended up on death row."

"No one ever taught me how to use magic." Her eyes are on mine, but her focus is somewhere in the past. "I discovered my talent for sorcery when I was fifteen, but I hid it from everyone, because it would have meant a one-way ticket to the gallows. Still, it was impossible to resist." She waves a hand in front of her face, and the air ripples, her complexion turning rosy, the shape of her cheeks augmenting before my eyes. Suddenly, she's Daphne again, exactly as I remember her. "My element is wood, which means my natural gifts include glamours, shape-shifting, and speed. At court, I read palms and told fortunes—and I tricked a lot of wealthy clients into believing they were being visited by the spirits of their departed loved ones.

"What I didn't know was that magic is like a pond, and touching it sends ripples in every direction." She mimics the motion with her fingers. "The analogy isn't perfect, but you get the gist. Basically, every time I pulled my little act, I was sending out a homing beacon to other sorcerers—until, finally, I was confronted by a rather powerful woman who ran a black-market operation selling dark magic and killings for hire to influential Parisians. I could either buy into her network or be publicly denounced as a witch."

"An offer you couldn't refuse."

"And I ended up on death row anyway." Viviane Duclos laughs at the very notion. "I never wanted to be a vampire until I was about to be hanged as a witch. When Erasmus Kramer came to my cell . . . well, *that* was an offer I couldn't refuse."

I give a distant nod—thinking of the proposition I made to Jude only minutes ago.

"While at court, I met the occasional undead, and I realized that the scary stories I'd heard growing up in a Brotherhood household were mostly nonsense." She shrugs. "Anyway, Erasmus had heard of me through mutual friends, knew what I could do, and . . . well, maybe he had a little crush. Either way, he offered me an escape, and more power than I could ever dream of, if I joined his cause."

"So you did." I sound absurdly reasonable. "Did you even believe in the Corrupter?"

"Not then, but it didn't matter," she says. "Kramer's group was small, and a shape-shifting sorceress whose glamours could disguise them and shield them from Sensitives was better to have around than another true believer."

"So that's how you kept me from being able to tell you and Gunnar were vampires."

"To be honest, Auggie, I'm still patting myself on the back for that, because I wasn't even sure it would work!" A goofy, conspiratorial grin splits her face, and I have to fight the instinct to smile with her. "Glamours aren't true transformations, just an interference with the field of perception." She waves one hand over the other, the air rippling, and I watch the varnish on her nails turn from black to red to silver. "It's essentially a smoke screen, and your access to the Dark Star's power is deepening every day. No matter how gifted I am, there's no way I could keep him from recognizing one of his own children forever."

My hands go still. "So you know who the Corrupter really is."

"Yes." Viviane hesitates. "I met Azazel once, Auggie—face-to-face. It was in France, more than a hundred years after I was supposed to die, and it changed everything." Her tone becomes hushed, even rapturous. "He knew me, knew everything *about* me. He said I had a destiny that . . . Well, it was the moment that my commitment to the League stopped being about repaying Erasmus and started being about something much bigger."

"That's why you want a global vampire takeover, and a . . . a deathless existence until the end of time?" I glare at Viviane Duclos, wishing I still needed my glasses so I could take them off and make Daphne's face disappear. "For your *destiny*?"

"No, Auggie." She frowns peevishly. "Believe it or not, aside from the Syndicate's relentless power-tripping, the League is pretty okay with the status quo. If you spent time with Gunnar, you know that the only thing he wants is to go surfing again and flirt with boys on the beach—to live normally. We don't want humans corralled into farms, and we definitely don't want hell on Earth. In fact, we seem to be the only ones who *don't* want that.

"Take a look around." She gestures broadly at the mall and everything beyond it. "Against all odds, human beings lucked into a complex nervous system and a sense of self-awareness, the ability to learn—opposable fucking thumbs!—and what are you doing with those gifts? You're poisoning your own planet! This dumb, blue ball rolling around all alone in the Milky Way has the precise and inexpressibly rare conditions necessary to foster life, and mortals are doing everything they can to destroy it." She slaps a hand down on the tabletop, her eyes flashing. "You flood your air with deadly chemicals, dump trash into the oceans, and bring back diseases that killed millions when I was still alive!

"Humans are a menace. No matter how many warnings your ancestors left you in your unending piles of history books, you're all determined to make their same catastrophic mistakes and learn those lessons the hard way." With an agitated flick of her wrist, she withdraws the Daphne glamour, her cheekbones regaining their dramatic angle. "There are no mortals left on the planet with a living memory of World War I, and even now, as the last veterans of World War II die off, your governments are reenacting all the same conditions that led up to it. The 'war to end all wars,' or so we once thought." Her eyes track the Sunday shoppers crossing the food court. "Humans are born with a self-destruct button and an itchy trigger finger, and you can't wait to damn us all to hell."

"You're . . ." I try to make sense of what she's saying. "This is an environmental thing?"

"Everything is environmental!" she exclaims, tossing out her hands. "How are any of us supposed to carry on if you all fuck up the climate so bad you starve to death, or resurrect some mutated strain of smallpox you can't stop?" A fly circles Jude's abandoned coffee cup, and Viviane waves it away. "Your leaders know what they're doing, and they don't care, because they're greedy—and because a hundred years from now they'll be gone anyway, and it'll be someone else who reaps the whirlwind. It'll be *us*."

I squint at her a little. "Just so I have this straight, your endgame is . . . solar panels?"

"Our endgame is *no end*," Viviane replies with passion. "The League of the Dark Star wants a future where life continues to flourish, side by side with the undead. What we want is nothing more or less than peace on Earth—a new age, where vampires don't have to hide, and mortals can't wreck everything we all depend on." She curls her hands into fists. "Humans are incompetent stewards of this planet, and they can't be trusted to run it any longer. If you *truly* value the life you have, Auggie, then the League of the Dark Star is your one hope."

My mouth is dry from the tips of my teeth to the pit of my stomach, because for the first time? Someone is making a case for my cooperation that isn't predicated solely on how much worse the world will be if I make the wrong choice—but on how much *better* the world could be if I make the right one. And I don't know if I have an argument against what she's saying. In a wobbly voice, I manage to ask, "Why me? Why is this happening to me?"

"I don't think there's an answer to that question." Her expression is genuinely torn. "The only thing the Risings we know of have in common is that, in each case, the vessel was someone destined for greatness. Kings and queens, warriors and intellectuals . . . names you would recognize if I told them to you."

"I'm only sixteen," I say, my eyes filming over. All I want, I think, is someone to acknowledge how unfair this is. Someone to tell me that I don't deserve it.

"When she was sixteen years old, Elizabeth Tudor had been declared illegitimate and stripped of her claim to the English throne. No one ever dreamed that she would go on to become one of history's most well-known rulers," Viviane rebuts. "Catherine the First of Russia was a housemaid, Joan of Arc was a peasant, Vincent van Gogh was an emo kid and a dropout . . . You've got no idea what sort of greatness waits inside of you!"

"And I never will, either." It's a challenge, but she doesn't rise to it.

"You might be the key to saving this planet for future generations, Auggie. You could easily be the most important historical figure of all time." Her expression is deadly serious. "I don't know what's going to become of Auggie Pfeiffer after the Ascension. I kind of hope you'll still be in there, because, believe it or not, I really do like you. You're the little brother I wished I had, back when I had little brothers and all of them were assholes. That probably doesn't mean anything to you right now, but it's the truth." She pushes a hand through the soft waves of her hair. "Regardless of anything else, if you commit yourself to the League of the Dark Star, you'll be saving the world. We don't want bloodshed; we want peace. We want a reality where mortals and vampires can be neighbors instead of enemies."

"Vampires *eat* mortals."

"You guys murder each other all the time!" she protests. "You need to have active shooter drills for your kindergarteners, for fuck's sake. Dogs kill more people each year than vampires do, but nobody makes sad Sarah McLachlan commercials about *us*."

"Azazel wants to turn Earth into his kingdom, like Lucifer did with hell."

"Azazel wants *dominion*," she counters. "Humans were given

dominion over the Earth, and they're doing a spectacularly shitty job of caring for it. But if you swear a blood oath to the League, we can make sure past mistakes are corrected. Before it's too late."

"If I still have the same blood," I answer. Then, "Besides, Azazel is an angel, right? What makes you think some puny little spell is going to make him do your bidding for eternity, anyway?"

"It's not about 'doing my bidding.'" Viviane frowns. "He wants a better world—he told me so himself when we met, and he said I had a part to play in it. It's just . . ." She flings out a hand, rolling her eyes again. "That was over two hundred years ago. Rasputin claims to have met Azazel in his last incarnation, and to have received some sort of benediction from him or whatever. It's all bullshit, of course, the guy is *not* dealing with a full deck. But . . . I can't leave anything to chance. The moment the Ascension occurs, I need to be able to look the Corrupter in the eye and know he remembers what he said to me. A blood oath binds people as tightly as family, and I need him to feel that."

"Rasputin has my family," I blurt, the words hurting my ears.

Her eyes widen and then close, and she curses. "That son of a bitch. I should have just killed him when I had the chance."

"He gave me five days to pledge myself to the Northern Wolf." I'm desperate enough by now that my next statement comes out with no trouble at all. "If you save them before that, I'll . . . I'll swear an oath to the League."

"I see," she murmurs, studying me shrewdly. "That could possibly be done. We don't know where Rasputin's headquartered himself, so we'd have to do some reconnaissance. We'd have to find out where your parents are, and how they're being guarded. We'd need manpower . . . It wouldn't be an easy operation." Her jaw shifts minutely. "Take the oath first, and you've got a deal."

Tears blur my vision. "If I take an oath to you, and he finds out—

which he totally will, because you said magic is a pond, and ripples and beacons and whatever the fuck else—he'll kill them!"

"If you commit to the League, not only will you earn all of our loyalty and all of our resources, but vampires around the world will jump at the chance to take down Rasputin and earn your favor. Even some of his own acolytes." She folds her hands together in her lap. "I know this isn't what you want to hear, and I'm sorry for taking advantage of a bad situation—but together we have a chance to make this the best of all possible worlds, Auggie. You just have to trust me."

26

I won't pretend my feet are steady as I walk away from Viviane Duclos and the offer she's placed on the table . . . even though I haven't declined it yet. My parents' lives in exchange for my body's endless servitude to an apocalypse cult is an arrangement that's terrifying, overwhelming—and *final*. Once I say yes, it is literally the beginning of the end, and no matter how badly I want to save my mom and dad, I'm not sure I'm ready for that. I'm not sure I'll ever be ready. But as I make my way to the Colgate Center's exit, I struggle to find even the smallest sign of something better to hope for.

You just have to trust me. What if Daphne/Viviane isn't lying—this time? I know Gunnar was being honest about his desire to live alongside humans, because I saw the truth of it when I was inside his head at the rave, so maybe saving the world really is the League's agenda. At least, after a fashion. No matter what, the vision she described is way better than what Jude foretold if the Syndicate gains control, and it's certainly better than what would happen if I give in to Rasputin's demands.

So maybe that's what my vision of Gunnar and the bowl of blood was about. Maybe I'm already destined to take the oath, to commit myself—whatever "myself" is in the approaching days—to Viviane's cause. Maybe my free will is an illusion, and all of this is already written out in a prophesy no one's discovered yet.

I'm so preoccupied with my thoughts that I'm not even aware of the man behind me as I push through the exit, until he catches the door before it can shut—and I don't take any special notice of the woman who gets to her feet from a bench outside the mall's entrance as soon as I emerge. I don't think about either of them until a second man steps directly in my path, and when I go to move around him, I find myself flanked on either side.

"August Pfeiffer." His hair is salt-and-pepper, and he isn't asking my name—he's telling me. "You're coming with us."

The man on my left and the woman on my right close in until they're touching my elbows, until a focused pressure against my rib cage from either side lets me know what it feels like to have a gun pressed up against you. My head spins. "You're with the Brotherhood, aren't you?"

"We are the ones sworn to protect humanity against the inhuman scourge," he reports in a tone devoid of emotion. "We are humankind's first and last line of defense against darkness and the creatures of the night." The man steps closer, one hand stuffed in his coat pocket—and the way it's pointing at my stomach makes me pretty sure that everybody brought a gun to the gunfight except for me. "I don't know how much of you remains August Pfeiffer, but I'm speaking to him right now. The entity that is inside of you is a threat to every mortal being on the planet, and it must be stopped."

"You're going to kill me." This isn't the first time I've faced death in the past couple of weeks, but surprisingly enough, it hasn't gotten any easier. The moisture that belongs in my mouth is making an icy streak down my back.

"If you live, the world dies," the woman on my right declares, her voice startlingly soft. "And we cannot let that happen."

"We are well past the point of caution." Salt-and-Pepper's eyes darken. "So if you resist, you die here, in spite of potential witnesses. But if you come with us, we will give you a chance to prepare messages for your loved ones."

Nothing about their guns suggests they're bluffing, and if I cooperate, at least I'll get a chance to say goodbye to my parents. At least I'll stay alive for a few more minutes. I nod my agreement, because I don't trust myself to speak, and the whole time I'm counting my breaths. How many more do I get to take? How much more time do I have to enjoy the smell of fresh air and the color pink?

I expect them to shove me into a van, to take me to a reservoir or an abandoned building, and so my panic redoubles when they lead me only thirty feet away—to a metal door set in the side of the mall, propped ajar with a stone. It opens into an unadorned corridor of painted concrete—a hidden part of the shopping center meant only for employees to use—and before we can encounter another human being, they hustle me through a second door and into a disused storeroom.

The space is confined, reeking of fresh paint, the walls lined by empty shelving units—and when I realize that this is it, the end of the line, my legs won't support me and I sink to my knees. I've never seen a gun so close-up before. It occurs to me to try and get inside Salt-and-Pepper's head, to see what I can do about exerting my influence on his free will; but somehow, I can't. He's protected by armor even stronger than Gunnar's.

"If you have any messages to impart, now's the time," the man says impatiently, my execution just another item on his to-do list.

The woman has her weapon pointed at my temple, and the second man—a sweaty guy in glasses—licks his lips nervously. "Let's just get this over with."

"Where are your swords?" I ask, because as long as I'm talking, it's a little more time to enjoy being on the razor's edge of explosive diarrhea. Won't they be surprised. "The last guy tried to kill me with a sword. I thought that was your thing."

"We use ceremonial weapons when we can, as tribute to our legacy, but they are impractical," Salt-and-Pepper informs me, attaching a silencer to his gun. "Clearly, it was a mistake to allow Galloway—your Mr. Strauss—the discretion to make that choice. We will not be so careless." He aims the barrel of his weapon at my forehead, and a choked whine squeezes from my throat. "If you have goodbyes to say, now is the time."

"Something's not . . ." The sweaty guy shifts his weight, glancing nervously around the small room. "I don't think we're alone, you guys."

I don't even want to allow myself any hope . . . but as he says it, a familiar whispering sensation passes across my skin.

"What are you talking about?" The woman asks, just as something moves in my peripheral vision: a small, gray mouse emerging from a narrow hole in the wall. It looks right at me, the whisper against my skin becoming a roar, and then it streaks forward. Leaping up, it erupts into a cloud of smoke that expands, unfurls, and reforms almost instantly into a very familiar shape, all before the armed Knights have a chance to react.

"Surprise!" Viviane Duclos announces cheerfully, her eyes a bright gold, her fingers extended into sharp ivory claws. With a blow from the back of her hand, she sends the sweaty guy flying across the tiny room, slamming into one of the shelving units with so much force the metal buckles and the cinder block behind it cracks; in the same fluid motion, she slashes open the woman's throat, blood geysering into the air. Salt-and-Pepper manages to fire at her once before she's snapping all the bones in his wrist, spinning him around and bending his head backward so that his neck is bared to her teeth.

Three whole seconds haven't even passed, and I'm still trying to process what's just happened as Salt-and-Pepper struggles to speak through his twisted windpipe. "Even if you kill us, you can't stop the Brotherhood of Perseus. More will come in our place!"

"I certainly hope so, love," Viviane purrs. "I'm starving."

"Wait!" I gasp, struggling onto feet that don't want to support me, shocked my underwear is still dry. "D-don't kill him!"

"Never show your enemy a mercy they wouldn't show you, Auggie." Viviane doesn't take her eyes off the jumping pulse in the man's exposed neck. "The first thing this man will do if I let him live is help the Brotherhood organize their next move against you. They'll know what pressures you respond to—and they'll know who I am and what I'm capable of." Salt-and-Pepper tries to say something, but she forces his head back farther, cutting off his air. "I'd like them to underestimate me for as long as possible."

"Daphne," I begin, because it's still the first name that comes to me, but I stop when I realize my mistake, startled out of my own train of thought.

"I promised I'd protect you, and I meant it." Her gaze meets mine over the writhing man's jugular, and despite the new angles to her face, I still see someone I know. I still see someone who cares about me—even if she cares more about the Corrupter. "Consider my offer, okay?" Her voice is calm, even as she holds a man pinioned so she can plunge her teeth into his throat. "And watch your back."

She waits until I've shoved my way out into the service corridor to start feeding, and the door clicks shut behind me on the man's dying screams.

The rest of the day passes like the unending moment in a car accident just before impact—a taffy pull of time filled with nightmares. I return to the food court, drinking one coffee after another, afraid to leave again before dark. The Brotherhood has already tried to kill me twice, and even if Viviane thinks she's delayed a third attempt, she could be wrong. For all I know, when Salt-and-Pepper fails to report in, another team will be on its way before sundown—ready to break my door down and slaughter me in my kitchen.

It takes forever for the sun to drop, the sky going gray and then black before I take my first hesitant steps outside. I feel the vampires watching me, my skin alive with whispers, and it's the strangest sort of comfort.

I don't even know if I want to go home, if I can face a night alone under my own roof—worrying about my parents, hoping that vampires I've never invited inside can protect me from home invaders—but the alternative is bringing my troubles to someone else's door. Ximena says she can protect herself . . . but can she protect *both* of us from the Syndicate, two cults, a group of gun-wielding Knights, and some ancient sorceresses? If either one us of woke up dead in the morning, Adriana would never forgive me.

Of course, figuring out where to go is the absolute least of my troubles. I'm running out of time, and I refuse to spend what I've got left just looking for the best hole to crawl into while I wait for the end. Maybe I can't save myself . . . but I won't go without a fight. I won't go without doing everything I can to at least save the people I love.

My house is fully dark when I pull up on my bike, because I didn't know to leave any lights on, and it already looks abandoned. I'm jumpy and nauseous as I hurry up the drive, rattled by a day of terrible revelations and missed meals, anxious to stash my bike in the garage and get inside where there are knives and locking doors. The police are useless against vampires, but if Knights broke in, maybe the police could help. If they got here in time.

"Auggie?" The voice comes from the shadows on the porch, and

I nearly blast out of my skin. So far I can read minds, sense vampires, and see the future, but the destroying angel inside me doesn't seem to come with any defensive capabilities.

Before I can start running—or dying—my visitor emerges from the darkness, and I relax just enough to start breathing again. "Gunnar?"

"I hope it's okay that I'm here?" He descends from the porch and stops, moonlight making art out of his dramatic bone structure, his plush lips. I hate how attractive I find him in spite of his duplicity, how little I regret kissing him—even if I'm going to die having only kissed liars, at least they were good at it. "Because if it isn't—"

"I guess you're the one she sent to guard the house tonight," I remark, punching in the garage code. We're surrounded by vampires, though, and Gunnar is still the only one I know that doesn't leave a mark.

"I asked for the assignment," he says quietly, his eyes on my feet. "She's not my biggest fan right now, but she figured you were entitled to an explanation—if you want one. If you'd rather not have me around, she can send someone else."

He says it like the League is doing me a favor—and I guess they are. Whatever their reasons, we all want to keep me alive. And there comes a point at which the number of people lying to you and plotting your demise becomes farcical, and holding a grudge against just one of them in particular is more work than pleasure.

"I guess if I need a babysitter, it's better to have one whose brain I've poked around in." I try to sound like I don't really care as I step into the empty garage—but my insides are knotted up so badly I'm not sure I'll ever get them untangled. I'm overjoyed that I won't have to be alone, that there'll be somebody in the house to protect me after all. At the same time, I'm hurt and angry for a host of reasons I can't even articulate.

I hold open the connecting door, and Gunnar moves past me, his scent on the breeze behind him. In spite of everything, warmth spreads through me, and I grit my teeth before I follow him into the house, full of emotions that won't make friends with each other.

He still knows things he hasn't told me, and I'm going to find out what they are.

27

I've never been alone like this before, I realize, as I rummage the fridge for something to eat. The whole house is mine—maybe for the rest of my life. I could drink my parents' wine, walk around naked, and do whatever I want until I'm either killed or expunged from my own body. I'm shoveling some sort of pasta leftovers into my face, eating so fast I can't even taste them, when I grunt, "You said you had explanations."

"I didn't grow up in a time or place where it was okay to be gay," he starts, sitting on one of the stools by the front window. "I didn't even know the word for it then—I just knew that if there *was* a word, I could never, ever use it, because people got killed for being what I was. So every time I felt something for another guy, I ripped it out and buried it. One chunk at a time, I created this huge void inside of me, and it hurt, and I hated myself.

"And then one day . . . Jude showed up." He gives his lucky necklace an instinctive tug. "It was the first time another guy had looked at me the way I looked at other guys. It was like . . . I'd been living in a house with a locked door, and then one day I found the key and discovered my house was twice as big as I'd thought it was." Gunnar shakes his head. "That doesn't even begin to describe it. All the parts

I'd torn out of myself? The first time Jude touched me, they slammed back into place and I felt complete for the first time in my life."

"Very romantic," I offer around a mouthful of food, because I can't tell what this has to do with all the lying and dying stuff yet.

"It wasn't romantic," Gunnar returns somberly. "It was . . . scary. I'd only been living half a life for sixteen years, suppressing something that I couldn't deal with. And when I couldn't do that anymore, I didn't know what *to* do. I didn't even know who I was. Do you understand what I mean?"

"I think so. Maybe." I put the pasta down. The truth is, I'm not sure I *do* understand. I know what it's like to be lonely, but that's not the same as being lonely and having to pretend to be something I'm not at the same time. When I figured out I was gay, I didn't stay in the closet for long, because I knew my parents would accept me.

"Suddenly I had all these feelings, and no practice for how to handle them. And then Jude told me he had to leave, and I just . . . I broke down, because him leaving meant ripping everything back out again, going back to the way it had been, and I just, I *couldn't.*" He looks up at me, twisting his necklace like he intends to strangle himself. "Once I knew what it felt like to *feel*, how could I stop? How could I go back into hiding and just . . . waiting to die? So I begged him to Turn me, to let me go with him."

Much of this story is still caught in my memory as well. "And he said yes."

"Eventually." Gunnar smiles at the memory, but his eyes are sad. "I thought I was in love with him. I mean, I did fall in love with him—but later. It took me decades to realize that half of what I felt for Jude was really just . . . loving myself for the first time." He looks away from me again, as if embarrassed. "Being in love with *loving.* It was such a relief to finally not have to be afraid of my feelings anymore, and because he was the first one I was ever with as the real,

253

complete *me*, all my emotions got tangled together. I'm sorry, I'm not putting this as clearly as I want to."

He looks abashed, but I'm starting to get it. The thrill and the tension that went through me when the two of them kissed at the rave, that feeling like flying a kite on a stormy day . . . I'm beginning to understand what it meant. "And then you guys broke up."

"It was a long time coming, and it wasn't easy," he says quietly. "But I needed time to tell my feelings apart. I needed to know what it was like to be me, by myself, without hiding. And no matter how much Jude loved being part of the Syndicate, I never fit in. I was always Jude's pet to them, and I needed a clean break."

"Is that when you went to Iceland?" I gesture at the necklace, his memory flashing across my mind, the dark sand of the beach and the cold wind.

"Yes." He looks down at the stone in his fingers, and finally releases it. "It's also when I met Viviane. She was after some carving from the Viking days, a fragment of a Corrupter prophecy, and our paths crossed. It was sort of inevitable, because it's not a big country, and vampires can't really stay out of each other's way. All she needed was one look at me, and she knew my whole story." He shakes his head. "She eventually offered to let me join the League, and I never looked back."

"But you didn't even believe in Azazel until you got here." I'm still mystified by all of this. Viviane did the League's bidding for a century before she decided Erasmus Kramer wasn't just some crackpot, and it took Gunnar thirty years to reach the same conclusion about *her*. What the hell kind of cult *are* they? "It takes three good episodes to get me to commit to a TV show, but you just . . . jumped right into a random day-walker cult?"

"It was more complicated than that," he replies peevishly. "And the League isn't a cult, okay? Viviane was a believer with a vision for the future, but it didn't matter to her if *I* believed or not. She wasn't collecting disciples—she was building a family. All the legends said that the Dark Star would grant eternal life to his followers, and that's not a gift you want shared with the kind of vampires who would do anything to get it. Even if I was never convinced, she was okay with that, because she liked me."

"Oh." I stuff some more pasta into my face, suddenly not quite sure what to say.

"After my mortal family, and then all those years with the Syndicate, I didn't even know what it was like to be *wanted* by more than one person until I became part of the League. Even if I had doubts about Azazel, I still believed in Viviane. She's the one who taught me to believe in myself."

"Aren't you lucky." There's something ugly in my tone, but I don't care. I'm sick of people explaining why they manipulated me, seeking my pity and forgiveness. *I'm so sorry your life sucked, I guess it's okay you decided to help ruin mine.* "It must be nice to be surrounded by people who aren't a bunch of fakes and liars, huh?"

Gunnar flinches. "Yeah. I don't have a better excuse than what you expect. I came here because I would do anything for Viviane, and I thought the Dark Star was a myth, so what difference did it make? But I asked you out because I got selfish, and that wasn't fair."

After a long moment, I admit, "I only said yes because I thought I was dying and wanted to know what being on a date was like. At least you told me you were a vampire before you kissed me."

"But I didn't tell you why I was in Fulton Heights, and that was also wrong." Our eyes meet, and something steals through me. The Corrupter's powers are definitely getting stronger, because without even trying to, I glimpse Gunnar's memory of that first kiss. It's different than mine—just as intense, but less chaotic, his guilt feeding his arousal. The pressure in my groin is sudden and unexpected, and I turn back to the refrigerator while he continues, "I know this is a shitty situation, Auggie. You've got no reason to believe me when I tell you that Viviane isn't an evil mastermind or whatever, but I swear to you she's not. If you need to, you can . . . you can check my thoughts to see if I'm lying."

He resisted me the last time, at the rave, and maybe I should be suspicious of his offer—or maybe he's hoping I'll call his bluff. But I turn right back around and follow the thread of that kiss, the memory still lingering in the air, straight into his mind.

It's even easier than it was last night, with Adriana. His happy moments come up first—a night of shared stories, the girl I thought was my math tutor laughing so hard she fell off her chair; a time Viviane said, "Here, you take the key," and how it proved she valued him, and how it made his heart swell; a guy he flirted with, the first one after Jude, and how nervous he was.

Viviane pops up again and again, telling jokes, talking about the future, and I realize that he feels about her the way I felt about Daphne Banks—and my heart hurts for the long-lost older sister I recently lost all over again. But I see enough to know that he's telling me the truth. Many nights spent talking about what the Ascension will mean, how they'll have to be audacious and smart if they want to change the status quo and maintain peace. Whatever lies I've been told, the League of the Dark Star does not wish to exploit the gift of true immortality to subjugate humanity and raise hell on Earth.

More of his memories call to me, his past a deep well filled with treasures I'm curious about . . . but I resist the urge to snoop. Instead, I turn the other way and push forward; while I have him, while he's willing, I want to know more about our shared future. I need to know if I'm going to swear an oath to the League, because I have no idea what to do right now, and I'm running out of what it takes to make impartial decisions.

The future is harder to reach than the past, however, the images shifting and unstable. I find that moment with the bowl and candle again, but this time it's different somehow—a shadow behind him that wasn't there before. And then I jolt forward again, the light lower, brick walls painted cinnamon by the warm glow. The air is heavy and sweet, and Gunnar's shirt is gone. His body is amazing, and I've got my hands on it, our lips an inch apart as he murmurs, *The choice is yours—just say the word.*

I jerk back, suddenly released from his memories, from the future we're going to share, and my heart races. Breathing hard, I adjust myself without thinking, my underwear in a Gordian knot. Gunnar's eyebrows go up. "What did you see?"

"I saw . . . a lot of things." I can't catch my breath, and I turn back around, embarrassed. The bowl is still there, the oath—if that's what it really is—but what was the rest of it? It wasn't the same as before, so does that mean the future has changed? Is that why it was Gunnar with his shirt off this time, instead of Jude?

"Auggie?"

"It's cool that the League of the Dark Star isn't a bunch of Batman villains," I say, fumbling for a glass of water. "I can't think who else I'd rather have ruling the world once my soul gets evicted—or incinerated, or whatever happens when Azazel takes the wheel."

"Auggie—"

"Did Daphne tell you that Rasputin has my parents?" I'm so unsteady that I don't realize I've called her Daphne until it's too late to take it back, until the fact that I still think of her as my friend is on the table between us, where Gunnar can use it against me if he wants to. "He's given me until the equinox to join Northern Wolf, or . . ."

Or . . . I'm not really sure, because he didn't say—but he didn't exactly have to. I've seen him with my own eyes, and just the thought of him anywhere near my parents makes my pulse go berserk. Soberly, Gunnar says, "She did. I'm so sorry. I wish—"

"Help me get them back." I blurt it quickly, my hands trembling. "They haven't done anything. Their lives are going to be hell anyway when I . . . when this thing Ascends, and they don't deserve any of this." Coming closer, I make Gunnar look me in the eye. He's not in love with me or anything, I know that . . . but he's attracted to me, he likes me, and he wishes he could have a chance to fall in love again. "Please, just . . . help me?"

He squirms, wincing, and I flip from desperate to furious before he even opens his mouth. "I'm sorry, Auggie, but I can't go behind Viviane's back and jeopardize my place—"

"This is *bullshit*!" I slam my hands down on the counter so hard that Gunnar jerks upright. "All of you have been crawling over me for weeks with ghost stories and fucking recruitment speeches, telling me it's so sad I'm gonna die, but I better do it the right way!" I slam my hands on the counter again. It hurts, but I like it. "Where's *your* sacrifice? You got your second chance, Gunnar Larsen. It took you almost forty years, but you got away from your shitty family and found one that loves you. I only get this one life, and the family that loves me is in the hands of a psychopath right now! And you *could* help them, but, wahh, what if you have to go make new friends because of it? You can go fuck yourself!"

I storm past him, my righteous fury carrying me all the way to the front door before I know what I'm doing, before Gunnar finds his voice. "W-where are you going?"

"Someone needs to save my parents," I snarl, filled with venom, ready to do damage and too angry to care who gets hurt—even if it's me. "And if no one will help me, I'm doing it by myself."

Flinging open the door, I march headfirst into the gloom, ready to become one of the many nightmares that fill this darkness.

28

'm not even to the end of the front walk before Gunnar blocks my path. "Don't do anything stupid, Auggie."

My laugh is so bitter it probably poisons the entire neighborhood. "You mean like trusting a vampire? Like counting on other people to do the right thing when they don't actually give a shit about what happens to me?"

He tries again. "I know this is a bad situation—"

"No, you don't," I fume. "You have no idea what I'm going through, or what I'm willing to do to make it stop. All you can think about is yourself!" Glaring at him, refusing to be cowed, I snap, "Get out of my way."

"I can't do that." He puts his hands on my shoulders—not using his strength against me, exactly, but making it clear that he's in control. "You can't fight Rasputin, and you know it. All you can do is give in to him, and I won't let you."

"You won't *let* me?" Anger thuds in my temples. "You don't decide what I do. My body's still mine—at least for now—and I'm going to find my parents. You can either help me, or you can get out of my way."

I try to move past him, but his grip tightens, his arms like steel girders. "I'm really sorry, Auggie. I don't want to do this, but it's for your own good."

"Let me go," I begin as calmly as I can, "or I will make you let me go."

"You're not strong enough to fight me."

"Yes. I am." I'm pushing my way into his mind before the words are out of my mouth. He struggles against the intrusion, but I know what I'm doing now, and the territory is familiar; within seconds, I've found the right strings to pull. His resistance takes a lot of work to overcome—but I manage it, and after a few moments his grip relaxes and his arms fall to his sides. I'm breathing hard, sweat warming my hairline, but I smile in grim triumph.

I march down the driveway, my head spinning. I've used the Corrupter's abilities before, of course, but I've never had to fight so hard to stay in control of them. Finally, I understand what Ximena meant about magic requiring energy.

"This is a really, really bad idea," Gunnar says, falling into step beside me, his eyes wide and worried. "You may have seen Rasputin in action once, but you have no idea what it's like to face him, Auggie—and I promise you don't want to!"

"He won't kill me." It's the one thing I'm actually sure of. I'm safer outdoors than indoors right now, because the undead hordes that have always plagued Fulton Heights need me alive. "And even if he kills me, so what? I'm going to die anyway, right?"

"You're not the only person he could hurt."

"I know. That's the whole point," I retort. I've witnessed Rasputin's appetite for violence, and I'm well aware that there exists no limit to the blood he wants to shed. At this point, the only way to save innocent lives may be for me to hurl myself straight into the lion's jaws—and make him choke on me. "If no one else is willing to care about what happens to me, *I'm* doing it. For once, I'm giving a shit about myself and what I want."

"Great, so what's your big plan? You gonna just walk around until his minions show up to snatch you off the street?" Gunnar's agitation stirs the air. "You don't know where he is! How do you think you're going to find him?"

I set my jaw. "Watch and learn."

Here's the thing: I actually do have a plan—I just don't know if it'll work.

I'm still figuring out that strange sensation I get when I'm close to a vampire, but I know it's growing stronger, its range getting wider. Now, using all the focus I've got, I flex the same muscles I used to read Gunnar's thoughts, and reach out into the space where I can feel the undead. Instantly, the whispering takes on a sharper focus, and I smile in grim triumph—for the first time, I can tell the different signals apart.

For a while, I wander without direction, just stretching my awareness and trying not to tire myself out—not knowing how much energy I'll need later. Some of the vampires I detect are familiar in a way I can't explain . . . until I eventually figure out that they're the ones who've been watching my house. Seven vibrations at seven unique frequencies, I've felt them all before, even if I didn't know it. I even manage to identify Jude among them, more familiar than the rest, and I wonder what he thinks of what he's seeing.

Gunnar's thoughts continue to buzz in my ear, accidentally caught in the unrefined web I'm casting out. *There's no way to stop the Dark Star from Rising.* It's something Viviane has said to him countless times, and he repeats it to assuage his guilt, but a timid, persistent thought keeps poking through nonetheless: *But what if there were?*

I look over at him. It's a bad idea to have a love story with a vampire, and I know it; but I kissed Gunnar anyway, and it was incredible. The truth is, I really do understand what he was talking about in the kitchen, and maybe it's because he's *my* first, but I kind of can't help wishing things were simple enough that we could both have what we want.

Just as I'm tempted to bring this up, another vampire registers on my radar—another signal I recognize—and it draws me up short. At the very perimeter of my awareness, nothing but the lightest touch, is a vibration that strikes right to my core. Somehow I know, *I know*, it's the man from Sugar Mama's.

"Auggie?" Gunnar's brows rise as I spin on my heel, following the source of that faint whisper, the sensation building with every step. "What is it? Where are you going?"

The closer we get, the faster I move, until I'm at a full jog—desperate to catch up with him before he pulls his spider-monkey act again and leaps out of range. But he stays where he is, and by the time we reach Fulton Heights High, we're so close I can practically smell him. Moonlight pours through shredded clouds, casting sepulchral shadows across the front entrance, painting everything in gunmetal tones of blue and gray.

Thirty yards along, down at ground level, the glass has been smashed out of a slim, rectangular window. It's one I'm very familiar with, because it looks into the art room . . . and my skin hums as I walk toward it. My worlds are colliding again.

"Auggie, what are you doing?" Gunnar asks in an urgent whisper as I get down on my hands and knees, gauging the distance to the floor. "It could be a trap!"

"It's not a trap." The window is just a dark rectangle, the shadows inside too dense for me to see through, but I'm sure I haven't been lured here. "There's only one vampire inside, and I need to talk to him."

"One vampire, and how many humans?" Gunnar asks, but he's a hair too late, because I'm already sliding through the opening and dropping into the darkness.

My landing is clumsy and loud, and Gunnar touches down

beside me before I've righted myself, his eyes glowing and his fangs extended—ready for a fight. It's brave of him, because he was right a moment ago; if the Brotherhood has sent more Knights to town, they might be here to look through Mr. Strauss's things. And if they really knew what they were doing, capturing a vampire I've had beef with and using him as bait to draw me out would be a smart move.

"I know you're here." My voice shakes a little, and Gunnar rises onto the balls of his feet. Moonlight slants through the broken window, and shadows bury the corners of the room—but two golden pinpricks hovering in the dark give my target away. "You have one chance to tell me where my parents are."

I can't see the man's mouth, but I know he's smiling. "Hmm . . . or else?"

"I'm older than you." Gunnar's voice is a deep growl I've never heard before, his face reshaped. "I could rip your head from your body with a flick of my wrist."

"Do it, then," the man taunts, stepping forward. The light picks him out—gaunt cheekbones and flyaway curls, dirty fingers clutching a tube of rolled-up paper. "Show me who's boss, pretty boy, and my master will show you the same."

"Your 'master,'" Gunnar sneers. "Do you know how ridiculous you sound? He was a fraud as a human, a starfucker so corrupt and self-indulgent that even the favor of an empress couldn't save him, and yet you grovel at his feet?"

"You do the bidding of a whore," the man snarls back, "who would see us all crushed beneath the boot of mortal tyranny forever." He's close enough to the light now that when he grins, his jagged teeth shine. "When the Ascension comes, she'll be the first to burn—and we will use her skull for a toilet."

Gunnar growls, and anger sparks inside me, raking my bloodstream. While these two measure their dicks, my life and death—and that of my parents—have once again been reduced to another unimportant detail in someone else's story . . . and I'm sick of it.

"Look at me, asshole," I seethe. "I'm not scared of you, and I don't care about your plans for the future. You won't hurt me, and if your head gets ripped off, I'll just track down one of your friends—so don't think you matter to me. Don't think you're leaving this school alive unless you tell me where my mom and dad are."

"Can you feel him?" His eyes grow bigger, his smile twisting wider. This is his true face, his cheekbones like daggers. "The Ascension is so close I can taste it. The Endless One claws his way through you even now, your sad, unworthy skin giving way to his glory!"

"I feel him," I confirm. "And if you won't give me what I want, I'll take it."

With that I lunge into his thoughts, burrowing as deep as I can. His name is William, and once upon a time, he was a musician—a normal person, if not a nice one, whose brain was damaged by substance abuse, then malnutrition, and then psychosis. He was exactly what Rasputin was looking for when they met: an embittered man without hope or morals, full of anger, desperate to feel powerful. He senses me running through the gallery of his thoughts, but he doesn't resist, because he knows I'll find nothing that matters.

He doesn't know where my parents are; he doesn't know where his master hides, or who's among his inner circle. He's nothing but a grunt, a foot soldier recruited to be one more body between Rasputin and his enemies—and William is more than happy to fulfill that role. He's been promised eternal life, dominion over the people he resents, and any sacrifice he has to make to get there is worth it.

I let him go, rage and desperation clashing in my heart like thunderheads, tears blurring my vision. William chuckles at my misery, his laugh a sound like bodies falling into a ditch. "All you have to do to save them is join the Order, August Pfeiffer."

"If I do that, he won't need them anymore." My throat is raw. "He'll just kill them."

"He'll kill them if you don't." William's smile stretches into a truly monstrous shape, an aspect of vampiric physiology I've never seen before. "You could at least give them a fighting chance."

"I could make you find them for me," I threaten, but his shoulders merely shake in silent mirth.

"The Endless One grows stronger, but you're no puppet master yet." He smirks at me. "You couldn't sustain that kind of compulsion, and I will never willingly work against he who Turned me." The air boils with tension, and William gives me a mocking salute, the tube of paper touching his temple. "Farewell, August. I'll see you soon."

He starts for the window, but Gunnar cuts him off, his own face full of dangerous angles. "Whatever you're holding, put it down, and you can go in peace."

"Peace is overrated," William purrs, and then he bares his fangs with a threatening rattle from deep in his throat. "You will step aside, boy, or you will die!"

"I died once already," Gunnar points out, holding up a hand so William can see the thin tendrils of smoke rising from his black-tipped claws. "It didn't agree with me."

Then, without warning, he surges forward, and the two of them collide in the center of the room. They smash against a table that splinters into fragments, their bodies spinning in a chaotic, violent dance, and I barely duck in time to avoid an airborne projectile. It's too dark, and they move too quickly for me to understand what's happening, but I hear the blows they rain down on one another—bones snapping and healing in the space of a breath.

If Gunnar dies, I realize, I don't know what I'll do. I don't know how to describe what's between us; we're not friends, enemies, or lovers, but some mix of the three. I know he cares what happens

265

to me, in spite of all the accusations I leveled earlier, and in this moment of literal life and death, I finally understand that I care what happens to him, too.

With a great roar, Gunnar flips backward, rolling and twisting in a way no human could ever move, and he flings William across the room. The vampire with the wild hair slams into the classroom door, tearing it off its hinges as he sails into the dark hallway beyond. His eyes burn against the shadows of the corridor for an instant—and then vanish.

"He's running!" I exclaim. Now that I've been inside his head, the connection between us is fibrous and tensile, stretching as he darts away. Fear overwhelms me, everything coming apart; I have so few days left, so few chances to save myself and those I love, and William is disappearing with one of those chances now. "We have to stop him!"

Gunnar moves reluctantly after me as I race for the door. "It's not worth it, Auggie. He doesn't know anything, and I promise we can figure out what he was here for."

I'm two steps down the hallway before wrath turns my blood molten. William is on the far side of the school already—I sense him preparing to shatter another window and escape—his glee ringing along the invisible cord between us. Gunnar may be content to let him go, but I'm tired of being lied to and walked on.

"Stop," I whisper. Reaching my thoughts across the distance of the school, following the thread that connects us, I sink back into William's mind before he knows to resist. The smell of the far stairwell rises around me, his senses becoming mine . . . and I pull.

Maybe my control isn't total, maybe I can't force him to work for me against his will, but I'm puppet master enough to make him dance tonight. He fights, and sweat rolls as I fight back, but my hooks are far too deep for him to cast them off. Despite his struggles, I have him, and step by halting step, he makes his unwilling return.

When he reappears at the bend in the hall, a tall shadow with fiery, golden eyes, his tone is equal parts curiosity and resentment. "I am impressed."

"You've got no idea what I'm capable of," I snarl, because it's true. Even *I* don't know what I'm capable of anymore. "Now, I'm giving you one last chance: Help me save my parents, and you might live long enough to see the Ascension."

William shakes with silent laughter, his eyes bright stars in the darkness. "You may be the Corrupter's vessel, but that's all you are—a filthy cup not worth the blood that fills it, a brat throwing a tantrum because it's bedtime and he doesn't want to go."

"Sorry—I can't hear you with my boot on your neck," I snarl, breathing harder. William is still fighting me, and holding him in place is more difficult than I want to admit, his mind a nest of snakes that wriggle and squirm in my grasp.

"Save your threats." He makes a dismissive gesture, claws spread. "Even if I could do what you wish, I wouldn't. I will never work against the Master—I would die for him!"

My fingers close into fists, my head whirling as rage spills from my heart. "*Then die!*"

I don't know what I'm doing as I plunge deeper into the channels of his brain, as I find new strings to pull—only that each choice seems obvious and inevitable. Somehow, it's as easy as breathing, an instinct that's harder to resist than obey. William's expression changes as the blood in his veins starts to vibrate, as his undead body begins to warm. At first, he's excited, the memory of being alive flooding back; he thinks it's a gift from the Corrupter . . . but I'm not done with him yet.

His expression shifts again as his temperature soars past one hundred, his blood racing and his skin turning pink with the rising heat. Sweat drips from me, and I dig deeper, watching with malevolent satisfaction as his eyes roll back and his body begins to thrash.

"Auggie?" Gunnar's voice is frayed by alarm, but I barely hear him. Blisters swell and burst across William's skin, his temperature passing two hundred and still climbing. Smoke rises from him in wispy threads, his skin splitting and crackling, the stench of cooking meat spreading along the corridor. My chest heaves, my heart pounds, but I don't let go.

Dark fluid is leaking from his nose and ears when the first tongues of flame erupt along his twitching arms—and then he is completely engulfed. White-hot fire consumes him from the inside out, liquefying his brain, instantly severing the magic that's kept him going since the day he died. Within seconds, his flesh and blood are reduced to ash, and all that's left is a smoking pile of dust and bone in the middle of the school hallway.

My limbs shake, sweat stinging my eyes, and a relentless pain hammers at my temples. The shadows swim and wobble, winding themselves around me, and the ringing in my ears is unbearable. Gunnar takes hold of me, shouting something—but he's too late. The shadows lunge down my throat and I drop away.

THE FELL OF DARK WAS AT LAST UPON THE HEATH, RENDER-
ing the low fog blue where it crept through heather and gorse.
Wrapping his cloak tighter around his shoulders, the bearded man
raised his lantern against the gloaming, and cast another furtive look
around. He was alone, of course; he'd been alone since he'd left the
outskirts of Inverness—but this body was depressingly vulnerable,
and even a common thief could pose a mortal threat.

Frankly, it was insulting.

He sensed the sisters long before he saw their fire burning, a
wavering glow in the distance that answered the light he carried, and
he hurried onward. The trio had made camp within the remnants
of an old abbey church—a long-abandoned ruin in the desolate
countryside, its walls crumbling and caked with moss. Superstition
was a plague in this part of the country, and the three women had
exploited it with admirable efficiency, driving away the curious with
unexplainable phenomena and eerie cries in the darkness.

The doorway to the abbey was an arched gap, a hole broken
through the side wall where hellish light danced, shadows bounding
like feral beasts. As pointless as the gesture was, he drew his sword
before making his way inside, an instinct this particular body found
it comforting to obey.

Firelight beat against the stone walls and rotted ceiling, the dark void of night visible where the roof gave way, and the odor of peat smoke clung greedily to the air. Long since reclaimed by nature, the nave of the old church was a corridor of trampled weeds and fractured statuary—at the center of which three shrouded figures gathered around a shallow pit dug into the floor. Ringed by stones, it cast up a column of bright flames that curled and twisted in unnatural shapes.

"By the pricking of my thumbs," one of the sisters remarked, her attention still on the fire, "something wicked this way comes."

"Is that any manner in which to greet an old friend?" The bearded man couldn't resist a sly grin.

Quick as a snake, the leftmost figure produced a weapon from the folds of her cloak, a long knife with a bone handle. Her head turned minutely in his direction, she stated, "We have other greetings to offer, Azazel. Don't tempt fate."

The Corrupter grinned wider, his skin prickling all over in the presence of his children—and what rebellious children they were. "Your blade is no match for mine, Brixia."

Drawing back the heavy veil that concealed her face, she at last favored him with a direct look. Her skin and hair were so pale they were almost white, but her eyes were dark as the night itself. "You are not the vermin this blade is meant for."

"We need no weapon to kill you," the woman in the middle reminded him, lifting her own veil. Dark skin, dark hair, lines tattooed beneath her bottom lip . . . this was Ket. She cast a handful of herbs into the fire, and they were consumed in a flash of blue sparks.

"If your death was our plan, you wouldn't have made it this far." The third witch revealed herself—Sulis, with tan skin, colorless eyes, and a crown of iron-gray braids. From her own cloak she produced a rat, already dead, and tossed its limp body across the circle. Brixia snatched it from the air, sliced open its gut, and wrung its blood into the flames. A ball of greasy black smoke belched out of the pit and rolled toward the ceiling.

"Your death will come, with or without us," Brixia added, wiping the blood off her hands with an old rag. "Already the sand slips out."

"Would you like to know your fate?" Ket asked.

"Perhaps he's seen it himself," Sulis suggested with a devilish smile.

"I've seen many fates." The Corrupter lifted his sword, running his fingers along the sharpened edge. It was no show piece; not so long ago, it had claimed the head of a king. "Some of them are yours. Death has grown impatient waiting for you three—perhaps it's time you joined your sisters."

"Is that what brings you here?" Sulis looked amused.

"Surely. not." Brixia was annoyed. "He's only trying to sound important." She waved her hands at the smoke and it quickly reshaped itself, forming the appearance of a head clad in a knight's helmet.

"He *is* important," Ket stated reasonably. "Mac Bethad mac Findlaích, Mormaer of Moray, King of Scotland. He leads the country—for now." She waved her own hands, and the smoke reformed again in the shape of a small child.

"Until the forest comes to Dunsinane." With that cryptic conclusion, Brixia made a ring of miniature trees sprout around the child's feet.

"Until he joins our sisters in death for another life." Sulis snapped her fingers and the fire leaped upward, swallowing the apparition whole before subsiding again.

"Is this what you three do?" The Corrupter gestured. "Thousands of years spent in this realm, performing puppet shows to entertain yourselves?"

"Mac Bethad mac Findlaích is the only puppet on this stage," Sulis purred.

Ket gave a nod. "And the show is hardly entertaining."

"We only watch because we enjoy the ending." Brixia stoked the flames. "We watch to make sure it always ends the same."

"One of these times, it won't," the Corrupter promised darkly. "Be it in a hundred years or a thousand, the Ascension will come. One of these times, the stars will be on my side, and everything will change."

Sulis shrugged, unconcerned. "Perhaps. But not this time."

"This time," Ket continued, "the blade you swung swings back."

"The stars don't take sides," Brixia chided him. "But Death will take you, gladly."

"Death has gobbled me up before, but it always spits me back out." The Corrupter smiled again, flexing his grip on the hilt of his sword. "And I don't intend to be dogged by you three forever."

"Ah." Brixia clasped her hands. "Now we are getting somewhere."

As in ages past, he reached for them with his mind—and as in ages past, an unseen wall crafted of magic kept him out. But Mac Bethad mac Findlaích was a very talented swordsman—a trained warrior who had led armies into battle—and his body handled a blade with natural intuition. The metal sang as he swept it up, smoke cleaving around its gleaming edge.

Which was as far as his advance got. Ket flung out her hands, something invisible rippling across the empty nave, a coil of air that tangled around the sword and wrenched it from his grip. Before he could run after it, Sulis gestured, and flames jumped from the pit. Streaking across the ground, they encircled the man and blazed up, forming a deadly curtain that trapped him in place.

"You waste our time and energy, Azazel." Ket narrowed her eyes. "We are not on Death's menu. Not tonight."

"Tell us your purpose here," Sulis demanded imperiously, a golden light gathering in her eyes, "before I decide to cut this puppet's strings myself."

The curtain of flame leaped higher, licking dangerously at the weathered boards of the collapsing roof, and the bearded man began to sweat from the heat. No matter how many times he died, each experience was freshly unpleasant. "My purpose here is simple. I have come with a proposition."

And there, backed by flame in a crumbling church, the Corrupter shared his design for eternity—and made each of them an offer . . .

29

The last vestiges of a dark dream cling to my thoughts when I force my eyes open, lids heavy as a lead apron—a lonely battlefield, churned earth, an army hidden by makeshift camouflage—and I know it's a memory from yet another life I never lived. A throbbing headache pounds nails into my brain, so sharp I want to vomit, and for just a moment I'm ready to give this body to the Corrupter.

"Auggie?" Gunnar hovers over me, his expression apprehensive. "How do you feel?"

"My skull is malfunctioning," I reply through gritted teeth. "Please remove it for me."

"I got you some water. I thought you might need it." He indicates a glass on the side table. "You were kind of . . . sweaty tonight. A lot."

I sit up, and my brain seesaws dangerously, everything unsteady. I'm on the couch in my living room, and the sky outside the windows is a slate gray. Dawn is coming. "What happened?"

He helps me bring the glass to my lips, his brows creasing with concern. "Do you not remember?"

My instinct is to tell him that's a stupid question—if I remembered, I wouldn't be asking—but as I think back, an image comes to me in a startling instant: fire. I can practically see it in front of me, towering, rollicking, smoke pouring up to the ceiling. "Something was burning?"

"Yeah, you could say that," Gunnar allows, forcing me to drink some more.

"It was in the church." Words echo in my ears, and I repeat them without thinking. "'The stars don't take sides.'"

"What?" Gunnar tucks a gentle hand under my chin, turning my face to his so he can look into my eyes, more worried than before. It's embarrassing how welcome I find his touch. "Auggie, what are you talking about? This was at your school."

When he says it, it's as if a filter is removed from my mind, and a new picture swims into focus. The hallway, those glowing eyes, that ferocious heat. "The vampire. William."

"Was that his name?"

"Yes." I reached too deeply into his memories, I think, because they're stuck to me. His rocky childhood, his surly adolescence, his descent into self-pity and retaliatory violence. "I killed him, didn't I?"

"You *immolated* him," Gunnar corrects softly. "Did you know you could do that?"

"No." I can't look at him. "And . . . yes. I think a part of me did." He doesn't have to ask which part. "I didn't . . . It's not why I made him come back. I just wanted some answers."

Reaching for something on the floor beside the couch, Gunnar says, "Lucky for you, then—William dropped what he was trying to steal when you made him explode."

The edges are singed, but when he unrolls the heavy sheet of paper, I recognize it immediately. It's the sketch I did the day I met Jude. "This is mine."

I'm not exactly surprised—there isn't much else Rasputin would be after in the Fulton Heights High art room. For days, I've been assuming it was locked in a Brotherhood vault somewhere . . . but, then, Mr. Strauss told me he wanted to take pictures of it. Watching me, Gunnar asks, "What does it mean? Who are these three women?"

"I don't know," I say, avoiding his eye. "I'm, like, ninety percent certain all these people are watching the Corrupter get executed in one of his lifetimes? But I don't know when or where—and I don't know why Rasputin would want it."

Self-consciousness heats my face as I carefully tell the lie. For the first time, I think I *do* know who those ladies are supposed to be. My mind is fixed on Ximena's account of the three undead witches who faced Azazel in the past, who have supposedly tracked him from life to life ever since.

Maybe Rasputin wants my practice sketches because he's a Corrupter fanboy, and this will be a great exhibit in his private collection someday. Or maybe he wants any information he can get about the sorceress coven that might stand between him and his dreams. The witches could be Azazel's worst enemies . . . or his biggest groupies—and until I know which it is, I can't afford to share what little I know about them.

"I can't wait to see the look on that gangly bastard's face when I make him combust." Just imagining it warms the cockles of my heart. He kidnapped my parents, terrorized my best friend, slaughtered people . . . I'm glad the only ability I have to stop him involves an incredibly painful death. "Wait till he finds out I'm not as helpless as he thinks."

Gunnar sits back. "You can't be serious."

"Why not?" Gesturing out the window, trees and rooftops taking shape against the sky, I state, "The sun will be up soon, and wherever he's hiding, he'll be stuck there until sunset. I've got all day to find and torture henchmen until one of them gives him up."

"Auggie, you need to listen to yourself." Gunnar is emphatic. "This is a bad plan."

"I'm learning to resist mesmerism, and I can destroy him without having to lift a finger." Just saying it is empowering. The Corrupter may be killing me, but at least I won't go alone. "You should want to help me. Doesn't getting rid of Rasputin mean less competition for Team Dark Star when it's finally Pop-Goes-Azazel?"

"You almost died tonight!" Gunnar barks, tossing his hands up. "Don't you get that? The magic you tapped into at the school is more than a normal human body is built to withstand, and it almost destroyed *you*! If you try using it against Rasputin—a vampire with some actual command of the dark arts himself—you might not survive." I open my mouth to argue, and he cuts me off. "He won't be alone. Did you think about that? He'll be surrounded by adherents just like William, and all of them will die to protect him."

"Good. Let them," I snap, harvesting anger in place of confidence.

"You still don't get it." Gunnar sets his jaw, shaking his head in disgust. "You barely managed to kill William before you blacked out. You don't have the control to handle ten or more vampires at once, and Viviane isn't going to just hand you an army to lead against Rasputin until you make her a commitment—in blood."

Our standoff lasts a tense moment, and then his eyes flit nervously to the window. The Mad Monk isn't the only one who'll be trapped by the sunrise, and I remind myself that Gunnar doesn't have to be here at all. Maybe he's not the guy I thought he was, but he got me out of the school and stayed with me while I was unconscious. Even if his loyalty is to the League, he's not really my enemy. But even so.

"I can't do nothing." I grip the couch cushions. "I'm not pledging my allegiance to anyone on an empty promise—you guys have all lied way too much for me to trust you'll keep your word once you get what you want. And whether I die fighting Rasputin or I die during the Ascension, what difference does it make?" As I get to my feet, I try to hide how dizzy I am. "Meanwhile, the Knights aren't gonna waste time organizing their next attack; so you can help me, or you can get out of my way, but you're not going to stop me."

Gunnar looks up at me, his expression a turmoil of angst and regret, and he manages a barely perceptible nod. "Okay. You win."

"I win?" I'm so shocked I sit down again. "Uh . . . what do you mean?"

"I mean you're right." He tugs his lucky necklace, raking his other hand through his hair. "A week ago, I didn't even believe in the Corrupter, and now . . . the closer we get to zero, the less I think I want any of this." Standing up, Gunnar walks a few paces and turns back. "I don't want to cross Viviane, but it's not like you getting caught by Rasputin will help her out. And . . . and I don't want you to die, Auggie." With a helpless shrug, he looks at my feet. "If you promise not to do something stupid, I'll help you save your parents."

"You will?" I nearly fall off the couch. Maybe I should pretend to be all cool, like I knew I'd get what I want, but I can't. "You'll really help me?"

Gunnar struggles with his words for a moment. "Believe it or not, I wish this weren't happening to you. Maybe that's selfish— maybe I should be wishing it weren't happening to *anyone*, but . . . you're special." Embarrassed, he continues to avoid my eyes. "I can't protect you from Azazel, but this is something I can do."

Before I can think twice, I'm off the couch and throwing my arms around him, so overjoyed that I don't stop to consider how awkward the gesture might be. Gunnar freezes . . . but then he hugs me back, muscles shifting under the fabric of his T-shirt. Suddenly, all I can think about is how his body feels against mine, and how he smells like linen and fresh mint, and how very recently his tongue was in my mouth. And then I start getting an erection, and it's incredibly inappropriate, because we were literally *just* talking about rescuing my parents from a murderous vampire, and *what is wrong with me*?

Gunnar pulls back first, and I wobble to the kitchen for another glass of water, my hormones and my brain cells crashing together like bumper cars. I still can't figure out the futures I've seen, the shifting images of Jude and Gunnar in similar circumstances; I can't figure out how I feel about either of them, or which vision I secretly hope comes true.

What if there is no destiny? What if there are multiple endings, all the time, and we just . . . stumble our way in and out of them? I don't know who or what I want. I don't know which of the two I'd rather kiss again. Truth be told, I think I want to kiss *both* of them—not because I'm developing feelings for them, necessarily, but because it turns out I really, really enjoy kissing someone I'm attracted to.

"The sun is almost up." Gunnar hovers behind me in the doorway to the kitchen, watching me anxiously. "I'll have to leave, and I . . . don't think you should be here alone."

The future might be staring me in the face, I realize. *The choice is yours—just say the word.* "Can you stay? I mean, there's only a couple of windows in the basement, and we can cover them to block the sunlight. Then, if Brotherhood dudes break in, you'll be here."

"And if they set fire to the house to flush you out, I'll die down there," he returns candidly. "Or we'll both die down there, or we'll both die trying to escape." The sky is gray, verging on blue . . . our time almost up. "I don't think being here is a risk either of us can afford to take. I'm sorry—I wish I could protect you, but . . . you said it yourself: The Knights aren't going to waste any time."

"Where am I supposed to go?" I ask the question reflexively, thinking of all the options I don't have—all the places my enemies will obviously look first.

"You know, if your power has progressed to where it will work on humans, you might be able to set up your own hideout." Gunnar traces the doorframe. "Viviane would break my neck for telling you this, but all you need is an empty apartment and a friendly landlord willing to hand over the keys just because you tell him to."

I offer a mechanical nod—but inside, something falls out of place. With everything else that's happened, it's silly that being forced to abandon my own home is what makes me want to cry. "Thanks for the advice."

Gunnar shrugs into his jacket and starts for the door, but then stops, turning back. Removing his necklace, he slips it over my head, pressing it to my sternum. He watches my lips, like he wants to kiss me but doesn't know how, as he says, "Pack a bag, but don't take too long. The farther you get before sunrise, the safer you'll be."

And then he leaves.

Pink is starting to show on the horizon as I slam my feet down on the pedals of my bike, speeding out of my neighborhood without any direction in mind. I won't be going to school today, and no one will be calling me in—and only if I'm lucky will I live long enough to face the consequences. How far should I go? Where am I going to hide?

The vampires watching over me drop off my magical radar one by one as the sun rises, and I eventually drift to a stop on an unfamiliar street corner, a cold breeze chilling my sweaty face. I've made a lot of bad decisions, turned to all the wrong people for help, and the only plan I've got now is to swindle my way into an empty apartment and hide. Even if I can somehow Mission: Impossible my parents out of Rasputin's clutches with nothing but Gunnar's assistance, I'm still going to die anyway.

Panicked adrenaline scours my nerves, my head spinning with mortal terror. I don't want to go, I'm not ready—and of all the bad decisions I've made, the worst one is still waiting. The only group I haven't turned to yet is the one I trust the least and fear the most, but also the only one that might be able to beat the Corrupter.

If that's what they want.

When Azazel Ascends, everything on Earth will change—and every choice I make now will affect whoever's left when the dust settles. I can't afford to be reckless . . . but I can't afford to play it safe, either, when the actual destruction of the world is on the line. I've got my phone in my hand, just about to make a call, when I hear a voice behind me. "The answer is yes."

Whirling around, my heart bursting like a confetti cannon, I blink frightened stars from my eyes until I recognize the speaker. Sitting in a car that's been parked at the curb this whole time, she gives me an awkward smile, and I blink a few more times. "*Hope?*"

"Hi, Auggie." Despite the circumstances, Hope Cheng does not look at all surprised to find me on this random corner at 7:00 a.m. on a Monday. Indicating my phone, she says, "You don't have to call—they're willing to see you. In fact, they're, um . . . kind of waiting for you right now. I'm supposed to drive you, if that's okay."

"You're supposed to drive me," I repeat, my fingers slippery and cold. The sun is up now, so she's definitely not a vampire. At least there's that. "To . . . where, exactly?"

"A meeting with the coven that supposedly cast out Azazel back in the Bronze Age. Or . . . something." She shrugs apologetically. "That's what you were going to call Ximena about, right?" She gives me a beat to answer, but I can't, and she goes on, "They want to see you, too. Also, you should probably get in the car quick, because I guess things are supposed to get really messy today in Fulton Heights if we don't leave on schedule."

My limbs shaking again, I reach for Gunnar's necklace, feeling the stone bite comfortingly into my flesh. "How could you possibly know any of that?"

And this is when the person in Hope's passenger seat leans forward into the light, another familiar face swimming into focus. It's early, but despite the shadows in the car, Adriana's face is unmistakably pale with worry. "Please just get in, Auggie. We'll explain everything on the way."

30

There's already space in the trunk for my bike, and Hope has the car in gear before my butt hits the seat, sleepy neighborhoods whipping by as she speeds for the edge of town. It takes me a minute to choose my first question. "Where exactly are we going?"

"The city," Hope answers, anxiety thinning her voice. "That's where they've been staying. They've been here for a while, but . . ."

More silence, more blurry neighborhoods, and I see signs for the highway when I finally lose my patience. "But *what*? Look, I don't mean to be rude, or whatever, but I am rapidly losing every last molecule of my shit back here, and I'd appreciate some details! How did you know where to find me?"

There's another brief silence, and then Adriana answers, "Hope can read minds."

"Oh." I stare at the girl behind the wheel. "You're . . . a sorceress?"

"The gift runs in my family," she allows uncomfortably, flipping on her turn signal. "My uncle's element is wood, and mine is water, which means that, yeah, I can read minds. I'm still working at it, though. Sometimes I can't turn it on, and sometimes I can't turn it off." Hope gives a feeble shrug. "I didn't come into my abilities until last year, so I'm kind of a novice, but it's the reason I moved here—so I could train under the Nexus."

Just like Ximena. I know I should be demanding more answers, but instead all I can think of is the number of vivid daydreams I had about Boyd Crandall during the independent art study Hope and I have shared all year long, and my stomach shrivels to the size of a raisin. My fantasies were *detailed*.

"Hope's uncle is one of the other two witches Abuela told us about," Adriana reports with a moody frown. "The ones training with the coven? Well . . . you need to tell him."

"Uncle Marcus said I had to practice, and he suggested using you as my subject," Hope blurts, glancing at me in the mirror as we merge onto the highway. "I swear I didn't know why! When I started picking up scary shit from you—people being beheaded and burned alive—I thought my power was malfunctioning. I didn't know it was . . . that—"

"That her uncle was using her to spy on you for the coven." Adriana is concise.

"It wasn't like that!" Hope stomps down on the gas pedal, and I grip my seat belt a little tighter. "Or . . . okay, it *was* like that—but I swear I didn't know what I was doing. You weren't the only one he told me to listen to; you were just the only one he cared about."

"It's okay," I mumble, thinking about the woodcut she sent me. Whatever else she did, Hope took a risk trying to help me out. "I'm not blaming you."

"They're the ones who told me where to be this morning," she reveals at last. "A week ago—after they did . . . whatever they did that they needed your hair for."

"A *week* ago?" My tone shoots up an octave or two. "Wait, you've known about all of this for a week, and you—"

"I didn't know." She's emphatic. "I didn't *want* to know, either.

My uncle said the witches wanted to see me, and I freaked out that a coven that powerful even knew my name. Being in the room with them was . . . terrifying? Overwhelming? I had all these questions, but I was too scared to open my mouth, and they knew things about me I had never shared with anyone." Hope shudders all over. "They told me to be at that corner this morning, and it wasn't a request. It wasn't until last night that they revealed all the who and why, and said Adriana had to be there, too—or 'darkness would fall upon the world.'"

She finishes in a choked whisper, and Adriana adds, "After dropping you off yesterday, Abuela went to confront them. Whatever they said to her, whatever they showed her . . . it scared the shit out of her. She believes them now."

"How can she be sure it wasn't more bullshit?" I ask, trying to control my rising panic. "Twenty-four hours ago, she said not to trust them, but now we're going to an emergency meeting with them?" Silence fills the car, and I start sweating some more. "What if it's a trap?"

Adriana grips her jacket a little tighter around her shoulders. "You didn't see my abuela's face after she got home, Auggie. It was like she'd seen a ghost—getting axe-murdered by another ghost. If there's even a chance you meeting them could stop whatever's coming? It's worth it. Anything is worth it."

We make the rest of the drive in silence.

Our destination turns out to be a high-rise on Chicago's north side, an ordinary building in a busy neighborhood, less than a mile from the lake. There are rainbow flag stickers on the doors of shops and restaurants—something I've never seen in Fulton Heights—and if I weren't currently terrified of being cursed forever by a group of undead mastermind sorceresses, I'd probably find it exciting.

I'm not too surprised when Ximena Rosales is waiting for us in the lobby of the building. She's accompanied by a man I assume to be Hope's uncle, and a petite woman I've never seen before, with a pale, bookish face and red hair. My skin prickles from the presence of vampires somewhere above us. Adriana's grandmother greets me with a somber expression, her hands firm where they grip my elbows.

"Don't be scared, mijito," she says, but if there's any reason I shouldn't be, she keeps it to herself. Instead, she gestures to the strangers beside her. "This is Marcus Cheng, Hope's uncle, and this is Lydia Fitzroy. They're the other witches that have been training with the women you're about to meet." She casts a glance in the direction of the elevators. "We're going up with you. What's to be discussed . . . it involves all of us."

"All of us?" Hope and Adriana exchange a glance.

"Not you two." Marcus Cheng is stern. "This is still a school day, remember?"

"We drove Auggie all the way out here, and now we have to go all the way home again?" Adriana is annoyed—but I know her well enough to see that, for once, she's happy about being excluded from witch stuff.

"What you two did was very important," Ximena begins patiently, "and so is your education. You girls will get a fancy dinner date on me as a reward, but right now you're leaving. Entiendes?"

Adriana relents, but before she and Hope go, she gives me one last worried look.

Together with the adults, I take the elevator up fourteen floors, sweating profusely. We walk down a windowless hallway that someone forgot to oxygenate, and we knock on a nondescript door. When it opens, we enter a small apartment lit by a single lamp with a golden shade, the windows shielded by velvet drapes. Four high-backed chairs face a small sofa—where three figures are seated, all dressed in black. I don't know who opened the door for us, because the room is otherwise empty.

"Hello, August Pfeiffer." The leftmost of the seated trio is the one who speaks first, her skin pale as alabaster, her eyes bottomless. "My name is Brixia."

"I am Ket," says the woman in the middle, her chin tattooed with a row of slender, vertical lines.

"And I am Sulis." The third woman, her colorless eyes glinting, gestures at the empty chairs. "Please sit. There is much to talk about."

We arrange ourselves, Ximena on my left and Marcus on my right, the air in the room practically vibrating with energy. Or maybe that's just my skin, the three undead witches tripping my radar with an intensity I've never felt before. They're surprisingly petite, and they've barely moved, but I still understand exactly what Hope meant—they're terrifying. It's in their poise, the ageless intelligence that sparks in their eyes, and the unmistakable aura of power that surrounds them. They're all dressed like Elizabeth II, modern but regal, and the effect is strangely imposing—a deadly tea party.

"You need not be afraid," Brixia remarks offhandedly. "Anything we might do to you could hardly be worse than what you face already."

"That's not exactly comforting," I point out, my tongue as cold and dead as an oyster on the half-shell.

"Nor should it be." Ket inclines her head. "The only fate worse than what you face is that which will befall everyone you leave behind."

"Thanks for the reminder." I narrow my eyes at her in spite of myself. Here I am, literally dying, and she wants to make me feel like a drama queen for it. *Adults.*

"Many lifetimes ago, we confronted Azazel," Sulis interjects, her tone commanding. "With his dreadsome power, he wrought havoc in this realm. His blood turned men to monsters, and his monsters made meals out of men."

"We were double our number then." Brixia stares nostalgically into the distance. "Our circle was complete, our sorcery unmatched. He had to be stopped, and we were the ones to stop him. Through wits, we trapped Azazel, and began the work of casting him out."

"But we were mortal then—the one truly fatal flaw." Ket sighs. "Even though we succeeded in wrenching him from his physical body, one of our sisters died before the spell could be completed and his banishment secured."

"He escaped into the ether, and those of us who remained took a vow to face him again upon his return." Sulis glowers. "Over the centuries, we lost two more sisters to those who would see the Corrupter triumph . . . but the stars align themselves again, and the battlefield is prepared."

"We will finish what we began." Determination gleams in Brixia's eyes. "It is time to close the circle."

Worlds die and galaxies are born in the breathless silence that follows. I want to believe they intend to stop the thing inside of me, but my hopes are fragile from too many trips down the stairs—too many burns from trusting the untrustworthy. Haltingly, I turn to Ximena . . . who gives me a reassuring nod.

"They revealed the ritual," she states in a hush. "I've seen it myself, mijito. It turns out this is what we've been training for all along."

"But I thought . . ." My eyes flood. I still don't want to believe.

"At the point of Ascension," Sulis declares, "when the Dark Star first realizes he inhabits a shell strong enough to support him, he will gather himself to Rise and tear asunder the bindings of mortality."

"He will cleave his entity from yours, and with his first breath he will purify the vessel of your soul and begin the Earth's subjugation." Ket's fingertips inscribe the air.

"But in the space between heartbeats, we will have our chance," Brixia promises. "As he separates, and before he breathes, he will become exposed . . . and we may seize him."

Lydia speaks for the first time, her voice soft and thin. "The ritual will bind Azazel, preventing him from taking that first breath while we extract him from your body."

Marcus Cheng is genuinely excited. "It'll be a surgical strike, and everything will hinge on the timing, but . . . it can be done."

"True sorcery requires a balance of six elements," Ket begins, "and to execute a spell as demanding as this, they must be wielded by magic-workers with an unparalleled degree of skill. Our circle is finally complete with earth, water, air, fire, wood, and metal."

Water is my element. I hear Brixia's voice in my head, although her lips don't move. *My gifts include telepathy, remote viewing, and the casting of illusions.*

"I am air," Ket says, rippling, vanishing, and then reappearing again. "Disapparition and the control of unseen matter are my domain."

"Mine is fire." Sulis raises a hand, and sparks gather above her palm, swarming into a ball. "My abilities speak for themselves."

Lydia is next, and when she claps her hands together, the air crackles. Sparks jump to life around her fingers, and my hair stands up. "Metal elementals control electricity. We also make excellent mediums."

I sit up a little straighter. I had Lydia pegged for the kind of person who sells homemade wind chimes at farmers' markets, not the kind of person who can kill you with a handshake. Hope's uncle is next, and even though I know his element is wood—and what powers that gives him—watching him shape-shift into a perfect double for Sulis is nonetheless remarkable.

When it's Ximena's turn, she merely shrugs. "I didn't come

prepared to give a demonstration, but earth witches possess great strength and are skilled with mesmerism."

"For generations, my sisters and I have stalked the Corrupter, playing sentinel—and our moment is finally at hand." Brixia steeples her fingers. "On the vernal equinox, four days hence, the planets and stars will be in their foretold houses. The Ascension will begin . . . and we will take hold of Azazel, casting him from this realm. We will banish him into hell at last."

All the planets and stars collect in my throat, and I choke on them. *Four days hence.* My life is due to end in four days. My brain chugs, revolving faster and faster around this fact, this blunt and brutal confirmation of my worst fears. "Why am I only hearing about this now?" I demand just shy of a screech. "You've had a plan for thousands of years, you knew about *all* of this, but you decided not to say anything until *four days* before I'm supposed to die?"

"We are the only enemy to pose Azazel a true threat," Ket begins, unruffled, "and two of our sisters perished long ago at the hands of ones who would see us fail. To show ourselves is to invite danger, to risk disrupting the necessary course of events."

"How am I supposed to believe you?" It's not an idle question; ever since I sat down, I've been trying to get inside these women's heads—to search their memories and examine their intentions— but, again, there's some kind of wall between us. "All I know for sure is that you're vampires, and that makes Azazel your one-way ticket to fun in the sun."

"We have had more than enough time on this planet," Sulis answers dryly. "We are among the oldest beings to walk the Earth, and our feet are tired from it. Eternal life is not the prize you seem to think it is."

"Almost a thousand years ago, Azazel offered to seat us at his right hand when he Ascended." Brixia gives a bored shrug. "We would be second only to him in his kingdom, sharing in inconceivable power. It was an attempt to sway us from our mission to destroy him—and we declined."

"We do not fear death." Ket lifts her chin. "And if dominion is what we sought, we have the strength to claim it on our own. We are here because nature demands balance, and we are Azazel's counter-weight. When he is gone, our time will be up."

"If we wished a place in his kingdom, all that would have been required of us was silence," Sulis notes. "The prophecy would fulfill itself, and our lack of intervention would have proven our allegiance."

This, at least, is a point I'm not sure I can argue. Rasputin, the Syndicate, the League . . . they all have visions for a future that depend upon controlling the Corrupter, but even if none of them interfered at all, they're still Azazel's children—they'd all have a place in his literal hell on Earth. Either these witches are telling the truth, or . . . well, or they're not. Maybe they really are planning to expedite the Ascension rather than stop it.

I'm aware that Brixia is reading my thoughts like ticker tape, absorbing them as quickly as they come to me, and despite her placid expression I squirm. "How do I even know this is possible? I mean, you've been following him around like groupies for thousands of years—if you can actually *do* this, then why haven't you zapped him already?"

"We've never had the chance," the alabaster witch answers simply. "When Azazel Rises, even when he takes over a body completely, he still shares it with a human soul. Mortality limits his power, prevents him from fulfilling his design for a hell on Earth—but it also shields him. Right now, your spirit and his are tangled together."

"If we were to reach into you and tear him free, we would uproot your soul as well," Ket elaborates, her tone reasonable. "And were we to then cast Azazel into hell, you would go with him, damned to a lake of fire for an eternity of incomprehensible suffering."

"Oh." My mouth tastes like cardboard and battery acid.

"'Vengeance is mine . . . saith the Lord,'" Sulis quotes with a wistful aspect. "We could take your life easily enough, but we cannot decide the everlasting fate of a mortal soul—even if we wished. Even if we judged your unjust damnation an acceptable cost. There are mystical boundaries on this plane that even the strongest magic cannot transgress."

"But this is the Ascension." Brixia's eyes inflame, a low, kindling light. "For the first time, Azazel will at last divorce himself from his host's humanity—he will finally become his own for a single, indefensible instant."

"All of this is foretold, though. I've got four different cults on my ass, and then you guys playing mind games, all because some prophecies say I'm the guy and the time is now." This is the heart of it—the thing I can't escape from—and my voice shrinks. "You obviously believe them, and it's not like any of the writings have been wrong, either. So . . . so why should I believe you're here to stop it, or that it can even be stopped at all?"

"Only a fool believes in fate," Brixia replies. "The future is a web, August Pfeiffer, not a line, and its construction changes all the time. Every day, some strands are built and some are plucked, and it is we who create the so-called inevitable."

"A week ago, you knew exactly where I was going to be this morning," I point out in disbelief. "But even *I* didn't know that! I didn't stop on that corner for any reason—it was totally random. It wasn't even on my usual route to school!"

"It was a matter of probability," she says vaguely, and the three of them stand up together. "Here." Brixia holds something out to me—a set of keys—and I blink up at her. "You've found your safe house. This apartment will remain empty and unbothered for the remainder of the week. We will wait to hear from you."

"Whether you trust us or not, we are the only ones who can give you what you truly desire." Ket gazes at me, unblinking. "Whatever happens in four days' time, the Corrupter will not survive the Ascension. But if you cooperate with us, we will do our best to see that you do."

With that, the three witches join hands and vanish, leaving behind nothing but a ribbon of vapor that gradually dissolves into the golden air.

31

f you cooperate with us. As if they don't already know what I'll do—as if I even have a real alternative. The Syndicate wants dominance, Rasputin wants chaos, Viviane wants utopia, and the Brotherhood wants a world cleansed of the undead . . . but the only thing none of them want is for me to walk away from this. Supposing the witches are lying, I've still got nothing to lose. And if they're being honest, they really are promising me exactly what I've lately been too scared to hope for.

Or, almost exactly. They said nothing about helping me get my parents back, and I don't think it was an oversight. Getting rid of Azazel without me dying in the process is an objective we all conveniently share right now, but that doesn't mean they've been hanging out for thousands of years just to do me a few special favors. My parents are collateral that only I care about, and no matter who I side with, no one is going to save them but me—and I have to figure out how before I'm separated from the Corrupter, one way or another.

Ximena offers me a few encouraging words, and then she departs with Marcus and Lydia, leaving me alone in the apartment. The silence is earsplitting, and I shove aside the thick drapes, daylight dazzling and cold over the endless blue of Lake Michigan. For a while I just stand there, immobilized, looking out over this neighborhood I don't know—tallying up the hours I've got left until the moment I either live or die.

A knock at the door sends my heart skyrocketing, and I spin on my heel, my chest so tight I can't breathe. Whoever is in the hallway outside, it's not a vampire, because I can't sense them; and if the Brotherhood somehow followed me here—

"Auggie?" The voice is muffled—but I know it. "Don't be scared, it's just us!"

When I fling open the door to find Hope and Adriana waiting tensely in the hallway, I burst into unashamed tears. "W-what are you guys doing here? Didn't you leave?"

"Not a chance!" Adriana pushes me back inside, throwing her arms around me.

"I didn't mean to eavesdrop on your thoughts," Hope says, her cheeks pink, "but I could tell how freaked out you were down in the lobby. We figured you might want some company afterward."

"We hid until Marcus and Abuela left, and then we came up." Adriana wraps her arms around me a little tighter. "This is the apartment where they met with Hope, too."

I'm a wreck; I can't stop crying, and I can't stop hugging them. We shuffle to the sofa as a unit and collapse into it, and within a few minutes I've told them everything. The girls hold hands while they listen, and there's a tiny ache in my heart, but this time only a fraction of it is envy. I'm glad they have each other. I don't want the world to end for them.

"I'm still not sure I trust the coven," I admit, squeezing my hands together in my lap. "But it's not like they're just going to leave if I say I won't play ball." A lump forms in my throat, and it takes me two tries to swallow it down. "Apparently, Friday night is when it's all supposed to go down, and they'll come for the Corrupter whether I make it easy or not."

"They're not the only ones," Adriana chimes in fretfully. "Those Knights won't care if this thing comes back in a hundred years, so long as they stop the apocalypse—and even if they learn about the coven, they won't take chances. They're still going to want you dead."

"And the vampires will want to keep you alive." Hope bites her lip. "They'll just raise the pressure—try to make you pick one of them before it's too late."

"Why are you *here*?" Adriana blurts the question, swinging her arms around. With the sun shining through the windows, the apartment is spare but cheerful; it has molded ceilings, exposed brick walls, and a small kitchen with a floor of checkered tile. "They could have taken you anywhere—like Bhutan, or Patagonia, or whatever. Somewhere nobody would ever think to look for you. We're not even an hour away from home!"

Hope shakes her head glumly. "All of this started with the Nexus—its power is what drew the Corrupter here, and they'll need it to drive the Corrupter out." Another faint smile pulls at her lips as she adds, "Secret information courtesy of my uncle's private thoughts. He, Lydia, and Ximena need the boost from the overlapping energy fields to wield the magic that'll be required. If Auggie leaves Fulton Heights, it won't prevent the Ascension from happening, but it might keep them from being able to stop it."

"Oh." Adriana blanches a little. "I like here, then. Here is good." There's a brief silence as she looks around the apartment again, squirming like there's something inside of her trying to get out. A tear rolls down her cheek, and finally, she blurts, "I'm so sorry, Auggie. I'm sorry this is happening, and I'm sorry I can't help, and I'm just . . . sorry. None of this is fair."

And that's when I lose it again, because of course Adriana would be the one person to say what I've needed to hear. It takes me a long moment to steady my breathing and get to a place where I can speak, and I clear my throat. "Actually, I think maybe there is something you can do. I might have . . . kind of a plan, and I need someone I can actually trust to help me."

"Anything." Adriana reaches out and takes my hand, linking the three of us together, and I feel a rush of love—and a little bit of steel.

I'm going to save my parents if it's literally the last thing I do.

32

After they leave, I look around, finding just enough food and supplies in the apartment to last me to Friday . . . and no longer. I also discover a trove of strange items under the sink that I don't understand—candles, rocks, a seashell, and some other things—and I leave them where they are, because the last thing I need now is to get hexed by a bunch of undead sorceresses for playing with their stuff. I have peanut butter for lunch, then mac and cheese for dinner, and I sit in the empty living room while I watch the sky go from rose to navy to black over the water. Stretching my radar as far as it will go, I reach out for familiar signals—but the vampires who watched my house for weeks haven't found me here, and I don't think they will. Cars stream along Lake Shore Drive, the sounds of the city drifting up from fourteen stories below, and somehow, impossibly, I start to hope again.

What if this could be my life? What if I actually survive until graduation, move to a city with rainbow-stickered doors, look through my own windows at a world that continues turning? Maybe my life doesn't have to end in tragedy and become someone else's story to tell, after all.

Maybe I'll actually get to tell it myself.

* * *

As the sun sets the next evening—three more days to go—I pull out that strange collection of witchy things I found under the sink. Over the past day, I've finally come to realize something I should have understood about them from the beginning. Somehow, despite seeing the future multiple times, I still missed what was right in front of me.

Clearing my mind, I reach out for my two remaining allies. I'm miles away from Fulton Heights, and this power is changing every day, but I've been inside both their heads before, and finding them again—even at a great distance—proves easier than I expected. All I have to do is plant a suggestion, and within minutes I know that first one of them and then the other is on the way.

The next time there's a knock at my door, that recognizable whisper is already traveling over my skin, and his scent even seems to hang in the air—lemongrass and cigarettes. When I open the door, Jude Marlowe appears nervous, his brow furrowed, his pouty lips turned down at the edges. He's wearing the same jacket and ripped jeans he had on the day we met, and I try not to check out his knees. I need to play it cool.

"August." He peers past me, looking into the empty apartment. "What . . . am I doing here? What are *you* doing here?"

"It's a long story." I don't elaborate, because whatever I think I can count on him for, it's still better to share only what's necessary. He still works for the Syndicate. "You can come in. I mean, if you need an invitation. I don't own the place, so . . ."

He crosses the threshold and stops in front of me, worried eyes studying my face. "You disappeared yesterday. I went looking for you, and you were gone, and I . . . I started to panic. I thought maybe Rasputin—"

"Don't worry, I'm okay." I'm stating the obvious, but I'm a little flustered. I'd planned on offering Jude a seat, playing the part of considerate host, but he's standing really close to me—his lips are *really close* to mine—and there's this constant *woogah woogah* siren coming from between my legs now. *I'm a mess.* "I kind of had to get out of town."

He nods automatically, and his expression doesn't change. "A group of Syndicate enforcers are due to arrive in Chicago tonight, and . . . there's going to be more of them than I was told to expect. According to Hecuba, the Syndics are breaking into unofficial factions—and to be perfectly honest, I'm afraid of what's coming."

"You're not the only one." My voice cracks, because of course it fucking does. I still can't believe a guy like this actually kissed me on purpose. "Um . . . I kind of need to do something a little invasive? And I hope it's cool with you. Because it's non-negotiable."

It's another thing I'm not even sure I can do until I'm actually doing it. Just like the web of time that Brixia described, Jude's memory is a complicated structure being built a strand at a time; with a bit of care and focus, I detach just the right ones. By the time he leaves this apartment, he won't recall where it is or how he got here—and if he tries to send any telepathic messages to vampires in his lineage, I'll overhear it. I think I trust him . . . but the less he knows, the less he can be forced to divulge later.

Just as I'm finishing up, that sensation prickles my skin again, and the air is suddenly scented with mint and linen—Gunnar is here. When I let him inside, he and Jude eye each other awkwardly, and the air thickens with their confused emotions. It's a conversation I can't help overhearing, a loud mix of hurt, longing, and resentful lust.

"Auggie?" Gunnar slides me a wary look, tousled hair falling in his face. The feelings he has for me are equally palpable, and I try not to blush as I register them. "I'm kind of afraid to ask what's going on. Is this your safe house?"

I mumble a yes noise, once again choosing to elide the details. "Thanks for coming. I brought you guys here because you both promised to help me at one point, and I . . . well, whatever chips I've got, I'm cashing them all in."

"Oh." Gunnar takes a seat on the sofa, and I catch myself staring at his legs. *What* is *it with me and leg parts?* "This doesn't have anything to do with all the Syndicate foot soldiers coming to town, does it?"

Jude starts visibly. "How did you—" He catches himself, his expression tightening, and he narrows his eyes. "Why is August wearing your necklace?"

"Because I gave it to him." Gunnar's tone drips with smug satisfaction.

"*Stop.*" I hold both of my hands up. "You guys have eternity to flirtagonize and pretend you don't still want to bone, but there's a really good chance that literal Armageddon is coming in a few days, and I need your help. So can you focus for a second?"

Chastened, Jude sits down in one of the chairs while I work my memory magic on Gunnar, and when I'm done, he states primly, "I know I promised to help you, August, but there are certain things I cannot talk about in front of him. The League of the Dark Star operates outside the Syndicate's directives, and that makes them our enemies."

"*Enemies,*" Gunnar repeats, rolling his eyes like there's a camera on him. "That's always how it is with you, isn't it? Either I do everything you say, or I'm the enemy. You're so obsessed with 'directives' invented thousands of years ago that you can't even imagine there's a way to exist without them and not be *evil*. You're such a Virgo, Jude!"

"Excuse me—"

"*Knock it off!*" I interrupt them both—again. "Back to your

301

corners, okay? Believe it or not, I didn't bring you here to play couples therapy."

"I'm sorry." Slumping back, Gunnar crosses his arms over his chest and glares. "I shouldn't have let him get to me like that."

He's being deliberately provocative, but I don't even care; two more minutes of this and I'll set them both on fire with my brain. Quickly, I state, "There's a chance that the Ascension can be stopped after all." When I have their attention, both of them staring, I feel a tremor of possibility. "I don't know how likely it is, but I'm going to take it, and if it doesn't work . . . well, you need to know I'm not letting this thing out into the world."

"Auggie." Gunnar reaches for his chest, seeming to forget he isn't wearing his necklace anymore. "If you're talking about . . . ending your own life, there's no point in trying—the Corrupter won't let you. When he manifests in a new body, he links his survival imperative to the vessel's subconscious. By the time you started dreaming about his past lives, it was already too late. Even if you tried, you wouldn't be able to go through with it."

"Don't worry, that's not what I mean." What's strange is that it isn't until just now that I realize I've never even seriously considered it, despite how obvious it is. I shudder a little, wondering just how much of my subconscious is actually occupied. "If the Ascension can't be stopped, then I'll go down fighting. I'll take on the entire Order of the Northern Wolf at once, if I have to, and I'll kill as many of them as I can until my body gives out."

"Auggie, you . . ." Gunnar stops and shakes his head with an agitated frown. "Even if it drains you like it did the other night, you might only lose consciousness again—and then they'd just grab you, and the Ascension would happen anyway. There's nothing in the ancient writings that says you have to be awake or responsive for the Dark Star to surface."

"I know." I cross my arms and look at the floor. "Using Azazel's power out in the open probably won't kill me . . . but the Knights of Perseus will."

Saying it out loud doesn't feel any better than thinking it. I don't want to die, but I still don't know if the coven really wants to cast Azazel out of me—or if they even can. But whatever else happens on Friday, I'm going to stop the Corrupter, even if I have to use my enemies to do it.

"About a half-dozen Knights staked out your house yesterday," Gunnar acknowledges. "And that's in addition to all the vampires that were already in place. Given the personalities involved, it's a miracle that war didn't break out."

"Those men were just the tip of the iceberg." Jude leans forward, clasping his hands together. "Ever since the death of Jesse Strauss, the Syndicate has been ramping up its intelligence operations against the Persean Knights. We've intercepted a flurry of messages over the past forty-eight hours that make it clear the Brotherhood is mustering all its forces for this. They essentially are preparing for a war."

"Good." Discreetly, I wipe the sweat off my palms. "I'm arranging one for them."

"Is that where we come in?" Jude cocks a brow. "You want us to convince Viviane and the Syndics to unite against Rasputin and the Brotherhood? Because honestly, August, you'd have better luck getting blood from a stone."

"Can you imagine?" Gunnar shares a glance with Jude, and for one unguarded moment they both giggle. "They'd be like cats in a bag."

"Trust me, I'm not expecting anyone to act out of character. There's actually something way more important that I need from you two." I cast a glance toward the kitchen, where the items I found beneath the sink are waiting to be used. "Tomorrow, I'm sending out word to Rasputin that I'm willing to join the Order of the Northern Wolf."

"What?" Jude goes still. "August, you can't—"

"I resisted his demands, I killed one of his minions, I fled town—"

"He doesn't know you were the one who killed William," Gunnar argues quickly. "We were inside the school, and away from the windows. His spies couldn't see us, and for all he knows, I—"

"That's not the point." I hold my hands up again. "Time's running out, things are escalating, and he's not going to be patient much longer. I don't want him to start sending pieces of my parents to the local newspaper in order to up the ante, you know?" Letting my arms drop, I exhale a shaky breath. "I mean, I'm obviously not going through with it, but I need him to think he's still in control before he starts to get worried.

"And that brings me to why you're here." Sinking down into the same chair I used when I met the coven, I grip my knees until my fingers turn white. "No matter what happens on Friday, my parents need to be rescued, and Azazel needs to be stopped, and . . . and you guys are the only ones I can trust to make sure that happens."

They exchange another look, and Gunnar begins, "Auggie—"

"I know: Your bosses have big plans, and you've been given orders, and blobbity blah. But I *know* you." I make eye contact with both of them. "Neither one of you came here wanting the Ascension to happen, and nobody knows what this thing inside of me is going to want when it breaks free." Squeezing my knees tighter, I add, "We're talking about the 'father of all vampires'—an actual angel who's spent all of human existence trying to get back here and assert itself. This thing isn't looking to take orders from its children, and making me pinky swear my allegiance and hoping it counts for jack shit later is nuts."

Jude's mouth curves into a hollow smile. "All right. You're not wrong—about any of it—but promising to help is . . . I mean, we still don't know where Rasputin is hiding, let alone where he might be keeping prisoners. Besides, the oath I swore to the Syndicate will prevent me from acting against their interests. No doubt Gunnar is in the same position."

"Actually," Gunnar mumbles, suddenly fixated on his fingernails, "I never swore an oath to the League."

Jude does an actual cartoon double take. "Wait, what?"

"Viviane never asked me to." Gunnar shrugs, his gaze flicking to Jude and then back down again. "Kramer made her pledge her blood before he would Turn her, and even though she eventually came to believe, she didn't want me or anyone else to be deprived of free will."

Jude continues to stare at him. "You mean you've had the ability to walk away at any time, but you've *chosen* to stay with them?"

"Obviously." Gunnar bites the word off.

"I still don't understand." Jude's massages his brow. "You joined them despite never believing in their central cause, and even though they hold nothing over you, you still do all their bidding anyway?" Gunnar doesn't answer him, so he presses, "How does Viviane Duclos know you won't betray her entire organization?"

"Because she trusts me, okay?" Gunnar finally explodes. "This isn't easy! I joined the League because Viviane was a friend to me when I needed one the most, and because she's never done anything but help me figure out who I am and what I want. Maybe that whole concept is alien to you—"

"Hey!" Jude rises to the bait instantly, his eyes smoldering. "When I Turned you without authorization, I put my position at risk and jeopardized all of the relationships I had with the only people that *I've* ever trusted—including Hecuba! How have you possibly forgotten that?" Tossing out his arms, he snaps, "You're so determined to cast me as a villain that you've decided you never mattered to me, and it's bullshit!"

"Rasputin is going to kill my parents if you don't help me save them," I interrupt loudly. Maybe I'm not sad I never had a boyfriend. "Letting innocent humans get slaughtered by a megalomaniac with a god complex won't help either the League *or* the Syndicate—and if my one shot at surviving this fails, then the Ascension proceeds and the whole world will be destroyed. Figure out how you feel about that."

There's a long silence, stars glittering through the tall windows, before Jude rubs his face. "Just . . . what is it you expect us to do? How are we supposed to pull this off?"

So I tell them—what parts of my plan make sense, and which I can safely share—and they listen with pensive expressions. There are a lot of critical gaps in my account, and by the time I'm done, I'm sweating. Without the full picture, it's an incredibly weak case, but I've got no other choice. "I know this is a lot to ask, and I'm sorry, but . . . I won't be able to just take your word that you'll help me. I need both of you to swear a blood oath."

Jude stills. "What?"

"I'm sorry," I repeat, scrubbing moisture from my hairline. "Even if things go perfectly, Friday night is going to be overwhelming, and Rasputin . . ." It takes a moment for me to work the kinks out of my voice. "He'll use my parents against me. I won't be able to focus unless I'm sure they're covered—and if the shit really hits the fan, I need to know that someone will push the reset button before I pop out the final boss." For the umpteenth time in the past few days, I reach up to adjust the glasses I'm no longer wearing. "Please do this. Please. I can't . . . I don't have a better argument than that. If the Ascension is stopped, we save the world; but these are two things I can't do by myself, and I *need* you. Please."

"August," Jude says again, but he can't seem to find any more words after that.

"You said the Syndicate doesn't even believe in the Corrupter—not officially." I'm pleading at this point, all but on bended knee. "So anything you might do to keep him from taking over isn't technically against their interests, right?"

Squirming, fidgeting, his expression miserable, Gunnar interrupts. "I'll do it."

"You will?" It's my turn for the double take.

"I've been thinking about what you said the other night—about all my chances, and how you only get this one? You were right: It's not fair. And Viviane . . . she's so close to something she's dreamed of for centuries that she's lost sight of her own principles." He looks around the room, like maybe it's the last time he'll ever see freedom. "She thinks we need the Dark Star to save the world, but maybe we don't. *She's* the one I've always believed in, not Azazel, and her dreams can come true without him." He gives me a melancholy smile. "I hope she understands, but . . . I promised you I'd help, and I meant it."

I turn to Jude, who has his clasped hands now pressed tightly to his mouth, but when he meets my eyes, he gives a minute nod. "Okay. I . . . okay."

"Really?" If anything, Gunnar is even more surprised than I am.

"You have no idea what kind of ground game Rasputin has, or how many lackeys he might have Turned by now, just to protect his objectives," Jude answers irritably. "If you try this alone, you'll get killed, and I . . . I won't let that happen."

Gunnar stiffens. "I know how to watch my own back."

"Of course you do—I trained you. But there's no way this is a one-man job. You'll need help." Jude rolls his shoulders. "Anyway, believe it or not, I don't want you to die, and I don't want the Corrupter to Ascend. If there's any way my entering into this pact will aid the plan to stop him, I'm on board, and that's all there is to it." With a defeated gesture, he adds, "Besides, Auggie is right: Absent a guarantee that they would control him, Azazel is a threat to the Syndics' entire power structure. So in my view—and Hecuba's—anything I do to prevent the Ascension *is* in their best interests."

"Okay." I bob my head, my insides careening around like a pinball game. Now that they've agreed, it feels like we somehow just took a massive leap closer to Friday. "Okay."

Mechanically, I retrieve my items from the kitchen and arrange them on the floor in a circle, following my instincts. I place a hunk of crystal in one position, to signify earth; in the next, I set a cone of incense, its smoke meant to call forth the element of air; then a bit of volcanic rock for fire, a seashell for water, and a budding twig for wood. The last element, metal, is represented by a coin so old its engravings are worn away completely.

Jude arches a brow. "You're certainly prepared."

"Sort of?" I don't want to admit just how much I'm winging it, here. Setting out a bowl and a group of seven candles, I then move around the apartment, drawing the thick black curtains across the windows—not for any particular reason, but because that's how I remember it. The exposed brick walls, the heavy drapes, the bowl and candlelight and smoking incense . . . My visions changed a little, but each time the room looked like this. I've got what might be a cyclone of bumblebees swarming in my guts, because my visions *also* consistently featured a lot of nakedness, and I still don't know if I'm ready for that.

When I turn back to the circle, to the two vampires who wait and watch, my heart thuds between my legs as I remember them without their shirts. I'm such a joke—about to enter into a mystical pact with the undead, on the precipice of literal doomsday, and I'm getting a boner. Life would be a lot easier if I could've been born a hermit crab or something.

Gunnar senses my hesitance and cocks his head. "Auggie?"

"I . . ." I'm at full mast now, and I'm not sure they can't tell. Maybe getting my soul immolated won't be so bad after all. "I don't really know how to do this."

"It's less intimidating than it seems." Jude smiles at me. "We can walk you through it. The ritual is essentially the same from one pact to the next, although the specific steps might vary depending on the participants."

"Okay." I force myself to come closer, and they hold out their hands for me, bringing me into the circle. They walk me through the steps, and together we light candles and invoke the elements. A warm glow beats the walls, the air sweet with incense, and the circle floods with energy as I fumble nervously with a sterilized lance.

"Remember: It's more about the intention than the words," Jude says softly. "Just speak from the heart."

Holding my breath, I prick my fingertip, drawing a bead of dark blood. Gunnar makes a noise in the back of his throat, and when I look up, both vampires' eyes blaze a bright, hot gold. As I squeeze a few drops of the thick fluid into the bowl, I struggle through a basic oath with their coaching. "May the blood I spill tonight signify my intent: to rescue my parents and halt the Ascension. Let those who would share my goal join their will to mine, bind their deeds to their word, and swear their troth by this act."

I pass the lance to Gunnar, who stares for a speechless moment before pricking his own finger. "May the blood I spill tonight signify my intent: to rescue Auggie's parents and halt the Ascension. I join my will to his, my deeds to my word, and I swear my troth."

Jude goes next, his blood mixing with ours, and he repeats the phrase. No sooner has he spoken than the puddle in the bowl turns black. It crackles and sparks, and a plume of smoke rises from it to mingle with the incense, leaving behind only a smudge of ashes.

Something sweeps through me, the thick energy inside the circle dispersing—and I can tell right away the magic has worked. The sensation is exhilarating and terrifying at once, because this was no entry-level spell; once again, I performed real-deal sorcery, something I could only accomplish because of what's gradually expanding inside of me.

"That's it," Jude declares quietly, once we've released the elements and closed the circle. "It's done."

Gunnar's eyes still glow, the tips of his fangs showing, and when I catch him staring again, he shrinks back. "I'm sorry, honestly. I didn't mean to . . . It's just . . . It's your blood. I've never smelled anything like it."

"It's the Corrupter." Jude speaks in a reverent hush, threads of golden light swimming in his eyes as well. "It has to be. He's so close to the surface, his magic is all the way through you."

"Oh." I look down at my finger, at the tiny puncture that hasn't had time to close, filled with anxious curiosity.

"I-is there . . . ," Gunnar stammers and shuts his mouth; then, "Can I . . . taste you?" Embarrassment suffuses his expression, but he continues, "Please? I'll be careful, I promise, but I just . . ."

I'm not sure what to say. I've always been taught to say no to a request like this, to never volunteer my blood to a vampire—because what if they lose control? But the way he asks makes my heart race, pressure building in my groin again as I consider the intimacy of such an act, and I'm holding my hand out to him before I know it.

He parts his lips, sliding his tongue across the tip of my finger, and sparks dance up my spine as his lids flutter closed in pleasure. I gurgle out a sigh when his lips close around my knuckle, as he draws a gentle trickle of blood from the puncture, and my pulse beats like a blacksmith's hammer. After a moment, Gunnar pulls back, his eyes glowing even brighter when they open again. "Jude, you have to taste this."

He passes my hand to his ex-boyfriend, who blinks heavily, his golden eyes fixed on mine in a stupor. When Jude accepts my finger, taking me into his mouth, my head spins with fear and desire. His cheekbones sharpen before my eyes, something about my blood pushing him deeper into his transformation.

Gunnar's hand slides over my chest, his lips brushing my ear, his voice rough as he asks, "Can we drink from you?"

I turn to look at him, and find him wearing the face he had the night we kissed in his car—all sharp angles and strange, terrifying beauty. "Is it . . . safe?"

"We'll take care of you," Jude murmurs against my fingertip, his lips impossibly soft. "Neither of us wants you to be hurt."

"If you have a little bit of our blood first, it'll help your body replenish whatever you lose." Gunnar's mouth grazes against the side of my neck, and every part of my body that can stand up is *up*. "We'll go slow, and we'll never take so much that you're in danger."

"When it's done the right way, feeding can be pleasurable for both humans and vampires." Jude removes his jacket and then his shirt, his skin polished by candlelight. His eyes meet mine. "We'll do it the right way."

"Turning involves much more than all this, so you don't have to worry," Gunnar adds, his mouth just below my ear. "Nothing has to happen tonight that you don't want, okay? The choice is yours—just say the word."

This is, of course, exactly what I'm worried about. It's almost ironic: Only days ago, I was asking Jude to make me into a vampire—to exploit a supernatural loophole, and save both me *and* the world. But now I've got a chance to live again, to save everyone, and I don't want to lose it. If this drinking game goes wrong, all my plans are destroyed. But I trust these two undead boys, I realize, and I think I want to know what Jude means when he says feeding can be pleasurable.

My nerves are snapping like castanets, and I can't speak—but I manage a staccato nod. I want to know what this feels like, and I trust them as much as I'm willing to trust anyone. "Okay. Yes."

"Say stop when you need to," Gunnar purrs against the beat of my jugular, while Jude sinks his fangs into his own wrist, breaking the skin and drawing blood to the surface.

"Swallow as much as you can," he advises me. "It'll make the experience last longer for all of us." He presses his slippery flesh against my mouth, and my tongue lights up with it, an irresistible current of energy pouring into me.

I knew what to expect, and yet it still takes my breath away, this heart-pounding taste of forbidden fruit. My body warms as I drink, my own blood stirring as it meets the magic, electricity spiraling through my limbs.

Gunnar's hand finds its way under my shirt, lifting it over my head as I release Jude's wrist, and his touch against my bare skin is a million feathers—it's a hard rain, a lightning storm—and a sound presses from my lungs. The air sharpens, candlelight climbing to the ceiling, as bright as their eyes. My back arches when Gunnar's teeth pierce the flesh on one side of my neck, the pain momentary and somehow exquisite, and Jude whispers just beneath my ear, "No matter what happens Friday, tonight only has to be about us."

He bites down, then, and as they drink, swallowing in time with the beat of my heart, the electricity jumps from my body. Tendrils of my expanding mind flow into the two vampires that feed from me, their thoughts spreading open like petals at the softest touch. Their memories and emotions run through me, a current that swirls and eddies, volatile and aching and filled with want. Jude's hand slides across my skin until it reaches Gunnar's, and their fingers interlock, pressing against my bare chest.

It's love and hunger, a temporary truce, a moment where they both relinquish the past and choose bliss. Tonight is about us.

Warmth pours out of me, lifting us up, and we float toward the ceiling.

33

Just before sunrise the next morning, after doing me one last favor, Jude and Gunnar depart. Despite the fact that they won't recall where they were, they will remember everything we discussed—and everything we did. I'm finally certain I can trust them; they could have bled me dry, feasting on the magic that fills my veins, but they controlled themselves. And with even their most carefully hidden feelings now written indelibly in my memory, I know they'll do what I've asked.

I sleep late into the afternoon and then spend some time reviewing my plans yet again. One of the requests I made of Hope and Adriana was to leave a series of notes around Fulton Heights with a message for Rasputin: *I'm willing to meet your terms, but first you need to prove that my parents are alive and unharmed.* With a dummy email address at the bottom, I scribbled out enough for them to tack up all over town—school, Sugar Mama's, Colgate Center, the abandoned factory, and even my front door.

Rasputin isn't the only one who needs to get the message, and scattering a few breadcrumbs is the only way I can think of to get everyone following the trail.

As the shadows grow long, the sky turning lavender above the water, the streetlamps blink on against the gathering dusk—and I finally leave the apartment. Head down and collar up, I strike out for the nearest library. Vampires roam the city—my radar strong enough now for me to detect even their moods—but none of them are here for me.

It's twenty minutes until closing when I hunker down at a public internet terminal and sign in to my new email account. I could use my phone for this, but I'm far too paranoid at this point. Five groups want to get their hands on the Corrupter, the newest of which is a century old, and all of them have had plenty of time to prepare—to hack my GPS or plant a source capable of tracking my cell usage . . . I'm not taking any chances.

My inbox contains a single email, a blank message with an attached video. Although I try to brace myself, there's no way to prepare for what I see when I open it. My parents, pale and wild-eyed, still dressed as I last saw them, sit side by side on plain wooden chairs. They don't look hurt—but they don't look well, either, their bodies rigid with fright. On either side, they're flanked by vampires with matching, blank-eyed expressions of cruel glee, and my finger trembles as I press play.

"Auggie . . ." My father's voice cracks as he says my name, and I start to weep, just like that, struggling to be silent. "We're okay. We're alive and unhurt. We're being treated well."

"If you pledge your loyalty to the Order of the Northern Wolf tonight, they'll let us go." My mother stares into the camera, her pupils so wide her eyes are completely black. They're being mind-controlled. "Come alone to the old metro station on Culver Avenue after midnight tonight. Please, Auggie. Please save us."

"If you don't, they'll kill us." My father hesitates. "They'll start with your mother, and they'll . . . take her apart slowly."

"Please save us," my mother repeats—and the video cuts off.

I sit there, sobbing quietly into my hands, for so long that a five-minute warning comes on over the library's speakers. Out of everything I've gone through, this is what almost breaks me, what almost makes me forfeit my ridiculous scheme and give in to Rasputin's demands. Even though my parents would die anyway, at least it wouldn't happen because of my hubris.

Quaking so badly I can barely find the right keys, I manage to type a response:

These are my terms: On Friday night, two hours after sundown, you will come to the west picnic grounds at Colgate Woods, and you will bring my parents. When I see them with my own eyes, alive and unharmed, I'll take the oath. If either of them has so much as a paper cut, or if you go anywhere near my friends in the meantime, you will die in agony. I have access to more of Azazel's powers than you think. Don't bother responding to this message.

After I hit send, it takes nearly all the time I have left to get myself under control, but I finally write one last message to Adriana, delete my account, and leave the library.

The next day and a half pass like a trip over Niagara Falls in a barrel full of broken glass, my hands constantly sweaty, every moment a new opportunity to second-guess my strategy. To hate myself for terminating any chance of further communications with Rasputin. It was the smart thing to do, I know that—my only leverage lies in my refusal to negotiate, my depriving him the chance to send me a video even worse than the first.

He needs me, I keep telling myself, and I laid out my conditions plainly. No matter how angry he gets that I didn't jump at his command, he wants control of the Corrupter more than he cares about hurting my parents. When he tries to reply to my email and it bounces back, he'll see that there's no point in lashing out at me by deliberately violating the terms, because I'd never know. I repeat it over and over . . . but I'm not very convincing.

Even if Rasputin thinks rationally, there's still plenty of horrible things he could do to my parents that won't leave a mark. He could break their legs, heal them with vampire blood, and then break their legs again—over and over, all to punish me for my insolence. Just thinking about it invites a panic attack . . . but if I give in to his demands, the world would be irrevocably doomed, and my parents along with it.

My clock is ticking loud enough to have an echo by now, and I'm beginning to feel the entity that's Rising inside of me—something moving just out of sight. The witches didn't say exactly what hour I should expect the Ascension, and I exist in a state of constant panic that it will happen too soon, that my big gamble will turn up snake eyes in the end.

On the other hand, they obviously need me present to perform their ritual—whatever its true aims are—and their understanding of how the future unfolds is precise enough to have accurately predicted my movements a week in advance. Maybe if they chose not to tell me something, it means they didn't need to. Given the many ways my night with Jude and Gunnar differed from the visions I'd had of that same event, I'm finally starting to believe destiny might truly be malleable; that Brixia was telling the truth when she said only fools believe in fate.

Maybe the coven can defeat Azazel after all.

Maybe.

On Friday evening, an hour before sunset, I clean the apartment, set the key on the kitchen counter, and then leave the building for the last time. My hands trembling and my gut tied up in frigid knots, I'm finally on my way back home.

34

Part of the Cook County Forest Preserve, Colgate Woods is one link in a chain of nature areas that meanders throughout Chicago's suburbs. Crisscrossed by streams and walking paths, it's a convenient escape from city life, and a vast clearing on its west end—at the base of an overgrown slope separating it from the former industrial sector of Fulton Heights—is a popular spot for picnics. Public and accessible, it's officially closed after dark, and the only light available comes from the moon.

This is the location I've selected for the Corrupter's final showdown.

The sky is clear and the air is glacial as I watch from the trees, everything clicking into place. Detecting the vampires that gather in the darkness requires no effort now, ghostly whispers scurrying back and forth across my skin, and I stick to the shadows, aware of how quickly the dominoes will fall once I show myself. Undead blood— from a vial Jude filled on Wednesday morning—pumps through my veins, amplifying my senses.

An hour early, the first of Rasputin's outriders dart past, three of them, their signals weaving through the birch grove on the north side of the clearing as they check the terrain. They look for me, but I'm not worried; they won't see me until I want them to. When they've completed their scouting mission, they retreat—and when the appointed time arrives, their golden eyes flicker to life in the gloom festering among the trees. Two by two more eyes appear, like fairy lights, as a small army of shiftless undead soldiers secure the field for their general.

"August Pfeiffer?" Wind shakes the branches, and traffic whooshes by on the main road, just out of sight, but Grigori Rasputin's heavily accented voice still sounds loud and clear across the picnic grounds. "Come out, come out, wherever you are . . ."

"I want to see my parents," I call back, and the golden eyes neither blink nor waver at my demand. There are seventeen sets, but I sense twenty-one vampires hiding in the birch grove. "Show me you complied with my terms, and I'll come out."

"Show me yours and I'll show you mine." His taunting voice circles the clearing like a boomerang, the source impossible to determine. He's using magic. "This little scene is more public than I care for, August Pfeiffer. Too unprotected. I do not wish to walk into a trap."

"Neither do I." We're all at risk here, and that's the point. The Syndicate and the League will do anything to stop me from making a deal with Rasputin—and the Brotherhood wants to see me dead no matter what. A meeting at Colgate Woods leaves everyone vulnerable . . . but there are dozens of escape routes, and few ways to rig the playing field. "The second I come out there, you'll probably grab me! And how do I even know you still have my parents? How am I supposed to know they're okay?"

"If you don't come out, how am *I* to know you did not lure me here to be killed?" He counters, his singsong voice still making eerie rounds over the clearing. "But if you insist . . ."

A moment later, another voice splits the night, ragged and heartrending. "*Auggie, whatever he wants, don't give it to h—*"

The warning cuts off abruptly, plunged into silence . . . but not before it has its intended effect. My throat closes, my vision wobbles, and for just a moment I'm six years old again. "D-Dad?"

"You will see your parents once I see you, August Pfeiffer." The Mad Monk's voice contains a wicked smile.

Freshman year, right after I came out, I had the classic recurring nightmare about being naked in front of my entire class. That sense of total exposure was nothing compared to what I feel when I leave the shadows for the moonlight, drowning in the vast openness of the picnic grounds. I'm radioactive with nerves, visible from space, with an angel uncoiling inside me. More whispers scatter across my skin, a snare closing, and I swallow hard.

The dominoes are beginning to fall.

"Okay." My voice is so thin it could splice atoms. "Here I am. Now it's your turn."

Shapes begin to form around the golden eyes that hover in the trees, bodies emerging from the darkness in unison. Seventeen figures, all wearing identical robes of flowing white fabric, step into the clearing—staring creepily, like those animatronic bears at amusement parks. I brace myself, readying for an attack . . . and that's when I hear the squeak and crunch of heavy wheels passing over dirt—when I sense three of the remaining Northern Wolf vampires approaching.

A wooden cart trundles into view, creaking and unsteady, from the mouth of a dark trail that snakes through the birch trees. Pushed by Rasputin's remaining stooges, its weathered chassis bears up a sizeable cage, like something meant to hold tigers for a traveling circus—only the trembling, pitiful creatures being held in captivity aren't animals. They're my parents.

"Auggie?" My mother's voice breaks when she sees me, her face gray, haggard with fear; and I take two frantic steps forward before I remember how much peril I'm in. I've got limitless opportunities to lose everything, but only one chance to save the people I love. To save *the world*. Rasputin wants to break me, to provoke me into charging, and I have to be smarter than that. Even if it hurts beyond enduring.

Just now, my heart sparking and explosive, I want to mesmerize these zombies into letting my parents go—to turn them against each other in a death match . . . but I don't try. Even with vampire blood in my system, I know instinctively that I can't control this many minds at once. The Corrupter's hour is approaching, and I can feel him pulling away; pretty soon, this body won't be big enough for the both of us, and one of us will have to go.

I'm starting to lose my grip on his power, and I'm running out of time.

My parents clutch the bars of their cage, crying out—but the only sound they make is my name, over and over: *Auggie, Auggie, Auggie.* The rest of their vocabulary has been stripped from them, certainly by magic, but those two repeated syllables are filled with anguish, love, and desperation. I'm sobbing when the birches give a sudden shake, a figure launching over the treetops, dropping in a graceful arc to land twenty feet in front of me.

Clad in a black tunic with embroidered occult markings, Grigori Rasputin leers at me with eyes like rolling lava. His followers shift behind him, straightening their shoulders, and a few of them even salute. Twisting his mouth into a smile, he intones, "We meet again. I wonder, will you run away like a scared child this time, as well?"

"Let my parents go." I can barely get the words out, my throat hot. "Until they're out of that cage, there's no deal, you son of a bitch."

"Such spirit!" He gives a condescending laugh, and his acolytes laugh with him, a blood-curdling Greek chorus that falls silent at a gesture from one of his spidery hands. His expression droops into a thoughtful frown. "I think, however, this is a condition I cannot meet. Without your parents under my protection, what guarantee do I have that you will honor our agreement?"

"Unless you set them free now, what guarantee do *I* have that you'll do it at all?" I make a tentative mind-push into Rasputin's consciousness—but I hit a brick wall. He's shielded himself with the same kind of magic the coven used. I wonder if he's bothered to protect the rest of his crew. "No more negotiating!"

My paranormal radar system is going haywire, my skin crawling from the inside out. Rasputin wants me to take this oath as a guarantee, but if he truly believes the Corrupter is on his side, then all he has to do is grab me right now. Somewhere above us, the planets are gliding into formation, and I probably have just minutes left to pull this frying pan out of the fire. I'm going to need all the luck the universe has to offer.

"It would seem, then, that we are at something of an impasse." Spreading his hands philosophically, the Mad Monk shrugs. "We both have something the other wants, and neither of us is willing to conciliate." And then he grins malevolently, his face darkening. "If only there was perhaps something I could do to change your mind . . ."

He makes another languid gesture, and one of the vampires that pushed the circus cart reaches into the leather bag that hangs from his shoulder—and pulls out a blowtorch. A spear of blue flame leaps from the nozzle with a hiss, and my mother yelps as she and my father jolt away from the bars, huddling together. Like they know it's meant for them . . . like they're already familiar with it.

Rage dissolves my reason, a red filter passing over the world, and I plunge my will straight into Blowtorch Guy's body. The Corrupter's gravity stirs his blood, and shock flares in his eyes as heat spills through him. Balefully, I growl, "Careful when you play with fire."

This isn't a smart move. This confrontation has barely started, and I'm already throwing the first punch—I've already let Rasputin destabilize me, and I don't know what the fallout will be. As the vampire's face turns pink, I hesitate, caught between the urge to stop and the urge to finish what I've begun.

And that's when the next domino falls.

"*Grigori Rasputin!*" Eyes blazing and cheekbones canted, Jude Marlowe bursts from a cluster of evergreens on the eastern edge of the picnic grounds. He's dressed in black and looks every inch a debonair killer. "You have violated the codes and precepts established by the Syndicate of Vampires, and on their authority you are ordered to stand down!"

The undead cleric rolls his eyes, his shoulders sagging in annoyance. "Oh good. An interruption." Dismissively, he answers, "I appreciate theatrics as much as anyone, but as you can see, we are busy here. Go play cops and robbers somewhere else."

"You led an unsanctioned raiding party that took numerous lives—mortal and vampire," Jude continues, his voice booming. "Your group's actions were reckless and unprovoked, and now our entire community is threatened by human retaliation." He avoids looking my way. I didn't put him up to this—the Syndics absolutely want Rasputin's head on a platter—but he only knew to be here because of me. "The Syndicate will not tolerate contempt for its directives, and as the self-declared leader of the Order of the Northern Wolf, you will answer for its crimes."

Anger finally tightens Rasputin's features, his brows pulling together. "You pretend to have authority over me? Your ridiculous organization makes a mockery of what our kind can be, what we are destined for! You crawl in darkness when we might all march in the light, and I reject your petty restrictions." He waves his hands, and eight of his minions turn toward Jude with a guttural hiss and a flaring of their eyes. "You may go. I am in a good mood, so I will even allow you thirty seconds before my children hunt you down."

"I'm not leaving without you," Jude returns darkly, his teeth stretching longer.

"Then you won't be leaving." Rasputin's claws extend, his face beginning to reshape. Behind him, those eight minions step out of formation to flank him. "I have business to attend to, and I fear no retribution—not from humans, and certainly not from you."

"Have it your way," Jude says with a feral grin—and right on cue, more figures come crashing through the pines behind him. Eyes blazing and faces sharpened like axe heads, two dozen new vampires appear, arraying themselves for battle with rehearsed precision. "I didn't come armed with words alone."

Rasputin's eyes flicker, and over by the rolling cage, the blowtorch extinguishes as silent communication passes between the master and his progeny. He's got twenty mindless, helter-skelter goons willing to die for him, but as he faces twenty-five of the Syndicate's hand-picked enforcers, he's starting to look like he might be at least a little afraid of retribution after all.

Hostility crackles in the air as the two factions square off, and I glance nervously around the clearing, thinking about my great escape. These gangs are ready for battle, but they're not going to forget what they're fighting over; and while Jude may speak for the Syndicate, he doesn't control the vampires backing him up . . . and plain as day, I can hear four of them thinking about their private orders to take me into custody at any cost. I'm not out of the woods yet—figuratively or literally.

The opposing packs advance on each other, and I step back. It's cold and getting colder—but my breath leaves no trace on the night air, and I'm hoping neither side notices. Sixteen of Rasputin's flunkies now fall in line as he closes the gap with Jude, while two stand guard by my parents' cage and two more focus their attentions on me. The cleric bares his teeth, about to speak . . . when a ghostly cry pierces the building tension.

An owl swoops across the clearing, its wings spread against the moonlight; as it circles, its call is answered, the treetops coming alive with a strange howling. The raptor banks sharply and plummets—coming straight at me, with dark vapor pouring from its feathers. When it's four feet away, the creature suddenly rears, erupting into a starburst of smoke that swallows it . . . and then dissolves to reveal a smiling Viviane Duclos.

"Hi, Auggie." She surveys the disagreement taking shape around us, and her eyes smolder to life. "Looks like we joined the party just in time."

The picnic grounds fill once again with that cacophony of eerie hooting, and then bodies begin to drop out of the trees. The birch grove shivers as eight vampires—including Gunnar—leap to the ground behind Rasputin's crew and eight more break free from the shadows atop the evergreens, landing to instantly outflank the Syndicate. The League of the Dark Star might be the smallest force on the ground tonight, but they've already got their foes surrounded.

Perforce, the other factions divide—splitting their focus again. Eight of Rasputin's sidekicks turn on Gunnar, while eight stay with their master, and ten of the Syndicate enforcers reverse position to counter the rear ambush. The four that were watching me earlier simply break ranks, their agenda here wholly different than that of their friends. When they inch in my direction, Viviane brandishes her claws, daring them to try.

My heart beats in my throat as I watch this all unspool, a tinderbox moment on the verge of exploding, and I take another step back. This chaos is just what I had in mind.

Bloodshed was always inevitable, the killers and cultists

dogging my footsteps, clamoring for violence from day one. All along I've known that I would be helpless in the end: one pathetic little art kid against a legion of vicious, undying monsters. The enemy of my enemy is still my enemy—but if I can force them to fight each other, they're useful, nonetheless. I gave Rasputin an ultimatum, and I told both Jude and Gunnar beforehand to make sure their sides would be present as well. All that's missing is the one group I have no "in" with, and I can only hope that the bread crumbs I arranged will lead them here.

"You must be Viviane Duclos." Rasputin evaluates her carefully, and I finally realize that the night they fought in the street, he had no idea who she was. Until now, what she really looked like had remained a calculated mystery, and the glamours she'd cast over herself to become Daphne Banks were sophisticated enough to fool even him. With mock formality, the Mad Monk notes, "We are ill-met by moonlight—again."

"Like old times." Viviane gives him a sweet smile with malice carved into its edges. "Sad to say, I won't be pulling my punches tonight. If you have any last words for your drones, you should probably get them off your chest now."

"A very good point." He rubs his jaw. My captive parents were his advantage, but they're now a liability; he still has to guard them, even while fighting a war on two fronts and trying to keep me out of enemy hands at the same time. With Viviane as my personal guardian, his job just got even harder. After a moment, he calls out, "My last words: Kill them all, and leave no one standing but the boy."

With a gesture, Rasputin signals the two minions he'd assigned to watch me, directing them to rejoin their brethren while he moves to face Viviane himself. Jude evaluates the change in lineup, his gaze moving from us to the cage with my parents in it, and, back among the birches, Gunnar is doing the same. I can practically hear the fuse sizzling as the tinderbox prepares to blow, and still the guest list isn't full yet.

The spark jumps suddenly, the twenty-one vampires of the Northern Wolf snapping their jaws open and hissing in unison—and then it's bedlam in Colgate Woods. All three factions surge together, a storm of teeth and claws and golden eyes, flesh tearing and bones shattering in a grotesque symphony. Those four Syndicate vampires finally make their move on me, but Viviane and Rasputin both whirl, lunging to intercept the attack. Their magic crackles, smoke threading under the moon as they streak through the air.

The Syndicate vampires don't stand a chance. The first quite literally loses his head, as well as a few vertebrae, when Rasputin decapitates him bare-handed—and the others fare no better. In two swift moves, Viviane produces a hidden stake, diving under one man's arm to thrust it into the chest of another. Then, she swings back in the same motion, impaling the first as he spins around to face her. Both enforcers drop to the ground, already rotting, just as the Mad Monk is polishing off his second victim.

The decks cleared, the two faction leaders eye each other again—and charge. More smoke rolls across open ground as they finally clash together in a furious display of feints and strikes. Their back-and-forth movements are hypnotizing, violence as choreography, feet and claws meeting like swords in a fencing match. My time is running out, I can feel it, but I stay put. Jude and Gunnar are both fighting their way closer to the traveling cage, and I can't go anywhere until I know my parents are safe.

Three of the four groups that have been stalking me these past weeks are currently on the field—and there's no warning when the last domino lands, and the missing faction that I've been expecting finally joins the fray. Viviane and Rasputin wheel suddenly apart, and the cleric reaches out in the nick of time, his grip stopping a fiery arrow an instant before it hits him. His eyes go from shocked to understanding, and then more arrows hurtle across the night sky, flames licking the stars and plunging down.

"*Brotherhood!*" One of the vampires shouts. Bodies are hit, the blazing missiles surging on impact, and the undead begin to scatter in panic. The first salvo is followed by a second, arrows crisscrossing overhead, their trajectory seeming to anticipate the disarray. More targets are struck, flames engulfing them with unnatural speed—but I hold my ground.

One of the arrows lodges in the wooden frame of the cart, the boards blackening as the fire threatens to spread. My parents yelp and whimper, huddling closer together, and my insides revolt in fear. Across the clearing, despite the confusion and the mounting danger, Jude and Gunnar are frozen in place. Their promise, and the magic of a blood oath, means they have to act—now or never.

They exchange a glance . . . and then break forward, racing across the picnic grounds, converging on the wheeled cart. At the same moment, black-clad figures come springing out of the trees behind me, agile and silent—at least fifteen of them, each wielding a sword. Polished metal flashing, their blades swing with deadly intent as they storm the field.

Viviane is closest to the trees, and the Knights reach her first, four of them bearing down at once. She pauses only a second before erupting in a cloud of smoke, shifting back into an owl and spiraling for the sky. Two more arrows launch at her from the trees, but she barrel-rolls, dodging both and flying out of sight.

Four others target Rasputin, rushing at him in an acrobatic advance, blades slicing loops from the air. The cleric vanishes suddenly, reappearing behind his assailants—snapping a Knight's neck before vanishing again when the others whirl to catch him.

As the Russian taunts his adversaries with a deadly game

of keep-away, Jude rips the lock off my parents' cage, and he and Gunnar dart inside. Two more flaming arrows carve bright tracks through the air, and I'm dizzy with fear, but their fiery tips hit the cart—missing flesh, both alive and undead.

I don't get to see if the rescue is a success.

Three of the Knights reach me at last, and I don't even bother to run. There's no point. The first to come within striking distance thrusts his sword straight into my chest, and the second plunges hers through my back. The metal edges meet with a terrific clang and then glance apart, vibrating where my body is supposed to be.

I see my own reflection in the tinted goggles of the man facing me, and I give him a cheery smile a moment before I glimmer out of sight.

35

My eyes pop open and I gasp for air, my face sweaty and body trembling. Beside me, her clammy hand locked tightly with my own, Hope Cheng looks even more wrung out than I feel. She's pale and breathing hard, her shoulders quivering—but there's a giddy smile on her face.

"It worked," she pants hoarsely, sounding almost astonished. "I can't believe it!"

Rubbing my forehead, I blink a few times. "You . . . didn't think it was going to work?"

"I had no idea." She gives a breathless shrug, combing her fingers through her damp hair. "A detailed, interactive illusion, cast from a distance? That's telepathy, projection, remote viewing . . ." She ticks them off on her fingers. "Honestly, I'm proud of myself if I can even match my socks in the morning. This was, like . . . a *shitload* of advanced magic."

I lick my lips, and wind tosses the branches around us. Behind their chattering, however, the drumbeat of violence continues loud and clear. "Just so we're on the same page . . . you told me you would do it, but you didn't know if you *could* do it?"

"I told you I would *try*," she corrects me. The color is already coming back to her cheeks, her hands steadying again as she pops the cap off a bottle of water. On Wednesday morning, Jude and Gunnar each left me a vial of vampire blood; tonight, I drank one and gave the other to Hope—and already it's replenishing the energy we lost from our intensive spell-casting. Wiping her mouth and nodding toward the chain-link fence that separates us from the trees, Hope adds, "And look: We pulled it off!"

A smile steals across my face at last, because somehow? We really did. We got Rasputin to bring my parents into the open, at a location of my choice, making a rescue possible; we lured all my enemies into a trap to fight one another—including the Brotherhood, thanks to the notes Hope and Adriana scattered all over town; and we projected the illusion of my presence on the picnic grounds long enough to set the conflict in motion. I'm still worried about my parents, but at least I know Jude and Gunnar have them now.

Seated together inside a chalk circle, magic symbols scrawled around us on fissured pavement, Hope and I huddle in the shadow of the Trapans Glassworks factory. Old crime scene tape is strung around its perimeter, the broken windows a haunting reminder of what happened here a week ago. At most, we're a quarter mile from the bloody skirmish being waged over the entity that continues to percolate inside of me.

"*You* pulled it off," I point out, giving her a hug. Euphoria is building inside me, endorphins riding a wave of vampire blood, and my nerves are beginning to vibrate with it. "I was just here to hold your hand. You know, literally."

The most critical step in my half-assed plan depended upon Hope's abilities as a water elemental—to cast illusions and hear things she's not supposed to hear. Without her, my parents' rescue would have been impossible. The coven would still do whatever it is they plan to do, of course, and maybe I would be saved . . . but my mom and dad would have been killed for certain. It turns out that Hope, appropriately enough, was my only hope.

Hand in hand, with her gift for sorcery and my borrowed magic—boosted by syzygy and vampire blood, and amplified by the Nexus—we powered a walking, talking apparition that fooled even a sorceress as strong as Viviane Duclos.

"*We* did it." Hope tilts her face to the stars and closes her eyes, breathing in the night. "And it was . . . incredible. I've never wielded magic like that before. Am I . . . I mean, am I an asshole for being just a little sad that it was a once-in-a-lifetime thing?"

"I get it." And I do. But our lifetimes might be over sooner than either of us thinks. As my senses sharpen, I detect something I've never felt before—a hairline fracture where I end and the Corrupter begins. He's starting to separate.

My eyes dart back to the trees, my good mood vaporizing instantly. Colgate Woods was the only location I knew of where a final battle could take place without innocent lives being lost in collateral damage. Meanwhile, the site of the ill-fated rave was the only one that offered both the privacy and proximity Hope needed to pull off a trick this complex. The strongest sorcery needs to be worked close at hand—the greater the distance, the weaker the magic. Which is something that both Viviane and Rasputin will know.

And even now, with multiple vampires crowding my awareness, I can sense the two faction leaders connecting the dots . . .

"Can you tell what's happening down there?" Hope interrupts my darkening thoughts, as if reading my mind. Or maybe she *is* reading my mind. "Are your parents—"

"I think they're okay." I spit it out quickly, because now that I'm reaching out with the Corrupter's radar, I can tell how rapidly things have deteriorated since I vanished.

Now that the flaming arrows have stopped flying, and the prize they were competing for has vanished, the vampires have turned on the humans in their midst—a common foe they can eat. With numbers on their side, the undead are swarming; and even as some of them disappear from my radar, falling prey to the Knights, I can tell by the pattern of their movements that they're prevailing.

Maybe I should feel guilty. The Perseans are human, and they want the same thing I do: to prevent the apocalypse. The only thing we disagree on is, you know, how dead I should be to get there. If they killed me, the world would be saved . . . for a while. But Azazel would just keep coming back. I'm the first vessel in generations with any hope of stopping him for good, and who knows when there could be another?

The Brotherhood volunteered to die for this cause, but nobody bothered to ask me. I want to live. I want a chance to make the world better, to do something beautiful. The Knights on the field always planned to die for their beliefs. I intend to live for mine.

"Jude and Gunnar are leaving the picnic grounds." I can feel them, darting through the trees along the streambed, a blur of speed. "They're heading toward Adriana."

A few blocks away from us—close enough to reach on foot—Adriana sits behind the wheel of Hope's car. She's the getaway driver, waiting for her girlfriend and my parents to fill the empty seats so she can take all of them as far away as possible.

"Then they have your parents!" Hope squeezes my hand again. She's made the same deduction I have, and I reach out with my mind, because I have to know for sure. It's Gunnar's thoughts I find first, and when I understand that he's carrying my mother as he sprints after Jude, my eyes well with tears. But there's no time to cry, because I'm picking up other thoughts as well—ones filled with malevolence.

"You should get moving," I say urgently. Rasputin's forces are dwindling fast; he's losing his followers, and no matter how satisfying he finds it to kill, he's losing his patience with the distraction of the battle. In fact—"*Go! Now!*"

Four of the remaining Northern Wolf vampires suddenly spring away from the clearing, each hurtling with impossible speed in a separate direction. I don't even have to reach into their easily accessible minds to know that this is a recon mission—that Rasputin wants to find me, and these are his advance scouts.

One of them is headed our way.

Hope pales, lurching to her feet, and she starts to run—but she barely makes it five yards before a figure rises into the night sky, arms wide and eyes blazing, soaring above the trees that separate the factory from Colgate Woods in a gravity-defying leap.

The Northern Wolf minion is still in midair when I raise his blood, speeding its atoms, until he erupts; he bursts into flames as he passes over the chain-link fence and crashes hard to the pavement, dead before he hits the ground. His body shrivels, burns, and disarticulates so fast that Hope still hasn't even made it to the main road before he's nothing but ash and bone—before I swivel and shout, "*STOP!*"

She stumbles to a halt and spins around, our eyes connecting. This time, I know she hears what I'm thinking. The telepathic connection linking vampires to their progeny means that the second his outrider spotted us, Rasputin knew where we were as well. And now he's coming, abandoning the battlefield, and bringing his remaining minions with him.

Hope and I sprint together, colliding in the cold shadow of the building, wrapping our arms around one another as tight as we can. Rasputin knows I'm dangerous now, that I have the power to kill, and yet he's still headed this way. Either he has a strategy to subdue me until the Ascension can take place . . . or he has no strategy at all—and I'm not sure which is scarier. That hairline fracture between me and the Corrupter is spreading wider by the moment, and I'm not sure how much longer I have.

Taking a breath, I reach for the magic I felt on Tuesday night—when Jude, Gunnar, and I floated together. I've practiced this trick since then, but our conditions are worsening fast. Hope and I rise slowly, bubbles pushing up through heavy fathoms of water, lifting past the barricaded entry points of the crime scene's first floor. One story up, most of the glass is still missing from the windows Rasputin's crew used to crash the party, and my head aches with the effort to propel us closer.

We reach one of the openings, sweat matting the hair at my temples again, and we've just passed through when something inside of me lurches. The hairline fracture widens abruptly, and we plunge through five feet of thin air before I can catch us again, our bodies twirling madly in the fragmented moonlight. Hope's arms dig into my ribs, her breathing frantic in my ear, and panic overwhelms me, gravity forcing our erratic descent.

Eight feet up from the concrete floor, I lose hold of this power entirely, and we crash down hard, sprawling. My ankle twists, a firestorm of pain shooting through me before it goes numb. Gasping, eyes bulging, I can already tell it's broken, a dull throb setting in.

"A-Auggie?" Hope is white as a sheet in the shifting darkness that surrounds us, struggling up onto all fours. "Are you okay?"

"I'm fi-ine," I wheeze through my teeth. It's a lie, but it'll be the truth soon enough. Even before the numbness has a chance to wear off, the heat and pressure begin to recede, vampire blood pulling me back together. "Don't worry about me . . . just hide!"

My undead radar is starting to shrink, the picnic grounds out of reach, the signals from Jude and Gunnar too hazy for me to interpret. But Rasputin and his backup will be arriving any second.

Hope hesitates, but she must still hear my thoughts, because we both look up at once. Jumping to her feet, she races for the devouring shadows at the edge of the room, and not a second after she's vanished from sight, two figures soar in through the shattered windows on opposite sides of the building.

White-robed henchmen drop from two stories up and slam to the concrete with an echoing *boom*, one landing on either side of me. Their eyes burning, their claws trailing tendrils of smoke that drift in the moonlight, they hang back at a wary distance. My heart hammers my temples. I don't know if I can take both of them—I don't even know if I can still take them at all—but when one darts a glance in the direction Hope just ran, I know I'm going to find out.

With everything I've got, I fling my influence at him, whipping his blood into a frenzy. His muscles seize as the heat rises, his golden eyes going round; but a moment later, he slips from my grasp. His blood slows and settles, and I dig deeper, trying again . . . but nothing happens. I can't get back in. Cold sweat limps down my spine, and another lurching sensation rocks me, stealing the breath from my lungs.

A muscle twitches in my hand, my fingers jumping, and I gape as it dances. *I'm not the one making it move.* Azazel is growing more defined by the second, his presence separating from mine like oil in water—and he's starting to figure out how to make this body work. Horror turns my stomach, bile singeing my throat. *It's happening.* All my dreams, all the moments I haven't lived yet, rush at me with terminal speed. No matter how many plans I laid for this moment, I'm not ready. I'll never be ready.

The Ascension is beginning.

Finally, at long last, I've got no time left.

"Oh my." The vampire I failed to kill splits his face in a monstrous, knife-toothed smile. "It looks like the vessel just might be full."

"The hour is at hand." The other intones his agreement.

The air crackles, and unpleasant sensations shiver through my body, more muscles twitching against my will. Desperately, gulping air, I sputter, "N-now. It's happening *now*."

"The Master will be pleased . . ." The vampire on my left giggles, a sound like a fork caught in a garbage disposal, and he spreads his arms to the heavens. My body jerks, my lungs burn, and hairs rise along my arms—and from high above us, another figure comes soaring through the windows and into the upper reaches of the warehouse. Embroidered robes flapping, his face carved in a maniacal grin, Rasputin has finally made his entrance.

36

He plunges with graceful precision, knees flexed, his clawed fingers trailing hellish, otherworldly smoke that shreds in the updraft. His minions exalt his glory, and I try to scramble backward—even as one of my hands lifts from the floor on its own, my head getting lighter. Rasputin's eyes streak through the darkness, meteorites blazing their way to Earth.

When he's only fifteen feet from landing right on top of me, however, the air wobbles suddenly . . . and he slams, hard, against an unseen barrier. Stunned and flung off-course, Rasputin crashes to the floor and tumbles away, while the shadows behind me swim and unfold—to reveal Ket. Her hand outstretched, the alchemical symbol for air is chalked beneath her feet.

"You are unwelcome here, Grigori Rasputin," she states without any particular emotion.

The Mad Monk glares up at her as he pushes into a crouch, his face twisted with rage. Over his shoulder, he barks an order to his disciples. "Kill her!"

They both charge at once, snarling, but Ket doesn't even flinch. Her hand twists, flicking one direction and then the other, waves of visible distortion hurtling outward and knocking both vampires off their feet.

The one to my left rockets backward, and when he crashes to the floor, the gloom where he lands unstitches to reveal Lydia Fitzroy—the metal sorceress—standing over him. She claps her hands together, sparks dancing to life between her fingers, building into a furious storm of snapping electricity that she flings downward. It surges through the vampire's body, his frame convulsing and smoking . . . until he bursts into flame.

Simultaneously, when the minion on my right hits the ground and rolls to a stop, the emptiness beside him swirls and fills with the figure of Ximena Rosales. *I didn't come prepared to give a demonstration*, she'd said the morning I met the coven, *but earth witches possess great strength*. I see what she meant at last when she squeezes one bejeweled hand into a fist, sucks in a breath, and then brings it down on the vampire's head with so much force his skull literally explodes. The floor trembles, bone fragments and brain matter scattering everywhere like the contents of a revolting piñata.

Adriana's grandmother, a woman who doesn't even like to step on bugs, rises back to her feet, flicking clumps of undead gore off her fingers. "I really hate doing that."

My ankle is healed now—and I only know it because my leg twists suddenly, and I barely catch myself before I'm sent face-first to the floor when my body weight shifts on its own. Pressure builds in my head, my clothes stuck to me with sweat, and I struggle to make my vocal cords move. "*It's . . . happening! You n-need to . . . hurry!*"

Ket sweeps her hands out in another fluid motion, and the rest of the coven is unveiled around me—Sulis, Brixia, and Marcus Cheng, all standing over chalk symbols reflecting their elements. They've been here all along, waiting for this moment, hidden by the camouflage of Ket's magic: *disapparition and the control of unseen matter*. Hope needed to be close to the picnic grounds, the coven needed space to perform their ritual, and the glassworks factory met all the requirements. In a brief phone call with Ximena on Wednesday morning, I'd formally accepted the witches' offer to exorcise Azazel, and this was the location we'd settled on to see things through. They wouldn't help me with my half-cocked rescue, or with the deadfall I was arranging for my enemies in Colgate Woods . . . but they'd at least agreed not to get in my way.

Rasputin scrambles to his feet just as Sulis launches a ball of swirling fire his way. He blinks out of its path, reappearing several feet over, but the sorceress seems to have anticipated the move. Like a boomerang, the miniature comet suddenly redirects, unfurling into a rope of flame—catching the edge of Rasputin's robes just as he reso- lidifies. The magical blaze spreads fast, leaping hungrily up his sleeve, and the undead cleric frantically tears the garment from his body.

"Forget him, sister," Brixia interjects calmly. "He's about to become quite too busy to bother us."

As she speaks, a small shadow darts silently into the moonlit reaches of the upper story, and then dives—dropping like a stone at Rasputin's head. Only when its wings snap wide to catch the air, two feet from its mark, do I realize it's a familiar owl. Bursting into an expanding plume of smoke, it catches the cleric's attention at last, and he whirls just as Viviane Duclos leaps from the twisting cloud, already lunging into an attack. Immediately, he reverts to his trusty disappear-reappear trick, but she's done pretending to be fooled.

Viviane's body moves in a way I can't comprehend, faster than should be possible. Her hips rotate, her spine bends, and her foot catches Rasputin in the chest before her hands have even cleared the space where he was standing a moment earlier. The cleric's body launches back as if blown from a cannon, smashing into an outside wall hard enough to break through. Bricks fly apart as he ejects from the warehouse, exposing a slice of night sky, demolished mortar dusting the air.

Swiveling around, Viviane meets my eye for just a moment. At the center of a magic circle, ringed by powerful witches, I sway to my feet—my body acting of its own accord. I'm a hostage in my skin, the Corrupter pressing upward with an ineluctable force, and terror washes my skin in a cold sweat. Viviane hesitates, her transformed face hard to read—but past the fangs and sharpened cheekbones, the golden eyes and angled brows, I catch a glimpse of Daphne Banks.

And then she whirls around, springing for the hole in the outer wall. Smoke trails behind her as she makes her choice—leaving behind the Dark Star and her vision for the future in order to chase after Rasputin. In order to protect me.

She isn't even out of sight before Azazel turns my head, directing my attention, using my eyes to examine the witches around us. He recognizes Brixia, Ket, and Sulis, and his sense of alarm sends adrenaline pumping through me. A memory that isn't mine disrupts my scattered thoughts—*six witches, a barren landscape, unendurable pain*—and I feel the moment that he steps over me.

I feel the moment that he Rises, at last.

I'm pushed down, sinking in my own body, a bit of flotsam caught in the swell of a bottomless ocean. The Corrupter opens my mouth to draw his first breath—the one that will end me, *the one that will end the world* . . . and then, as one, the coven speaks.

"*Kulamāje maljo draugo!*"

Instantly, my body is pinioned, magic snapping fast around me. Muscles lock in my legs and arms, my chest constricting so tightly my lungs can't expand. Azazel fights back, electricity licking the underside of my skin, and my heart thunders.

"*Skaro anmenndho draugo!*" the witches chant together, and my insides give a violent twist. Pain shears through me, unlike anything I've ever experienced. It's a blade slamming through my neck, fire eating my flesh—a hundred gruesome deaths at once. My immobilized lungs burn and Azazel rages . . . we're trapped together, he and I.

"*Steigoawa nāmante draugo!*" Their eyes closed, the coven lift their arms, and sparks tear through me. The circle sputters to life with a gas-blue shimmer, flickering, pulsing, growing stronger. My body still can't breathe, and the lack of oxygen sends panicked signals on a cannonball run through my nervous system. Dark spots freckle my vision, and it takes a moment for me to realize the unearthly glow is coming from me.

From *us*.

"*Kulamāje maljo draugo!*" the witches repeat, the air beginning to stir in the gutted factory, moving in a lazy spiral. "*Skaro anmen-ndho draugo!*"

Something intangible at my center wrenches apart, searing heat cauterizing my insides; but I stop sinking. The great ocean of the Corrupter froths and surges, but within him, my consciousness reverses course. The pressure in my chest is suffocating, and my heartbeat strobes behind my eyes . . . but now, suddenly, *I'm* the one who's Rising.

"*Steigoawa nāmante draugo!*" Those sparks break the surface of my skin in a rush, bursting into the air, and the glow around me intensifies. Pins and needles stab my fingertips, pressure mounting behind my eyes, and my chest burns like it's filled with hot coals. Just as I fear I'm going to black out, there's another vicious tug at that unseen part of me, and the force compressing my lungs lets go.

I suck down air in ragged gulps, my head spins . . . but it's me breathing, not Azazel. My arms and legs are still frozen, and I feel him clinging to me—*but the spell is working.*

"*Kulamāje maljo draugo. Skaro anmenndho draugo. Steigoawa nāmante draugo!*"

My head snaps back, jaws open, and sparks geyser from my

throat, the air filling with the odor of brimstone and burnt hair. Memories that aren't mine blitz through me—an armored king felled in battle, a queen paraded to the guillotine, a girl trapped in a basement stinking of gunpowder—and I gasp for oxygen. Inside myself, I begin to expand.

The air swirls faster, dust and paper scraps dancing as the witches chant louder, their expressions taut. Azazel is pulled further away, but he pours his visions into my mind. I see my parents huddled in the back of Hope's car, Adriana behind the wheel, terrified, wondering where her girlfriend is. I see Jude and Gunnar sprinting back to the battlefield, racing each other, their relationship more complicated than ever.

"Kulamāje maljo draugo, skaro anmenndho draugo, steigoawa nāmante draugo!"

His consciousness is crushing, too great for me to process. I relive dozens of lives in a single moment; I see countless potential futures. In one, Azazel presides as emperor of a scorched planet, hordes of emaciated undead crawling its surface; in another, mankind ruins the Earth with no help at all; but in yet another, Viviane's dream comes true—we save ourselves and prosper. We all become Chosen Ones. We all rise to the challenge.

"Kulamāje maljo draugo, skaro anmenndho draugo, steigoawa nāmante draugo!"

The light around me is nearly blinding now, density gathering in its shifting center as the witches continue to chant. With a ripping sensation, my tongue is freed from its paralysis. I realize in amazement that *this* is the Corrupter—this thrashing, spectral glow leaving my body in increments is the very enemy I've been fighting. Sucking in another breath, I start chanting as well, pushing against Azazel with everything I've got.

"No!" The panicked cry resonates through the factory, echoing

over the swirling wind. Rasputin is scrabbling back through the hole his body made in the outer wall, his flaming eyes wide and stricken. "The Ascension must proceed!"

His face is a mask of undiluted hysteria, and the blue light arches sharply above me, twisting and spiking. I can feel Azazel's own anger and despair, his roots being torn out, and I shout at the top of my lungs. "*Kulamāje maljo draugo!*"

I don't know what it means, but the pressure in my head lifts with each word, my body casting out its unwanted passenger.

"No, no, *no!*" The bearded vampire leaps and vanishes, smearing across the space between the wall and the magic circle, materializing again behind Brixia. Her eyes shut, her focus is on the spell when he grabs her head and twists, all in one swift motion.

Still frozen in place, I hear the hollow pop of her neck breaking, and can do nothing but watch as the ancient water sorceress—a witch who sacrificed her humanity for the chance at seeing this moment through—topples to the ground. Lifeless.

The Corrupter's light surges wildly, flinging sparks in all directions as the elements are unbalanced, and a percussive blast catapults Rasputin across the room again. The wind races around the circle, my temperature climbing as Azazel starts to reach his way back inside; I fight as hard as I can, but I've got no magic of my own now.

The floor shakes, cracks spreading through the concrete and up the walls, and the remaining witches struggle to maintain the chant. Their faces shining with sweat, their eyes closed in concentration, their hands tremble with effort as they reach for the sky . . . but still the rollicking blue fire shrinks as it eats its way back into my body.

Witnessing the chaos, Rasputin's greed for more is written on his face as he regains his feet; but just as he starts forward, a column of smoke twists into the air before him. A hand reaches out, ivory claws snapping closed around the cleric's throat, and Viviane Duclos takes shape. Her face carved in deadly angles, she growls, "Not so fast, mon biquet—we're not done yet!"

She whirls, flinging him into the darkness on the far side of the factory . . . but the tide has already turned. The pressure in my head intensifies, squeezing my thoughts sideways, and the human witches are starting to go pale from the relentless drain on their energy. Azazel's memory pours back into my brain—a confrontation from eons ago, when he faced this same peril and killed one of the witches to escape. All he needs is to gain control of me long enough to draw his first breath, and this battle is over. With Brixia dead, the circle is incomplete . . . it's only a matter of time.

"*Skaro anmenndho draugo!*" A fresh voice rings out above the roar of blood in my ears. "*Steigoawa nāmante draugo!*"

Emerging from the shadows at the back of the warehouse, racing for the magic circle at a dead sprint, is Hope Cheng. Skirting Brixia's inert form, she plants her feet on the symbol for water—their shared element—and lifts her hands. "*Kulamāje maljo draugo!*"

My body lurches again, and the blue light flails as the balance is suddenly restored. The Corrupter's fury burns my throat, his grip deep and painful, wriggling in places I have no name for. Metal creaks as the hurtling wind rattles catwalks overhead, and the hole in the wall widens, the building shaking from its foundations up. One word at a time, Azazel is ripped back out of me, the air so thick with the reek of smoke and sulfur I can hardly breathe.

"*Kulamāje maljo draugo . . . skaro anmenndho draugo . . . steigoawa nāmante draugo . . .*"

Viviane and Rasputin continue their vicious battle in the shadows, dancing on the turbulent air and exchanging blows, but the coven is barely standing at this point. Ximena and Marcus are swaying, Lydia trembles, and the strain of this ritual has pushed the two undead witches to the limits of their physical transformation—their brow bones sharply arched, their lengthening claws bleeding smoke into the whirling cyclone around us. I chant louder, reaching for what I can of Azazel's magic, using it to push him out.

I feel it. When the last thread breaks—when he loses his grip and severs from me with one final, agonizing snap, when my body is somehow mine and mine alone again, for the first time in weeks—I feel it. My legs give out and I hit the floor, gasping, trembling, and hot; a cloud of volatile, brilliant light churns around me, swelling like a thunderhead . . . and yet I could float. My body is weightless, light as a feather and stiff as a board.

I'm alive.

When Hope suddenly collapses, though, losing consciousness, I feel that, too. The circle unbalances again, the cloud seething and deforming, and the Corrupter's sparks surge into lightning that strikes past the magical boundaries chalked on the floor. The witches battle to keep this chaotic energy contained, but it's too much for them to bear at this point.

Ximena sinks to her knees, followed by Marcus, and the catwalks dance until they come apart. Metal and concrete rain down as more cracks spread across the floor, and a bolt of electrical discharge leaps from the circle and slams into the compromised outer wall. Vibrations roll to the ceiling, bricks falling like loose teeth, and the screaming winds tear the remaining glass from the windows. When Ximena finally goes slack, toppling onto her side, the violent, glowing presence above me pitches and expands.

The world might be saved, but disaster is still imminent.

"*No!*" Rasputin's anguish is barely audible above the terrifying sound of a building coming apart, a disembodied angel heaving against the restraints of a failing spell.

When Marcus faints, followed by Lydia, the Corrupter whirls madly—and then contracts. For a brief moment, the suggestion of a face appears in the raging mass of light, furious jaws spreading wide . . . and then it rushes at me. There's an explosion, an earth-shattering *boom*, and a blinding flash fills the gutted factory all the way to the roof. Energy rolls outward, and the walls give way.

Abandoning the spell at the last moment, Ket sweeps her hands out, and a dome of shimmering air snaps open above the circle. With a deafening roar, the entire structure comes down around us— on top of us—a deluge of brick and steel, glass and concrete. I've got only enough strength left to curl into the fetal position as it all crashes against the invisible, impossible membrane of air magic, and tumbles aside. Sulis links hands with her sister, and the protective bubble grows, forcing the gathering wreckage back.

As the din subsides, moonlight touches my face . . . and some-how, I'm still alive. Stars show beyond a thick plume of dust that rises up above us, drifting endlessly into the dark, naked sky, and a stiff breeze makes me shiver. When Ket at last releases her invisible shield, she slumps to the ground, taking Sulis with her.

Trees rustle, people shout, and police sirens are already croon-ing their distant response to our many disturbances—but for a moment, peace settles over me. The Corrupter is gone and I'm still here. Somehow, against all odds, I have a future after all.

The debris shifts, rubble resettling, fragments of brick and mor-tar skittering through unseen pathways. Fallout from the dust cloud begins to subside, coming down like a fine snow. I'm just wondering what we're going to say to the cops—when the debris shifts again, stirs . . . and then erupts.

Two slabs of concrete burst apart, flipping like coins, and an angular figure rises from the unsteady ruins. His wild hair and scraggly beard gray with disintegrated mortar, his garments hanging in rags from his rawboned frame, Grigori Rasputin snaps his own dislocated jaw back into alignment—and then turns his deranged, incandescent glare on me.

He lunges, smearing across the space between us, soot tainting the air. When he snatches me up from the ground, the tips of his claws pierce my flesh, and a burning sensation tumbles through my blood. The pain is excruciating, suffocating; I can't even manage a cry for help as he tightens a massive hand around my throat and presses my windpipe shut.

"You filthy brat," he snarls thickly, froth gathering at the corners of his horrible corkscrew mouth. "*You miserable little mongrel shit!* I spent one hundred years preparing the way for a true god to rise, and *you* have destroyed everything!" His eyes are so bright they hurt to look at, and his face is disfigured with pure hatred. "Can you even comprehend what you have done? I was to be his anointed—I was to bear a title in Azazel's court, and sit at his right hand! You robbed me of my destiny, and now I shall introduce you to the hell you deserve!"

His claws sink deeper into my flank, and blinding pain shoots through me, a flurry of razor-edged stars. Pressure mounts in my ears, my lungs throb, and I shut my eyes—this agony will only get worse. The gruesome sound of tearing flesh and snapping bone makes my stomach convulse . . . and then Rasputin's grip abruptly loosens, and I drop like a stone to the fractured concrete. Air sweeps down my bruised throat, and I choke on it, coughing violently as I blink and look up.

Rasputin still towers above me, eyes wide and glazed, jaw hanging open—and in the center of his chest gapes a dark, ragged hole, spilling old blood. Staggering to one side, the vampire pivots on unsteady feet—to reveal Viviane Duclos. Once again, she wears the face of Daphne Banks—the blond hair and apple cheeks, the sly glint—and she gives the cleric a smile. In her upraised hand, she holds the ugly black mass of his heart. "Pardon me, sir, but were you looking for this?"

Rasputin stares, horror-struck, his fingers trembling as he reaches. "*No!*"

349

But he's too late. With her other hand, she produces that stake of hers—and plunges it straight through the organ in her slimy grip.

Rasputin lurches violently, stumbling to his knees as his legs desiccate instantly beneath him and the joints fail. His hair and beard blanch and grow, his shoulders separating and his jaw swinging loose, all his tendons shriveling. He pitches forward, and by the time he hits the ground, he's nothing but bones, his remains scattering between us.

Viviane casts aside the leathery scrap that's left of her enemy's heart, brushing off her hands, and then peers down at me. My heart is still racing. She just saved my life—again—but I don't know where we stand. Centuries of her own plans were just foiled as well, and I'm still the one to blame. When she snaps out her fangs, I flinch and hold my breath, stifling a whimper—but then she sinks her teeth deep into her own wrist.

"Here." She kneels down beside me, offering me her arm. "You really need this." Blood wells in the fresh wounds, but I just stare at it in a daze, until she gives me a sad smile. "Go ahead, Auggie. Trust me."

And the thing is . . . I think I do.

LITTLE WHITE PICKET FENCES

Once you've survived multiple vampire attacks, a collapsing factory, and getting inappropriately touched by an angel, you develop a kind of hubris about your threshold for suffering. But if I may be honest, the oppressive silence in the Fulton Heights High library might be what finally does me in. That, and Algebra I. Again.

Two weeks after living through a brutal, near-apocalyptic showdown that leveled an entire building and left Colgate Woods littered with corpses, I'm sitting at a table near the reference section, facing off against my dreaded archnemesis: the quadratic equation. The clock ticks ominously as I screw up one practice question after another, and every time I try to ask Adriana for help, the librarian glares at us. It's times like these that I almost miss being constantly on the brink of death, because at least I wasn't bored.

In the end, I accepted that offer of vampire blood. No matter what doubts I had, the police were closing in, and they were going to have lots of questions I wasn't sure I wanted to face. At some point during my brief and harrowing moment at Rasputin's mercy, all of the witches had simply vanished—leaving Viviane and me alone in the middle of an exploded building, near a clearing full of dead bodies. Eager to leave, and too weak to move on my own, the choice kind of made itself.

"I'm sorry, Auggie," Viviane says as we wander through a quiet neighborhood after sprinting from the arriving cruisers—a reenactment of our escape from the rave. "I guess I'm not sure what else to say. I'm sorry you went through this, and I'm sorry I tried to use your parents against you. When I met him back in the seventeen hundreds, Azazel told me he intended to create a world of harmony and peace, where vampires would no longer be confined to the darkness. And I believed him." Smiling up at the stars, she shrugs. "It was exactly what I wanted to hear, told to me exactly the way I needed to hear it. Well, who knows? Maybe that really was his plan all along."

"But you saved me." I study her, her face still Daphne's. "When Rasputin sabotaged the ritual, and when he tried to kill me, you stopped him."

She's silent for a moment. "When I pledged myself to the League, Erasmus Kramer's objectives were to cure himself of his vulnerabilities, and to surround himself only with those he felt were also deserving of immortality. While he was alive, because of the blood oath, his goals were mine; and the one time I met the Corrupter in person, Erasmus was with me."

"And when Erasmus died?" As we walk, I'm aware of a lightness I'm not sure how to describe. Until the very end, I could never sense the Corrupter . . . but now I feel his absence.

"At that point, I was more zealous than ever. Honestly, Auggie, you have no idea how charming Azazel can be—how convincing he was. I fell completely under his spell. Our group had spent centuries reconstructing and studying the prophecies, and I was ready to see them fulfilled." A troubled frown disturbs her features. "I knew Rasputin claimed to have met the Corrupter, too, but I always assumed he was just another egomaniac obsessed with day-walking. This is embarrassing to admit, in retrospect, but I never seriously considered the possibility that Azazel could have encouraged him the same way he'd encouraged me."

"It makes sense, though," I say lightly. "He wanted a kingdom, which meant he needed subjects—and soldiers to protect him from Knights and witches and whoever. He probably tried to gather new followers every time he Rose."

She lets out another laugh, full of self-deprecation. "Did I mention how embarrassed I am that I didn't figure that out sooner? Clearly he made promises to Rasputin—and I don't care what their outfit says, I'm starting to think there's not a chance in hell that Azazel never revealed himself to a vampire with Syndicate lineage at some point, either." Light flickers in her eyes, a quick flash of smoldering anger. "The closer we got to the Ascension, the more I started to feel like I'd been played—like we'd all been played."

"Wow, you mean it turns out that a guy so notorious for spreading bullshit that his nickname is literally the Corrupter might have been sorta dishonest with you?" I'm taking a lot on faith that she doesn't actually plan to kill me. "Who would've thought?"

To my relief, she just laughs again. "I still don't know what Azazel intended—and as long as we're being honest, Auggie? He was so convincing that if I met him again I bet he would explain all of this away and have me right back on his side, like that." Viviane snaps her fingers. "When I saw the witches working that ritual, when I understood what it could mean . . . it might have been the first time I realized that the League doesn't have to follow Erasmus's vision anymore. I can set my own path, and maybe it's time I did."

"Lucky for you, you've got the time." I nudge her, and she nudges me back, and for just a moment, things are like they used to be.

"So do you, Auggie." She gives me a serious look. "I meant what I said before: You've got no idea what kind of greatness might be in your future. There's still time to save the world, and maybe the reason you survived—maybe the reason you were the prophesied vessel to begin with—is because you're meant to be part of the rescue mission. Mortality limited the Corrupter; but maybe mortality is what gives you your strength."

I twist my mouth. "I seriously hope the world can do better than an art nerd with questionable taste in guys."

"I'm pretty sure the world is lucky to have you." We stop walking, and with a start, I realize that we're in Ximena's neighborhood. Viviane gives me an affectionate smile and says, "It was an honor getting to know you, August Pfeiffer. Take care of yourself, okay?"

Before I can say goodbye, she spreads her arms, bursts into smoke, and becomes a storm of bats hurtling up into the night sky. As they vanish over the trees, I yell, "Show-off!"

"Do you guys wanna get coffee or anything?" Adriana asks as we walk down the empty hallway after our unproductive study session. With finals approaching, the library stays open an extra half hour after classes end for the day, for those who need the space and quiet time. Since I don't have a tutor anymore, it seemed like a useful thing to sign up for, and it's nice to spend time with my friends. Even if we have to do it in *total silence*.

"That sounds fun." Hope smiles brightly. "I've still got about an hour and a half left before my curfew starts and I get locked in like Bertha Mason."

"It's so unfair," Adriana grouses. "I can't believe you're still being punished. You literally saved the world! Literally!"

"That was my argument, too!" Hope spreads her hands. "But my uncle is all fixated on how I lied about where I was going to be that night, drank vampire blood, did sorcery I wasn't trained for, and almost got myself killed."

With a frustrated grunt, Adriana rests her head on her girlfriend's shoulder in sympathy—which only lasts for a few paces, because it's hard to do that and walk at the same time. "Well, he can't stay mad at you forever."

"Actually, there's a pretty good chance that he can," Hope replies, looking at the floor. "He's, uh . . . thinking about joining the coven. Permanently. On, like, an undead basis?"

"Wait, *what*?" I stop walking altogether and stare at her.

"Yeah. Believe me, there are no arguments that work against that one, either, because I've tried them all."

"Your uncle is seriously thinking about becoming a *vampire*?"

"I collapsed before we could complete the ritual, which means the Corrupter is still out there," Hope reminds me, her expression turning somber. "Best-case scenario is he'll be back in a hundred years—and so on and so on, until he finds another body that can withstand an Ascension. Uncle Marcus thinks he has a responsibility to protect the world, and stuff." With a miserable hitch of her shoulders, she adds, "Out of the original six, only three sorceresses lived long enough to face Azazel a second time—and even though they were joined by the strongest mortal magic-workers they could find, everything still went wrong. He says he won't do it until after I graduate, but . . . he's taking it really seriously."

Hope still doesn't know what happened after the building came down—how Ket and Sulis managed to evacuate her, themselves, and all the other witches out of the ruined factory in the blink of an eye. All she knows is that she woke up in her own bed a few hours later, with a splitting headache and a royally pissed-off uncle.

"Am I the only one who *doesn't* ever want to face Azazel again?"

I squirm inside my skin. We're right at the bend in the hall where I made William go kablooey.

Adriana grunts. "Actually . . . my abuela was thinking about it, too." I snap an incredulous look her way, and she puts her hands up. "Hey, I told her she could do it over my dead fucking body, and I got a whole lecture about duty and 'don't use that language with me, young lady,' and . . . blah blah blah, I don't know, I yelled too loud to hear the rest." Tugging at the ends of her hair, she won't look at either of us. "She finally told me she won't do it, but . . . if she changes her mind, it's not like I can stop her."

After the factory collapsed, Adriana drove my parents to her grandmother's house—our predetermined rendezvous point— fueled by panic. I got there only a few minutes after she did, and we all sat up for hours until Ximena walked in the door. She wouldn't tell us where she'd been, or what the coven had talked about in the aftermath of the ritual, but she wasn't much happier about Adriana's participation in my scheme than Marcus Cheng was.

I haven't heard from the coven myself since that night, but I'm certain Brixia eventually recovered from her broken neck, just as Viviane recovered from her own; and in fact, over the past couple of weeks, I've come to realize something. The water sorceress—who could read minds and accurately predict the web of time—had to have known that she might not make it through the ritual. I can't help but think about how they had Hope pick me up that day, and how she had to reveal her secret to me as a result. I can't help but think about how the whole idea I devised for the battlefield ruse came out of that revelation.

Brixia knew, or at least suspected, that she would die—and that another water elemental, strong enough to stop the Ascension, would be on hand to take her place.

356

"So . . . coffee?" Adriana tries again. "We don't have to go to Sugar Mama's."

We all have mixed feelings now about our formerly favorite café. Gunnar doesn't work there anymore, but I think about him every time I go in—and it makes me sad in a way I don't totally understand yet. With a shrug, I say, "Sorry, I can't. I have to go home and help my parents pack shit up."

"Nooo, I don't want to hear this!" Adriana claps her hands over her ears, pouting and stamping her feet for good measure. "I don't want you to go anywhere. You can't leave me!"

"I don't want to leave you, either," I say, matching her pout. The statement is factual, insofar as I wish I could take her with me. But beyond that? *Get me the fuck out of here.* "But we're not moving anytime soon. We still have to find a new place, and my parents need to sell our house—which, you know, isn't exactly easy in Fulton Heights."

"Still." Adriana wraps her arms around me, and we shuffle down the hallway like that. "The friend part of me is sad, even if the *good* friend part of me understands."

"How are your parents doing?" Hope asks with a polite cough.

"They're okay," I reply, lying through my teeth. My mom and dad aren't the same people they used to be. They barely sleep anymore, and when they do, they have night terrors so violent that they wake up screaming. Neither of them has been able to talk about what happened when they were in captivity, but I'm not sure I could handle knowing about it, anyway. Almost dying was easier than watching them suffer. "They're just, you know, super ready to get out of Dodge. Hence all the early packing."

"I get it." Hope's tone is soft. "Do you know where you're moving to?"

"Nope. Right now, the only guidelines are A) no supernatural nexuses, and B) within our price range. Although you'd be surprised how much that narrows things down."

"I'm going to miss you so much." Adriana squeezes me a little tighter. "This shithole isn't going to be the same without you."

"Let's hope not," I quip.

As we pass the art room, I keep my eyes averted. I haven't set foot in there since the night Gunnar and I confronted William, and even though the school district hired a sub to replace Mr. Strauss, I still prefer the library over finishing my independent study. The Corrupter is out of my body—I know that—but I can't shake the paranoid fear that I'll lapse into another trance if I try to draw something while I'm still living under the Nexus.

I also can't bring myself to trust the new art teacher. She's, like, eighty, and I have a hard time picturing her as a part-time ninja, but . . . I'm not taking chances. Lots of Persean Knights were killed in the Battle of Colgate Woods, but I've got no way of knowing what the survivors reported back to their organization. I don't know if any of the prophecies gave a hard date for the Ascension, so I can't be sure the Brotherhood is even aware that the danger is officially over now. No one has tried to kill me in at least two weeks, so they probably figured it out, but . . . still.

When we push through the side exit, the parking lot and its few remaining cars bathed in spring sunlight, I grimace theatrically. "Oh shit—my history book is still in my locker! I need to go back and get it."

"Do you want us to wait for you?" Adriana asks, clearly hoping the answer is no.

"I got it covered." I give them both hugs. "Go have coffee and do girlfriend stuff. I'll text you guys whenever I get bored of packing boxes. So, like, constantly."

We say goodbye, and I start back up the hallway—and when

the door slams shut again and I'm sure they're not watching, I stop. For a long while, I sit with the silence of Fulton Heights High, breathing in recycled air and looking at the floor where someone must have had to sweep up the remains of an incinerated vampire.

I don't think I feel bad about what I did to William. He was a monster, literally and figuratively, and even if I hadn't exactly killed him in self-defense, he had plenty of blood on his hands, and he'd been proud of his viciousness. The world is better, safer, without him in it . . . and yet. The way I think about vampires has shifted a lot in the past month, and taking a life—no matter what kind of life it was—isn't easy to process.

When the light coming through the windows of the side exit turns amber with the setting sun, I finally leave the building. A breeze sweeps the parking lot, loamy and green—scented with new life—and I drink it in. When I hear the door click shut behind me, I count to five, and turn around.

"Fancy meeting you here." Jude Marlowe leans on the wall beneath the overhang, safe from daylight in its slender shadow, with a little smirk I still can't quite resist.

"It's been a while," I agree, appreciating the shape of him. It makes me think about all the things that happened that night in Chicago—and a few of the things that didn't.

"And yet you're almost acting as if you expected me to show up."

"In a way, I think I'm always expecting you to show up." It's the truth, even if I'm avoiding a direct answer.

We watch each other for a companionable moment before he says, "I'm heading back to Europe tonight. The Syndicate needs my final report, and it's going to be kind of a doozy. I guess I just wanted to see how you were doing. Before I go, I mean."

"Aside from all the trauma, I'm great." I get a laugh out of it, but then I turn serious. "Thank you. For saving my parents, I mean. I never got the chance to say that."

"You don't have to thank me for that," he points out. "I was magically compelled to do it, remember?"

"Okay, fair point. But you would have done it anyway." I know this now, for sure.

"Perhaps." He glances down, a little shy, and a delighted shiver tickles me. Now that I have nothing he needs, I feel the chemistry between us more than ever. It sucks that this is a goodbye.

"Do you know if the Brotherhood is still planning to kill me?" I blurt the question quickly, because I need to know, and he's the only one I can ask.

"According to our sources, they've gone to ground," Jude answers, not seeming to think it's a strange thing to ask. "Given the circumstances surrounding the factory's collapse, and the way vampire activity in Fulton Heights has plummeted since the confrontation in Colgate Woods, they've realized that the Ascension was thwarted. Plus, they left behind multiple bodies with forged identities, which the authorities are still trying to investigate. They'll lie low for a while."

"And the Order of the Northern Wolf was completely destroyed," I note. "The Syndicate must be in a pretty good mood."

Jude takes a moment, producing a cigarette and lighting it up, watching the smoke from his exhalation catch the sunlight. "Actually? Things are pretty . . . tense in the Carpathians just now. The Syndicate is about as close to dissolving as it's ever been." He meets my gaze with a wry smile. "It turns out one of the Syndics was . . . keeping a few crucial secrets from the rest of us."

"Oh?" I do my best to look surprised, but I remember the disloyal enforcers in the clearing—and Viviane's words ring in my ears:

There's not a chance in hell that Azazel never revealed himself to a vampire with Syndicate lineage at some point.

"It's a long story." Jude turns his gaze to the treetops, their branches studded with burgeoning leaves. "Let's just say that someone with a lot of influence had good reason to believe the prophecies, but decided to withhold the information, because he was expecting to be held in the Corrupter's favor after the Ascension." He picks a fleck of tobacco from his bottom lip—and I try not to think too much about what that bottom lip feels like. "I was expected to bring you back to Transylvania . . . and if I failed, this particular Syndic had a plan to smuggle you out under my nose so he could reap glory in a changed world."

I reach up to adjust my glasses—forgetting that I still don't wear them anymore—and move my hand to Gunnar's necklace instead. "So I guess they've changed their official stance on the existence of the Corrupter, huh?"

"Oh no, not at all." Jude lifts his brows. "Some of the Syndics are more committed than ever to insisting it's all a myth—the last thing they want is to encourage future Rasputins." Flicking ash off his cigarette, his expression clouding, he adds, "As for the rest of them . . . well, that's part of why I need to go back. A lot of decisions have to be made."

He falls silent, and the air between us hums with unsaid words. When I can't take it anymore, I ask, "Have you heard anything about . . . the League of the Dark Star?"

Jude smiles sympathetically. "If you're asking what I think you're asking, the answer is: He's already gone. I'm sorry. Gunnar Larsen has always been terrible at goodbyes."

"Oh." I'd kind of figured as much, but I'm still a little crestfallen anyway.

"If it makes you feel any better, he'll be back." Jude cuts me a look from beneath his long eyelashes, and I can see we feel the same. "A year from now—maybe less—he'll start thinking about all the things he should have done but didn't, and he'll want to see if it's not too late." With a shrug, he looks away again. "Like I said, he's terrible at goodbyes."

"What about you?" I try not to make it sound flirtatious, even though it kind of is. "Will you be back?"

"There's a chance." He casts his cigarette to the ground and grinds it out. When he looks up again, something passes between us, a shared current, and he smiles. "I've got a feeling the three of us will never manage a proper goodbye."

The air is practically vibrating, that current lifting the hair on my arms. It feels like something secret, something I'm not supposed to bring up, but I do anyway. "You feel it, too, don't you?"

"Of course I do," he answers softly. "We fulfilled the oath, but the three of us will always be joined now—by blood, by magic. On some level, we'll always feel it." With a knowing look, he says, "Be good to yourself, August Pfeiffer. Maybe I'll see you around."

"Don't be a stranger," I reply, but only because I can't think of anything else. The truth is, he and Gunnar will both be back in my life before long—but I can't really explain how I'm sure of it without making things unnecessarily complicated. So I turn around and start walking for my bike ... and the peculiar whispering sensation that bothers my skin vanishes in an instant as Jude slips away behind me.

It's the strangest thing. The witches purged Azazel from my body, and I know he's not coming back—at least, not in my lifetime— but a few days after the exorcism, I started to discover that he left behind some parting gifts. My undead radar has returned, almost as strong as before; and lately, I've begun to realize that I can still explore other people's thoughts . . . and catch limited glimpses of their potential futures.

It's an ability I try not to abuse, of course, because that would be wrong—but I will absolutely use it to save my ass on this algebra final.

Unlocking my bike, I start for home as the sun dips lower on the horizon, only a few hours left before the fell of dark.

ACKNOWLEDGMENTS

Right out of the gate, my number one thank-you goes to the amazing Saundra Mitchell, editor of *Out Now*—an anthology of contemporary short stories celebrating queer voices in young adult fiction (which is, conveniently, out now!). When they contacted me about being a contributor, I jumped at the opportunity . . . and then struggled to come up with a premise. What I *wanted* to write was a tale of two social enemies forced to work through their lust/hate issues while hiding from a vampire invasion—and I was sort of shocked when Saundra gave my idea an enthusiastic green light.

I came to love that short story so much that I actually scrapped a manuscript I had already fully outlined and put together a frantic pitch for a different book entirely: "What about vampires, but *gay*?!" I am so lucky to work with Liz Szabla, who keeps helping me hone these concepts into books I'm proud to put my name on—and so grateful to Jean Feiwel for believing in me and my ideas enough to put *her* name on them as well.

My magnificent agent, Rosemary Stimola, sees that my dreams come true over and over again, and I am so grateful; and many thanks are due to Allison Remcheck and the rest of the Stimola Literary Studio team for unwavering support and all-around awesomeness!

The book in your hands was made possible only by a staggering amount of work. My (literal!) months and months of writing were only the beginning. From edits and revisions to design, execution, and promotion, I've been aided and abetted by an incredible team at Macmillan. Brittany Pearlman, Molly Ellis, Mandy Veloso, Kim Waymer, Mike Burroughs, and Ashley Woodfolk are all heroes and magicians; and I owe a debt of gratitude to Erin Stein, Allison Verost, and Jon Yaged, as well.

I am not without my enablers, of course, and I need to thank my own personal League of Dark Stars: Adam Sass, Kevin Savoie, Phil Stamper, Kosoko Jackson, and Ryan La Sala. And thanks, also, to my Syndicate of Glampires: Julian Winters, Alex London, Mark Oshiro, Adib Khorram, Lev AC Rosen, Shaun David Hutchinson, Sam J. Miller, Adam Silvera, Kristen Simmons, Tom Ryan, Kiersten White, Zoraida Córdova, PC & Kristin Cast, Tim Floreen, Dahlia Adler, Erick Smith, Zack Smedley, John Corey Whaley, and Cale Dietrich. And yet more thanks go to the Mystic Order of Friends I Cannot Believe I Still Have Yet to Meet in Person: Derek Milman, James Brandon, Shawn Sarles, Riley Sager, Greg Howard, and Abdi Nazemian. Every last one of you is an inspiration!!

Upon occasion, I've encouraged my friends and readers to contact their elected representatives. You might be surprised how effectively you can drive meaningful change by voicing your opinions for the officials who represent you at all levels of government. A big thank-you to Angele McQuaid, Anna Wetherholt, Jennzah Cresswell, Brendan Patrick, Kathryn Fox, and Erica Sirman for contacting their reps when I asked my Twitter followers to pick up their phones! And another thank-you to Anna Wetherholt, who has been tirelessly supportive—you remind me that what I do matters.

If you have not yet read the Engelsfors trilogy by Mats Strandberg and Sara Bergmark Elfgren, you absolutely should. It's a brilliant series about a group of reluctant witches who have to stop a terrible evil, and the trilogy's complex magic system was a massive inspiration for the one you find in this book. Thanks are also owed to the cast, crew, and writers of the greatest TV show of all time: *Buffy the Vampire Slayer*. If you're as big a fan as I am, check out the Slayerfest98 podcast for an episode-by-episode deep dive! (And a shout-out to Ian Carlos Crawford, who is the inimitable host of said podcast, and the nastiest girl in Sunnydale history!)

Writing this book was a lot harder, and took a lot longer, than I initially anticipated. Through it all, my family and friends put up with my perpetual agonies and centrifugal panic attacks, and I am eternally grateful. Love you all!

Best for last, as always: Uldis, this year has been completely bananas, but we're still here. Through thick and thin, from the Polar Vortex to the Potter Globus, we're a team—and I wouldn't have it any other way. Es tevi mīlu, Ulditi.

THANK YOU FOR READING THIS FEIWEL & FRIENDS BOOK.

The friends who made

THE FELL OF DARK

possible are:

Jean Feiwel, Publisher

Liz Szabla, Associate Publisher

Rich Deas, Senior Creative Director

Holly West, Senior Editor

Anna Roberto, Senior Editor

Kat Brzozowski, Senior Editor

Dawn Ryan, Senior Managing Editor

Kim Waymer, Senior Production Manager

Emily Settle, Associate Editor

Erin Siu, Associate Editor

Rachel Diebel, Assistant Editor

Foyinsi Adegbonmire, Editorial Assistant

Mike Burroughs, Senior Designer

Mandy Veloso, Senior Production Editor

Follow us on Facebook or visit us online at fiercereads.com.

OUR BOOKS ARE FRIENDS FOR LIFE.